FALL OF FORGOTTEN GODS

RYAN KIRK

WATERSTONE
MEDIA

For Taylor

Here's to many more writing adventures!

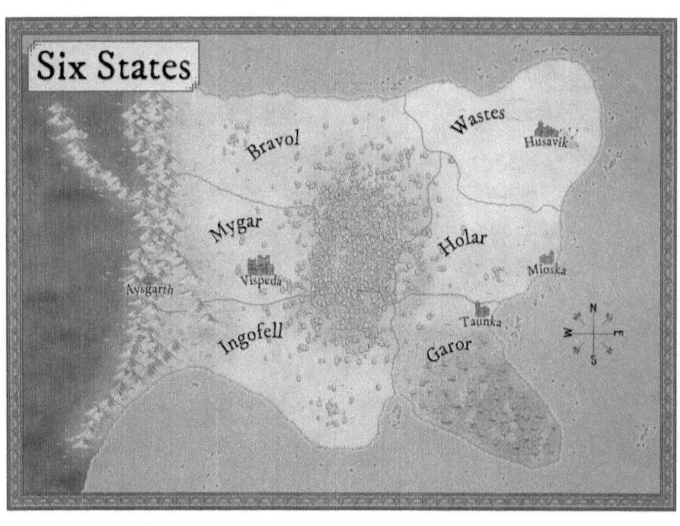

Six States
Bravol
Wastes
Husavik
Mygar
Holar
Mioska
Aysgarth
Vispeda
Taunka
Ingofell
Garor
N
W
E
S

AUTHOR'S NOTE

I recently read a series in which the author introduced each new book with a brief retelling of the events in previous volumes. The stated purpose was to avoid forcing characters into recounting situations from previous books in awkward and unnecessary scenes. After listening to reviews from my wonderful advance readers, I've done the same here.

Band of Broken Gods opens on a father named Hakon, searching for his daughter. Once the fearsome leader of a legendary band of warriors, he has started a new, more peaceful life with his late wife and now-grown daughter.

His daughter, Cliona, has left home and has been studying and living at an academy in the rapidly growing city of Vispeda. A curious soul, she is one of the foremost interpreters of a long-dead language spoken by the gods of myth and legend, the stamfar. However, she recently disappeared, leaving no clue as to her destination. Hakon braves a vicious wilderness and old foes to seek her out.

As he travels, he hears the first rumors of a possible war, set in motion by a name he hasn't heard in almost a hundred years. Damion is a powerful warrior, a kolma like

Hakon, building a force of tehoin far to the west of the six states in the secluded stone fortress of Aysgarth.

While Hakon searches, Cliona is working at an archaeological site, led by a cantankerous older scholar from her academy. They seek the home of a famous stamfar, hoping to uncover the mysteries hidden within. She's joined by Zachary, a noble son exiled from his house for murdering his sister's abusive fiancee.

Their dig is a success, and they find the home buried deep underground. Not long after the discovery, Cliona learns the academy didn't fund their dig, as she'd assumed. Their actual benefactor is a mysterious and powerful man named Damion.

Damion convinces Cliona to come with him to Aysgarth, where she can study the ancient texts, searching for references to an object lost long ago. She agrees to go, and Zachary accompanies them.

Back in the six states, Hakon suspects his daughter has gotten entangled with Damion's schemes. He discovers that the academy in Vispeda is run by another familiar face. Solveig, a warrior who was once part of his band, has become an accomplished scholar. She leads him to Ari, a quiet and yet skilled assassin who was also one of the band.

Together, Ari and Hakon find the dig site, as well as the corpses of the academics who worked it. Damion had them killed to prevent word of his efforts spreading.

There is no love lost between Hakon and Damion. They once fought on opposite sides of a great rebellion, and Hakon knows that if Damion discovers Cliona is his daughter, her life will be forfeit. Fortunately, Cliona herself doesn't know who her father really is. He's never told her of his long life before he settled down with her mortal mother.

Hakon, driven by necessity, reunites his old band. First,

they find the master swordsman Irric, followed by Meshell, the only other kolma who can manipulate teho like Hakon.

Once together, a strange stamfar named Isira visits them. She fought the band in the past, and once imprisoned them for the crimes Hakon committed. She is the only foe they fear more than Damion.

The band convinces the stamfar to spare them, though she makes it clear she is watching their every move. Finally, the band travels west to rescue Cliona from Aysgarth.

In Aysgarth, Cliona meets an enormous dragon, a creature long vanished from the six states. Damion controls it, making him an even more fearsome leader. Over time, her trust in Damion erodes. She finally finds the secret Damion has been searching for. Instead of revealing it to him, she escapes Aysgarth with Zachary by her side.

After a dramatic escape, aided by Damion's dragon, Cliona and Zachary meet up with the band on their way to rescue them. Cliona sees her father fight and realizes he is not the man she thought he was.

The reunion between father and daughter is bittersweet. Hakon has his daughter back, but she is wounded by the lifetime of lies he's told her about his past.

Together, the group decides they must travel to Husavik, the place Damion has sought for years. It is an abandoned city deep in the wastes, and Cliona is certain it is the burial place for a stamfar named Ava.

Once they reach Husavik, Zachary betrays them. The young man reveals that Damion has blackmailed him since the beginning. Damion captures Cliona as his troops flood into the old and nearly forgotten city.

Forced to work for Damion, Cliona eventually finds the burial site. As Damion moves to secure it, the band attacks. They intend to both rescue Cliona and prevent Damion from reaching Ava's grave. But they are vastly outnumbered, and Damion has brought his dragon.

It is a fierce battle, and in the fighting, Zachary is gravely wounded. All looks lost, especially when Damion deals a fatal wound to Cliona.

Though her body dies, Hakon is certain some part of her lives on in the dragon, which she freed from Damion's control. Hakon mounts the dragon, and in one final blow, ends Damion's life.

After, Isira appears on the scene, and agrees with Hakon there is something strange surrounding the events of Cliona's death. She takes Cliona's body for safekeeping. The band was victorious once again, but at a cost much higher than anyone was prepared to pay.

PROLOGUE

When Sigurd looked west, all he saw was freedom. That goal kept his spirits high, even when the wild tried to bury his dreams in mud.

He closed his eyes and breathed in deeply through his nose. Scents of wet grasses and meadow flowers mixed with the far less pleasant odors of tired humans and exhausted horses. Behind them, to the east, a low rumble of thunder accompanied the constant flickering lightning that illuminated the bottoms of dark clouds. From a distance, the rain looked gentle, a gray veil that dropped from cloud to grass.

It hadn't sounded so gentle as it pounded on the shield Gleb had formed for them. The old vilda had complained, but Sigurd had insisted. The party was near to breaking, their morale as low as Sigurd had seen it since they'd left Vispeda. Getting soaked was a small inconvenience, but sheltering under Gleb's shield had brought weak smiles to weary faces. Once they stopped for the night and Gleb enjoyed an extra mug of ale as thanks, the vilda's complaints would fade, too.

Unfortunately, Gleb hadn't been able to protect the rest of the land from the storm. The caravan's pace, decent through most of the day, slowed to a crawl. Heavy wagons sank in mud, and the horses, already tired from countless miles, struggled to pull them farther.

Sigurd pulled out his maps and grimaced. He'd hoped to make it to a small settlement by nightfall, but the sun already approached the horizon. They would be hard-pressed to set up camp before dark, much less cover the six or seven miles that remained between them and the settlement.

Gerd motioned for him from the wagon. He angled his horse toward his wife, soon riding close enough they could speak softly without being overheard. "You'll be setting up camp tonight, then?" she asked.

Sigurd glanced again toward the sun, relentlessly marching toward the conclusion of the day. Then he nodded. Gerd spent even more time with the maps than he did. She understood the situation. "Any thoughts on where we might stop?"

"There's a spot marked on one of your maps from a previous caravan. A clearing near a bend in a stream. We'll have fresh water, and maybe even fish."

Sigurd didn't remember any such camp, but he didn't doubt Gerd. These days, his attention was torn between a dozen competing problems at any time. Wagons fell apart. Horses got injured or were pushed too hard. Families within the caravan argued with one another over meaningless details.

But soon, this too would pass. One more week, and then they'd reach their new home.

The thought brought a smile to his face. He'd have just as many problems there, but he'd be free, in control of his own fate. No more taxes to authorities who then wasted his coin. No more haggling on prices that continued to rise.

It would just be them against the wild.

He didn't delude himself into thinking it would be easy. But there was a purity to that struggle that day-to-day living in Vispeda lacked. Out there, life would be as simple as survival.

"Sigurd!" Gerd snapped.

He blinked and brought himself to the present. More often, now, he'd found his attention wandering. Like the others, he was tired, and his thoughts sought refuge in pleasant dreams of the future. If he was to experience that future, though, he needed to focus on solving problems now. One at a time, beginning with where to camp.

If Gerd believed it a good spot, that was enough for him. "Where?"

She pointed northeast. "Maybe half a mile."

He tipped the brim of his hat toward her. "My thanks, love."

She waved him off, and he nudged his horse toward the front of the caravan. He spoke briefly with the scouts, and the caravan turned, like an oversized snake crawling through the grass.

Gerd spoke true. As the edges of the sun kissed the horizon they came upon evidence of an earlier camp. Blackened and cleared dirt was evidence of a past cook fire, and a lazy stream softly babbled fifty paces to the north.

Tired or not, the travelers prepared camp in short order. Most settled for sleeping in their wagons, but a few tents went up around the wide circle. One family started a fire, responsible for the meal tonight. Sigurd supervised the preparations, but in truth, there was little to do. They'd performed the same routine nearly every night for the past four weeks. He and Gerd chose to sleep in their wagon, so he lent his strength to any family that needed help with preparing shelter.

Gleb sought him out before long. "Wards tonight?"

That Gleb even asked the question kindled Sigurd's anger. The vilda was making enough money from escorting this caravan that he would be able to drown his memories in whole caskets of ale when he returned to Vispeda. But he still argued against too many of Sigurd's demands. Of course they needed wards. The wilds never rested, and neither could they. It was why they'd hired the vilda in the first place.

Sigurd bit back his retort. Though he'd never admit it out loud to anyone besides his wife, he understood Gleb well enough. The vilda had been a soldier, like Sigurd, but had served for much, much longer. Tehoin were too useful to be discharged early.

He'd seen the same in some of the other soldiers who served for years. Prolonged service in the armies could sap a warrior's will if they weren't able to find a deeper purpose. Soldiers fought against bandits, against the wilds, and sometimes, against neighboring states. But they were always fighting, or marching to a fight, or training for a fight. It wore a person down, planted exhaustion somewhere deep in the bones, where it never left. He was glad he'd gotten out as early as he had. Gleb hadn't. If the vilda had no greater goals than seeking answers in the bottoms of countless cups, Sigurd wouldn't judge the man.

But he would ensure the terms of their contract were carried out. "Wards tonight," he confirmed. "Full ring."

Gleb's eyes flashed, but the older man's exhaustion

snuffed it out fast enough. "Yes, sir." He shuffled off to begin his work.

Sigurd watched him retreat, then returned to his own tasks. Before long, the camp was ready, the food was cooking, and the families were relaxing around the fire. The clouds cleared, revealing the constellations that had been Sigurd's companions no matter how far he traveled.

After the meal finished, the families turned, one by one, to their shelters. Their first nights, they had brought out instruments and told stories. But as the days turned into weeks, there were fewer entertainments around the nightly fire. Sigurd didn't feel the urge to sleep quite yet and contented himself with ensuring the others retired safely for the evening.

Gleb remained up, too, his mug of ale not quite finished. The two former warriors watched the last of the coals slowly burn down, each lost in their own thoughts. Gleb finished his ale with one powerful swig, belched, then stood up. "Going to check the wards once more before I retire."

"Thank you," Sigurd said. The others had been leery about hiring Gleb. The man's reputation as a drunk was well known around Vispeda. But other caravans kept hiring him, and Sigurd had found no fault with the vilda's work. He complained enough for five travelers, but he followed orders, and a lifetime of soldiering had driven good habits into him. Gleb never drank more than two mugs of ale a night, which he handled with ease. He always double-checked his wards, and as far as Sigurd knew, none of the wards had failed yet.

Sigurd climbed into his wagon and lay down in the small space reserved for him. Gerd was still awake. She entwined her hand with his and gave it a squeeze. "Not much longer," she said.

"A good thing, too."

She squeezed his hand again. "You've done well to get us this far. If this is the worst we experience, we should count ourselves lucky."

His wife was right, of course. Sigurd knew he was self-critical. There was always something he could do better, and leading this caravan was no exception. He'd made dozens of mistakes, and those were only the ones he knew about. But no one had died, and they'd made consistent progress west. They'd done well, and other caravans hadn't been so lucky. The wilds were particularly vicious this year.

If Sigurd had one worry about Gleb, it was that the tehoin was only vilda. A nelja would have been better, but such strong warriors were almost impossible to find, and came with an appropriately high price. Sigurd and the others would have had to save for years to afford one.

Gerd snuggled closer against him, and he ran his hand up and down her back. When they built their new home, they would try for a child.

Sigurd smiled and felt his eyelids grow heavy.

The air flickered, an unnatural red light, banishing any thoughts of sleep.

Sigurd sat up and threw off his covers. Gerd complained about the cold air and wrapped the blankets tighter around her. "What is it?"

"Something's testing the wards. I'll go see what it is."

Sigurd clambered out of the wagon. The night was cool enough he could see his breath. The wards flashed red again, and this time, Sigurd saw where the light had originated. He crossed the circle of wagons and hurried to the western edge of their camp.

He was surprised to find Gleb there. The vilda crouched

close to the ground, his eyes focused. Sweat beaded down his forehead. His lips moved, but no sound escaped.

Sigurd let him finish the new ward. He looked out and saw the corpses of two small foxes. They'd fallen dead almost on top of one another.

Movement in the distance caught his eye. Shadows danced in the tall grass. He leaned forward and squinted. For a heartbeat, all was quiet. The shadows settled, and Sigurd doubted he'd ever seen anything.

Then a fox burst from the grass, followed by another, then another. Within the space of one sharp intake of breath, a whole skulk charged at him.

Despite knowing he was protected by Gleb's wards, Sigurd flinched away.

The foxes charged without a sound, as though they were spirits on the wind. The first fox hit the wards mid-stride, in the exact place the two foxes already lay dead. Gleb's ward flashed red, bright against the dark of the night sky. The fox died, killed by the teho contained within the ward.

Their leader's fate did nothing to deter the others. One after another, the foxes slammed into the wards. Red flickered like lightning as the wards endured the beating.

Sigurd took a step back. Rumors of similar events were whispered in taverns back in Vispeda, but he'd never believed the tales. Fox after fox died, and Gleb clutched at his skull, groaning. His forehead dripped with sweat, and his cheeks were more flushed than they were after several mugs of ale.

The attack ended as silently as it started. More than a dozen foxes lay piled on top of one another. The last ones in the line had jumped over their dead brethren to sacrifice their lives uselessly against the wards.

Gleb's wards held.

Sigurd kneeled next to the vilda. "Are you hurt?"

Gleb shook his head but didn't let go of it. He rocked back and forth. Sigurd stood, not sure what course of action was best. Was this it, or did the wild have more surprises lying in wait?

He fell back on his military training. When in doubt, extra caution was never a poor choice. They would establish watches throughout the night. Several in the caravan were proficient in the bow, and there was at least one other former soldier who could be trusted not to accidentally stab herself with a sword.

He turned back to the circle of wagons, but was stopped before he could advance more than a step.

It wasn't a sight or sound that froze him in place, but a feeling. All the hairs on the back of his neck stood straight up and his stomach twisted in watery knots. He almost fell to his knees. His breath came in ragged gasps.

He turned, somehow certain what he would see, but unable to believe his own eyes.

Far off in the distance, still miles away, a small shadow passed in front of the stars.

Sigurd gripped the hilt of his sword with his left hand. He tried to shout, "To arms," but his voice came out as a hoarse whisper.

What did any of their efforts matter? Even if they were all nelja, their fate was sealed.

The shadow grew larger.

Beside him, Gleb cried out in agony. His rocking intensified.

Sigurd wouldn't die like that. He cursed the world and his time on it, but he would die with a sword in his hands and his friends by his side. He stood straight, cleared his throat, and shouted, "To arms!"

He repeated the call until the whole camp was awake. Men, women, and children stumbled out of tents and wagons. Bows were pulled taut. Swords emerged from sheaths. They formed up on Sigurd, but hadn't yet sensed the danger.

Gerd stood next to him, kitchen knife in her hand. "What is it?" she asked, loud enough for all to hear.

Sigurd couldn't bring himself to say the words. He hoped he walked in a dream, and feared that if he spoke, his nightmares would be made real. He pointed his own bared steel toward the sky.

The shadow had grown. It looked far too large to fly, and yet it soared through the air with an ease a hawk would envy.

Some in the caravan gasped. Others began offering prayers to the stamfar.

Gerd reached for Sigurd's hand. He took it, disappointed in all the days they would no longer have together.

The dragon's course never wavered. It came straight for them, swooping down low as it approached. It raced across the prairie, the force of its passing flattening every blade of grass. Enormous jaws opened, revealing rows of sharp teeth. It roared, and the sound of a hundred thunderclaps pummeled Sigurd's ears.

His strength, forged over a lifetime of battle and training, fled. A lone arrow shot into the sky but fell pitifully short of the beast.

The dragon hit Gleb's wards, which flashed red once and vanished. Sigurd ducked as the jaws snapped at him. They closed instead on the families standing behind him. He heard the wet sound of teeth rending flesh, bone, and viscera.

The monster passed them in the blink of an eye. Sigurd

fell, slammed to the ground by the wind. Bodies tumbled, screams carried away by the force of the gale.

Sigurd blinked. It took him several moments to understand he still lived. He rolled over and forced himself up onto hands and knees. Gerd was nowhere to be found. Long gouges had been carved in the ground to either side of him.

The caravan was no more. One pass from the dragon had wiped out a year of planning and preparation. People were missing, and the wagons were in pieces, the physical reminders of their lives scattered in every direction.

His heart still beat, though, and his limbs still served his command. Hope remained, slim as it was. They could recover from this.

Howls came from behind him.

Sigurd turned.

At first, they looked like wolves, but that assumption was quickly dispelled. They were too large and too dark. And there were dozens of them. Without Gleb's wards, the settlers had no chance.

Sigurd closed his eyes and prayed that he would meet Gerd on the other side of the gates.

CHAPTER 1

Hakon blinked as he and Ari appeared in the middle of a field. He let go of his friend's hand, and together they began the search. A bird had arrived that morning, sent from a settlement far to the northwest of Vispeda. A caravan had been expected but had never shown up. Eventually, the news had reached Solveig, as all news in Vispeda did, and she'd asked Hakon and Ari to investigate.

The two worked quickly, falling into familiar habits. This was far from the first caravan that had gone missing in the past few months. Ari's ability to transport was invaluable, as it allowed them to search vast distances quickly.

The assassin could have done the work alone, but Hakon had needed something to distract his attention, and it did make sense for Ari to bring company.

Hakon held out little hope they would find the caravan alive and well. Not after what he'd seen so far this year. The wild was pushing back, and humanity lacked the strength to fight.

They found the evidence of the dragon before long, eliminating Hakon's last slim hope they might find survivors. They followed the flattened grass and came upon the remains of the caravan.

Hakon walked slowly through the scene, giving his eyes time to notice any small details that might shed light on how, exactly, the caravan had perished. The ground had been soft during the attack, allowing Hakon to easily note the various tracks. The information helped little, though. What he really desired was one witness, one person who could speak to the events of that tragic night. Alas, every single soul had passed through to the other side of the gates.

Ari walked parallel to him, half a dozen paces to Hakon's right. They came upon the marks left by the dragon's talons. Hakon compared them to others he'd seen recently.

"Same one?" Ari asked.

Hakon shrugged. "Size seems right." But that alone didn't serve as sufficient evidence. They needed survivors to confirm or deny their guesses.

The pair of friends continued through the carnage, only stopping when they reached the center of where the wagons had been circled. Even those had been torn down. Splinters of wood lay everywhere. Axles that had endured hundreds of miles of travel were broken as though they were twigs. Shreds of the heavy canvas that had once covered the wagons flapped in the wind.

Only blood and the occasional bone remained. The wild had devoured the bodies. Hakon spotted eight types of predators in the tracks, and there may have been more. One type of track surprised him more than the others. He frowned as he looked up to Ari. "Aren't we beyond the range of shadow wolves?"

"Two years ago, I would have said so," Ari answered. He

came over to confirm Hakon's discovery. "These days, I wouldn't be surprised to see a shadow wolf in Mioska."

Hakon snorted at the thought of one of the terrifying creatures strolling down the streets of the continent's largest city. He repeated the question Ari had asked him. "Do you think it's the same one?"

"I hope so. Otherwise it means we have more than one hunting these lands."

Hakon let an exasperated sigh escape. He was tired of questions that had no answers. So, he asked one that did. "How many tehoin were with this caravan?"

"One vilda. An old, retired soldier named Gleb. Competent enough." The assassin left the rest unspoken. No matter how competent the former soldier might have been, it didn't matter much when faced with the overwhelming power of a dragon.

"Not enough to attract a dragon on his own, then."

"Probably not," Ari agreed. "The dragon would have had to be directly overhead to care, and we know that wasn't the case." He gestured toward the wide swath of grasses bent and broken by the dragon's passing.

A familiar storm of emotions rose in Hakon's gut, the same feelings he'd been battling for months now. He clenched his jaw and let his hand drift up to his chest, where a necklace hung.

He wanted to shout at the sky. Tear something apart with his bare hands. He wanted to know that what he was doing mattered. That he wasn't wasting his breath. That somehow, his days and efforts brought him closer to answers.

Closer to her.

Unfortunately, life wasn't in the habit of making such guarantees. He was as confused and as lost as the day he'd carried his daughter's still body from the ruins of the temple in Husavik.

Eight months had passed. Seasons had come and gone, and the six states had celebrated the new year. In that time, he'd crisscrossed the continent, usually transported by Ari. He'd pillaged the libraries of a dozen academies. He'd learned plenty, but he'd answered nothing. If anything, he had more questions now than he did then.

Ari noted his frustration. They'd fought side-by-side for decades. Even if they hadn't, little escaped the assassin's notice. His friend was kind enough not to say anything, though. Ari walked farther afield, giving Hakon space.

A simple enough gesture, but one Hakon silently thanked his friend for. He looked to the sky and closed his eyes. He evened out his breath, counting the heartbeats of both his inhale and exhale. Grief had been a constant companion long before Cliona's death, and he knew how to push forward.

Once he felt solid again, he opened his eyes. Ari had wandered to the west side of the camp and gestured for Hakon to join him.

He trudged through the site of the massacre. A pile of dead foxes lay undisturbed at Ari's feet. The predators of the wild had eaten and scavenged every other scrap of meat in three hundred yards, but the foxes remained untouched. A small shiver ran up Hakon's spine.

This wasn't how the wild behaved. Food was never wasted.

Ari kneeled and hovered his hand above the creatures. "Killed by wards," he said.

"All in the same place," Hakon added.

He let his eyes wander the horizon. He and Ari were alone out here, and Hakon had long since outgrown his fear of the wild. Certainly, there were creatures that could harm him, but they were few and far between. Still, he felt uneasy as he stood next to the foxes.

Ari stood. "It's just as Zachary reported."

Hakon nodded. It wasn't that he doubted the young man's account. The boy had spent many of the last eight months on the frontier, seeking his own answers around Cliona's death, and by all accounts, had acquitted himself well. But the reports he'd returned with portended terrible times ahead.

There was little else for them to learn here. The foxes had probably attacked first, but the vilda's wards held. Then the dragon came, followed by the rest of the wild. The caravan never had a chance.

"Ready to return?" Ari asked.

The resignation in Ari's voice lit Hakon's frustration on fire. He clenched his fists. "What do we do, Ari?" He swept his hand across the scene they'd just explored. "There's so few of us left, and there's no will in humanity for the fight that is coming. If this is a harbinger of what's to come..." His voice trailed off.

Ari didn't flinch away from Hakon's outburst. "I often feel the same," he admitted, "but I hold onto hope."

"How?" Hakon had been holding onto the thinnest strands of hope for months now, and his grip was failing.

"The five of us are back together, and Isira hasn't killed us yet. That's one miracle already."

Hakon's anger fizzled away at Ari's stolid answer. He cracked a grin.

The assassin turned serious. "Solveig has dozens of the best minds in the six states seeking answers. All of us are doing what we can. Even Zachary saved a settlement on the frontier, and he can barely form a shield." Ari paused. Had the assassin been a different type of man, Hakon imagined he would have come closer and put his hand on Hakon's shoulder. But Ari wasn't one for reassuring contact. "It looks bleak. Hell, it is bleak. But we'll fight. It's what we've always done."

"Fight until we fall?" Hakon asked. It was a saying Irric had once been fond of.

"Fight until we fall," Ari agreed.

CHAPTER 2

Zachary sat in a tavern, watching the street through the window next to his seat. Perhaps it was just him, but the streets of Vispeda seemed quieter than in his memories. People smiled less. Mothers, fathers, and children scurried from one errand to the next, eager to return to the imagined safety of their homes.

Or, he thought as he took a long swig of his ale, he was simply in a bad mood.

The sun was close to setting by the time he saw them, and Zachary felt the three ales already in his stomach. He didn't leave the tavern, preferring to remain unobserved.

They were in worse shape than he'd feared. Their uniforms barely looked like they deserved the title. Most were stained, blood and mud obscuring the light blue that represented the honor of the army.

Zachary clenched his mug of ale tight enough that his knuckles turned white. Those who remained in the streets had full view of the army's defeat. The soldiers walked with their heads down, their shoulders slumped. A full unit had left, fifty trained warriors sent out to battle the wild. By his estimation, only thirty or so had returned, and at least another ten of those were injured enough to require serious care.

Someone, years ago, had decided to locate the barracks near the center of the growing city. Useful, perhaps, while the unit's main occupation was protecting the young settlement. But now their primary responsibility was to sortie out into the wilds, to protect new settlements and beat back the predators that threatened humanity's advance. A wiser magistrate would have built new barracks near the edge of Vispeda, giving their soldiers easier access to the wilds and saving their troops from this humiliating return.

Word would spread, as it always did.

Zachary finished the last of his fourth ale with one quick swig. He wanted a fifth. The ale put his busy mind to rest, allowing him to pass peacefully at night into the realm of dreams. The thoughts that tormented him from sunrise to sunset seemed less important after a few drinks.

But that was a dangerous path. He pressed his hands against the table and pushed himself to standing. He left both hands planted for another moment to ensure he wouldn't fall. Once he was confident in his balance, he left the tavern, following the same route the army had just taken.

Their procession cast a pall over the city. Those still walking the streets were quiet, their eyes downcast. Few spoke of it, but everyone knew what these returns meant.

The mood on the streets improved once Zachary turned onto a different route. It wasn't quite the boisterous atmosphere he remembered from his earlier days at the academy, but it was still a sight better than the main thoroughfare. The taverns were doing a brisk business.

Young academics and merchants drank and debated. Once, those had been two of Zachary's most enjoyable pastimes.

He walked past them all, feeling like a stranger in the place he'd called home for years. He came to the short walls of the academy and passed through the main gate. Once on the other side, the feeling of being a stranger grew even stronger. Despite the lateness of the hour, scholars still prowled the grounds, noses stuck deep in obscure texts.

Such study had never been his way, and he'd once looked down on his peers for their obsession with knowledge. He shook his head, amazed at how foolish he'd once been. Cliona's passion for translating stamfar texts had been the first arrow to pierce his comfortable worldview. Then he'd seen gods battle over ancient knowledge and watched the wild attack in ways that shouldn't be possible.

His sense of superiority had long since crumbled to dust. Strength couldn't save them, at least not any strength he could imagine. Humanity's refuge from the advancing storm would be the knowledge they acquired. Unfortunately, if the conflict to come was to be decided by learning, Zachary was striding onto the battlefield less prepared than the soldiers who had just returned to Vispeda.

He ran his left hand through his hair, which reminded him he needed to get his hair trimmed soon. More and more recently, he'd found his thoughts turning down dark paths. He wished he felt more optimistic, but after months in the wild, he couldn't summon the feeling. Optimism had become nearly synonymous with delusion.

He had rooms within these walls, and he was more grateful to the academics than ever before, but this still wasn't home. He didn't belong here. The band was gracious enough to him, thanks to his brief relationship with Cliona, but he was no more one of them than he was an academic.

He wasn't strong enough to fight, nor smart enough to study. So how did he help?

His reverie was interrupted by a scholar he'd noticed standing watch near the front gates. When he'd passed her a few moments ago, she'd been engrossed in study, but now her footsteps pounded behind him. "Zachary!" she called.

He didn't recognize her, which meant she'd probably arrived at the academy within the past year. She wouldn't look up to meet his eyes. "Solveig sent me to keep watch for you. She wanted you to visit as soon as you returned."

Message delivered, the girl scampered back to her studies. Zachary figured he wasn't more than a few years older than her, but somehow that gap seemed a chasm.

He didn't particularly want to visit Solveig. There was only one reason why she would summon him. Once, he might have flouted such a request, flexing the power he imagined he held. Tonight, he just sighed and walked toward the administration building. Petyr manned the desk at the entrance, as he often did. The scholar tilted his head, indicating that Zachary was allowed to proceed. Zachary walked down the hallway behind Petyr, feeling a little like he was walking toward a hangman's noose.

When he entered Solveig's study, she was buried deep in a stack of papers. Without looking up she said, "Close the door."

Zachary did, then took a seat across from her.

Still focused on her work, she pulled out a drawer and retrieved a sealed envelope. She handed it to him without breaking her gaze from the papers before her. Zachary leaned forward and grabbed it, glancing at the familiar seal. He ripped the envelope open and read the missive quickly. Then he tossed it on her desk.

Finally, she looked up. Her eyes looked tired. "I can't

keep lying to him forever. The only reason you've avoided him this long is because you're never here for more than a few days before leaving again."

Zachary grimaced. Half a dozen retorts came to mind, but none of them were worthy of Solveig. "I don't know what to do," he confessed.

"Would it be so bad to return?"

"Even if my father speaks true about ending my exile," Zachary made sure his tone indicated just how much he believed that, "I would be even less useful there than I am here."

"Having another ally at court would be useful for our aims," Solveig argued.

"Unless that ally is me. My father ensured that when I left, I renounced all claims to his position. I'm not even sure I'd be allowed to speak to the council. If anything, close association with me will turn my father's alliance of magistrates against you."

"All the same, I can't keep sheltering you. If your father finds out just how long I've misled him, we may very well lose what meager influence we have. You know we need every resource we can scrounge together."

"I know." Zachary looked up and stared holes into the ceiling. "What do you think I should do?"

"Honestly?"

Zachary nodded.

Solveig gestured to his father's summons. "Answer it. Return home. You're a grown man, Zachary, with no obligations save the ones you bind yourself with. You are more capable than you think, and I do not think you would be ignored if you returned to court." She held up a hand to stop his protest. "Even if you decide to leave for the wilds once again, you'll eventually need to confront your father."

Zachary managed a wan smile. "Here I was hoping that maybe you would send me on an expedition so far away even my father couldn't reach me."

Solveig pushed the letter back toward him. "You know you have friends here, no matter what happens with your father. But this is a choice you need to make for yourself." She glanced back down at the never-ending stack of papers on her desk. "Now, I need to return to work. Please let me know your decision once you've made it."

Zachary picked up the letter and envelope and left. Outside, the first stars were just beginning to appear, and as he'd done so many nights before, he looked to the skies for answers.

And just like every other night, the sky refused to answer.

CHAPTER 3

Hakon and Ari reported to Solveig as soon as they returned. She took the news like a broke merchant hearing all their debts were being called in. She didn't even take notes, as was her custom.

They finished their tale, and she leaned back in her chair. They sat in silence.

Solveig clenched her fist, then realized what she had done. She opened it and shook it out, placing it deliberately on her desk. "We're running out of options," she said.

Neither of the men spoke. The truth was written plainly for all to see.

"I received a letter from Mioska's council yesterday," Solveig said. "They denied my request for more troops."

The refusal came as no surprise, but Hakon still grimaced. "What reason did they give?"

"That academics have no right to request military support."

Hakon gripped the arm of his chair so tight he feared he might break it. "They would have answered more politely if they knew who you truly were."

Solveig shook her head. "I don't think they would. Out east, the appetite for exploration wanes. They see the casualty lists from the local troops, and see little reason to risk lives for so little personal gain."

"Every step we get beat back by the wild is one step closer the wild approaches their precious cities."

"What do they care? They're hundreds of miles away. Even if they did believe your claim, which they don't, they'd feel no rush to act." Solveig saw Hakon's outburst building. "I know, it's foolish, but it's the world we live in."

Hakon growled. "They're cowards."

"In their defense," Ari pointed out, "if dragons are returning to the frontier, it doesn't much matter if they send all their troops. Better the warriors remain out east until we know how to use them."

Silence enveloped them again. They'd done all they could since Husavik, but they still lost ground with every passing day. Hakon stood. They'd create no new strategy tonight. Solveig looked as though she was moments away from using the pile of papers on her desk as a pillow. He looked to Ari. "Would you mind one more transport tonight? To Meshell?"

Ari shrugged. "Sure." To Solveig, he said, "I'll return soon. Then I'm going to force you to get some rest."

Solveig nodded, and Ari reached for Hakon's hand. He took it, and they were gone.

Hakon found himself in a pine forest, surrounded by trees almost as old as him.

Ari pointed south. "The main road is about six hundred feet that way. If they're still on schedule, they should be a few miles west of here tonight."

"Thanks. I'll plan on accompanying them the rest of the way."

"See you in a few days, then," Ari said. The man vanished, back to Solveig. Hopefully, he could get her to rest. Hakon forgot, sometimes, how much this mysterious campaign wore on all the others.

He followed the direction Ari had pointed, and just as the assassin had promised, he came upon the road. He turned west and kept walking.

Though he was hundreds of miles from where he and Sera had built their home together, this forest had much the same feel as that one. Exposed granite and gnarled roots poked through the soft carpet of pine needles, threatening a twisted ankle if he strolled too far off the road. Birds sang to one another, the distinctive call of a nearby owl louder than all the rest.

He could have hurried, but treasured the time to himself. They were all wearing themselves out, running in circles. He let his mind wander, almost daring the wilds to attack him.

Whether through coincidence or wisdom, though, nothing approached. It wasn't more than an hour before he came upon the caravan. A younger woman was on watch, and he held his arms up as he approached to demonstrate that he meant no harm. He stopped just outside the line of wards. "Would you mind waking Meshell?" he asked the guard.

The woman looked like he had asked her to put her head in the mouth of a shadow wolf. Which, Hakon supposed, he had. "Tell her it's Hakon. She won't be too angry at you."

"No need," a voice said from behind the guard. Shadows shifted, and Meshell emerged. "I felt Ari transport in and out." She smirked. "Care to test my wards for me?"

"I'd really rather not."

Meshell approached her wards and unraveled the section in front of Hakon. He stepped through and she reformed them. "Any trouble here?" Hakon asked.

"Nothing out of the ordinary. It's been a quiet trip, thankfully. How about you?"

Hakon glanced back to the woman, now watching them and trying to pretend like she wasn't. "Perhaps we could go to your tent?"

Meshell shot him a mischievous grin. "That's quite forward of you."

Hakon fought the urge to roll his eyes.

Meshell led him to her tent, a small construction at the edge of camp. She crawled in, and Hakon joined her. They lay down next to one another, and she rested her head on his arm. "What is it?"

"Another caravan, quite a way south of here, was attacked yesterday. Ari and I investigated when it missed its rendezvous. Looks like it was a coordinated attack from the wilds, similar to the type of attack Zachary was telling us about." He took a deep breath. "And a dragon was involved."

Meshell stiffened. "Her?"

"I don't think so. Hard to tell, but it seems like it was a bit smaller."

"Mathematics was never my strength, but by my count, that makes more than one dragon wandering around. And if there are two, there's probably more."

"The thought had occurred to us as well."

Meshell swore. "Almost makes you wish we hadn't spent so many years killing ourselves."

"Ari doesn't believe humanity has the strength to repel the dragons again."

Meshell nodded. "It pains me to admit it, but I agree. I don't know how many kolma remain, but it must be less than a dozen. And I've never heard of anyone less than a kolma killing a dragon. Hell, it takes several of us to even scratch one of the elders." Meshell reached for Hakon's right hand, resting on his chest.

He squeezed her hand. "We'll find a way."

"We better."

They allowed the sounds of the forest to wash over them. In time, Meshell's breathing slowed and she fell asleep. Hakon absently ran his hand through her hair. How many nights had they once spent like this? Huddled together in a tent, unsure of what the dawn would bring?

Some nights, when she slept in his arms, he dared to imagine a happy future for them. It was a new development for him, a sign, at least in his own mind, that he was beginning to move past the grief of Sera's death.

He couldn't say if those imagined futures would ever come true. His betrayal remained a barrier between them, one he wasn't sure Meshell wanted to fall.

He knew his own mind, though. Whatever Meshell ultimately decided, Hakon wanted to spend the rest of his days fighting by her side. Never again would he break an oath.

It was up to her to decide whether that was penance enough or not.

He felt his own exhaustion pulling him closer to the realm of dreams. But just as he was about to drift off, the hairs on his arms stood on end. The ground beneath him quivered gently. He placed his palm on the ground and felt the subtle vibration. A force of unbelievable power approached.

He shook Meshell awake.

"What?" she asked, instantly alert.

"We have company," Hakon said.

CHAPTER 4

The morning after his meeting with Solveig, Zachary woke up no closer to an answer. Despite her trust in his abilities, he didn't believe his return home would make any meaningful difference to the band's efforts. The rift between him and his father wasn't the sort of argument that healed with time. Most days, Zachary was convinced that only blood could settle their differences.

He couldn't guess why his father stretched out his hand after all these years. It wasn't in friendship, nor genuine reconciliation. If there was one constant in his father's behavior, it was that he only acted out of self-interest. But Zachary hadn't followed the news of events back home, especially in the past year, so he couldn't say what motivated his father.

Solveig was right about him needing to decide, though. He'd been fortunate to avoid his father's long reach for this long. But the magistrate didn't take "no" for an answer. If he continued to delay, Solveig and the academy would suffer as a result.

No amount of sitting and thinking was going to solve his problem, so Zachary dressed and left the gates of the academy. He had no destination in mind. He wanted nothing more than to wander the streets and search for an answer.

His feet carried him through places he knew well. The bright, cloudless sky mocked his dark mood. Children played in the alleys, shouting as they chased after one another. Zachary cracked a smile at their antics. He longed for the days of his youth and the lack of concern that made peace so much easier to grasp.

Watching the children did inspire one idea. He could disappear. He could head out west one last time, putting everything behind him. There was a simplicity to the frontier that appealed to him, a lack of artifice. He'd acquitted himself well on his previous outings. Perhaps he hadn't shifted the course of history. No one would sing songs about his deeds, as they did of the band. But he'd saved lives, and wasn't that enough?

Eventually, he found himself in front of his favorite tea house. He stepped out of the busy streets of Vispeda and into a tranquil room. His favorite table near a window was open, so he sat there.

The owner's daughter, a young girl of perhaps fourteen or fifteen years, waited on him almost immediately. "Your usual?"

"Yes, please."

The girl scurried away, and Zachary watched the street. This tea house was a block off the nearest thoroughfare and almost always quiet. Only a handful of people passed by outside.

The daughter came with the tea, setting a tray down gently before him. He thanked her and poured the first cup.

He inhaled the aroma, letting the grassy, almost floral scent fill his nostrils. When he'd been a true student in Vispeda, the taverns had been the only places he frequented. But both ale and wine had lost most of their flavor. It was tea he craved, though he couldn't say why. He took a sip and sighed in contentment.

The front door to the teahouse opened, and Zachary's eyes naturally traveled to the new arrival. He noted her physical characteristics first. Her hair was cut short, but like her eyes, was dark as a moonless night. She stood a few inches shorter than him, but the way she carried herself took his breath away. She had a presence he could feel as soon as she entered the room. The sword at her side looked like it belonged there, and he had little doubt as to her occupation.

Her eyes met his, and she walked right to his table. "May I join you?"

An odd request, what with the number of empty tables, but he wasn't one to deny the requests of an attractive woman without cause.

"Not sure I'll be great company, but please." He gestured to the empty chair across the table from him.

She took the offered seat and waved away the owner's daughter when she approached.

"My name is Hel, and I've come here for you," she said.

Zachary barely managed not to choke on his tea. Such directness from a stranger was unusual, to say the least. "Why?"

"I was one of Damion's commanders," she said. He swore he hadn't yet seen her blink. "And we'd like you to join us."

He was glad he'd had the foresight not to continue drinking his tea. He certainly would have choked on it at that pronouncement. "Why would I ever do that?"

"You're vilda. You belong with us."

She said it as though she was telling a child the sky was blue. That the fact was so obvious anyone should be able to figure it out on their own.

Once his surprise faded, though, the anger grew. He considered forming a teho sword and slashing at her right there. But if she had been a commander under Damion, she was almost certainly tehoin. She'd entered knowing full well he was a vilda. She was prepared for him.

Besides, he didn't want to see any harm come to this tea house. There were few peaceful places left in his life. No point in destroying one of them.

"Damion kidnapped and then killed my friend. Why would you think I would ever come with you?"

Hel looked as though she'd been waiting for just that question. "Because you don't think she's dead. Because you're running around the frontier, risking your life in a desperate pursuit of purpose. And, finally, because if there are answers to the questions you're asking, they are found in the libraries of Aysgarth."

Each point stabbed like a needle. "He killed her."

"And Hakon killed Damion. Unlike the band you spend your time with, I hope you can look beyond the events of the past. I'll make no excuses for Damion. He did as you say. He was a man with a vision and the will to make that vision a reality. Though he is dead, his vision lives on."

"What vision?"

"To save the world."

Zachary scoffed. "He was nothing more than a power-hungry kolma. He might have obscured his intent with noble words, but all he wanted was to rule."

"You speak as though you knew him." Zachary didn't miss the hint of anger in Hel's response.

He pushed harder. "I barely spoke with him. When I did, it was usually because he was blackmailing my sister, or threatening me. He was no different than the magistrates I grew up around."

Hel clenched her fist as she visibly struggled to master her emotions.

Zachary gathered his teho, ready to strike.

She stretched her neck and took a deep breath through her nose. Her hand relaxed. "How far would you go to save Cliona?"

It was his turn to clench his fists.

"Would you blackmail the conceited son of a magistrate? Would you fight those who stopped you? Or would you stick to your own illusions of nobility?" She leaned forward. "I know you look at me and believe that I cling to a mirage. But I look at you and see the same. You've been to the frontier. You know what's happening. The wild is fighting back, and it's defeating the six states. It doesn't care if you've lived by some arbitrary rules you've adopted. This is a battle for our survival. Damion saw it earlier than anyone and tried to save us."

Hel leaned back. "I didn't come to fight. You're a skilled vilda, and after Damion's death, our plans have changed. We no longer have any designs on the six states. We've focused our efforts in Aysgarth. We're going to build a place where humans can finally live in peace. We could use you. In exchange, you would have access to some of the best scholars in the world. If anyone can figure out what happened to Cliona, it's us."

Hel stood up.

Something about this whole meeting struck Zachary as wrong. As she was about to leave, he figured out what it was.

"You've clearly been watching me since Husavik. And I can't believe you make this effort for every vilda you come across. Especially knowing I might go back and report everything to the band. Why me?"

Her expression barely changed. Only a small flicker of emotion gave her away. He'd hit on something, and she was reevaluating him.

"Two reasons," she said, raising two fingers. "First, because the council that has taken Damion's place in leading Aysgarth has been impressed by what they've seen of you. Word of your deeds has spread throughout the frontier, and you have more friends out west than you might think. The fact that you are a magistrate's disowned son has appeal, as well. You represent a potential path to a more peaceful relationship with the six states."

"And two?"

"We want to know what happened to Cliona almost as badly as you do."

He was out of his chair before he realized it. "If you think you can threaten her—"

Hel didn't back down an inch. "I never said that. I said we want to know what happened. Perhaps, if you join us, I'll be at liberty to tell you why."

"How do I find you?"

A smile flashed across her face. "I'm staying at an inn about a half-day's walk west of here." She gave him directions. "I'll be there for another two days, and then my work will carry me into other parts of the six states. If you'd like to learn more, come there."

She left, and Zachary stared at her as she walked away. He released the teho he'd been preparing since she'd told him who she was.

He collapsed back into his chair. Leaving everything behind and wandering the frontier had never sounded more appealing.

But somehow, it looked like fate wouldn't allow him the peace he so desperately sought.

CHAPTER 5

Hakon and Meshell burst from Meshell's tent like a pair of arrows launched from a longbow. Meshell ran to her wards, strengthening them with an additional layer. Hakon, whose meager wardwork ability would do no one any good, bellowed for the sleepers to wake.

The camp erupted in confusion. The woman on watch was the only one to have seen Hakon, so the others woke to a massive stranger, wearing an enormous sword, shouting at them in the middle of the night. Several of the travelers thrust pitchforks and old rusted blades in his direction. Hakon ignored them as he searched the sky.

The vibration of the ground increased, but Hakon saw no evidence of the creature that caused even the stone beneath his feet to tremble. Tall pines blocked his view of the horizon. In this small clearing, he wouldn't know where the monster was until it was right on top of him. His eyes darted across the sky, but all he saw were the stars and moon looking back down on him.

Meshell finished her wardwork and joined him. "Seen it?"

He shook his head. "How are the wards?"

"Two layers deep. Considered a third, but that's a waste of effort. They'll buy us a bit of time."

Seeing their hired guard speaking with Hakon deepened the travelers' confusion. The pointed instruments aimed for his heart faltered. Hakon gestured to them as he questioned Meshell. "You know them best. What should we tell them?"

She answered him by shouting commands. "Everyone, gather as close to the cook fire as you can! Whatever happens, don't flee. It'll only make it harder for us to protect you."

Hakon grimaced. He would have told them to make a run for the trees. The dragon would most likely only be interested in him and Meshell. But then he thought of the doomed caravan to the south. If this attack was like that, spreading out would only seal their fates. So long as they kept close, Meshell and Hakon had a slim chance of keeping them alive.

A group of songbirds burst from one of the nearby trees dived into Meshell's wards. They hit the invisible barrier and died. Meshell cast an annoyed glance their way.

"It's more than just the dragon," Hakon said. Meshell had made the right decision. He turned to the travelers. "Truly, if you want to live to see the sunrise, don't flee."

It put the burden of many lives on their shoulders, but theirs were the only ones who could bear it.

A pack of wolves emerged from the shadows and prowled in a circle around the wards. They howled, and several travelers whimpered in response. Neither of the tehoin paid the animals much mind. The animals could charge the wards all night and accomplish nothing. If the wards failed for other reasons, Meshell could kill them all in a moment. They were no threat to the kolma.

Hakon stepped toward the wolves, and Meshell followed. He spoke low, so that the travelers couldn't hear. "When it comes, I'll fight it. Help if you can, but focus on protecting your caravan."

Meshell grunted her acknowledgment.

The wolves scattered as the trees rocked back and forth, blown by invisible currents of power.

It was close.

A few moments later it flew overhead, roaring as it passed. It blocked out the light of the moon, and several of the travelers fell to their knees. Even Hakon felt his legs weaken as the dragon passed. He'd faced nearly a dozen in his long life, and they still terrified him every time. Only a fool would feel otherwise.

Not for the first time, he wished he'd been born in a more peaceful era.

The dragon flew on, as though oblivious to the intruders below. The trees stilled and the vibrations under the soles of Hakon's feet faded. But the wolves didn't return, either. For several long seconds, the forest was quiet.

Had the dragon truly passed them by?

A cry from one of the men dashed Hakon's desperate hope. A moment later, Hakon saw the reason for the alarm.

In the distance, the dragon rose on powerful wings, flying so high it seemed to soar among the stars. It drifted lazily, far above them.

Then it folded its wings and dove.

Meshell swore.

"It's not an elder," Hakon said, trying to sound more hopeful than he felt. "Will your wards hold?"

Meshell didn't answer. Twin teho blades appeared in her

hands.

Hakon drew his own sword, taking comfort in its familiar weight. He filled body and blade with teho and braced himself for the impact.

As the dragon dove, it shifted so that it fell claws first. Enormous talons flexed and Hakon swore the beast aimed straight for him. He crouched, ready to meet the dragon with all his strength.

"Try not to die," Meshell said. "I'd be annoyed."

"Annoyed? I'd be heartbroken if anything happened to you."

She flashed him a brief smile, and then there was no more time.

The dragon struck Meshell's wards. Powerful muscles absorbed the impact of the landing as the talons squeezed against the strength of the teho. The force of the dragon meeting the wards blasted the surrounding pine trees from the ground, shredding them as though they were paper. Farther away, trees cracked and split, all of them falling away from the clearing where the travelers had made their camp.

Meshell cursed again and grimaced as her first level of wards bore the brunt of the assault. They collapsed after only a moment. The dragon hit the second level, and as it squeezed its talons, those wards shattered as well.

The moment they did, Hakon launched himself upward. The dragon had left its neck exposed, and Hakon swung as he passed. The teho enveloping his sword bit into the dragon's armored scales.

The dragon snarled, turning Hakon's insides to water. It snapped its head around and struck Hakon in midair.

The force of the blow tossed him away from the others like a child's doll thrown in the middle of a tantrum. He hit the ground hard. If not for the teho flowing through his muscles and bones, he would have broken into pieces. Instead, his limbs left gouges in the dirt as he tumbled to a stop.

He growled and pushed himself to his feet.

Fortunately for the others, his actions earned him the dragon's sole focus. The creature flapped its wings as it twisted to face him. Wagons blew over, and several travelers fell. The dragon landed between Hakon and the others, giving Hakon his first good look at his enemy.

The dragon was no elder, but wasn't a hatchling, either. Probably a youngling, based on its size. Hakon's cut had drawn blood but wasn't even close to fatal. Hakon met its eye and extended his sword toward the beast.

It spread its wings and launched itself at Hakon. It moved with a speed that seemed impossible for a creature so large. Hakon swung, aiming again for the long neck.

Before sword met scale, the dragon screeched. It flapped its wings chaotically, as though beating off an invisible enemy. Hakon's cut struck nothing but air and he barely braced himself against the winds.

The dragon gnashed its sharp teeth as it struggled against an unseen force. It screeched again, reminding Hakon of the death wails he'd sometimes heard from the creatures. It thrashed in midair, then climbed into the sky. The farther away it flew, the steadier its flight became.

Hakon watched the scene, rooted to the spot. He looked down at Meshell, wondering if she had somehow fought the creature off. But she was watching the dragon's flight with as much confusion as him. Then she shook off her wonder and began a new set of wards. She gestured for Hakon to join them, but he shook his head. The wards wouldn't last more than a moment, and perhaps his presence away from the others would distract the dragon's attention. Meshell looked like she wanted to argue, but then she shrugged and resumed her work.

High above them, the dragon circled once, then dove toward them.

Hakon braced himself, flexing his fingers and tightening his grip on the sword.

This time, the dragon didn't even get close. Hundreds of feet in the air, it emitted the same screech Hakon had already heard twice that night. It struck out at invisible enemies and began to plummet out of the sky.

Hakon was just about ready to regret not ducking under Meshell's wards when the dragon regained control and gained altitude once again. This time, it flew away, roaring with an anger Hakon felt in his bones.

After a few minutes the vibration in the ground stilled. Hakon shifted his weight, and it felt as though he'd actually grown roots. He walked to the line of wards, where he met Meshell. Behind her, the travelers were gathering their scattered belongings. He saw a few cuts and plenty of limping gaits, but it appeared everyone had been spared from serious harm.

The sky above them remained clear.

"Is it gone?" Meshell asked.

"Seems that way."

They looked around. The forest around Meshell's wards had been flattened for dozens of paces. Beyond that, trees lay cracked and broken. The destruction had scared off whatever creatures had lurked in preparation for the attack. Hakon couldn't see any movement in the trees.

"Do you have any idea what just happened?" Meshell asked.

Hakon shook his head. "Not the slightest."

CHAPTER 6

Zachary paced outside the administrative building, drawing curious looks from a fair number of passing scholars. More than once he caught himself muttering out loud. His former instructors probably thought he'd cracked under some difficult academic problem.

When he'd woken, the choice had seemed so easy.

Hel's offer gave him the opportunities he desired. He'd started packing his bags and considered, briefly, leaving without informing Solveig. If she didn't know where he'd gone, she wouldn't have to lie to his father when he pressured her.

But he had never appreciated secrets, especially after watching the effect they'd had on Cliona. She had been devastated by Hakon's hiding of his past, and then Zachary's betrayal shattered what little trust remained.

Besides, Hel had never demanded his silence. He couldn't guess at her reasons, but she didn't seem concerned about the band learning anything she'd told him. Once his bag was packed, he marched to the administration building, intending to speak to Solveig as soon as her door opened. When his hand reached the door, though, doubt had seized him.

The building had been open for nearly a half hour, but he remained outside.

He had one question he couldn't answer.

Was he traveling to Aysgarth because it was the right action, or because he was fleeing his father?

He clenched his fists. Stared at the door to administration as though it were a mortal enemy.

The door didn't flinch from his glare.

Then he realized he was being a fool. He didn't need to decide on his own. Though he suspected the band tolerated him more than they welcomed him, they might have their own thoughts on his choice. Maybe, for the first time, he could be useful to them. He stepped inside the building.

Petyr, as usual, was at the desk.

"I'm here to see Solveig," Zachary said.

"She's meeting with a small group of administrators right now," Petyr said.

"Any idea of when she'll be done?"

Petyr gave him a look. "She's meeting with a small group of administrators."

"Ah." In other words, it was possible she would be occupied until the end of time. Fortunately, Solveig was immortal. Zachary didn't have that luxury.

"I could let her know you stopped by as soon as the meeting ends," Petyr suggested.

He couldn't just sit here waiting for the meeting to finish. He'd tear out all his hair while they debated minutiae no sane person would concern themselves over. "Thanks," he said.

He turned to leave, but before he reached the door, the

floor began to shake. The tremor only lasted a moment, but it stopped Zachary in his tracks. He'd experienced several earthquakes growing up in Mioska, near the coast. But he couldn't recall one this far west.

"Was that an earthquake?" asked Petyr, his voice shaking.

When Zachary turned, he saw the normally composed academic had wide eyes as he stared at the floor. Zachary stifled the urge to laugh. Petyr looked as though his oldest friend had just broken an oath. The ground wasn't supposed to shake.

Petyr had grown up outside of Vispeda, though. His reaction to the tremor confirmed Zachary's own suspicions. There were no earthquakes here.

The floor rumbled again, this time hard enough to shake mounted paintings off the walls. A group of administrators and academics crashed out of one of the rooms behind Petyr. Solveig ushered them out, her face white.

That was when Zachary knew they were in real trouble. He couldn't imagine Solveig frightened over an earthquake.

She looked like a shepherd herding frightened sheep, but within a minute she'd directed everyone to safety outside the administrative building. Zachary followed the crowd.

The courtyard of the academy was in chaos. Some scholars hid under benches, as though worried the sky would fall on them. Others hugged trees. But most scurried about. Impromptu groups formed as they argued over the cause of the earthquakes. From beyond the short wall that separated the academy from the rest of Vispeda, Zachary heard screams.

The ground shook again as a shadow passed overhead. Zachary looked up and almost fell to his knees. A dragon flew low in the skies above Vispeda. Memories of Husavik overwhelmed him, and he wondered if there wasn't a little more space for him under one of the benches.

He wasn't alone in his fear. Some scholars cried as others collapsed to their knees. Groups scattered, only to realize the walls of the academy now served as their cage. A few scholars fainted. Zachary forced himself to watch the dragon. It flew with impunity over the city. Not a single arrow or spear rose to greet it, though it was well within range. He looked to Solveig, who was also staring at the creature.

Behind Solveig, back in the administration building, teho bloomed. A moment later, Ari appeared in the doorway Zachary and the others had just fled. His appearance snapped Solveig out of her momentary reverie, and she ran to meet the assassin. Zachary knew there would be no safer place than near them, so he chased after her.

Ari spoke to Solveig. "You felt it?"

"I did. Not sure why there's a dragon overhead, though."

"Hard to believe it's a coincidence."

Solveig grunted, and Zachary wished they would slow down long enough to explain. But they paid neither him nor his desires any mind. Ari retreated into the administrative building, and Solveig was only a step behind. They didn't invite Zachary, but they also hadn't forbidden him from joining them, so he followed on Solveig's heels.

They walked to the back of the administrative building, a place Zachary had never seen in all his years at the academy. They came to a small room that looked like a private library. Every wall had shelves that stretched from floor to ceiling, and every shelf was filled to bursting with books and papers. Zachary couldn't imagine what was so important in this room they needed to visit while a dragon flew above them.

Ari flicked a thin but powerful line of teho along the corner of the wall across from them, and Zachary heard a latching mechanism disengage. Ari and Solveig pushed together against the far bookshelf, and it opened like an enormous door. Behind the bookcase was a small plain room with a hole in the middle of the floor. The light of the stamfar came from the hole.

Ari vanished in a burst of teho, and Zachary felt him reappear beneath their feet. Apparently, ladders were too much work for the assassin. Solveig climbed down the ladder. Zachary hurried after her.

The room hidden below reminded him of Marjaana's home, the abandoned stamfar building that had been the subject of the expedition that had changed his life. Here, the walls were plain, but a short hallway led to a larger room with one feature.

Zachary froze in place when he saw why Solveig and Ari had come. A long tube, made of materials Zachary didn't recognize, held a figure he did. The last time he'd seen this relic it had been underneath a temple in Husavik. Since that day, he'd wondered what had happened to it. Now he knew.

Ava had been moved. She'd been right beneath his feet all this time, and he'd never known.

The others didn't give him time to be angry. They rushed to the tube.

Zachary saw all he needed from a distance. The clear material that made the top surface of the tube was cracked. Now that he was closer, he understood what Solveig and Ari had felt. Teho leaked through the fractures. A very slight amount but growing more with every passing heartbeat.

"Should we move it?" Ari asked.

Solveig hesitated for a moment, and it cost them everything. The ceiling cracked. Ari looked up, eyes wide. He grabbed Solveig and vanished. A moment later, they were standing next to Zachary. The ceiling groaned and began to cave in. Ari roughly grabbed Zachary's arm, and the next thing Zachary knew, he was out in the courtyard of the academy.

He blinked quickly, his mind questing for an explanation of what he saw.

Where the administration building had once been, there was now nothing but imploded rubble.

Then a dragon broke free of the shattered stone and rose into the air. Ava's tube was clenched in its jaws. Higher and higher it climbed, and Zachary could see the enormous muscles of its jaw gnawing on the tube.

Ari formed a group of teho darts, but Solveig held out a hand. The assassin shook his head. "It's too late now." His darts chased the dragon into the cloudless sky.

A long teho spear from Solveig followed a heartbeat later.

Either of those attacks would have torn through stone or flesh with equal ease. They barely scratched the dragon.

For a moment, Zachary wondered if the dragon was her, if it was the woman he'd spent so much time searching both land and sky for. But the color and size were wrong, and he couldn't imagine her attacking the place she'd once felt such an attachment to.

He formed a teho sword, then felt foolish. The dragon was hundreds of feet in the air. No sword would reach it, and even if he could, what good would it do? He possessed only a fraction of Ari's strength, and even the assassin couldn't bring the dragon down.

A sharp crack rang out above them, and the tube that

had held Ava for hundreds of years broke into pieces. Her naked body dropped from the sky, surrounded by the remains of the tube.

Zachary ran forward to catch the body, but stopped after two steps. Teho bloomed from the corpse, and Zachary suddenly realized Ava wasn't nearly as dead as he'd thought she was. Beautiful and intricate stands of teho sprang from her back, and she landed softly in the courtyard.

The power flowing from her was terrifying.

Over the last few months, Zachary had become accustomed to the strength of the kolmas.

But this had nothing in common with the strength of the band.

Zachary took a step back. Even the dragon seemed pathetic next to this.

Ava looked around the academy, then up to the sky. She gave the dragon a brief nod, and it turned and flew off.

Every eye in the courtyard was on Ava, and she basked in the attention. Her nudity didn't bother her in the least.

Then she vanished in a burst of teho.

The courtyard was perfectly silent. The scholars had finally seen something they couldn't explain.

But Zachary could.

They'd just witnessed the resurrection of a god.

CHAPTER 7

akon felt their stares, the same as he had every day since the dragon. Their gazes felt like ants crawling up and down his back, and he had to constantly fight the urge to reach back and wipe them off. Though they walked through the middle of a thick pine forest, he felt as exposed as he would facing a dragon on a wide-open plain.

Meshell walked beside him. "You look like a man searching for a cave to hide in," she said.

"It doesn't bother you?"

She glanced back to the travelers following in their wake. "Not too much. I'd rather avoid the attention, but doesn't this feel more honest to you? We don't have to hide what we are."

Hakon thought of the life he'd built once with Sera. True, she'd known who he was, but she had been the only one. Those days didn't feel like a lie to him. "We're more than just our strength, though. They look at me and see nothing but my sword and what I can kill with it. They don't know that I raised a family, or that once I was a young child obsessed with honor and justice and serving the empire. None of them care that you sing beautifully."

"Granted," Meshell agreed. She took his hand in her own. "But we've never had to hide those aspects of ourselves. We have had to hide our strength, and fear what would happen if we were discovered. Haven't you been the one who's been arguing that we need to be more public? Admit it. There's a part of you that enjoys the attention."

He grimaced but couldn't quite bring himself to confess that she was right. The attention made him uneasy, but he'd gotten used to it once. There were days when he had enjoyed the fame, too.

He forced the matter from his mind. What was done was done, and there was no point crying about it. If not for the frightened travelers trudging behind them, Hakon could have convinced himself that he and Meshell were out for a scenic walk. A stream flowed along the trail, bending through the pines as it snaked its way toward the prairies to the east. Songbirds filled the air with their voices, and the scent of pine filled his nose. Today was one of those days where the wild hid its claws and revealed its incredible beauty.

Those in the caravan probably didn't feel the same. Though there had been no casualties the night of the dragon attack, it had scarred them deeply. No one was the same after a dragon attack. The fear they instilled was almost as dangerous as their claws.

The greatest loss the caravan suffered was their belief. They traveled west because they were certain they could overcome the wild. It had been done before, in the places they had been, and they believed they could do it again.

The dragon stole that from them. It was a force few humans alive could comprehend, much less fight against.

How many of these once-optimistic travelers now believed they were marching to their doom?

The worst of it was, Hakon wasn't sure they were wrong. Had the situation been different, he might have encouraged them to turn around. But the closest safety was their destination. After the attack, he wasn't certain they had enough supplies for the journey back. He hoped they didn't end their journey at a destroyed settlement.

Since the attack, they'd kept a brutal pace. The faster they reached their destination, the faster they could put sturdy walls between them and the wild. Hakon and Meshell kept them safe, though few threats appeared. The travelers had tried giving the pair offerings worthy of kolma, and it had taken no small amount of persuasion to convince the offerers they desired nothing.

That afternoon, they came upon the settlement. It had been carved out of the forest, and Hakon was reminded of Dagrun's village a few days outside Vispeda. A wooden wall surrounded it. It wouldn't withstand even a basic siege, but it protected the families within from the wild. Several dozen homes had already been built, and there was plenty of space for more.

The two kolma led the caravan all the way in. They'd discussed leaving the travelers outside the walls but decided against it. Fortunately, the settlement was well into the frontier, so news of their presence would be slow to spread.

Besides, the idea of a roof over their heads was too tempting to pass up. Ari wasn't scheduled to arrive for a few days to pick them up, so they figured they might as well spend the days in relative comfort.

The caravan was expected, and they were greeted with enthusiasm by those already settled. More hands made work lighter, and there were a handful of skilled laborers among the new arrivals. Hakon and Meshell watched from a distance. In the chaos of greetings and welcomes they were largely forgotten, which served them both just fine. Hakon guessed they would receive more attention soon enough.

The settlement didn't have a proper inn, but it did have an expansive longhouse where community meals were served. There were a few rooms within for guests and new arrivals, and they gratefully accepted one. The travelers and the settlers worked together to make a quick feast, and everyone in town gathered for the meal.

After several days on the road, the food raised Hakon's spirits. Fresh fish from the stream accompanied heaps of potatoes, and a cask of ale that had survived both the journey and the dragon was cracked open.

Eventually, the travelers told the story of their trip. Hakon declined an invitation to speak of the dragon, but there was no shortage of witnesses to fill his silences. Hakon watched the original settlers as the story was told. When one of the older travelers described the dragon, he saw no disbelief among the assembly. His heart sank.

"We've seen the beast," one of the elders of the settlement said. "It's left us alone thus far, but we see it in the sky once or twice a week."

All eyes turned to him and Meshell when their part in the story was revealed. Hakon lifted his mug when thanks were given, but refused any greater acknowledgment. The mood in the hall darkened as the story ended. The joy of meeting fell prey to the fear of the future. Conversations died as people focused on the ale in front of them.

Hakon stood, drawing every eye.

He fought a grimace. The act had been an impulse, a memory of a time long past. Once, he had led the band. He'd inspired armies. He thought he'd put that all behind

him, but his body and spirit remembered. The corner of
Meshell's mouth turned up in a hint of a smile.

That was all the encouragement he needed.

He turned to his sword, resting in the corner of the
room. "That blade has crossed paths with nearly a dozen
dragons," he said. His voice was deep and clear. A voice that
sounded like it would carry for miles. "And every time, those
creatures have terrified me."

The travelers and the settlers glanced among
themselves.

Hakon continued, before they lost all hope. "No man can
honestly promise you an end to fear. But you are not
children, needing the comforting lies of parents to drift into
the realms of sleep. What I can promise you is this." He
paused, letting the suspense build. "No matter how terrified
I might be, I will fight until all the strength in my arm is
gone. I will fight until the moment my soul is pulled, kicking
and screaming, through the gates."

Heads nodded, but mere agreement wasn't enough.

Hakon thrust his mug into the air. He lowered his voice
until every soul in the longhouse had to lean in to hear him.
"My name is Hakon, and I fight dragons."

He paused again, then issued his challenge.

"Who will stand with me?"

He waited. As the echoes of his challenge faded to
silence, he saw the men and women of the settlement
looking to one another.

This was the moment. A leader was nothing without
people to lead. Too many believed the leader was the most
important person in a movement. They were wrong. The
most important person was the first one to pledge their
loyalty. The first follower.

An elder of the settlement stood and raised his mug. "I'll stand by you," he said.

His proclamation was the falling pebble that started a rockslide. One by one, the others at the tables stood, until they were all standing, holding their mugs aloft.

"Yes!" Hakon roared. "Together, we'll make even the dragons fear!" He quaffed his ale, and a cheer went up among the settlers.

Musicians went to their instruments, and the brief spell of gloom was cast off. Tonight, they celebrated being alive.

Hakon met Meshell's eye, and she joined him on the dance floor.

When Hakon had his fill of dancing, he stepped outside to take a turn watching the walls. The couple patrolling the wall offered their gratitude, then hurried in to join the festivities. Hakon watched them run off, then took a deep breath of the piney air.

The woods were quiet tonight, and the sky was clear. Hakon looked to the countless stars twinkling above. Not for the first time, he wondered what lay in the vast distances between the stars. What other secrets lived in the darkness of space?

The smell of the forest and the silence of the night made him suddenly homesick. When Cliona had been much younger, he and Sera fought a nightly battle to put her to sleep. But once the battle was won, they often retreated to a pair of chairs Hakon had built not long after he finished the house. Their neighbors always locked themselves in their homes at night, as was wise, but Sera hadn't feared the night with Hakon at her side.

How many nights had they watched a sky just like this one? He would reach across and take Sera's hand.

Sometimes they would talk in voices just above a whisper. But more often, they sat in the silence of their own thoughts.

Those nights had seemed perfect, even at the time.

He wanted to have her at his side again, watching the stars. He'd always known she would die before him. But she'd been taken too soon.

His thoughts were interrupted by the sound of footsteps approaching the wall. Hakon turned to see the elder who'd first rose to Hakon's challenge. "May I join you?"

Hakon nodded, and the older man climbed the ladder with impressive grace. He joined Hakon, and together they patrolled the walls. "It was a good thing you did in there," he said.

"It was not so much," Hakon said.

The elder gave him a disapproving glance, and Hakon bowed his head in apology. There would be no false modesty between them.

"It was important, and no one else could have done such a thing," the elder insisted. "You know it, too." He gestured to the sword on Hakon's back. "You're really him, aren't you?"

"I am. Will that be a problem?"

The elder thought for a moment. "I don't think so. You saved that caravan, so they'll not speak against you, and it's earned you no small amount of goodwill among my own people. In more peaceful times, some might object to your presence, but with the dragons in the air once again, I can't imagine you'll hear any complaints here."

"Please let me know if there are any. We will not overstay our welcome."

"I will." They walked for a while longer, making it halfway around the walls before the elder spoke again. "What really happened to the band?"

Hakon looked to the stars. "The legends are true enough. Some is omitted, but what lies in the past is best left buried."

"Even though there are many who hate you for abandoning the world after the rebellion?"

"Even then."

"I knew who you were, even before your speech," the elder said. "I would stand by your side, no matter the battle."

"I'm honored by your trust."

"Is there any chance you and Meshell might stay?"

"No. I would stay for a time if I could, but unfortunately, there is much for us to do. Yours is not the only settlement to have spotted dragons in the air. And other predators, besides. We need to find the reason."

The elder stopped in front of Hakon. "For what it is worth, I'm glad I got a chance to meet you before I make my own journey to the gates. You are not as the legends would have us believe."

With that, the elder left him and descended the nearest ladder.

Hakon watched the man until he disappeared back into the longhouse. After so long away from the world, he hadn't stopped to consider how messy the band's return would be. He grinned at a thought.

Solveig was going to be furious when she found out. Returning to public eye risked Isira's wrath.

Hakon understood the danger, but the times called for them to shoulder that risk.

Meshell emerged from the longhouse soon after the elder entered and made her way toward him. From the way she wobbled on her feet, she'd enjoyed several more ales since they'd parted. She joined him on the wall. "Making friends?"

"The elder knew who we are."

Meshell grunted. "Doesn't exactly take a scholar to figure it out. Your sword might as well be an announcement. Especially when you use it to fight off dragons." She laughed. "Solveig is going to be furious at us."

"I was just thinking that."

"They're still talking about you back there," she said, gesturing to the longhouse.

Hakon grimaced.

"I didn't think you had it left in you," she admitted. "Not after Sera, and definitely not after Cliona. But they'll stand and fight, now."

"It doesn't matter. If that dragon does come here, they'll have no chance."

She glared at him. "It does matter. They might die, but they won't break. That's something."

"It's not enough."

"So, we'll keep fighting. Same as we always have."

Hakon shook his head. Even after all these years, Meshell hadn't changed in any way that mattered. She remained pragmatic, realistic, and stubborn. "We will," he agreed.

He reached for her hand, and together they watched the stars in silence.

CHAPTER 8

There were days—a lot of days, it seemed—when Zachary was sure that if he pinched himself hard enough, he would wake up and find himself in his bed at the academy, the adventures of the past year nothing more than a rapidly fading nightmare. Who was he, to be here, among such company?

A stranger, glancing into the private dining room Solveig had reserved at a restaurant, wouldn't see much out of the ordinary. They might look twice at Hakon's enormous sword resting in a corner of the room, but there was little else that signified the importance of this meal. This was no grand hall of the magistrates. No courtiers lined the wall, listening to every detail. The band looked like nothing more than five friends, huddled together discussing something important.

The stranger would walk on, most likely never giving the assembly a second thought.

But Zachary would bet that more lives hung on the outcome of this meal than any assembly in court. Gathered in this room were the powers that truly shaped both the past and future of the six states. He fought back the urge to smirk. How many of his children would his father sacrifice to have a say here?

More than one, that was certain.

If his father knew what Zachary intended, he would strangle his oldest son.

Which made Zachary certain he'd chosen well.

But the time to make the announcement hadn't come yet. The band was still catching up with one another, and the stories being told seemed like they were pulled straight from legend. Had Zachary not seen the dragon with his own eyes, he'd be halfway convinced he was in the company of the mad. Ari had transported Irric into Vispeda last night, and Hakon and Meshell had transported in this morning to view the devastation at the academy.

Of the band, Irric was the only one who hadn't fought a dragon in the past month. Like Meshell, he'd been accompanying a group of settlers heading west. He'd heard rumors of dragons in the air but had escaped their attention.

After the stories came the questions. Why were the dragons attacking now? What had happened to the dragon Hakon and Meshell fought? How was Ava involved? What were Ava's plans, and where was she?

So many questions, and although the kolma explored every possible angle, Zachary already knew they wouldn't find any answers.

He had none, either. He didn't even have guesses, so he kept silent as the discussion swirled around him. As he watched the band debate back and forth, a certainty settled in his stomach. It was a thought he'd had before, and some part of him had always known it was true. But he felt it clearly now.

He didn't belong among the band.

He didn't belong here at all.

The thought didn't carry any pain or sorrow. It was just true. He belonged here as much as a bird belonged underground, or a fish on dry land.

Which, again, simply confirmed his decision.

His heart felt more at ease than it had for weeks. He watched the band, tried to imprint them into his memory. He was fortunate to be here, even as nothing more than an observer.

They fascinated him. On one hand, they were walking legends. They possessed a strength that boggled his mind. And yet, they were still so very human, Hakon maybe more than any of the others. They were all tired, as confused about what to do next as anyone else would be in their position. For all their strength, for all their history, he couldn't bring himself to feel any special reverence for them.

Bitter memories of his own father intruded on his thoughts. When he was six or seven, Zachary had asked to go see a particular warrior in the arenas. The other students in the sword school couldn't stop talking about him, and Zachary had wanted to see him in person. He sounded like a great hero.

His father had sneered, then waved him away, eager to return to his correspondence. "Never meet your heroes, boy," he said. "They'll only disappoint you."

Zachary looked among the band, still seeking their elusive answers. The band was not what he had thought, but he wasn't disappointed by them. He looked up to them. He learned what he could from them and acknowledged their weaknesses without judgment. Everyone was human. Even the stamfar.

A long silence settled over the room.

Irric chuckled. Of all the band, he was the one least

prone to falling into despair. "We're not getting anywhere, are we?"

Hakon answered. Something had changed in the giant man since he'd returned from his battle with the dragon. Maybe it had awoken a part of him long dormant. Since Zachary had come across the band, Solveig had been in charge. She still was—Hakon deferred to her yet, but he asserted himself more than he had before. Hakon had once led the band, and now Zachary began to understand why. The man radiated a quiet strength that even the other kolma acknowledged. "We can wonder as long as we want, but we don't know enough. So, the question then becomes, 'What are we going to do?'"

Solveig rubbed her eyes. "Just say it," she said.

"I want to go west," Hakon said.

Solveig sighed. "We've talked about this. A lot."

Hakon pressed his argument. "Before the dragon came for Ava. Their return to the six states isn't coincidence. If anything, they are at the heart of it all."

"And because you still think the dragon from Husavik is there."

"I won't deny it. It makes sense that the dragon, freed from Damion's control, would head home. Cliona has to be there."

The mention of Hakon's daughter's name chilled the room. Zachary saw it on every face and wondered if Hakon did, too. The others all called it "the dragon from Husavik." Only Hakon named it different. Hakon's belief couldn't be shaken, but the others couldn't be convinced.

Zachary spoke for the first time during the gathering, hoping to ease the sudden tension in the room. "How far west?"

Hakon looked as though he'd forgotten Zachary was there. "As far as it takes."

"As far as Aysgarth?"

Across the room, Ari chuckled. "Boy, if Hakon had his way, Aysgarth is where his journey would start."

Zachary blinked, and again he experienced the powerful feeling of not belonging. Aysgarth was so far west most travelers would consider it an almost suicidal destination. As far as the six states were concerned, the world *ended* at Aysgarth. And Hakon wanted to use it as a place to *start*?

Solveig, who didn't miss a detail, asked, "Why do you ask?"

Zachary swallowed hard. He'd come here with the intent to tell them, but with all five of them now staring at him, lying seemed far preferable.

He sat up straight. "I've received an offer to travel to Aysgarth, and I intend to accept it."

Meshell's response was perfectly flat and expressionless. "What?"

"Recently, I was approached by a stranger named Hel. She claimed to be one of Damion's former commanders. According to her, they are rebuilding Aysgarth to protect the tehoin who live there. She invited me to join them and offered me access to Damion's library if I did."

His announcement was greeted with mute stares. His cheeks flushed, but he refused to look down.

Then he was hit with a barrage of questions, the band turning their full attention to him and the offer he'd received. He answered as well as he could, but he didn't know much beyond what little Hel had told him in the one meeting.

Eventually, the questions faded. "Is any of this even something we need to worry about?" Ari asked.

"I don't think so," Hakon said. "If Damion's surviving followers want to build a commune outside the six states, I don't see how it's our problem. Damion was, and we killed him."

"It's not so easy," Solveig replied. "First, we don't know if Hel was telling the truth. Second, even if she was, Damion had assembled the largest army of tehoin in the six states. If the dragons are returning, those tehoin would be invaluable. If they do nothing but hide in the mountains, they're as good as dooming the six states."

"We can't spare the attention," Hakon argued. "Even if you did somehow recruit all the tehoin, it doesn't matter. If the dragons return with the force they once had, humanity doesn't have the strength left to go toe-to-toe with them. We need to go west. Any answers to the dragons are there."

"Or in Damion's library," Solveig countered. "The man had a greater collection than almost anyone."

Zachary raised his hand to get everyone's attention. "If you don't mind me saying, you don't need to choose. I want to go, and if Hel spoke true, then I can communicate with you freely."

"And if she didn't?" Solveig asked.

"Give me one of Ari's stones that you all carry. I'll learn what I can, then use it to summon aid."

Ari shook his head. "Even though Damion is dead, his wards around Aysgarth remain. I can't just transport in and save you."

"He's got a point, though," Hakon said. "I want to go west, but there's no need for the full band to go with me. We can afford to split our attention."

"What about Ava?" Solveig said, exasperated. "If she acts, it's going to take all five of us to even have a chance against her."

Three arguments erupted at once around the table as everyone tried to speak over one another.

Just as Zachary began to feel that all hope for a compromise was lost, Hakon stood so fast he knocked his chair over. He slammed an open palm onto the table, threatening to break it in half. The motion silenced the others. A storm of emotions played over Hakon's face, and Zachary was glad Cliona's father didn't have his legendary sword in hand.

After a few moments of silence, Hakon vanquished whatever demon tormented him. He looked straight at Solveig. "There's only five of us."

Zachary had a sudden, maddening urge to remind them he was here, too, raising the number to six. He pressed his lips together to prevent making that mistake.

Hakon continued. "We can't do everything, nor can we save everyone. But I still might be able to see my daughter again."

The giant man's voice quivered. Zachary didn't dare to breathe.

Hakon raised his hand and clenched it into a fist. Zachary feared the table only had a few seconds of service left. But Hakon never struck. He took a deep breath and put his hand back down. "We need to choose, and I choose Cliona."

With that, Hakon left the room. No one followed.

The others leaned back in their chairs, exhaling slowly, as though they'd just escaped an ambush. Irric said, "He's right, at least about not being able to do everything we want."

"I'll go with him," Meshell said. "I'll do what I can to keep him from getting killed."

Irric chuckled. "No small task, that."

All eyes turned to Solveig, whose gaze had been locked on the table since Hakon left. Her fingers tapped lightly against the oak, intricate patterns Zachary couldn't follow. Then her fingers stopped, and she looked up. "The rest of us should travel with Zachary," she said.

He almost spit out his tea. "What?"

She shrugged. "Hakon is right, painful as that is to admit. I've been balancing too many threats. We don't know anything about Ava right now, so there's no point in us chasing our tail in that regard. My collaborations with other scholars are going nowhere useful. And you've given us an opportunity. We should meet with Damion's tehoin. They're powerful, and if they're organized, they can't be ignored."

"Hel didn't invite anyone else," Zachary protested. For once, he'd had an opportunity to strike out on his own. To make his own way.

"She also didn't demand you keep it a secret from us," Solveig pointed out. "I suspect she considered the possibility. Wouldn't you like some company?"

"Of course, it's just—" How could he tell them he didn't feel like he deserved their company?

"Then it's decided," Solveig said.

"What about rebuilding the academy?"

Irric chuckled again. "All the senior scholars know now what Solveig was storing in secret, and more than a few have connected the dragon attack to it. I don't think too many will be upset if Solveig decides to travel for a time."

Solveig looked down again, and Zachary chastised himself. He wasn't paying enough attention to how events were unfolding. He kept getting lost in his own selfish considerations.

"I should at least go talk to Hakon," Zachary said.

"Why?" Meshell asked.

"I—" Zachary hesitated. "I want him to know that I'm also going to do everything I can to find Cliona."

"He knows," Meshell said. "And it might not be the best time to speak with him."

"It's decided?" Solveig asked. There were nods around the table. "Get prepared, then. As soon as we can, we'll meet Hel and let her take us to Aysgarth."

The group dispersed without fanfare, leaving Zachary alone in the room with his tea. Just like that, Zachary thought, the fate of the six states was decided.

CHAPTER 9

When Hakon's frustration subsided, he found himself in Cliona's old room at the academy. No one had quite been sure what to do with it, but with no pressing need for space, the other administrators were perfectly comfortable letting the matter slide for now. For that, Hakon was grateful. If Cliona still lived, he wanted her to have her home to return to.

Although, he thought with a wry smile, the place had changed since she lived here. She'd probably not approve of the lack of an administration building.

The arrival of the dragon had disorganized the room. Several books were on the ground, and Hakon picked them up and replaced them on the shelves. He made sure to put them back where they'd come from, a task made easy by his daughter's rigorous organization.

When he stood in this room it felt as though she was standing right next to him. Her essence permeated every inch of space, from the organized shelves to the jewelry on top of the dresser. The necklace he'd taken from the dresser pressed lightly against his chest, hidden underneath his tunic. He used it as a reminder, to keep Cliona close. He looked around and felt hollow inside, as though he was nothing but skin and skeleton wrapped around an endless hole.

Hakon sat on the edge of her bed, the wooden frame creaking under his weight.

He didn't know how much longer he could go on like this.

Two hearts beat within his chest. One lived here, in this room. The heart of the concerned parent. The grieving father and widower, the man who would do anything to see his daughter smile at him one more time.

The other lived out there, in the wild. It had stood in that longhouse and boasted of its great deeds. It stood against the dragon, proud and unbroken.

The scene from the forest came rushing back to him. How he'd faced the dragon, sword in hand, death one wrong move away. In those moments his fingers tingled with excitement. When he stood right beside the gates was when he felt the most alive.

He couldn't be both. Fighting dragons and traveling with Meshell were betrayals against the grieving father. How dare he feel so alive when his family suffered so?

There was a soft knock on the door, and it opened gently. Meshell slid in. "May I?"

The two hearts warred within. One wanted desperately to see her, to take her in his arms and borrow some of her strength as his own. The grieving father recoiled from the thought. Meshell was from a different life and had no part in this.

She didn't wait for his permission. She shut the door behind her and sat next to him. "Talk," she commanded.

"I'm a mess."

"That's putting it gently."

Gods, but he loved that about her. She didn't pull her punches, even when they were verbal. She was, perhaps, one of the most honest people he'd ever known.

She deserved no less from him.

He gestured out Cliona's window to the west, a soft growl escaping from the back of his throat. "I want to be out there, sword in hand. I want the dragons to fear my coming."

"And that's a problem because..." She waited for him to finish the sentence.

"Because I'm Cliona's father!" He clenched his fists and closed his eyes, forcing his voice lower. He opened his eyes and exhaled slowly. "I hid my sword under our house. I buried my past for her, because she deserves better."

Meshell began to retort, then caught herself. She'd been about to say something cutting. It was her nature, the way she protected herself from the very pain he now experienced. Like him, she took a moment, then tried a gentler approach. "Do you still believe that burying your past was the right way to parent her?"

Hakon hadn't forgotten the arguments between him and Cliona during the brief time they'd been reunited prior to Husavik. Those memories rose, unbidden, several times a day. He hated that of the short time they'd been reunited, so much of it had been acrimonious.

Despite his best intentions, his lies had put her in far more danger than if she'd simply known the truth.

Meshell didn't wait for his answer. "Do you believe that continuing to bury your past—burying who you are even now—will help Cliona?"

A lump formed in Hakon's throat. He confessed the truth he hadn't spoken to anyone. "I fear that if I embrace who I once was, I'll lose the parts of me that made me a good father."

Meshell was silent for a moment, but Hakon had little difficulty imagining what might be going through her head. She confirmed it a moment later when she swore and stood up. "Gods, but you can be a frustrating brute."

She turned on him. "Do you hear yourself?" She deepened her voice in a parody of his own. "If I embrace who I once was, I'll lose who I am." Her voice returned to its normal register as she swore again. "You sound like a child."

Anger sparked in Hakon's chest. What did she know of what he was going through?

She didn't give him a chance to argue. "I don't know where this idea of you being one person or the other came from, but it's foolish. You're *Hakon*! You're a legendary warrior *and* a father. Why do you believe you have to choose?"

He stood, too, so that he could tower over her. "Because they can't both exist!"

She didn't back down. "Why not?"

"Because—" And he realized he didn't have an answer. He'd spent so long thinking of himself as two different people, the simple idea of just not doing that confused him.

"Grieve your daughter's loss. Remember fondly your time with Sera." Hakon saw her wince at that sentence, but Meshell pressed forward. "Fight dragons. Inspire settlers. The Hakon I know can do it all." She poked her finger in his chest. "You don't have to choose."

The wall that he'd built over the years, the barrier that separated before and now, cracked. He was a fool.

He wrapped her up in his arms and brought her close. Their lips met, and after a moment of surprise, she returned the kiss.

A moment later, he realized what he'd done and broke the kiss off. He looked around his daughter's room. He knew he should be horrified.

But he wasn't.

All he could think about was that Meshell hadn't pushed him away. Even after all he'd done.

The grief that had threatened to consume him faded. It didn't vanish, but if Sera's death had taught him anything, it was that the grief would always remain. It would linger, and he would welcome it as a reminder of what they had shared.

His thoughts, now undammed, flowed freely. He looked at Meshell and his eyes narrowed. "Why are you here?"

"The rest of us talked after you stormed out. We decided that you should travel west. And I'm going to accompany you."

"They'll need you here, especially if Ava or the dragons attack."

Meshell shrugged. "Then we better find what we're looking for quickly."

She should stay here. With him gone, she was the best chance they had against dragons or stamfar. But he was grateful that she'd elected to travel with him. He bowed his head. "Thank you."

She nodded and turned to leave. "I'll start gathering supplies. Find me when you're ready. Ari said he'd transport us whenever."

Once she left the room, Hakon turned to take in his daughter's room one more time. He still felt her beside him, but the gloom had been banished from the room. It took him a while to figure out what he felt stirring inside his chest. It had been absent so long.

It was hope.

CHAPTER 10

Preparing to leave didn't take Zachary long. He'd never truly reconnected with his old friends after Husavik, so there were no goodbyes to endure. There'd never been many in the academy he'd call friend, anyway. Those who were close to him tended to be those with an eye for political favor, thinking Zachary might someday bring them with him if he rose to the position of magistrate.

He almost had fewer clothes than friends. Since his first trip to Aysgarth, he'd lived off a set of supplies that could be carried easily in a pack. And he'd already been packed before the dragon attacked. All he had to do was replace anything that had escaped his pack since then. The whole process didn't take more than a few minutes.

Even so, he was among the last to join the band. Except for Solveig and Hakon, they'd lived nomadic lives for hundreds of years. Leaving was easy when there were no roots to pull.

Neither Meshell nor Hakon were present. When

Zachary asked, he learned that Ari had already transported them as far west as he was able. The pair were on their own.

Zachary was glad they had left, for he knew how soon Hakon had hoped to leave. But still, he would have liked to say something to Cliona's father. Hakon accepted his presence among the band, but he'd never forgiven Zachary for his betrayal. Zachary wanted another chance to prove how bad he felt over the choices he'd made.

There was nothing for it, though. He had to trust that Meshell spoke true, that somewhere, deep in that enormous chest of his, Hakon understood. Zachary, like the rest, had come to believe Cliona was dead. A strange death, perhaps, but final all the same. Still, he wished Hakon well in his own quest for answers.

Together, the group left the academy. Their departure from the main gate wasn't even remarked on. A band of legends, their tales told in almost every household, and not a single soul came to wish them well. It was unjust, and yet none of Zachary's companions said a word.

It didn't take them long to put the busy streets of Vispeda behind them. They traveled west, following the directions Hel had given Zachary what seemed like a lifetime ago. Today was the last day of her visit to Vispeda.

The inn was one Zachary had become familiar with over the past eight months. He'd come to prefer it himself. It sat close enough to Vispeda he could reach the city with ease, but gave him enough distance to feel like he was separated from his past life. He'd often used the inn both as a beginning and an ending to his journeys.

He was the first to enter the inn, and she was the first person he saw. There was something about Hel that drew his eye. Even in a common room with half a dozen customers, she might as well have been the only one there.

She smiled when she saw him, and then her eyes widened when she saw who entered next.

The reaction was brief. Barely a flicker of emotion, but he'd seen it clearly. She hadn't expected the band. Then she smiled wider, and it looked like relief to Zachary's eye.

He approached her table, checking every corner of the room for surprises. Although their arrival was noted by every patron, no one paid them much mind. Hel gestured for them to sit. "I didn't expect you to bring company."

Zachary trusted his instincts. "You might not have expected it, but you hoped for it."

"I did." Hel turned her attention to the others. "Thank you for accompanying Zachary. Are Hakon and Meshell going to join us, too?"

Solveig spoke for the band. "No. They had other matters to attend to. Why did you reach out to him?"

Hel swallowed. "I did not lie. For most of us, all plans involving the conquest of the six states have vanished. We want only to protect ourselves. Recruiting Zachary alone would have been a success. We know his value. But we hoped that by approaching him, you might also be interested."

"Most of you?" Solveig hadn't missed the use of the phrase, either.

Hel grimaced. "While most of us have abandoned any thoughts of conquest, there are those who hold more tightly to the letter of Damion's teachings. There are those who hate you. I cannot guarantee your safety if you return with me."

Irric flashed his most winning smile, and Zachary was surprised to find he was jealous when Hel returned it with one that was equally dazzling. "Trust me, dear," the swordsman said, "we didn't think that returning to Aysgarth would be without danger."

Solveig cut Irric off with a wave of her hand. "You're still avoiding the question. Why are you seeking even more tehoin?"

"It would be best if I showed you," Hel said.

"Then lead the way," Solveig suggested.

Hel left coin on the table for the innkeeper, then brought them outside. Clouds built on the western horizon, and Zachary couldn't help but see the formations as a warning. The group gathered in a circle. Hel said, "There will be a handful of guards in the place where we will appear. So long as you make no aggressive moves, they shouldn't react. I'd urge you to avoid conflict whenever possible. It would be helpful to me."

She reached out and took Zachary's hand. He grabbed Ari's, and soon they were all touching. Hel met each of their eyes one more time, then nodded. Zachary closed his eyes. His last thought before Hel took them was that she was stronger than he had guessed. To transport this many made her nelja.

He felt no sense of motion, but he knew when they'd transported. The experience made him feel sick in his stomach, and the wind against his skin changed. The air was colder here, and thinner, appropriate for the higher elevation of Aysgarth.

He opened his eyes. Hel had transported them to a high platform with a view of the valley below. Guards surrounded them, and for a moment, he feared he had led the band into a trap. Their arrival startled the guards, but after several tense heartbeats when no one struck, both sides came to an unspoken truce. Hel stepped forward to talk to the commander, and Zachary let his gaze travel to the valley below.

Several of the homes in the valley had been flattened to rubble. Dark furrows had ripped up enormous parts of the fields. As his eyes traveled across the breadth of the damage, the wall that protected the valley came into view.

When he'd last seen the wall, part of it had been destroyed by a dragon in the escape he and Cliona had designed. Now it barely resembled a wall at all. Broken stone lay all around the foundation, scattered as though by an angry, oversized child.

Only one creature could cause such destruction, and Hel confirmed his guess. "Welcome to Aysgarth. As you can see, Vispeda was not the first city the dragons visited."

CHAPTER 11

Ari left them with little more than a nod. Hakon checked his gear one last time, and Meshell did the same. Once satisfied, they left the small clearing to find the road to Aysgarth.

In a more perfect world, Ari would have been able to transport them somewhere farther west, or at least somewhere farther away from Aysgarth. But the transport point that served them best was the same one they'd appeared on when the band had launched their last expedition to retrieve Cliona from Damion's fortress. Any other destination would have added days, if not weeks, to their travels.

Hakon set a quick pace. He and Meshell both believed their best course was to get through Damion's former territory as quickly as possible. They made no attempt to hide, but quickly realized there was no need. Despite their sharp watch, they saw no guards, nor travelers. As near as they could tell, they were the only people on the road.

They passed familiar landmarks, and Hakon's thoughts turned to his last journey through these lands. The band had fought off dozens of tehoin and rescued his daughter, their first action together in over a hundred years. He remembered how good it felt to fight by their side again, and how ashamed he'd felt when he realized Cliona had seen him battle.

He'd been a fool to hide his past from his daughter.

They walked for another hour. Eventually, the path turned north and rose steeply. From Ari's description of the road, this was the final ascent into the valley that housed Aysgarth. The pair broke from the road and continued west instead. There was no need to get too close to Aysgarth, no matter how curious Hakon was about what happened within its walls. The others would find out soon enough.

Their progress slowed after they left the road. It took them the rest of the afternoon to summit a pass in the mountains.

When they dropped down on the other side, they were attacked by the same creatures Cliona had reported in her story. Strong and quick, they swung from tree limb to tree limb with incredible grace. Meshell and Hakon endured two assaults before the creatures realized they were not prey.

Hakon still heard them, paralleling their steps in the trees. No doubt, they waited for the travelers to rest. They'd be in for another surprise when they encountered Meshell's wards.

As night fell, a pack of shadow wolves passed no more than a hundred paces in front of the pair. Hakon had his hand on his sword, but the shadow wolves ignored the travelers. Hakon couldn't guess why, but he was grateful not to have to fight them.

If there was one thing Hakon had forgotten in his years within the six states, it was how wild the wild actually was. The home he'd built with Sera so long ago was considered wild by most standards, but the untamed lands of the six states were far different than the untamed lands farther west. In the six states, living apart from a city was a calculated risk, but one that could be managed by most anyone with common sense.

The mountains that surrounded Aysgarth and bounded the six states to the west were another story entirely. Hakon's old neighbors, skilled at surviving the forest they called home, wouldn't have lasted a day here. Beyond Aysgarth, humans had never been able to settle in these mountains.

Hakon didn't think it was outside the realm of possibility, but it wouldn't be anytime soon. There was still plenty of land in the six states, and building larger settlements in the mountains would require a huge investment in both people and supplies. Back in the days of the empire, it might have been organized, but not now.

He imagined Solveig chastising him for being an imperialist again and grimaced.

Meshell noticed. "What is it?"

"Nothing," Hakon said. "Just wondering if the empire ever would have settled out here if we hadn't brought it down."

"Probably," Meshell said. "I know Torsten planned on eventually using Aysgarth to launch settlements farther west."

"It's frustrating, sometimes, to think of all the consequences of what we did."

"Do you regret it?"

"Not the rebellion, no. That was just. But I'll admit that there are things about the empire that I miss."

"Me, too."

"Really? When I even implied as much to Solveig, she just about bit my head off."

"That's because she's always dealing with one plot or another to restore the empire. It's a recurring problem in her life."

They crossed a small stream, using teho to jump over without getting wet. "What do you miss?" Hakon asked.

"The feeling of purpose that came from serving the empire. Especially in the early days, before we'd seen what we did. I felt like I mattered."

"As did I."

Their stroll through the memories of their past was interrupted by a shadow emerging from the clouds far to their north. They both spotted it, their heads turning in unison.

"Well, that's certainly no bird," Meshell said.

Hakon grunted and followed the flight of the dragon. It flew from east to west, majestic even when seen from miles away. Hakon had long believed that they were the most beautiful creatures in this world, even with their terrifying strength. Though he'd never spoken the truth, not even to the band, the moments when he'd flown upon the dragon over Husavik were some of the greatest in his life. Partly it was because of the link with Cliona, but partly it was because he'd always dreamed of flying. "Think it attacked another settlement?" he asked.

"Likely." Meshell pointed in the direction the dragon had flown. "So, we're going that way, then?"

Hakon grunted again, then said, "Second thoughts?"

Meshell scoffed. "I passed the point of second thoughts a long time ago."

They shifted their direction, following the dragon to whatever faraway land it called home. Hakon kept expecting Meshell to protest the foolishness of their quest, but she never uttered a complaint. He was grateful for her presence, in more ways than one. Her wards were far superior to his own meager efforts, and her ability to protect them with ranged teho weapons made the task of traveling much easier.

She also made him feel less of a fool by her presence alone. He knew his reason was compromised by Cliona. If anyone would tell him when he'd gone too far, it would be Meshell.

It wasn't until the sun was setting on their second day of travel that she asked the question he'd been dreading. "What, exactly, are you hoping to discover? Even if we do find where the dragons are coming from, I'm not sure how that helps us."

He'd fielded that question in the past from Solveig, and his answer remained unsatisfactory.

"I don't know," he admitted.

Meshell didn't sigh, but she looked like she wanted to.

"I'm hoping we find the dragon from Husavik again, at the least. If I can touch it, I'll know for sure. Otherwise, I'm just hoping we'll find *something* that leads to Cliona."

Meshell rolled her eyes. "So all you want to do is *touch a dragon*?"

"You think I'm mad."

"Not mad, exactly. I understand your reasoning well enough. But we have no clearly defined objective. You want to wander around until you find something. We could end up out here for months."

"It's one of the reasons why I'm glad you're here. I expect that you'll keep me honest."

They walked for a bit before Meshell replied. "I'll help you, because I want you to find her. But if I tell you we need to leave, will you listen?"

"I'm not sure, but you're the only one who has a chance of making me."

He wished he could promise more, but he wouldn't give up on Cliona. Not when even a single strand of hope remained.

That night, Meshell's wards endured constant attack from the wild. They watched the wards flicker as creature after creature met their demise. No matter how many died, more kept coming. Even a nelja's wards would have collapsed under the onslaught. "Guess we won't have to worry about food," Meshell said.

On the third day, they descended into a wide valley. For the first time since they'd left the road leading to Aysgarth, the attacks from the wild stopped.

They followed the path of a stream. It flowed gently over smooth rock, and if not for the sound of the water, the whole valley might have been perfectly silent.

Meshell responded with wariness. Her pace slowed and her head roved back and forth. Hakon was much the same, and his hand itched to have the comforting weight of the sword within its grasp.

The valley turned gently to the north. Meshell, in the lead, froze. Hakon stopped beside her. He was about to ask why they were stopped, but his eyes picked out the reason soon enough.

A dragon lay, perhaps a half-mile away. For several long minutes, Hakon and Meshell watched, barely daring to breathe.

"It doesn't look like it's moving," Hakon said.

"It doesn't even look like it's breathing," Meshell agreed. "Approach it?"

"Sure. So long as you're in the lead."

There was no point trying to hide from the dragon if it

was alive. It would sense their teho as they neared. Hakon strode forward, the blood in his veins boiling with the familiar excitement that came when facing one of the terrifying creatures.

The rush faded as they got closer. It was not a sleeping dragon, as Hakon had first thought. Terrible gashes ran along its side, and a large chunk of its stomach had been ripped out.

Hakon thought of all the times he'd used all his strength, only to have his sword bounce off the armored scales of a dragon. The amount of both force and teho required to tear out so much flesh was almost beyond his imagination.

Almost.

Meshell swore softly under her breath. "I never thought I would see such a thing."

Hakon agreed. "Dragons are fighting other dragons."

CHAPTER 12

Zachary woke in a small room built from the stone of the surrounding mountains. He shivered as a chill ran up his spine. Memories of his last visit to Aysgarth were still too fresh. How many hours had he spent helping Cliona in the libraries, knowing all the while he would betray her if she ever found her answers? How many times had he almost confessed, only to bite his tongue for his younger sister's sake?

Though he didn't know what else he would have done, returning to Aysgarth reminded him that he had been a coward. That he had folded against Damion while others fought.

He shook off the memories and stood, dressing quickly. His room held the essentials: a bed, table, and chair, but it had no windows to let in light or air. Although the door locked from the inside, it still felt like a prison.

A guard was posted outside his room, slumped in a chair and looking bored. Although Zachary couldn't blame her for her lack of enthusiasm, the lack of discipline did surprise him. When he'd last been here, Aysgarth had been bursting at the seams with purpose. Everyone had walked quickly, a fire in their eyes and a bounce in their step.

Now the city reminded him of a battered fighter, injured and bleeding internally, but too strong and stubborn to surrender. Damion's death reverberated through the halls of Aysgarth, and Zachary feared for what might still result from that fateful day in Husavik. He gave the guard a small bow of thanks for protecting him as he slept, then made his way to the nearest dining hall.

When he reached it, the hall was quiet. The members of the band sat together on one side of the room, and the residents of Aysgarth sat all the way on the other side. The sight was so awkward Zachary almost laughed.

Solveig greeted him when he approached their table. "Eat quickly. The council has requested an audience with us."

Zachary looked down at the remnants of the food on the band's plates. It looked unappetizing, and he thought he caught the slightest whiff of rancid plant matter. He took another look at the others in the room, but even the citizens of Aysgarth looked like they were regretting their decision to eat breakfast. Now that he was looking for it, he noticed that they didn't look all that healthy, either. They weren't emaciated, but they weren't far from it. "Maybe I'll pass."

Irric grinned. "A wise choice, lad. They did apologize to us before serving it, but the dragon attack destroyed most of their food stores, and their harvest isn't looking promising. They claim their evening meals are better, with fresh game."

"Not the worst we've ever eaten," Solveig observed.

Ari shot her a withering look. The band rose and returned their plates to the kitchen. Irric thanked the servers for the meal, and his charisma was such that even though everyone present knew it was a lie, it still sounded genuine.

Zachary was about to offer to lead them to the throne room, but Solveig led the way without stopping to ask for directions.

Even in such a small thing, he was useless to the band.

Irric reached out and put a hand on his shoulder. Their eyes met. "It's good that you brought us here," he said.

Zachary didn't see the situation the same. They'd been brought by Hel, and he'd only been used as a tool. But Irric spoke with such conviction Zachary felt better, regardless.

Though there were more important problems to discuss, he couldn't help but quiz Irric. "Why did you never seek office? With your strength and your way with people, you could have become a powerful magistrate, or even a governor."

"We were locked away," Ari hissed. The "you fool" was unspoken but clearly implied.

Zachary grimaced. Truthfully, he'd forgotten, and felt as foolish as Ari believed him to be. When the governments of the six states were being formed, the band hadn't even been around. But still, although Zachary wasn't sure of the exact dates, he knew Irric was active for at least three or four decades since his release. There had been plenty of time for him to rise to power.

"Peace, Ari," Irric said.

Ari glared at Irric but obeyed. The small exchange further convinced Zachary the swordsman should be a governor, at least. If anyone could get the dour assassin to listen with so little effort, they probably deserved the rule of all six states.

"Several reasons," Irric said to Zachary. He ticked points off the fingers of his right hand. "First, any bid for political power would probably attract Isira's attention, and she's the rare woman whose attention I'd rather never attract again. Second, my being kolma is problematic. Most believe us to be nothing more than myth, but it would be terribly difficult to explain why I don't age while everyone around me does. Third, I love people, but I hate the intrigue of the court, as you can well imagine."

Zachary did. The court ruined people. It rotted them from the inside, even the best of them.

A part of him still longed for it, though. His father remained a problem, but should that problem ever be solved, Zachary planned to return. He wanted to lead because he believed he would do it well. No matter what happened, he wouldn't let himself be corrupted by the politics and the greed.

Of course, all it had taken was Damion threatening his sister once to get him to betray all his values. But Damion had been exceptional.

Irric continued. "While all that is true, none of those reasons are actually why I've avoided office." He shrugged. "The truth is, I know I'm not a leader. I'm best with a sword in my hand, and it's in the midst of battle that I feel most alive. That is what I treasure, and what I'll always seek."

Zachary nodded. Though Irric had answered him, he'd only given Zachary more questions. He had more questions for everyone, in fact. But there was no time or place to ask them.

The band reached the throne room and were stopped by a handful of guards. One guard left the group to check inside and returned a moment later. The band and Zachary were allowed in, and they received their first look at the heart of Aysgarth. The cavernous room, made from the same stone as every other room and hall in Aysgarth, was both what he expected and not. Although he'd known the room's location, he'd never actually been inside during his previous visit.

Wide, glass-covered openings in the ceiling allowed sunlight in, which made the room feel even larger than it was. The walls held giant banners that depicted the four seasons, each in their passing cycle. The stone floor was polished, giving the room a silvery sheen that reflected the light from above.

Zachary noted everything, but his attention was drawn to the front of the throne room where a line of chairs faced them, most of them filled with warriors. The chairs looked large and comfortable, carved from a heavy wood, and topped with cushions. In the center of the line of chairs stood the throne, made of black stone. There were no cushions, and even more curiously, the throne had many chains hanging from the arms, legs, and back.

There was a woman sitting on the throne, dressed in rich silks. The clothing threw Zachary off, and it took him longer than it should for him to realize who he was looking at.

Hel sat in the throne. "Welcome, all. We are honored by your presence."

Zachary overcame his shock as he watched the other warriors of the council. Many of them kept their expressions closely guarded, but a few had easier faces to read. Some looked at the band with hope in their eyes, but at least one councilman glared at the visitors as though he was about to form a teho sword.

Hel had warned them that their arrival would be contentious. Zachary braced himself. His best defense here would be sharp observations and quick thinking. Though he'd been years away from his father's court, the mindset returned quickly. It fit him like an old, comfortable coat.

Solveig stepped forward and spoke for the band. "Thank you for the invitation. How may we assist?"

The glaring councilman gritted his teeth and clutched the arms of his chair so tightly his hands paled. The sight tempted a smile, but it was easy for Zachary to keep a carefully neutral expression. The man was only a few sentences away from attacking the band, but no matter how strong he was, he was no match for any of his guests.

Before Hel could respond, the door behind the band slammed open. Every eye turned to the entrance, where two more warriors stepped through. Zachary frowned. He'd seen these two before, but struggled to place them.

When the angry councilman practically sagged with relief, Zachary knew they were in for trouble.

The two new arrivals stopped behind the band. They didn't give Hel a chance to speak. "What's the meaning of this?" the woman demanded. Her hair was dark and cut short, and her eyes sparked with anger. She took two more steps forward, her boots thumping against the stone floor like drums calling an army to war.

The crowd assembled in the throne room backed away and fell completely silent. Zachary stared at the woman, unsure of what to make of her. The way her dark hair contrasted with her pale skin made her seem almost otherworldly, but it was her eyes that really made Zachary pause. They were so dark it was hard to tell where the iris ended and the pupil began. The quick flick of her eyes over the room was sharp and assessing, and so quietly precise he knew she missed nothing. Even outraged, she spoke with assumed authority, her question demanding a response.

"Peace, Valdis," Hel said, the words an echo of Irric's. But

Irric's had carried enough weight to silence Ari. Hel's sounded more a plea than an order. "The band is here, as we agreed."

"There was no agreement," Valdis said. "There was a hasty vote, taken when many of the council members were still reeling from the attack. They are here because of your manipulation and nothing more."

"We'll make no progress if we continue to squabble amongst ourselves," Hel said.

Valdis cut her off, and Zachary remembered where he'd seen the pair before. Valdis and Gunvald were their names. Two of Damion's most trusted lieutenants, back when he'd been alive. "No," Valdis said, her reply cold enough to freeze stone, "we'll make no progress so long as we seek outside aid, begging for help when we should be taking what we need."

Valdis stepped past the band. Zachary was reminded of a performer on a stage, preparing to astound her audience. She formed a teho blade, and the tension in the throne room grew even thicker. Now even the band was prepared for a fight.

Perhaps he'd walked them into a trap after all.

But Valdis didn't attack. She pointed her blade at the band. "These are the men and women responsible for all the ill that has befallen us. Because they killed Damion, we were too weak to fend off the dragons. Because they killed Damion, we argue among ourselves instead of following the path he laid before us. Everyone here knows my mind. I've spoken freely and without reservation. If the council was to give me the authority, I would order them killed where they stand."

She let her challenge echo in the chamber, and Zachary didn't dare to breathe.

Hel tried desperately to salvage the situation. "Join us, Valdis, and take your rightful seat among the council."

Valdis spat on the floor. "The lot of you don't deserve to do anything beyond lick these stone floors clean with your tongues. I'll take no part in this mockery of true rule. When this city we built through our sweat and blood collapses around you, come find me. You know where I am."

Valdis spun on her heel and marched back toward the door. She stopped before Zachary. "You're a traitor and a coward and should be killed for your crimes. If you have any honor at all, come find me, without these nursemaids that hover over you. You can either redeem your name, or at least die with some measure of dignity."

She leaned forward and growled, then brushed past him. A moment later, both her and Gunvald were gone, the doors slamming shut behind them.

Zachary looked to Hel and around the room. By all appearances, the stranger who had found him in Vispeda was still in control of the council. Barely, though, and who knew for how long?

Valdis hadn't used her teho against anyone, but Zachary still wondered if she'd just managed to doom them all anyway.

CHAPTER 13

Meshell swore as another flock of birds swept down at her. She swatted at them, then formed a small shield to protect them from the next diving attack. Though she tried to hide it, Hakon saw what the effort cost her. She faltered on her next step, a momentary loss of balance that she quickly recovered from.

He almost asked her if she needed to rest but shut his mouth before he could make such a mistake. If he asked, she would think he was accusing her of being weak. She'd angrily tell him that she was fine, then push herself beyond the brink of exhaustion, endangering them both. If he said nothing, there was at least some small chance she would admit, in her own time, that she needed rest.

Eight days had passed since they'd found the corpse of the dragon. Eight long days of travel, using teho-enhanced muscles to traverse more ground than any ahula would dream of traveling in a day, through rough terrain that was almost as dangerous as the animals that called it home. That they were on their feet at all was a testament both to their strength and determination.

Eight days without an answer. Without so much as a clue.

They'd seen more dragons in the sky. Hakon believed they were getting closer to the dragon home, though he couldn't guess how far they had yet to go.

Every morning, Hakon was certain Meshell would end their expedition. They'd been gone too long with too little to show for it. But every morning she shouldered her pack, never uttering a word of complaint. Even on days like today.

The sun had barely passed the midpoint, and already exhaustion was taking its toll. The birds didn't sense Meshell's shield, so their next dive was a suicidal one. He watched the dead birds slide off the shield and onto their path. Meshell let her shield drop, and they stepped over the poor creatures as they continued west.

Hakon couldn't help but feel guilty as he watched Meshell forge onward. When the whole band traveled together, his own weaknesses mattered little. There were plenty of others who could pick up his slack. But when it was just the two of them, Meshell ended up bearing most of the burdens of travel. Surviving the wilds west of Aysgarth required shields and strong wards, both impossible for Hakon.

It was why she was exhausted, and he was merely tired.

No single attack posed much of a threat. The worst they'd faced yet was a small pack of shadow wolves. But the wilds wore them down, and only needed them to make one fatal mistake to win.

They walked in silence, mosquitos swarming around their heads. Ants crawled up their legs, and one afternoon, a whole hive of bees had stung at them. When people usually thought about the dangers of the wild, they thought of the larger predators, but in this war, the insects were just as likely to lead to that final mistake.

Hakon couldn't remember experiencing assaults like this in his previous expeditions. Back in the day, the band had accompanied no small numbers of caravans west, and the wild had always been a force to be reckoned with, but not like this. This felt like a malicious intelligence, like the world itself was coordinating a siege against them.

Late in the afternoon, Meshell held up a hand to stop their advance. Hakon crept closer. "What is it?" he whispered.

She pointed toward a thick clump of trees and brush ahead of them. "A sleuth."

Hakon squinted. After a moment, he saw the shadows moving through the pines. He counted four bears prowling near the path. He pointed to the south. "We could just detour around them."

Her look was skeptical. "You think they'd just let us pass? They're waiting for us."

As if to confirm her claim, the bears stood in unison and growled.

Meshell sighed. "Told you."

The bears charged toward them, cutting the distance between them in half in only a few seconds.

"We could run away," Hakon pointed out as he drew his sword and reinforced it with teho.

Meshell launched two teho spears as the bears came within her range. "They'll just pursue." One spear hit a bear in the flank, but it did little more than slow the bear down. Hakon frowned. Two more spears appeared in the air above her, but they lacked the focus Meshell usually possessed. She threw them, but even as they began their flight, Hakon knew they were going to miss.

Even at distance, one hit out of four was unlike Meshell. He stepped in front of her. "Let me take these."

She swore at him and stepped forward, so they were side by side. "And let you have all the fun?"

He shook his head. Her pride would be the end of her. But there was no time for a rational and nuanced conversation. She was more than capable of taking care of herself. Still, as the bears came within fifty paces, Hakon bellowed a war cry and rushed forward, hoping to kill some of them before they got close to her. Two more teho spears flashed overhead. One hit the lead bear in the front shoulder. The other missed.

Such a strike should have killed the lead bear, or at least brought it to the ground. But again, all the spear did was slow it. Hakon filled body and blade with teho and leaped at the first bear. He swept his sword across, parallel to the ground, as he passed to the side of the beast. His sword bisected the bear, cutting through muscle, bone, and organ with equal ease. Hakon felt the resistance as nothing more than a gentle tug on the blade.

He landed hard, his feet digging gouges in the dirt as he slowed. His powerful legs flexed with the impact, but by the time he came to a stop, the bears were already past him. He sprinted after them, closing the distance between him and the last injured bear in half a dozen steps.

He made his cut, severing the bear's spine as he sliced it in half, too. Then he resumed his chase.

He'd hoped, when he'd launched his charge, that he would kill at least three of the bears before they reached Meshell. But he'd been too slow. The first bear smashed into Meshell's shield.

Hakon's eyes widened when he felt her shield collapse

under the impact. She sagged, just for a moment, as her shield dropped.

But that one moment was the only one the next bear needed. It struck Meshell at a full charge, knocking her back several feet. As she tumbled to a stop, the bear swiped at her with its enormous claws.

Hakon shouted. The bear attacking Meshell ignored him, but the other bear turned to regard him. He swung his sword and cut through the stunned bear without slowing.

Meshell fought the bear on top of her, but her counterattacks were too weak. At best, she was angering it. It never saw Hakon coming, though, and his sword once again cut through the bear with a single swing. He shoved the parts of the bear off Meshell and looked down in horror.

The bear had bitten clean through Meshell's right shoulder and had clawed her arms and legs as she'd defended herself. Nothing looked immediately fatal, which meant she would probably live. But it had been a close thing. Far closer than it should have been for a skilled kolma.

Flies began to swarm around them, ignoring the dead bears. Hakon studied Meshell for a few more moments, then made his choice. He pulled out one of the stones that Ari had given him. Maybe, in time, they could return and find Cliona, but Meshell needed aid.

"Don't you dare," Meshell croaked.

"You're hurt badly," he said, as though she wasn't perfectly aware of that fact. "Solveig can heal you."

"If I'm not dead now, I'm not going to be dead anytime soon. I just need to rest."

"We're leaving," Hakon said.

Her hand snapped up and grabbed his wrist. "Like hell.

I'm not returning and letting them know I got beat by a bear. Anyway, we need to find your daughter."

Hakon hesitated. He wanted to listen to her, even though it was a terrible choice. If they went back, there was no telling what would happen. Solveig could probably heal Meshell inside of a day, but depending on where the band was and what they were involved in, it might be a long time before he and Meshell could return west.

Even injured, Meshell seemed to understand his thoughts. "You know you want to stay. I'm not going to be the one who slows you down."

The retort came back before he realized what he was saying. "Too late for that, unless you think you can keep up with me now."

She laughed, then writhed in pain. She swore.

Hakon wiped away the flies that gathered around her, though they just returned a moment later. He sheathed his sword and picked her up gently in his arms. "Let's go, then."

He was fortunate to find a cave before the sun set. He laid Meshell inside, set his meager wards around the entrance, and collected wood for a fire. By the time he returned, he found that she had crawled to the entrance of the cave and was designing her own wards. "You really are terrible at this," she complained.

She didn't sound much stronger than she had earlier, but it was pointless to fight her. He brought the wood in and started the fire while she finished the wards. Their meal was cooking by the time she crawled back to the fire.

While their meal cooked, he used a knife to cut her clothes off her. She grimaced as he reopened some of the cuts that had been sealed by coagulated blood and her clothing. Once she was naked, he wet a rag and cleaned off what blood he could. Fortunately, while many of the cuts she'd suffered were deep, most had just sliced through skin and muscle. Her shoulder worried him, but that was all. "Bandages?" he asked.

"Around my shoulder."

Hakon took a long strip of fabric from his pack and wrapped it around her shoulder, trying to be as gentle as he could. He thought of Sera's skill at wrapping bandages, and while the memories ached, they didn't carry the same sharp edge as they usually did. He tied the bandage off and studied his work. The sight brought a smile to his lips. He didn't think he'd have a future as a healer anytime soon, but it would suffice.

"I think I'll be good to travel tomorrow," Meshell said.

"No." Hakon crawled toward the fire and began serving their meal. "Tomorrow we rest. We'll continue the day after."

He cut off her protest with a wave of his hand. "You got sloppy, and we both know it. You've been enduring most of the attacks and could use a break, not just to heal. A day won't make a difference."

He handed her a bowl of stew. Like his bandages, his cooking wasn't anything to brag about, but it sufficed. He missed the band. Irric was a tremendous cook, and they'd always eaten well on the road. Each of them was plenty strong alone, but together, they were something else.

"I didn't think you'd let us keep going," Meshell said.

"Why not?"

"You've gotten too cautious in your old age."

Hakon rolled his eyes. "You're twenty years older than me."

"Twenty-one. But I'm younger at heart."

"You clearly need your rest. You're talking nonsense."

She flashed him a rare smile and reached out to take his hand. "It's good to have you back."

"And you're getting sentimental. The bear must have hit you over the head, too."

Meshell chuckled, then finished her meal. She made her way slowly to where their bedrolls had been laid out, side by side, near the back of the cave. Hakon cleaned the dishes and built the fire up for the night. The evenings got cool this high in the mountains.

Meshell stretched out and patted the bedroll beside hers. Her look was mischievous. "What are we going to do all day tomorrow in this cave?"

Hakon shook his head. All these years, and still so little had changed. He put the dishes away and walked toward the bedroll. "I'm sure you'll come up with something," he said.

CHAPTER 14

Zachary had endured his fair share of mind-numbing gatherings. From his childhood in his father's court, suffering endless platitudes from sycophantic courtiers with a smile on his face, to his years in the academy, where most scholars believed the greatest value was gifted to students when they lectured the longest, he was no stranger to boredom. Even with all that experience, though, the meeting between the council of Aysgarth and the band taxed his ability to remain alert.

They met from mid-morning until supper bells rang through the halls. As near as Zachary could tell, the hours of negotiation had resulted in two very basic agreements: the two parties weren't going to kill each other today, and they would speak again in the morning. As the band left the throne room, Zachary idly wondered if perhaps taking Valdis up on her offer of a duel wasn't preferable to another day of negotiations.

Even Irric's cheerful demeanor sagged once they left the throne room. "Aysgarth won't survive the coming winter," he said.

Ari snorted. "They won't survive the month."

Solveig didn't rise to the insults. She was already lost in thought.

The problem was easy enough to see. Damion's death wreaked havoc, even today. The kolma had considered himself invincible and had never planned for how his vision might live on after he traveled through the gates. From what Zachary could gather, the council had been formed as a last gasp of desperation by the survivors who couldn't agree on how to move forward. Each faction, loosely defined, had a spokesperson on the council, and they took votes on any contentious issue.

It had allowed Aysgarth to stumble forward, and in time they might have settled on some agreement. But famine and the dragon stole what little stability they'd come to rely on.

The council couldn't even agree how much power it had. The majority still wanted the band present, to protect against the dragons should they ever return. But a vocal minority insisted they be sent back to Vispeda.

Or just killed where they stood.

Zachary sped up until he walked beside Solveig. "With Aysgarth in such disarray, you'll never find a better time to recruit tehoin. Everyone here knows what's coming."

Solveig stared ahead. "I was thinking the same. My fear is that the attempt to do so will result in further bloodshed, which I would avoid if I could. Tehoin are becoming increasingly precious."

Hurried footsteps echoed in the hallway. Zachary turned and saw Hel chasing after them. She pulled up short and bowed. "I'm sorry for today. Several of the council and I have promised to meet again early in the morning before you join us. I am hopeful we'll be able to reach more of an agreement then."

Zachary wasn't so optimistic, but there was also no reason Hel needed to hurry after them to inform them. If anything, she'd harmed her cause by letting them know. So why was she here?

She answered the question for him soon enough. "I was hoping that I might borrow Zachary for the evening."

Solveig raised a skeptical eyebrow. Irric coughed, and Zachary shot him a withering glare. Solveig shrugged and turned to Zachary. "Up to you."

The decision was an easy one to make. Truthfully, he hadn't been looking forward to another meal with the band. "I'd be honored."

He broke apart from the band, and Hel led him in the opposite direction from the one they'd been heading. "I hope you don't mind eating someplace private. After a day with the council, I'm afraid I have little desire to be around crowds of people."

"Makes sense." He grunted as he thought again about the day. "So, you rule Aysgarth?"

"If you can call sitting at the head of the council 'rule,' then yes. Although you saw for yourself what that looks like." She tucked her hair behind her ears. "I'm sorry for the deceptions in Vispeda. I wanted the band here, and it seemed the only way."

"I'm used to being used," Zachary replied, unable to keep the bitterness out of his voice.

His reply surprised her, but then her eyes narrowed, and she nodded. "I understand, and I'm sorry I contributed to that."

Her sincerity caught him off guard, and she continued. "I am head of the council not because anyone wanted me in the position, but because I was the one least offensive to the most people. No one supports me, but no one hates me as much as they do each other."

"You didn't seek the throne?"

Hel's laugh was bitter. "No one was more surprised by the final vote than I was. At first, I was foolish enough to feel honored, but it didn't take me long to realize why I'd been chosen."

"But you said you were a commander."

"True enough, but I commanded a small unit, usually on patrol around Aysgarth. The first real battle we saw was at Husavik. I rarely had any interactions with Damion. I wasn't like Valdis."

Zachary had more questions for her, but he figured they might be sensitive, and were better held until their meal. They passed several people in the halls, and Zachary noted the wide variety of reactions Hel inspired. Many looked grateful for her presence, but a few looked like they might stab her in the hall and whistle as they walked away. He changed the subject to something he figured she could discuss freely. "Why the chains on the throne?"

"Damion claimed they were to remind whoever sat there that they were enslaved to the good of the people."

Zachary didn't miss the way she phrased her answer. "Do you think he meant it?"

"I couldn't say. I never knew him well." They turned a corner, and she opened the door to a small room. He stepped inside a cozy study. "Food will arrive soon," she said. She gestured to a table, where they each took a seat. "I want to believe Damion meant the chains to be taken seriously. Sometimes, listening to those like Valdis, who knew him best, I think that Aysgarth was nothing more than his bid for power. But I never saw it that way."

Zachary leaned forward, curious now. "How did you see it?"

"Much the way it was described to me when I was first recruited. A place for the tehoin to start again, to found a state that respected our powers. It was supposed to be a place of learning, not just through the study of texts, as so many academies do in the six states, but through experience and experimentation. Damion wanted to know why tehoin existed and why we were going extinct."

"But don't you think that all of that was still in pursuit of power?"

Hel nodded. "It's possible. Probably even likely. But I choose to believe that even Damion's quest to rule the six states was to better protect everyone from what is coming."

Zachary leaned back, watching Hel's face carefully. "Do you truly believe that?"

She didn't flinch. "I choose to, yes."

There was a knock on the door, and their food was delivered. As the band had promised him in the morning, the food looked to be of considerably higher quality than their breakfast. His stomach growled, reminding him that he hadn't eaten all day. He hesitated, his fork hovering over a piece of venison.

Hel took a bite of her food and smiled at his hesitation. She offered him her plate. He appreciated the gesture, and it probably would have been wise to accept it, but it also seemed rude. He cut into his own meat and took a healthy bite.

After his hunger was sated, he returned to the questions that bothered him. He made an expansive gesture, taking in all Aysgarth with a sweep of his arm. "So, what is it you hope to accomplish with all of this?"

Hel thought for a moment. "Despite everything that's

happened, I believe Aysgarth still represents something unique in the history of the six states. First, as you can imagine, we need to survive. But I would like to see us become the seventh state, as Damion intended, although without the designs to rule the other six. I would see us lead, instead of command."

He remained silent, hoping she would elaborate.

She took a sip of wine, then did. "The six states, as they are now, can't survive. Damion believed this, and I do, too. In the places where decisions are made, wealth has become the most important consideration. That's not all bad. On average, people today live better than they ever have. But something is missing."

"Purpose," Zachary said.

She nodded. "Wealth is a fine goal in a time of peace, but those in the cities have forgotten the true danger of the wilds. Protected by their walls and their guards and a whole mass of humanity that has pushed west, they no longer respect this world. But you've seen the wild pushing back, an effort which has culminated in the return of the dragons. Our wealth will do nothing against such threats, and the six states will fall unless something is done."

"And you think Aysgarth represents the answer?"

"I do. Damion saw it as a herald to a return of the times of the empire. My own thoughts are not so grand. The empire fell to the rebellion for a reason. Instead, I believe that Aysgarth could represent a middle way."

Zachary took a long sip of his wine. "It's a grand ambition for someone who was surprised to find themselves as head of the council."

"I didn't ask to be put in this situation," Hel replied. "But I'll make the most of the opportunity that I have."

Her words stirred something in Zachary's heart. "I'm

impressed."

"Don't be. If anything, you're the one responsible for how I've decided to proceed."

"Excuse me?"

His reaction brought a smile to her face. "You really don't know, do you?"

"I'm almost scared to ask."

"One project that Damion doesn't get enough credit for, even among those of us who survived him, is his web of informants around the six states."

Zachary wasn't sure where Hel was going with any of this but was curious where it was leading.

"He used your sister to blackmail you for information. This, we both know. You can probably guess, though, that you were far from Damion's only target. He was receiving information from sources throughout the six states, all delivered by a collection of tehoin who could transport at will."

Zachary remembered, what seemed like a lifetime ago now, how quickly Damion had removed the library from Marjaana's home. He hadn't given enough thought to how such an organized ability could be used in other contexts. Though Damion had been separated from the rest of the six states, he probably knew more, faster, than even the governors of each state.

"I've inherited that web," Hel said, "and so I know what you've been up to in the months since Husavik. And I'm not the only one."

"What do you mean?"

"Despite your efforts to remain anonymous, word of your deeds has spread. No small number of people in your father's court know that you've been wandering the frontier, protecting settlements. You've become something of a hero."

That didn't make any sense. Even if the word had spread, few would care. Until Zachary considered the idea from a different angle. "My father."

"You'd think, listening to him, you are singlehandedly saving the frontier."

Zachary closed his eyes, connecting the dots. He could see how his father would play it. The details of his exile had always been a private affair, and his father had finally found a way to spin the truth so that it served him. "He claims that he sent me out here to protect the settlements and to send back reports. That it was all his idea, and that I've succeeded beyond his wildest dreams."

"Close," Hel said. "Too many people know you were sent to the academy. He claims that your travels served two purposes: to educate you and to give you an opportunity to observe how the governors of the western states are protecting the borders." Her eyes narrowed. "So, why were you sent to Vispeda? I suspect it has something to do with how Damion blackmailed you, but I don't know for sure."

"A family matter," Zachary answered. "But you are not wrong to doubt my father's word."

"He's been trying to reach you for some time."

"He can keep trying."

Hel tapped her fingers against the side of her wine cup. "You really do feel used, don't you?"

"I'd argue I have plenty of evidence to back up my feeling."

She gestured around the room. "You believe my efforts here fall into the same bucket."

He nodded. "You wanted the band, not me."

She frowned at that, as though she was confused. As always, her expression returned to neutral quickly, but there had been something there. Zachary didn't think she was acting. "You don't know, do you?"

"Know what?"

"Why your father is trying to reach you."

"You've already told me. He's made me into a hero, and now he wants me back by his side to show me off to his court."

Hel's fingers drummed faster against the side of her cup. She bit her lower lip. "That's not entirely true." She hesitated a moment longer. "Yes, when I reached out to you, I had hopes that the band would come with you. But that was not my only objective. You were important, too."

She didn't seem like she was lying, but Zachary didn't believe her. What use was he when those like the band existed?

"In your absence—"

"Exile," Zachary corrected.

Hel tried again. "In your exile, you've become one of the most important figures at court. Think what you want of them, but they aren't fools. They know the border is collapsing, they can't agree what to do about it, and their distance robs their debates of urgency. Your father has positioned you as the one with the answers."

"Why? My brother will inherit the house."

"Your brother has proven himself gluttonous and incapable of leadership. Your father's power teeters on the brink of collapse, and he rightly believes you are the only one who can keep the house alive."

"He'd never give me the house," Zachary said. "He made that very clear when I left."

"Zachary—" Hel hesitated again, not wanting to share something, but having no choice in this conversation. "Your father is dying."

CHAPTER 15

As the sun rose and warmed the cave, Hakon stirred to wakefulness. Beside him, Meshell snored contentedly, wrapping the covers more tightly around her as Hakon sat up. He wiped the sleep from his eyes and stared out the cave's entrance, where a pile of dead animals lay stacked against the wards. The attacks had been constant throughout the previous day, and from the number of animals piled together, it looked like they hadn't let up much overnight.

The sight sent a chill down his spine. He'd been alive a long time, and his eyes were no strangers to all the horrors that life could offer.

But this? This challenged everything he believed to be true.

He rose from the bed and packed for their journey. He didn't look forward to leaving, not when a quick glance told him what awaited him beyond the wards. Not when the memories of this place were still so fresh and warm in his thoughts.

Meshell stirred and sat up as he moved about the cave,

letting the blankets fall off her. Hakon didn't mind giving in to the obvious temptation.

"You had a dark look on your face there, for a moment," she said.

He gestured to the wards. "I've long believed that the worst things I've witnessed were caused by human cruelty and shortsightedness. I always found some measure of peace in the wild because no matter how dangerous it appeared, it always felt indifferent. It felt natural, like that was the way it was supposed to be."

Meshell nodded as she, too, stood from the bed, giving him a full view of her tempting figure. "It feels wrong to have the wild seem so malicious, doesn't it?"

He grunted. "Makes me feel like the whole world has gone sideways and there's nothing we can do about it."

"Don't let anyone ever tell you that you aren't a bundle of joy to wake up to in the morning," Meshell grumbled.

Hakon apologized, but he saw her eyes dart toward the wards and the nightmare just beyond.

They broke their fast quickly and left the cave. Hakon studied the collection of dead animals as they stepped over it. Birds, snakes, lizards, and deer lay dead, victims of Meshell's vicious wards. Hakon pursed his lips as he looked at the scene. It wasn't just the number of animals, but the variety, as well. The whole world was turning against him, and all the evidence he needed to prove his claim was right here.

He shook off the chill that threatened to settle in his bones. The sun crawled across a cloudless sky, and off in the distance, Hakon heard songbirds singing to one another. He was grateful, at least, that there wasn't an immediate line of animals resting outside the cave waiting for them to emerge.

Whatever guided these creatures, it wasn't human. It

had intelligence, but nothing quite like what Hakon would expect from a human opponent.

As before, Meshell led the way, and Hakon's spirit lifted when he saw that her pace was quick and her eyes sharp. Though she'd never admit it, she needed the day of rest. It wasn't long before they were tested by a murder of crows, but Meshell dealt with them with her customary ease.

The days passed, and they progressed west. Dragons became a regular sight in the sky now, but they didn't seem interested in the traveling pair. Hakon tried to catalog the dragons, to have some sense of how many there were, but he gave up the task before long. Up close, there were almost always markings and differences that identified a dragon, but from these distances, he could judge only their size, and it wasn't sufficient to guess their number.

The mountains became more treacherous. Given the number of days they'd traveled, the number of passes they'd climbed, and the sheer number of miles they'd put beneath their feet, Hakon figured they would have passed over the mountain range and into whatever lay beyond. In this, too, he was proven wrong. Jagged peaks stabbed into the sky for as far as his eyes could see.

The mountains were a strange mixture of serene and dangerous.

On the one hand, the mountains seemed to give off a kind of quiet song. The air here was clearer, fresher even than the wilds Hakon was more familiar with. The sounds of the wind moving through the trees, the birds in the trees, the sounds of whatever small animals scurried about the underbrush, all ebbed and flowed in gentle, calming waves. The smell of the mountains was wonderful, piney, and fresh.

On the other hand, the mountains put Hakon on edge,

and it wasn't just the animals that attacked them throughout the day. The peaks grew even higher, the air thinner. Their progress slowed as even they labored from exhaustion. The trails they followed were narrow, hugging the sides of the mountains, often with steep drops to the side. At times, he felt like the chasms were reaching for him, trying to pull him down. More than once, he caught himself leaning too far over the edge of a trail, about to lose his balance.

It was in these high places that they began to find the caves. These weren't caves like Hakon had ever seen before, though. They were too uniform, too symmetrical to be natural.

The first one they found towered over them, stretching twice as high as they were tall. The stone had been polished to a glassy finish. Hakon didn't know what this place was for, but it felt like an abandoned temple.

The caves only added to Hakon's growing unease. The wilds were worrying enough on their own, but the caves added yet another layer of mystery to a world that Hakon was increasingly realizing he knew nothing about. As far as he knew, humans had never traveled this far west. If some small expedition had gotten this far, they'd certainly never honeycombed this mountain with caves.

The stone inside the caves was smooth, too—smooth beyond any work Hakon had ever encountered. Sometimes he would run his hands across a wall, seeking even the smallest imperfection. He searched in vain.

He and Meshell camped in the caves almost every night. Though the tunnels went deep into the mountains, they never went more than a few feet in. Meshell would ward both the entrance and the tunnel behind them, protecting them from whatever lurked on either side.

One night, they discovered something new. After a day

filled with treacherous hiking, they searched for shelter. It didn't take them long to find a cave, ringed with smooth stone the way they all were. Hakon and Meshell stepped inside and then froze in place at the sight.

This cave wasn't empty.

Every other one had been, at least to the depths that they'd explored. They were perfect mysteries, carved into the mountains without a trace of their makers.

This cave wasn't as deep as the others. It only went about twenty feet into the side of the mountain, where it ended in a wall that was just as smooth as every other strange wall they'd seen. But that wasn't what caught their eyes.

There were bodies here, skeletal remains older than Hakon dared to guess. He saw four full skulls and what looked to be the remains of a fifth. They appeared to be human, and they'd been ravaged by something. Meshell squatted down next to the bones and plucked samples out at random, tossing them over her shoulder when she was done with them. Finally, she stopped and tossed one to Hakon. "Look at this."

It was a large bone, probably a femur. Hakon saw what had caught Meshell's attention. There was a gouge on the bone, of a size Hakon was familiar with. His gaze met Meshell's, and she nodded. "Dragon," she said. They searched through the rest of the bones, seeking some clue that might shed more light on the mystery.

Hakon found fragments of something that wasn't bone, but he couldn't identify the material. "Do you think they were stamfar?"

Meshell finished her study of the bones before answering. "No idea. You would think a group of five stamfar would have been able to kill a dragon."

Memories of Cliona lecturing him bubbled to the

surface. "Maybe. Cliona once told me there are some scholars who believe that not all the stamfar were tehoin. Or, more accurately, that not all people who were alive in the time of the stamfar were actually stamfar."

Meshell shook her head. "I never really understood why Solveig wanted to study history as much as she did. I'm starting to think that perhaps I was the fool."

"I know how you feel."

Meshell swore softly. "Also, don't ever tell Solveig I said that."

Hakon grinned. "I make no promises."

"Just for that, I'm making us stay here tonight," Meshell said.

Hakon groaned. He wasn't superstitious, but he wasn't in the mood to spend the night near old bones that shouldn't be here. Meshell knew it would bother her far less than it would him. "That's cruel."

She ignored him, quickly setting up wards, one at the entrance and one between them and the bones. When he gave her a questioning look, she shrugged. "Just to be safe."

He was glad he wasn't the only one who feared what those bones meant.

CHAPTER 16

Zachary shivered as the cold mountain wind blew his coat open. He tied it closed and hugged his arms tight to his body. Although autumn was several months away, the wind that came off the snow-covered peaks seemed perennially frozen.

Despite the chill in the air, Zachary had a smile on his face. After days cooped up within the halls of Aysgarth, it felt fantastic to be outside and stretching his long limbs as they hiked across the mountain valley.

Ahead of him the three warriors of the band were accompanied by nearly a dozen council members and commanders. Their eyes were on the fortifications that surrounded the valley, and the commanders pointed eagerly at sites they wanted the band to understand the importance of.

Zachary found that he had little interest in the tour. Partly, it was because there was little need for him to understand Aysgarth's defenses. His own meager ability would do nothing against the threats that they faced, and he was no strategist that could solve the problem that dozens of commanders had studied before him. He'd only been invited because he came with the band.

The other part was a malaise that had settled over him ever since Hel had informed him about his father. Learning that the old man was to die brought him no great sorrow. He'd long ago lost track of the number of times he had wished for this. He wouldn't miss his father. What fond memories Zachary had of the man were so far in the past the magistrate might as well already be dead.

And yet he still felt as if somebody had placed him in a jar and shaken him until he didn't know which way was up. What plans he'd made were scattered to the wind now, and he had no idea what he might do next.

So, he walked behind the crowd, content to observe.

In a way, what he observed was remarkable. A few months ago, any one of these commanders would have been drawing their sword and screaming for blood if they'd seen any of the band walking free in Aysgarth's lands. Now they freely shared the details of their defenses, as if they had been stalwart allies for all of living memory.

The sight stirred mixed feelings in his chest. It proved that, when necessary, people could come together despite their differences. But he was also disappointed, because if not for the dragons, none of this would have come to pass. He wished there were easier ways to bring people together.

Gradually, Hel broke apart from the rest of the pack and let herself slow until she was walking beside him. "You have the look of a man deep in thought," she said.

"I'm afraid it's all a deception," he replied, "an act I developed in my years at the academy to convince the scholars I was a student worth having in their classes."

The corner of her lips turned up in a smile, and Zachary felt his heart beat a little faster. "And did it work?"

"I'm afraid not. They saw through my ruse with ease."

Her smile faded. "I'm sorry if the news I shared has troubled you. It was not my intent to be the one who informed you, but there seemed to be no other way."

He shook his head. "I appreciate your consideration. I am troubled, but not because I'm a dutiful son." She reached out and grabbed his hand, and although he was surprised by the gesture, he didn't pull away. Her hand was warm in his.

"You will find no judgment here," she said. "When I was young, and my parents discovered I was tehoin..." Her voice trailed off. "Well, I can say truthfully that I have no fond memories of my parents after the age of five."

Zachary looked at her, surprised by the confession but not by the events she implied. More and more in the six states being a tehoin was considered shameful. Hel's story, although tragic, wasn't uncommon. His own father had been embarrassed when Zachary had shown he was tehoin. Of course, his father had only added it to the list of reasons he was embarrassed by his son.

"If you don't mind me asking, is that how you ended up here?" Zachary was curious what led so many people to Aysgarth. Being a tehoin was sometimes difficult in the six states, but there were easy opportunities for money, so he was surprised as many had taken up Damion's offer as they had.

"It is. Aysgarth, and Damion specifically, promised me a place where I would belong, and I will always be thankful for the fact that he took me in and gave me an opportunity to prove my worth. He was one of the first people who did."

He thought of her differently then. Most of the people he knew who wielded power had been born to it in some way. He certainly had. Unlike him, she had earned her place here. Curious, he gestured to the party in front of them. "What do you think of all this?"

"I'm glad the band is here. Despite everything that has come before, Aysgarth is my home, and seeing what the dragon is capable of made me view our world differently. I'm not sure how long this tentative alliance will hold, but I am convinced it is the only hope we have of surviving the wilds."

Zachary hesitated before asking his next question. "Do you ever fear that even our cooperation may not be enough?"

She nodded. "But then we will have at least died on our feet, and I find that future acceptable."

He squeezed her hand. "In this, we also agree."

They continued their walk, higher up into the valley, the mountains closing in on both sides. Zachary glanced from one side to the other and couldn't help but feel like the mountains tightened their grip on the pass like an ancient dragon's jaws. He looked back at Aysgarth, peaceful at a distance, and hoped his premonition didn't come to pass.

She broke his reverie. "What will you do?"

Zachary shrugged. "I've been asking myself that question for three days and I'm no closer to an answer than when I first learned about my father."

"Your voice could be invaluable among the other magistrates," she said.

"I am not so sure that's true," he admitted.

"Why not?"

"I've seen the efforts my father has made to maintain what power he has. I could not reach so low, nor strive so hard, for something that means so little."

"There are other ways to win hearts."

"Perhaps, but not among the magistrates. Whatever

nobility I might attempt to hold onto would be taken advantage of by those willing to act as my father does. Besides, if I returned, what would I even say? The gods are real, and dragons are returning? I would be laughed out of the hall so fast my seat wouldn't even have time to get warm."

Hel smiled but didn't let the subject go. "This world has no shortage of people capable of saying the right words, but very few who do the right thing. Organize expeditions. Make the other magistrates see the truth with their own eyes. Show them the destroyed villages and the starving citizens. The change you seek will happen slowly, but it will happen."

When he listened to Hel, he could almost envision the future she spoke of. It was not an easy path. Perhaps it was even an impossible one, but the challenge inspired him. She made him believe it was worth the effort to try.

Before he could give her a better answer, there was a commotion up ahead. He felt blooms of teho in every direction, and he swore as he formed his own sword. His first thoughts were of an ambush, a trap long in the setting. One glance at Hel, though, told him that if it was a trap, she was one of its victims, too. Sword and shield were at her side in a moment, but Zachary did not yet see their enemy. Up ahead, the feeling of teho was as strong as he had ever felt. Stronger, even, than what he'd felt in the ruins of Husavik.

Out of nowhere, a figure appeared, floating in the air. At first, he thought that the figure was very distant, but as he squinted, he realized that wasn't the case. The figure was only a few dozen paces in front of the band, but it was simply small. A child.

The voice that boomed across the valley and echoed off

the mountains was not that of a child, though. The sound alone almost drove him to his knees.

"What is the meaning of this?" she demanded.

It took him a moment to realize that he had seen this figure before, albeit very briefly. The god that even the band feared.

Isira.

And she had come prepared for a fight.

CHAPTER 17

Hakon woke before the sun rose over the mountain peaks. He hadn't slept well, knowing the bones were behind him. Meshell would mock him, but he kept imagining the bones returning to life, flesh knitting over skeletons as though the river of time was flowing uphill.

By the time Meshell woke, Hakon had their camp packed. She eyed him, a sly smile spreading across her face.

"What?" he asked, more gruffly than he intended.

Her smile grew wider. "Nothing," she said, her dark eyes dancing with delight.

"Get ready quickly," he demanded. "I'm hoping to put many miles behind us today."

"Of course," she answered. She remained in bed, stretching languorously.

Hakon growled and she laughed.

The sound warmed the cave and banished his thoughts of reanimated skeletons. Hakon spun on his heel so she wouldn't see the grin on his own face.

After another minute of rest, she got dressed, and before

long they were on their way west once again. They followed a narrow trail leading from the cave, and if Hakon's step was a little faster than usual, Meshell made no mention of it.

"I don't suppose you have any idea where those bones came from?" she asked.

Hakon glanced back at the cave, now fading from sight behind them. "I'm certain humans have never been this far west. Just as I'm certain those were human remains."

"Last night, I kept trying to come up with a story that would explain the bones," Meshell admitted. "I don't know where they came from, but I think they were digging the tunnel when the dragon killed them."

The story fit the slim evidence on hand, but it left them with more questions than it answered. "I've never seen stone worked in such a fashion. Perhaps the stamfar knew of such a technique, but with such strength, I believe no dragon would have posed a threat to them." He sighed heavily. "Besides, I know of no stories of stamfar journeying this far west. Given the extent of the caves, it seems like some legend would have survived."

The trail they followed lost elevation, dropping into a thick forest of pine. The trees seemed to crowd in, forming a tunnel that reminded Hakon uneasily of the cave they'd just left. The pines here were old and massive, branches forming a canopy high above that blocked the sun from view. Off in the distance, they heard a shrill cry, carried on the wind.

"Eagle?" Meshell asked.

Hakon nodded.

It was the cry of the eagle that alerted him to how quiet the woods they walked through were. They walked unopposed, too, not bothered by anything, not even a mosquito. "Do you notice that?" he asked.

"What?"

"We haven't been attacked all morning."

Meshell spun in a slow circle, the realization dawning on her, too. "That doesn't seem good, does it?"

"Carry on?"

Meshell shrugged. "Not much else to do, is there?"

The trail eventually turned back up the mountain and they gained some of the elevation they'd lost. After another mile, the forest began to thin, and Hakon enjoyed his first clear views of the skies in hours. He pointed. "I think I know why we've been left alone."

Two dragons flew through the skies, passing through puffy clouds as though they were playing. "Younglings," he said.

They watched the dragons in silence. Though they ranged over the sky, Hakon noted that they never ranged more than three or four miles from a point to the northwest, over a small pass from where they now stood.

Meshell noticed the same. She pointed to the pass. "Think that what we're looking for is over the pass?"

"Maybe," Hakon said.

"If so, I have a hard time believing they're just going to let us walk up to it."

"Too late to back out now." He wished he felt as confident as he tried to sound.

"Two dragons against the two of us? Not great odds."

"They're younglings."

"Right." Meshell shook out her limbs. "Fast or slow?"

Hakon studied the dragons for a few moments longer. "Slow. They've been ignoring us thus far. Maybe they'll keep ignoring us if we don't present a threat."

Meshell's snort told him what she thought of that idea.

They broke from the tree line and ascended toward the pass. The wind picked up, blowing their long hair straight back. For several long minutes, Hakon thought his idea might just work. The dragons circled overhead, chasing one another across the sky.

Halfway between the top of the pass and the trees, the dragons turned toward them.

"Hold," Hakon said.

There was some small chance they might still pass overhead.

As the dark shapes grew larger, their destination clear, Hakon drew his sword and breathed teho into the edge. Together, the dragons let out an angry screech. The sound turned Hakon's stomach to water, and fear threatened to steal the strength from his limbs.

Long ago, he'd learned that anger purified. Rage, properly nurtured, left no room for any other emotion. It had guided his weapon once before, making him a legend even among the kolma. So, he thought of Cliona, and of the dragon that had taken her from him, and his fear faded. He charged, yelling loud enough to challenge the dragons. They dove faster, folding in their wings as they fell.

Meshell ran beside him, keeping an easy pace, her steps light across the rocky terrain. She was the only one in the world who could match his speed.

An instant before the dragons hit the ground, they spread their wings and tore down the side of the mountain. Enormous jaws opened wide.

Meshell launched a single teho spear, thrown with every bit of strength she could muster. It cracked through the air, lost to sight as it sped toward the dragon.

Hakon couldn't follow the spear, but he felt it shatter against the dragon's armored hide. It screeched in response, but didn't change its course.

The forces approached at incredible speed, and when

Hakon judged the moment right, he launched himself into the air, angling so that he might pass to the side of the dragon. The jaw snapped behind him and Hakon swung.

The dragon twisted, unbelievably fast. Sword met armored scale, but Hakon knew, the moment he made contact, he hadn't hit the dragon hard enough. The youngling swiped at him with a claw, sending him hurtling through the air.

Hakon instinctively filled his body with teho. He slammed into a boulder, breaking it in half as he passed through it. He tumbled end over end twice before sliding to a stop, his ears ringing. His dragon flew straight into the sky as its companion circled warily around Meshell.

He pushed himself to his feet and almost fell again. That impact would have turned an ahula into jam against the side of the boulder, but even with all his teho, it felt like he had cracked some ribs. He shook it off as best he could. He hadn't been hit that hard in a long time, but this battle was far from over.

Hakon looked up to watch the dragon he'd collided with. He thought he saw a gash along the side of its neck. Not deep enough to be fatal, but he wasn't the only one who'd come away from the exchange with a wound. Unfortunately, at this rate, he'd run out of ribs long before the dragon bled to death.

Meshell and the other dragon still tested one another. The dragon flew in low circles, occasionally darting in with its long sinuous body, swiping at her with its jaws. Those were the moments Meshell threw her spears, holding onto her attacks until the dragon exposed its vulnerable throat. The dragon was wary, though, twisting away whenever she launched a spear.

Hakon's dragon didn't give him enough time to help her.

It dove again, aimed straight at him, its speed breathtaking. Hakon leaped to the side as the dragon spread its wings a moment before it crashed. Claws tore the air in front of him, and he cut at the first exposed target he saw. His sword clunked against the armored scales and Hakon retreated before the dragon shred him into small pieces.

The dragon had no interest in letting him escape. It pressed him as he retreated, jaws constantly searching for the first bite of its next meal. Hakon dodged, barely keeping his limbs away from the sharp teeth.

The dragon lunged forward, its long neck extending to its full length. Hakon slid to the side, twisting and cutting as he did. His target was the dragon's eye, but it flinched away at the last moment. His sword struck the dragon across the side of its head. It wailed in pain and launched into the sky. The blast of air almost knocked Hakon from his feet.

Hakon spared a moment to check on Meshell. Her dragon was on the ground, relying on its jaws and claws in an attempt to tear her open. She danced around its teeth and claws, teho flashing as she sought any weakness in the young dragon's armor. Though she made little progress, the dragon wasn't winning, and that was a victory in its own right. Watching her fight was always an awe-inspiring spectacle. He'd never, in all his years, found anyone who fought with the same combination of agility and power.

Meshell's dragon eventually grew frustrated enough to leap into the sky where it joined its sibling. They circled, and Hakon felt like prey in the sights of a much more dangerous predator. He wandered closer to Meshell, who mirrored the action. They both kept their eyes on the sky, but when they were close enough to speak without yelling, he asked if she was fine.

"I am. You?"

"Think I cracked some ribs."

"Will it be a problem?"

"I'm a bit slower than I should be. Hopefully not enough to make a difference."

"Maybe next time, don't charge one head on."

They watched the dragons together. Hakon was surprised they hadn't attacked again. He didn't get the sense their earlier duels had frightened the creatures.

"What do you think they're waiting for?" Meshell asked.

"Maybe to throw ourselves on a spit for them?"

He couldn't bring himself to laugh at his own joke. Their behavior worried him.

His worries were justified. Farther to the northwest, a deeper roar carried through the thin air of the mountains. Hakon and Meshell both swore in unison. They were fighting younglings.

But that roar made it sound like an elder approached.

CHAPTER 18

Zachary's thoughts, which a moment before had been skipping between different plans for his future, suddenly froze. He felt like a startled deer, realizing a precious second too late that a hunter was nearby. Who was he to dare to plan, when such powers roamed over the planet?

The first time he saw Isira, he'd been confused by her appearance. It wasn't until later, a night when Irric had drunk too much, that he learned something of her history. They believed her to be the last of the stamfar, now that Torsten was dead. She'd been a child when she'd come into the fullness of her power, and for reasons none of the band knew, had halted her aging as a youth.

All that Zachary understood was that the band feared her, in a way they had never feared either Damion or the dragon at Husavik. And they'd both terrified Zachary plenty. When he'd seen her in person, he'd been unimpressed, then furious when she took Cliona's body. Outside of the teho required for the transport, though, he'd not experienced her strength.

He understood now. The band feared Isira because it was right for them to do so. When he'd first come across Damion's power, Zachary had realized just how weak he, as a vilda, was. The band was to Isira what he was to them. Nothing more than a nuisance.

As a child, Zachary had heard all the stories of the stamfar. How they'd moved literal mountains, founded cities, and fought dragons for sport. They were fanciful tales, stories that, even as a youth, Zachary had known couldn't be true.

Today, he believed every one.

Isira floated in the air, her voice still reverberating in his bones. Teho flowed from her as if bursting constantly from a dam. Zachary respected the band, but if all of them were to work together, they'd have as much luck bringing her down as a gentle breeze might have destroying a fortress. Zachary barely felt their teho in the midst of Isira's maelstrom.

His thoughts started to run again. Solveig was shouting something to the floating god, but Zachary couldn't make out a word. Solveig paused, waiting for a response. When none came, she shouted again. It didn't look like Isira was interested in debate, though.

How did one kill a god?

Attacking head-on was as suicidal as sticking his head in a hungry dragon's mouth. He'd been called a fool for plenty of good reasons, but wasn't going to make it that easy for Isira. He looked left and right, finding no inspiration. Then he looked up. He turned to Hel. "Can you teleport me above her? High above her?"

Hel nodded.

"I'm going to need a sword."

She frowned, but he anticipated her question. "I don't want to use a teho blade. In case she senses it."

A moment later, one of the guards handed Zachary her sword. She grimaced as she offered it to him, but said nothing. He thanked her, then nodded to Hel. "Better to do this before I have time to realize how foolish it is."

Hel grabbed his arm. Her grip was firm. "Try not to die, at least."

She closed her eyes, focusing on the transport. He was about to ask her if she'd ever transported into midair, but before he could, the world around him shifted, and he was no longer standing. Hel let go of him and vanished, and he fell. His stomach twisted as his body fought to orient itself to its new circumstances. Vomit rose in his throat, but he choked it back down.

Hel was as good as her word. He fell headfirst, and he saw Isira floating far below him. He pointed his steel sword down, not trusting himself to time a swing accurately enough.

The speed of his descent surprised him. As a younger boy, he'd often secretly jumped off of any high ledge he could climb. He remembered loving the momentary sense of flying, as well as the private pride that came from landing and rolling safely every time. His punishment, had he ever been caught, would have been severe. Father never approved of unnecessary risks.

This fall was nothing like the jumps he'd taken as a child. He kept falling faster, the wind whipping his hair straight back and making his eyes water. He squinted, focused only on keeping Isira in sight. She continued to hover, and Zachary knew his plan would work.

He wouldn't survive, though. His speed was too great. Even his strongest shield couldn't protect him from the impact. He didn't believe the stamfar were gods, but old traditions returned at the end, and he said a quick prayer, wishing for protection for his sister.

Isira looked up, and there was no surprise in her eyes. Zachary swore as she simply floated back, away from the path of his descent.

Zachary had felt the fool plenty of times in his life, but never so much as he did in that moment. Surprise had been his only weapon, and he'd never actually possessed it. He'd die, a smear on the land of Aysgarth, having accomplished nothing.

Just as his father had predicted, so long ago.

Zachary closed his eyes as he fell past Isira.

So be it.

The bands of teho that wrapped around his ankles were stronger than anything he could have formed, and they immediately slowed his descent. He opened his eyes and saw Irric and Solveig focused on him.

If not for the constant pressure on his ankles, he wouldn't have believed it. The power itself was incredible, but the control of that power was beyond his imagining. How many lifetimes of training would be required to accomplish such a feat?

His descent slowed, and for the first time, he began to believe he might just survive his own stupidity.

Then teho exploded behind him, like another sun being ignited in the sky. Isira readied an attack, and two of the three band were focused on saving his life instead of protecting their own. Ari vanished, but Zachary had no idea where the assassin had gone.

If they were going to have any chance, they needed to forget saving him. "Let me go!" he shouted. "Save yourselves!"

Apparently, all they had needed was his encouragement.

The teho around his ankles vanished, and they turned their attention to the sky.

The ground rushed up to meet him as Isira and the band prepared to battle.

CHAPTER 19

Before long, Hakon caught sight of the new arrival. It was darker than the younglings and kept close to the contours of the land, denying either of the kolma a clear view. It shot over the summit of the pass at high speed and dropped, spreading its enormous wings wide as it reached for them.

Meshell danced away from the creature's grasping talons, but Hakon's injuries prevented him from doing the same. Besides, they couldn't run from dragons. They could either fight or call for Ari to save them, but if they turned tail, they were nothing more than entertaining prey.

Hakon swung down at the claw as it grabbed at him. His sword cut through the dragon's armor, slicing through the flesh beneath.

The cut wasn't more than an inch or two deep. But dragons were at the top of the food chain and weren't used to their prey striking back. The younglings' parent roared, and the force of the dragon's teho sent Hakon tumbling backward.

Somehow, Meshell kept her feet, skipping back as the

waves of teho buffeted her. She formed a spear and flung it at the dragon's face as it retreated. The dragon avoided the speeding projectile, but it flapped its wings and flew away, joining the younglings in the sky.

Hakon grimaced as he found his feet again. "Don't suppose they decided to give up?"

Meshell grunted. "I'm sure they're terrified. So far, we've managed to give them the equivalent of a paper cut. And now all three of them are together."

"Should we call for Ari?"

Meshell stared at the sky. "That would be the wise choice."

"But?"

She pointed over the horizon. "There's something there. And from the way they're flying, I think they're protecting it."

Hakon followed the line of her finger. He'd also noticed the dragons weren't circling directly overhead. Their flight was centered on a point farther northwest. "How do you know there's something there?"

"My fight against the first youngling took me to the top of the pass. You can see it from there. No idea what it is, but it's big. Shame to give up when we're this close."

Above them, the flight pattern of the dragons had changed. "They're coming," Hakon said. "What's your plan?"

"Can you make a dash for it? I'd guess it's about two miles away."

Hakon almost snorted with disbelief. Two miles, injured, with dragons chasing them? He didn't give her the pleasure of an outright denial. "What's the terrain like?"

"Rocky downslope leading to a pine forest." The corner of her mouth turned up in a grin, and Hakon had no doubt she knew exactly what he was thinking.

The dragons descended toward them. Hakon figured he had less than a minute before they struck again. Running was foolish. But they'd never find answers if they kept retreating. When he looked at Meshell, he felt like a much younger man, ready to throw himself at anything, no matter how foolish it seemed.

History told no tales of the cautious.

He sheathed his sword. "After you."

Her grin widened. "Like you could run fast enough to be in the lead."

With that, she was off, darting across the rocks like a gazelle. Hakon filled his body with teho and followed.

For a few heartbeats, it was just him and Meshell, running freely toward the mountain pass. So far as Hakon knew, they were the only two alive who possessed the ability to use teho to strengthen their bodies, so they were the only two capable of such speed. The wind blew his long hair back, and it felt like freedom.

The dragons shattered the illusion with their earth-shaking roars. He glanced up and saw three shadows falling from the sky. The two younglings fell toward Meshell, and the adult aimed at him.

The younglings reached Meshell first, a bit more agile than their parent. One came at her from the west while the other approached from the east. Hakon grimaced, his own danger temporarily forgotten, as the three rushed together in what appeared to be an inevitable collision. The youngling from the west passed first, swiping at Meshell from behind and blocking her from Hakon's view. Less than a heartbeat later, the dragon from the east cut across Hakon's sight, twisting to avoid its sibling.

Hakon blinked as Meshell came back into view, somehow still running. She dropped over the summit of the pass and disappeared from sight again, the two younglings chasing after her.

The parent snapped at Hakon as it passed, and he leaped forward. The jaws missed, but the power of the passing dragon knocked him off his feet. Hakon rolled, biting back a yell as pain shot up his side. He came to his feet and stumbled. For a moment, he thought he would fall and lose all momentum.

But the next step came easier, and the one after that even more so. He picked up speed and reached the top of the pass.

The sight of the valley on the other side almost froze him in place. If not for his momentum, he might have stopped to stare.

Meshell hadn't been lying when she'd said there was something on the other side. And it was nothing like Hakon had ever seen in his life. Long and gray, it jutted high above the trees, with two cavernous openings reaching up to the sky.

That was all he had time to observe. His speed had carried him over the pass, the summit of which was only a few feet wide. Now he was descending, and he saw that Meshell's description of the terrain had also tended toward understatement. The downslope was steep, almost vertical in places. Much of the stone felt loose underfoot. A sensible person would back down slowly with a partner, using a thick rope for safety.

Instead, Meshell ran down the slope.

No, that wasn't right.

Meshell wasn't running. She was falling, somehow remaining in control the entire time. Her feet skipped across the stone, each impact doing just enough to keep her from tumbling down the rest of the mountain.

The younglings didn't dare try to catch her. They'd broken off pursuit and were making passes above the scree below, waiting for Meshell to come to them.

Hakon swore as the stone underfoot gave way. He leaped, trying to mimic Meshell's grace. His foot landed on a solid boulder and he bounced down to the next solid-looking stone. His strong legs flexed as they absorbed drop after drop.

Just when Hakon believed he might make it safely to the scree, a shadow blocked the sun overhead. He risked a glance skyward. The parent, it seemed, wasn't so interested in letting the kolma make it to the bottom unopposed. It dove down, hugging the ground just like it had on its arrival.

It wasn't flying quite close enough to swipe at them, but it didn't need to.

The creature was too clever for its own good. The force of its passing knocked Hakon off course. He landed hard, dislodging several stones as he fell forward. Somehow, he managed to keep his feet under him as he fell again. The second impact was less kind. His landing wasn't clean, and his feet slipped. He slammed into a pointed stone, then tumbled down a rocky decline about twenty feet before being stopped by yet another rock.

Hakon groaned and flipped over so that he could look downhill.

Meshell had just about made it to the scree when the dragon passed overhead. She fell, but somehow managed to make even that look graceful. She returned to her feet a moment later, jumping on top of the scree and half-running, half-sliding down the loose stone. The two younglings saw their opportunity and dove toward her.

Hakon pushed himself to his feet, regretting the decision as soon as he did. But if he didn't move, he'd be the adult's next meal. One look at the sky told him he wasn't wrong. The parent was circling back, its large eyes focused on him.

Hakon dropped down to the next stone, then to the next. Each impact sent a wave of agony up and down his spine. The parent flew overhead again, but this time Hakon moved slowly enough he could simply hold still while it passed.

The scree was close. Maybe fifty feet down. Hakon leaped again. Forty feet.

Thirty.

The dragon came again, its attitude different this time. Hakon was moving too slow. It was going to try to grab him.

Hakon swore. As the dragon approached, he leaped as far as his legs could propel him, and hoped he'd thrown off the parent's timing enough that he wouldn't be snatched out of the air. The dragon passed behind him, the force of it propelling him even faster toward the scree.

Hakon didn't try to fight gravity. He tucked his limbs in close to his body and filled himself with as much teho as he could summon. He hit hard, but he just squeezed his eyes shut and hoped for the best. His body tumbled and slid, the descent a never-ending series of bone-jarring impacts.

Miraculously, he was still conscious when he slid to a stop at the bottom of the scree. He opened his eyes. The pine forest began maybe three hundred feet away. Meshell was almost to the cover of the trees, the younglings swooping in close behind her.

Hakon couldn't find a part of his body that didn't hurt. Cuts decorated his bare arms, and his pants were torn from shin to thigh. Blood seeped from dozens of wounds.

But teho still coursed through his body, and the now-broken ribs were the worst of his injuries. He sucked in a deep breath and pushed himself to his feet. The world tilted. He stumbled, but kept himself upright. He didn't run so much as fall forward and hope his legs would catch him.

Behind him, the parent was coming around again. Hakon looked back and swore. He ran faster, but he wasn't going to make it to the cover of the trees. He didn't think he had the strength left to fight, either. They'd bet everything on fleeing, and he was too slow.

Hakon figured his odds were still better running, though. If he stood his ground, sword in hand, the dragon would have no problem overpowering him. He heaved, every breath shifting his ribs, sending a fresh wave of agony through his chest. He didn't dare look back again, but he felt the dragon coming closer and closer, its teho remarkable.

A long spear of teho erupted from the trees, passing no more than a foot above Hakon's head. He twisted around in time to see the dragon pull up, taking the spear in its armored neck instead of risking anything vulnerable on its face.

The dragon looped, returning for Hakon, anger glinting in its eyes.

Hakon found one last burst of speed and made it to the trees. Meshell was ahead of him, bounding among the tall pines, graceful as a deer. He careened from tree to tree, his balance still not fully returned to him.

A moment later, trees exploded behind Hakon as the dragon tore through them. Tall pines, some which must have stood for almost as long as Hakon had been alive, erupted into spreading spheres of splintered wood. The dragon might not be able to see them, but the trees were thin protection indeed. As wooden shrapnel embedded in his back, he wondered if they wouldn't have been safer out in the open.

As the dragon lost momentum, it toppled trees instead

of destroying them. The forest boomed and cracked as trees died like front-line soldiers standing against a charge. Trees crashed behind him, and Hakon didn't dare risk a glance back, certain that he couldn't spare even the moment it would take.

But where were the other dragons? Hakon and Meshell might be hidden from sight, but the canopy of the forest was thick enough to block most of the sky, too. They might not notice an incoming dragon until it was too late to do anything about it.

The parent behind him must have taken to the sky, because the sounds of trees toppling faded. For several precious seconds he was able to run without fear. Meshell had slowed, and he soon caught up to her. They took no break. Meshell led them through the forest, always angling northwest. Hakon coughed and splattered blood across the trunk of a nearby pine.

Hakon's focus narrowed. He watched Meshell as she darted through the trees. He kept an eye on the ground ahead of him, avoiding roots and exposed stone half buried under dead brown pine needles. If he was going to become a meal for the dragons flying overhead, it wouldn't be because he tripped.

Why didn't they attack again? They'd had plenty of time to circle the area, and the trees were little more than an annoyance.

Meshell skidded to a stop so quickly Hakon had to angle toward a tree to make sure he didn't run right over her. Before he could ask the reason, the forest in front of them erupted in chaos. Trees blew apart and toppled, but through the storm of pinecones and branches, Hakon saw one of the younglings tumbling to a stop. It raised its head and roared, dark blood leaking from several deep gashes.

It gathered its legs beneath it and launched back into the sky.

Hakon traced its path upward. High above, the parent appeared to be wrestling with the second youngling.

He stared. He'd never seen such a sight. Had never even imagined it possible.

Meshell tugged on his arm. "Don't want to be underneath them if they fall again."

She pulled him through the clearing the youngling had made, and he decided she was absolutely right. Once again, he returned his focus to her and to the careful placement of his footsteps.

The forest remained silent except for the brushing of the wind against the pines and the sounds of their footsteps. Meshell's were quick and light, his heavy and labored. He kept glancing skyward, but once again the canopy blocked his view.

The trees ahead of them bent, and another roar split the air, so loud his ears rang after. A blast of wind tossed dead branches and pine needles into the air, but no dragon joined them in the trees. Meshell never faltered, and Hakon didn't let himself fall more than a few steps behind her.

The next time Hakon looked up, he could see no more than he had on previous glances, but the sky felt different. For the first time in what felt like years, it seemed empty, the menace vanished like a morning fog exposed to the bright rays of the sun.

If Meshell thought the same, she gave no sign. Her pace was as quick as ever, and it was all Hakon could do to keep up. The longer he ran the harder it became to breathe. His ribs and chest ached from his wounds, and he coughed blood every dozen steps or so.

Blackness crawled into the edges of his vision. He didn't have long.

"Meshell," he croaked, just before stumbling to a halt.

He leaned against a tree, feeling the ribs in his chest with every breath. He didn't even notice when Meshell came up beside him. When she questioned him, her closeness almost made him jump. "Can you move?"

"I just need a moment."

Meshell looked to the sky, and though she said nothing, the glance meant everything. They didn't have a moment for him to waste.

"This is going to hurt," she said.

That was all the warning she gave before she picked him up and heaved him over her shoulder. Though he knew she wasn't trying to be unkind, the impact almost caused him to pass out from the wave of pain.

Then they were moving again, and all Hakon could see was Meshell's boots as she carried him the rest of the way.

CHAPTER 20

Zachary formed a shield just before he hit the ground. It shattered the moment he hit, but it served his purposes well enough. He landed hard, the air expelled from his lungs as though he'd been squeezed by a giant. As he fought for breath, he rolled over.

The teho emanating from Isira terrified him. It drove thought from his mind and left him lying there, speechless. He watched Solveig and Irric form shields, but that was nothing more than a final act of defiance.

Isira didn't kill them. "You dare attack me?" she asked.

"Forgive the child," Solveig said. Now that Zachary was near them, he could hear them clearly. "His courage exceeds his intelligence." She shot him a glare, and he withered beneath it.

He'd thought his sacrifice noble, his attempt heroic.

She'd called him a child, and he hadn't felt so much like one in years.

He'd needed to be saved again, just like Cliona had saved him in Husavik, over and over. When would he be strong enough to fight for himself?

He wanted nothing more than to dig a grave to lie in.

Tears blurred his vision as he clenched clumps of dirt in his hand. He buried his face in the grass.

"Where are Hakon and Meshell?" Isira asked.

"West. Seeking answers."

Zachary was forgotten, as it should be. There was a long moment of silence, and when he looked up, he saw that Isira no longer floated. She now stood before Solveig, and it was as bizarre a sight as any Zachary had ever seen.

Solveig stood tall before Isira, not as the academic Zachary had known for so long, but as the warrior and kolma he'd come to recognize her as. She appeared to be in her early to mid-thirties, her limbs strong and graceful. In contrast, Isira looked like nothing more than a child. Her arms were thin, too weak to wield a steel sword properly. And yet there remained something greater about Isira.

It wasn't just her teho, either. Despite her appearance, she possessed a presence that demanded respect.

Though they spoke more softly, Zachary could still hear the two of them.

"After all these years, you still fight?" Isira asked.

Solveig's grin was tinged with bitterness. "It's what we do."

"To what end?"

"Same as always. To save as many as possible." Solveig paused. "Why now?"

"She's in Husavik. When I sensed you in Aysgarth, I feared there was a connection."

Solveig nodded, but Zachary didn't have the slightest clue what they were speaking of. "Do you have any idea of her intent?"

Isira shook her head. "But I think we're about to find out.

I think we caught her attention. Gather yourselves together."

Solveig turned and started shouting orders for the council members and commanders to close ranks. Zachary saw Ari near the back of the delegation, ushering people together. He'd not even felt the assassin transport there.

Then Irric's strong hands were lifting him up. "Injured?" he asked.

"Nothing serious."

"Then join the others. And try not to do anything quite so stupid again."

Zachary half-ran, half-limped toward the rest of the group. Hel rushed out and supported him. "I thought you were done for," she said.

"You're not the only one."

Another source of teho bloomed, higher up the valley. Zachary turned in time to watch Ava appear, surrounded by a shield of teho. He shook his head in disbelief. He was pretty certain he could drop a whole mountain on that shield and it wouldn't so much as tremble.

How had the world survived the age of the stamfar? Such power was beyond human. One errant tantrum and a whole neighborhood would be nothing but debris.

Isira turned, putting the Aysgarthians and the band behind her. She called out in a language Zachary didn't understand.

Ava considered for a moment, then floated to the ground. She let her shield drop, but her grasp on teho was as tight as ever. She spoke, her language indecipherable. Though Zachary didn't know what she said, the challenge in her statements was obvious.

Isira responded in the same language. Ava tensed.

Irric whispered to Solveig. "Shields?"

Solveig gave the barest hint of a nod. Zachary felt them grasp teho, although they didn't shape it. Without looking back, Solveig said, "You too, Zachary. Every bit of strength might be needed."

He held teho, and several of Hel's commanders did, too.

Ava spoke one more time, and her tone was one of finality.

Isira didn't answer for a long time, but when she did, her answer held the same tone. Ava formed a shield, and Isira teleported.

Ava twisted as Isira appeared beside her. A spear of teho appeared in Isira's hand.

"Shields up!" Solveig yelled.

As one, the tehoin of Aysgarth and the band formed a shield between them and the two stamfar.

Zachary grimaced as he added his strength to the wall. Compared to the kolma, it was next to nothing, but it felt better than actually doing nothing.

Isira's spearpoint met Ava's shield.

The air around the point of impact warped as the energies collided. The combatants froze in place, their powers perfectly balanced. Isira's thin arms trembled as she held her thrust. Ava gritted her teeth. Air swirled and bent as though reality was melting and reforming.

A white light appeared where spear met shield. For less than a heartbeat, it was nothing more than a burning pinprick. Then the whole world went white.

The impact hit the shield a moment later. Zachary dropped to a knee, his head pounding like it had just been hit by a brick. If not for Irric and Solveig, the blast would have shattered his shield without slowing.

Strong as the blow was, it only lasted for a moment and then vanished. Zachary looked back to see most of the

Aysgarthians slowly returning to their feet. Remarkably, no one seemed injured.

Then Zachary looked around. To either side of the party, the ground had been blasted away, five or six feet deep. They stood on a peninsula in the middle of a crater.

In front of them, Isira and Ava floated, their attention completely on one another. One bead of sweat trickled down Isira's brow, and Ava's hair was mussed. Otherwise, they gave no indication they'd just destroyed a quarter of the valley.

Ari appeared next to Irric and Solveig, who'd been driven to their knees by the blast and were slow to get up. They both appeared haggard. Ari helped them to their feet. "It's not settled," he said.

"The next one will be worse," Irric agreed.

"Can you transport us?" Solveig asked. Her voice cracked as she asked.

Ari cast a glance back at the assembled party. He swallowed hard. "Maybe. I have my doubts."

Zachary's attention drifted to the two stamfar women, still floating in the air. They were talking again, and it didn't strike Zachary as a conversation between friends.

"Who are we supporting here?" Irric asked Solveig.

"Isira, I think," Solveig said.

"Sure?" Ari asked.

"Reasonably. I can't make out everything, but I think Ava likes us even less than Isira."

"Did Hakon kill one of her friends, too?" Irric inquired.

Ari actually laughed. Then his voice lowered. "Want me to try?"

Zachary looked at Ari and barely recognized the man. It was as if he'd drawn so far into himself he'd become a void. The kolma stood only a few feet in front of him and

Zachary could barely see him. His eyes just slid off the assassin.

Solveig glanced over at Irric, who inclined his head. "One chance," she said. "We can take one more hit, then you need to get us out of here."

Ari turned his attention to the stamfar, and Zachary followed his gaze.

The discussion between the two had died. Though they stood still, they reminded Zachary of trained fighters circling one another in the arena.

How did stamfar fight? How did these stamfar fight? Ava had been imprisoned for centuries, and Isira had stopped her aging in the guise of a child.

Everything happened in the blink of an eye, and it wasn't until later that Zachary made sense of what he'd seen.

Ava flickered and was suddenly behind Isira, an enormous teho sword in hand. She swung the sword down, and Isira vanished, reappearing above Ava with her spear pointed down. She stabbed, and Ava's shield appeared. Again, the space around the stamfar flexed.

Ari crouched low as Solveig called for shields. A knife appeared in his hands, made of steel, not teho.

A pinpoint of light sparked where spear met shield. Space rippled around the stamfar.

Irric and Solveig built their shields. Zachary and the Aysgarthians joined them.

The world went a blinding white.

Ari vanished, leaving only two silhouettes standing between Zachary and the gates.

The impact hit, the force even greater than before. The shield broke, but not before absorbing the deadly force. Blood poured from Zachary's nose and his head felt as though it might crack wide open with every heartbeat. His legs turned to water and he fell, barely catching himself with his hands.

He looked up as Irric and Solveig fell, but his attention was on the scene farther up ahead.

Ava was caught between Ari and Isira.

The stamfar the band so feared was impaled on a teho sword through the side of her stomach. Isira's spear had broken through Ava's shield and through Ava's shoulder. Ari crouched behind Ava, his dagger in her back.

Had they done it?

Zachary remained conscious long enough to see Ava vanish and Isira drop from where she'd been floating.

Then he gave up and let darkness consume his thoughts.

CHAPTER 21

Once Meshell picked Hakon up, they made considerably faster progress, even if it was at the expense of a few more ribs. The woods remained silent, as though the world were holding its breath. Hakon kept waiting for the songbirds to burst into their melodies, but the only sound was that of Meshell's steady steps.

She came to a stop with a grunt. "Going to need to put you down," she said.

He heard no exhaustion in her voice. "Are we there?"

"Close."

She squatted down until he bore some of his weight on his feet. Then she repositioned herself so that she could stand under his armpit. Together, they turned to stare at the mystery.

Up close, it made even less sense than it had at a distance. It wasn't natural, and it was easily the biggest structure he'd ever seen, dwarfing even the ruins of Husavik. He guessed it stood ten times his height, and that was at an angle.

It had come from the sky. The reason Meshell had to put him down was because a ridge of broken rock stood before them, pushed aside by the impact. Its—front, Hakon guessed—was buried beneath the stone. How much of it was hidden from view?

They picked their way up the ridge of rock, Meshell supporting Hakon with every step.

Whatever had happened here had happened long ago. Soil had settled in the displaced stone, and old pine trees clung for purchase on the steep slope.

They reached the top and took their time studying the object. The material along the surface reminded him of steel, but it didn't look quite right. There were round holes in lines up and down the surface, reminding Hakon of windows.

"What is it?" Meshell whispered.

"I wish I knew."

Meshell's pragmatism didn't take long to assert itself. "Is it what we were looking for?"

Hakon looked to the sky, which remained empty. Strange as this object was, he didn't think it was the object of their search. If it was, the dragons never would have let them get this close. Besides, if he'd estimated the range correctly earlier, the dragons had been circling a location a few miles farther to the northwest. "I don't think so, but it's worth investigating."

They picked their way down the other side of the slope and Hakon shuffled toward the area where the object had buried itself in the ground. His chest was hurting worse than ever. Before long he would need to rest and let his body heal.

As he neared, he saw a rectangle with rounded edges cut into the material perhaps five feet from the ground. It was a thin cut that reminded him of stamfar doors, a technology he hadn't seen since exploring Marjaana's home with Ari. Similar shapes had been cut higher up in the structure.

Meshell broke away from him and ran her hand along the surface. When her hand passed over a section near the door, the surface lit up with two colors, red and green. Meshell pressed her thumb against the green light, and the material inside the cut recessed and slid aside with a quiet hiss.

"Teho?" Hakon asked. The lighted panel reminded him of other stamfar inventions. But he hadn't felt her use any.

"No," she said. "Something else." She looked up at the door, then glanced at him, her question obvious.

As much as it pained him, he was in no shape to explore. She'd have to either lift or pull him into the structure, and he feared he couldn't risk it. "Go," he said. "I'll stand guard."

Her snort of derision let him know just how useful she thought he'd be in that role. Then she climbed up into the door and disappeared. Hakon watched the hole for a moment, then turned around and leaned against the structure. He glanced up at the sky, grateful to see there were still no dragons overhead.

He felt lost, small, and insignificant. All he knew was that he knew nothing, and Cliona seemed farther away with every passing day. This world was not what he thought it was.

Then Meshell reappeared at the edge of the door, her foot only a few inches away from his head. "We'll need torches," she announced. "I'm sure there's a way of lighting up the inside, but I can't figure it out. Nothing within is powered by teho."

Yet another mystery. And they still hadn't found the

place dragons called home. "Mind if we look around a little more?" He had to believe they were close.

Meshell dropped down from the door, landing softly. "Probably not a bad idea, although you'll need to rest soon."

"I know."

They made their way around the structure. Meshell kept her pace slow enough that Hakon could keep up. Their route brought them under the structure. Hakon looked up at the enormous object as it angled over him. His perspective of the object changed again. He had known, since the first time he'd seen it, that it was big. But looking at it now, he realized it was even more expansive than he thought. A small town could be fit inside.

They reached the other side of the structure, Hakon still half in a daze over the sheer improbability of the thing he was walking around. He knew of nothing like it. He'd never even heard any stories of anything like it.

The other side held no more answers. It looked much the same as the first side they'd approached.

Meshell's hand on his shoulder caught his attention. He needed only a moment to see what Meshell wanted him to see.

His first instinct was to reach for his sword, but that would do him no more good than shouting at a thunderstorm to go away.

He knew, now, why they'd been able to find this spot. Why they'd come across two younglings and a parent.

Perhaps two miles away, another line of mountains pierced the horizon. Tall, jagged, and snow-capped, they looked like a place Hakon would fear to visit.

And that was based on the geography alone.

Never mind the dragons flying in lazy patterns around the mountains. He watched as dragons flew into the mountains, and with their flight leading his eye, he could make out the caves that dotted the steep cliffs.

That was their home. The place they'd been searching for.

He stared for a whole minute, wondering what to do next. He was so close. If Cliona was there, he had to continue. But he needed to rest.

From inside the mountain, a dragon roared.

The sound was deeper, more powerful than the cries of even the parent they'd just fled. Hakon swore he felt the ground vibrate beneath his feet.

His heart also skipped a beat. *He knew that sound.* He'd heard it before, in the skies above Husavik. Teho swirled through his limbs, responding to the dragon's call. They'd been connected once, and that connection still pulled at him.

"It's her," Hakon whispered.

Meshell's look nearly stole the last of his strength. She said nothing, but her stare spoke volumes. She thought he'd gone mad, that grief and pain had finally pushed him too far.

And what could he say? How could he explain the pull of teho, the certainty he possessed in every fiber of his being? He had nothing the band would believe, and yet he knew.

"I think we need to summon Ari," Meshell said.

Hakon shook his head, gently at first, then more violently. "No. We need to set up a camp, rest for a day or two, and then go up there."

"You need healing, not just rest. Ari can set up a transport locus here, and we can come back after we're healed. We've done enough for now."

"She's there!"

"And look!" Meshell jabbed her finger in the sky. "We barely survived two younglings and a parent, and there's far more than that in those caves. Even if you're right, we need the band."

"If we leave, I'll never convince the others to return."

"If you don't, you'll never survive. We need them, Hakon."

Hakon swore, his eyes fixed on the mountains. He was so close! How could he leave? He shook his head again. "I'm sorry, Meshell. I can't leave Cliona. Not when she's so close. I'll go alone if I have to, but I can't turn back."

"I know."

There was a deep sorrow in her voice, and he broke his gaze with the mountain just for a moment. She was looking down at her feet. She continued. "I can never decide if you're the most inspiring man I've ever met or the most frustrating. You just never stop fighting."

He frowned, not sure what she was going on about. He returned his stare to the mountain, starting to plan how he might assault the caves.

"I'm sorry," Meshell said.

He paid her no mind, his thoughts already turning to the task ahead.

He never saw the blow that knocked him unconscious.

CHAPTER 22

Zachary paced his small room, grateful the floor was made of stone. By now, he feared he would have paced a hole through a wooden floor. Since the attacks, he'd found it nearly impossible to stay still. At night, sleep only came after hours of tossing and turning. He'd taken to wandering the halls of Aysgarth long after everyone else was asleep.

How many times could his world be turned on its head before he finally surrendered? The stamfar were real, and he'd lived to see them duel. His father was dying and wanted him home. He was in exile no longer.

Almost everything he believed true a year ago was proven false. So much of what he thought impossible had become reality.

What did a person do, when they had no solid foundation to start from?

No matter how far he walked at night, though, his mind refused to settle.

Lately, Hel had made a habit of joining him on his nightly wanderings. She was a steady presence, a rock when everything around him seemed to be the waves of the sea tossed about by a violent storm. Their conversations wandered as widely as their routes. Often, they spoke of the events of the day. Hel continued to tiptoe along the edge of a razor. Ava's attack had thrown Aysgarth into an uproar, and the factions were at each other's throats daily.

The band, wisely, had removed themselves from sight. Their meals were delivered to their rooms and they rarely ventured out. Zachary hadn't found the courage to visit them yet. He was still embarrassed by his antics during the attack, and he'd gotten the sense, after the battle, of the band closing ranks. Their world was as uncertain as his, and they leaned on each other, gently pushing everyone else away.

Tonight, Zachary didn't even bother with the pretense of wandering. He'd heard the news. He made straight for Hel's study, where he knew he would find her working late into the night.

A single guard was posted outside her door, Hel's only concession to her safety. Zachary argued she should have more guards, but Hel believed that if she started walking around with a collection of guards in her own home, she had lost whatever scrap of legitimacy her leadership possessed.

The guard, who knew Zachary, nodded and let him pass. Zachary knocked on the door, and at the sound of Hel's voice, entered.

As he expected, she was buried deep in paper. Her days were filled with meetings with council members and keeping the peace. It was at night that she fought her least glorious but most important battles. This was where she decided which supplies would go where. Where she read and analyzed the information that allowed her to keep Aysgarth alive.

There were bags under her eyes, but when she looked up at him, her smile was wide. It faded, just a little, when she saw the expression on his face. "You've heard, then?"

He slumped into the chair on the other side of her desk as an answer. "What could she want?"

"I haven't the slightest idea."

It was obvious Hel was bothered. Isira had demanded an audience, not just with the council, but with all of Aysgarth. Given that one did not deny a stamfar their wishes, Hel had arranged the audience for the next day. Isira had given no clue of her intentions to anyone. "Have you talked to Solveig?" Zachary asked.

"Briefly, but she's as in the dark as I am."

That had been Zachary's only hope. He suspected the band knew Isira as well as anyone alive. If they were similarly adrift, everyone would be walking into the audience tomorrow blind.

"You will be there, won't you?" Hel asked. "I would have you with us."

Zachary nodded, and he thought he saw Hel's body relax, just a little. "You want to get out, just for a bit?"

Hel's smile fell. "More than anything, but I can't tonight. Council was worse than usual today, and we argued far longer than even I anticipated." She gestured to the pile of papers on her desk. "If I don't get this done, it'll only be worse tomorrow. And somehow I need to find the time to sleep before the audience tomorrow. Otherwise I'll be napping while everyone else is drawing swords over whatever Isira says."

Zachary laughed at the thought. "Anything I can do to help?"

He could tell she was about to say no, but she stopped before the answer left her lips. "Could you double-check my figures on our food supplies? I think my sums are correct, but it would be nice to have another eye look over them before I present them to council."

If anyone else had asked him to check their sums, Zachary was certain he would have run out the door. And Hel didn't need the help. She had a gift for numbers that would have put most academics to shame. He didn't have a doubt in the world that her sums were correct. And he still had an urge to be out walking, to burn off this nervousness that wouldn't leave his body.

But he couldn't tell her no. He wanted her company more than he wanted to walk the cold, empty halls of Aysgarth. So he pulled his chair to the other side of the desk so they could sit side by side, working late into the night.

THE NEXT MORNING Zachary broke his fast in the dining hall alone. He'd been curious if the band would show today, before the audience with Isira, but they stuck to the pattern they'd established since Ava's attack.

Zachary stared at the runny sludge on his plate. It was also possible they'd just decided to skip the early meal and break their fast on real food later in the day.

The mood in this dining hall was different than before. Yesterday, factions had sat on opposite sides of the room, speaking in hushed whispers among themselves. Today, the factions still sat apart, but the room was loud. Zachary had no problem hearing snippets of all the conversations, and every mind was turned toward the audience later this morning. The slow-moving crisis at Aysgarth was coming to a head, and there were many who were expecting a resolution today.

He listened to plenty of wild theories. Isira was planning on ruling Aysgarth. She was gathering them so she could destroy them all. One woman wondered if Isira would somehow resurrect Damion.

Zachary finished his meal early, scooping up every bit of the sludge he could. It tasted even worse than it looked, but it was food, and he had a feeling he was going to need all the energy he could gather today.

Then he made his way to the open-air amphitheater. He fell in beside others who also wanted to arrive early. Zachary was among the first to arrive, so he was able to secure a good seat. Hel had offered to let Zachary sit up on the platform with other non-council officials, but he'd declined. He craved the anonymity the crowd provided.

Before long, the amphitheater was filled close to bursting. Fortunately, the sun was out today, and the air was warm for Aysgarth. The council took their seats up on the platform, and murmurs ran through the crowd as they awaited the stamfar's arrival.

Solveig arrived to the audience first, and Zachary was surprised to see that she was alone. Where were Ari and Irric?

Zachary wished he'd had the courage to meet with the band. Then he'd at least have some idea of what they intended.

Solveig walked down the middle aisle of the amphitheater toward the stage, radiating a calm authority. Murmurs silenced as she passed. She took her seat behind the council, leaving only one open chair on the stage.

If the crowd calmed for Solveig, they fell absolutely silent when Isira appeared. She was dressed in the same clothes Zachary had seen her in every other day, and she still looked like nothing more than a disheveled child. Her injury from the battle had already faded, and Zachary wondered if she'd healed herself or if Solveig had aided her.

Then she embraced teho, leaving no doubt as to who, and what, she was. Though she was surrounded by a fair percentage of the strongest tehoin in the six states, Zachary wouldn't bet against her in a fight. Aysgarthians seated near the center aisle scooted away from her as she passed.

Isira took the last seat, and the whole crowd seemed to exhale at the same time.

Such power hadn't been gathered together since the time of the empire.

No one knew what was to come, but the sense of anticipation was palpable. When great powers joined, history trembled.

Hel spoke first. Her tone was casual, as though she was speaking to a friend in a tavern over drinks. But as she stood, all eyes were on her. For the moment, at least, she commanded the amphitheater. "We gather today to listen to the words of a stamfar among us. Let us listen with an open mind, then decide our next steps with a wise heart."

Isira stood quickly, and Hel flinched back. The stamfar waved Hel back to her seat. Her voice was that of a child, but her words carried to every ear without problem. "There's no need for any of your ceremony here," she said.

Had such rudeness come from anyone else, Zachary suspected the amphitheater would have been in an uproar. Everyone, including him, was leaning forward. Only the display of Isira's power kept order.

Isira addressed the crowd, ignoring the council completely. "Ava is a stamfar, and she wishes to wipe humanity from the face of this planet. If you hope to live, you'll need to fight together. Though I doubt it will matter. The choice is yours."

Then Isira started to walk off the stage, and the whole amphitheater exploded into chaos.

Hel stood first among the council, as she'd just barely sat down. "Isira!" Her voice was louder and more commanding than Zachary had ever heard.

The chaos subsided as the stamfar turned to face Hel.

"You tell us of a threat, greater even than the dragons, yet give us nothing. Will you fight with us?"

Isira stared at Hel, and Zachary feared the brave nelja would soon be dead. But Isira answered Hel's question. "No. Your fight is none of my concern." She held up a hand to stop Hel's response. Then she pointed at Solveig. "If you wish to have any hope at all, follow her. She's the most level-headed and far-sighted of you all."

Solveig looked as surprised by the comment as the rest of the amphitheater.

Isira walked off the stage, and the chaos erupted again.

Zachary ignored the shouts of his neighbors and kept his eyes on the stage. Solveig acted first. She followed Isira off the stage.

Hel spoke quickly to some of the council, the members Zachary recognized as her closest allies. Then she, too, followed after Isira, followed by Valdis.

Zachary swore. Gunvald, as well as the other council members, were trying to shout over the crowd, but their voices were being drowned out. The fact Gunvald was helping the rest of the council was telling, though. No one wanted a fight to break out. Working together, Zachary had the feeling they would eventually settle the crowd.

He refused to be left out of whatever conversation was

about to happen, though. If Hel wanted him to be useful at his father's court, he had the right.

He didn't dare charge the stage, though. At best, he'd be restrained. At worst, he'd be the one who tipped the crowd over the edge. Instead of trying to follow everyone off the stage, he retreated, pushing his way out to the rear of the amphitheater.

Aysgarth wasn't too large of a city, and Isira still embraced teho. If Zachary moved quickly, he could find her before it was too late.

CHAPTER 23

Hakon woke in a dark, windowless room. He groaned, then froze. The movement hadn't hurt.

Which meant Solveig had healed him.

Which also meant he was in Aysgarth.

He swore. Though he couldn't see her, he knew she was there. "I was going to save her."

"You were going to commit suicide," Meshell replied.

Hakon swore at her.

"How are you feeling?" she asked.

"Fine," he admitted. "You and Ari carry me all the way back?"

She snorted. "No. Ari has a new transport point right outside the wards. He transported us there, and we got a litter for you. And before you ask, yes, he built a transport point next to the structure. You'll be able to return any time."

"How about now?"

"I might recommend waiting a bit." Meshell caught him up on events in Aysgarth. "The council is gathering to meet with Isira now."

"Why aren't you there?"

"We decided it was best if only Solveig went. And Ari and Irric are next door in case you try anything foolish."

He groaned again. "I hate that you did that."

"Your apology is accepted."

He let out a string of curses, several of them directed Meshell's way. He'd been so close! Thoughts of Cliona, up in that mountain, led to him grasping teho and filling his limbs.

Next door, he felt Irric and Ari do the same. Meshell hadn't been lying, it seemed. She was the only one who didn't prepare for a fight.

The rage blew out nearly as quickly as it had flared. She'd saved his life.

He would still find Cliona. This was only a temporary delay. It took him several minutes, but he regained control of his reason. "Thank you," he said, gruffly.

"You're welcome. I'm glad you're feeling better."

She moved and lit a lantern, and soon the room was filled with friends and food. Hakon feasted as he caught up with the others.

Their reunion was rudely interrupted by a messenger. "Hel demands your presence, now."

Hakon gave the messenger a withering glare. No one demanded their presence.

But Ari and Irric jumped to their feet, robbing Hakon's glare of its strength. He stood and followed, pulled along by the currents of recent events.

The messenger led them through the labyrinthine passageways and stopped in front of a door. He beckoned for them to enter. The band stepped through. Hakon saw he'd led them to a room perhaps twice as large as the bedrooms they'd been given as guests. An enormous table, carved from the local granite, dominated the middle of the space.

They were a strange group of people, gathered here. There was Hel, of whom he knew little. But she matched the description Irric had given of the ruler of Aysgarth. Irric said that Zachary spent a lot of time with her, and Hakon could see why. Then Isira, who until recently had been the only stamfar in the six states. There was Hakon and the band, followed by Valdis on the other side of the table. Less than a year ago, they'd all tried to kill one another. He still shuddered at the memory of what Valdis and Gunvald had done to him.

From the look on her face today, she was possibly thinking about repeating the feat.

Hel was closing the door when another pair of footsteps could be heard sprinting down the hallway. Hel poked her head out, and a smile lit her face.

Zachary appeared, face flushed. He put his hands on his knees, took a few heaving breaths, then waved weakly with one hand. "Didn't want you all to start without me."

Hel's grin grew, betraying her feelings. It disappeared when she saw Hakon's gaze on her.

All eyes turned to Isira. Hel asked the first question. "What was that all about?"

The young woman was bold, to speak to Isira that way. "I did what I could to help."

"Help?" Valdis interjected. "You think telling us to follow *her*," she pointed at Solveig, "will help?"

Hakon found himself completely lost. Fortunately, when he looked at the rest of the band, they looked equally confused.

"I'm lost, too," Solveig said. "While I appreciate your support, I hardly think I'm in a position to lead Aysgarth."

Lead Aysgarth? What was she talking about?

"You're the only choice that makes any sense," Isira said. "And that should be obvious to anyone."

Before Hakon could explode with questions, Solveig interrupted. "Perhaps it would be best if we started with the events of a few days ago. What exactly happened between you and Ava?"

Isira leaned back in her chair, and for the first time, Hakon thought she actually looked like the little child she appeared to be. "Ava wants to destroy humanity. She claimed as much when we fought. She wanted to know if I would join her."

"Do you know why?" Solveig asked.

Isira stared down at the table. "I do not. I know no more about her than you do, and maybe even less."

Solveig continued the inquiry. "You fought because you refused to join her?"

"I told her that I wouldn't help her, that I've removed myself from the affairs of humans. I believe she took it as a challenge."

"Can you beat her?" Ari asked.

"I don't know," Isira admitted. "As near as I could tell, our strengths were perfectly balanced. It would come down to a matter of technique, and I'll confess that I am out of practice. If not for your help in the duel, I'm not sure what the outcome would have been." She gave the assassin a small nod, which was as much acknowledgment as Hakon had ever seen her give.

"Why did you tell my people to follow Solveig?" Hel asked.

"Because she's the strongest tehoin I would trust with anything more than a pointed stick."

Hel frowned. "But what about you?"

"I just told you. I don't involve myself in humanity's affairs."

Zachary figured it out faster than Hel. "Wait," he said. "You're saying that you're not going to help us, even though Ava said she wants to kill all of humanity?"

Isira looked at him as though he was the slowest student in the room.

Zachary either forgot that he was dealing with a stamfar or was too foolish to care. "How could you? You have the power to—"

Irric put a hand on his shoulder, interrupting him. "Best to let this one go, lad."

Zachary looked between Irric and Isira. He shook his head. "No. There are hundreds of thousands of lives at stake. I'm not going to let this go. She has the power to help!"

Ari wasn't so friendly. "Let it go," he ordered.

Zachary looked around the room, and Hakon wondered just what was going through the young man's head. He looked like he couldn't decide on who to interrogate next. He settled on all of the band. "How could you? I know you care about humanity. You've risked your lives fighting for it time and time again. Why aren't you upset?"

Hakon spoke. Hopefully if it came from him, Zachary would understand. "We don't have the right to make demands of Isira."

Zachary shook off Irric's hand. He slammed his palms down on the table. "No! I've put up with your damned mysteries for too long. We all have. How can you expect us to move forward while you allow yourselves to be bound by whatever happened in the past?"

Hakon felt the fire in his chest burn a bit more brightly. "You don't need to know. What happened in the past is buried. We need to focus on our problems now."

Zachary thrust an accusing finger at Hakon. "You!"

Though Hakon hadn't spent that much time with Zachary, he'd never seen this level of anger from him. Despite being arguably the weakest warrior at the table, by no small amount, he looked like he was ready to hurl himself at Hakon.

Zachary forced his words out through gritted teeth. "How dare you. You lost your only daughter because you wouldn't tell her the truth of your past. And you *dare* to tell me the past doesn't matter?" He tilted his head toward Isira. "As near as I can tell, she's the only one in the world who's useful against Ava, and you're just going to let her walk away? NO!"

He returned his palms to the table, and it looked like he was trying to squeeze water from the stone. He mastered himself and looked around the room. "It's time for you to tell us what happened to make the world like this. Make us understand why you all seem content to doom us."

It was only when Zachary finished that Hakon realized he had balled his fists so tight his knuckles had turned white. His nails dug into his palms so hard they almost drew blood.

He looked to Meshell, trusting in her guidance when his own reason had fled.

She nodded.

His hands relaxed. He shook them out, and took the opportunity to glare at Zachary. Perhaps the boy was right, but Hakon wouldn't forget this. It was a story he had hoped he would be able to take to the grave.

Or, at the very least, he wanted to tell it with Cliona

present. He didn't know if she could forgive him, but perhaps she would understand him a little better.

But now was the time.

The others settled deeper into their chairs, including Isira. She'd never heard the story from his perspective.

Hakon cleared his throat, coughed, and began his tale.

THE BAND 1

Hakon rapped on the door, two quick strikes, just the way his training officers had demanded.

"Enter." The voice from the other side sounded as though he'd just woken someone up from a long mid-day nap.

He took a deep breath, checked his uniform one more time, then opened the door. He stood straight as a sword and snapped his sharpest salute, a fist over his heart, a sign of his loyalty to the empire.

Silence greeted his entrance. Hakon waited for a few moments, suspecting a test. When there was still no response, he looked around.

The room he stood in was a disaster. Papers were scattered everywhere, and empty bottles of what he suspected had been liquor were the most common decoration. He was, without a doubt, the cleanest thing in the room. And he had, indeed, woken someone up from a nap.

The woman sat in a chair, back against the wall. She rubbed her eyes and yawned. When she saw Hakon, standing straight in his crisp uniform, one of her eyebrows went up.

Hakon assumed she was one of the staff for the fort. She wore no uniform, and given the state of the room, she was probably here to clean it. "I'm looking for commander Brynja."

"You my new recruit?"

Hakon startled when he realized who he was speaking to. His new commander noticed. "Not what you expected?"

"No, ma'am." When he'd gotten his orders, he'd been led to believe this unit was something special. And he believed he'd deserved no less for his performance.

"Well, you're honest, at least." Commander Brynja stood up, and Hakon couldn't help but notice how graceful her movements were. She eyed him. "Fresh from training?"

"Yes, ma'am."

"Brynja. There are no titles here."

"Yes, ma— Brynja."

"You'll get used to it." She gestured for him to follow her out the door. "They told me you were top-ranked in your class."

"I was."

"Did it matter to you, being the best?"

"Absolutely."

"When did you learn you could manipulate teho?"

"When I was six."

"And how old are you now?"

"Nineteen."

The answer stopped both the rapid questioning and their progress through the fort. She turned and looked at him. "You're as old as you look?"

"Yes, ma'am."

She glared at him, but only for a moment. "You're going

to be younger than everyone here. A lot younger than most. Will that be a problem?"

He shook his head, but she didn't look convinced. Then she shrugged and resumed their journey. They stepped together into a courtyard where a small group of soldiers were training. All activity stopped when they saw Hakon.

"New recruit," Brynja announced. "Figured we'd see what he could do."

The group formed into a loose circle, and Hakon got his first good look at them. None of them looked like the soldiers he had spent the past three months with. None wore uniforms, and there wasn't a single scar among them. They couldn't have been more different than his training officers.

Of course, his training officers had been ahula. Men and women who had no choice but to carry the scars of battles they'd fought.

Here, everyone was tehoin. So there would be no scars. At least, not visible ones.

A man stepped forward, as tall as Hakon but easily twice as strong. A staff of teho appeared in his hands. "I'll challenge him."

Hakon looked down at his uniform. He thought he'd been prepared for his first day with his new unit. Beside him, Brynja chuckled. "You won't be needing that again, so don't worry about getting it dirty."

"May I have a weapon?" he asked.

"Teho only. Unit rules." She shoved him into the circle.

Hakon's opponent spun the teho staff easily in his hands, his experience obvious. He waited for Hakon to form his own weapon. When Hakon didn't, he glanced to Brynja. She nodded.

The warrior attacked, giving Hakon no quarter. Hakon

retreated two steps, but it barely gained him a moment. The warrior cut off Hakon's retreat with a vicious strike aimed at Hakon's midsection. Hakon strengthened his arm with teho and blocked the blow.

It should have broken his arm, but instead, the teho staff bounced harmlessly off.

Hakon heard the collective intake of breath around the circle, but couldn't afford to spare the group his attention. He had one heartbeat to make his mark. The warrior was surprised, not sure what had happened. Hakon guessed he would recover quickly.

Before that could happen, Hakon stepped in, delivering several quick body blows. He took the warrior down and pulled a punch an inch from a very surprised face.

The man would suffer no more than a few bruises. Hakon opened his fist and turned it into an extended hand. His opponent stared at it for a few seconds before he realized Hakon's intent. He took the hand and Hakon helped him to his feet. "Never seen that before," he said.

The muttering around the circle made it clear no one had, although that was hardly a surprise. Hakon was the only one he knew of capable of using teho as he did. He was also the only tehoin he knew who couldn't use teho for any of its more common purposes.

"You choose not to use weapons?" Brynja asked.

Hakon shook his head. "I can't, ma—. I can only manipulate teho in my body."

She studied him for a moment. "Someone get this man a sword."

A few moments later he had one in hand. Brynja looked at another soldier. "Irric. You're up."

Again, Hakon found himself in the center of the circle.

He looked from Irric to Brynja. "If I strengthen the sword, I might hurt him."

The warriors around the circle laughed, although Hakon wasn't sure what they found funny. No other unit in the army was this lax. He was certain of it.

He wondered, for a moment, if he'd gotten the wrong orders. This didn't seem like the place for him.

"It's a risk I'm willing to take," Brynja said.

Hakon glanced at Irric, who looked perfectly unworried. "Are you sure?"

"I'll be careful." A hint of a smile tugged at the corner of Irric's lip, but he hid it quickly.

Hakon got the sense he was in for more than he expected. Still, he strengthened the sword with his own teho and attacked Irric. If he beat Irric, he'd start his tour with this unit as a respected warrior.

He understood the laughter soon enough.

He considered himself a decent sword. Perhaps in the top quarter of his class overall. He was used to winning far more fights than he lost.

Irric never let him come close to drawing blood. The man's sword almost cut faster than Hakon could track, and before long he was staring at the sky, his head ringing from Irric hitting him with the side of his blade.

This time it was Irric who extended his hand. "You lasted longer than anyone else on their first try."

Hakon took it. "It couldn't have been longer than five seconds."

Irric smiled. "It wasn't."

He clapped Hakon on the back as the rest of the circle closed in to greet him. "Welcome to Brynja's army."

THE BAND 2

Hakon woke well before the sun rose. He'd acquired the habit from working the fields with his father, when every moment of daylight was precious. It had served him well in training, and three weeks with Brynja's Army had yet to destroy his personal routine.

Though they certainly tried. His head pounded from the festivities the night before, and the thought of crawling back under his covers held a powerful appeal.

But if he succumbed to temptation once, he would again.

He rolled from his bunk, his steps silent. On his first morning with the unit, he'd not been careful in the unfamiliar surroundings. He'd made a racket that woke several of the others, and he imagined he could still feel the bruises they'd left him as a gentle reminder to be quieter.

He was still tempted to put on his uniform, but that routine had been driven out of him. Brynja's orders. No uniforms among her unit.

Hakon suspected an unspoken reason, but couldn't guess at it.

Brynja's army, as they called themselves, lacked any discernible routine or structure, but he'd also observed that everyone was constantly training. Whereas his companions in the training unit sought any excuse to avoid extra effort, here, he was always being asked to join in one more sparring match, or go for one more run.

Brynja herself was a mess, drunk as often as she was sober. The other kolma often made fun of her, but their barbs were gentle. In his weeks here, he had yet to hear a genuinely angry comment directed toward her. Not even at her back. When she gave an order, they jumped to it, and Hakon suspected several of them would willingly leap into the jaws of a dragon at her word.

He'd respected his commanders from training. Scarred veterans of both the frontier and the various rebellions that sprung up around the periphery of the empire, they radiated authority and confidence. Brynja inspired none of the same, though.

More than once, he considered submitting a request for a transfer. But there weren't many places for a kolma in the military. Normal units didn't work well with tehoin, and commanders throughout the army hated dealing with transfers. What if the next unit he found himself in was even worse?

Lacking better options, he vowed to make the most of his time here. The unit was filled with skilled tehoin. He was the youngest by far, both in age and experience. He learned something new every day. Thanks to the patient instruction of others, he believed he was close to being able to create weak wards. They weren't much, and they took all his focus, but before he'd joined this unit he thought any such manipulation of teho was beyond his ability.

He closed the door to the dormitory behind him, then

walked across the fort to the training ground. As always, at this time in the morning, it was empty, which suited him just fine.

Hakon pulled a wooden sword from a rack and started, as he always did, with the forms taught to him by the sword masters at training camp. He moved slowly, letting the familiar motions banish the last lingering effects of sleep from his arms and legs. The pounding in his head slowly faded away.

Once his heart was pumping, he worked on some of the forms that Irric was teaching him. The man was the best sword Hakon had ever seen, better even than the instructors he'd had in training. Irric didn't hold Hakon's previous instructors in high regard. On their first day of training together, he'd compared Hakon's technique to that of "a duckling waddling backward through mud."

Hakon didn't think his skills were quite so poor, but he appreciated having a wide variety of styles and techniques in his repertoire. Irric's instruction did make him a far stronger sword than he had been, and that was only with a few weeks of practice.

Hakon finished when his forms became sloppy. Poor practice was a waste of time. He put the sword back on the rack and began morning calisthenics. He carried large rocks around the perimeter of the training grounds. Pushups, pull-ups, and squats with the rocks were repeated until he couldn't move anymore.

Hakon had come to the unit light and fast, able to run for days. He hadn't considered himself weak until he compared himself to the others here. Brynja's warriors demanded more from their bodies. Even Brynja, so drunk she couldn't walk straight, had beaten him one night at arm wrestling. The defeat had led to yet another vow, which was to become strong enough he'd never suffer such a humiliation again.

Motion near the gate of the fort drew his attention. A woman entered, her long blonde hair braided almost all the way to the small of her back. She wore the same uniform Hakon now left folded neatly and stored in the chest at the foot of his bunk. She looked lost.

He approached. "Can I help you?" It had been rude of the guards to let her in without an escort, but they were near the end of their watch, and the relationship between the ahula guards and Brynja was chilly at best.

"I was ordered to report to a unit here before morning mess," the woman said.

"Reporting to Brynja?" The poor woman looked like she would be eaten alive by the unit. Hakon almost hoped she'd gotten turned around and was at the wrong fort. It would be embarrassing, but perhaps best.

She nodded.

"Fresh from training?"

She nodded again, and he suddenly felt like a seasoned veteran. "Commander Brynja runs this unit a bit differently than most. Mess isn't for another hour or so. But I can show you where to stow your gear and then take you to the mess hall."

"Thank you. I'd appreciate that."

Hakon offered a short bow. "My name is Hakon."

She returned the bow. "Solveig."

He led the way, feeling sorry for the new recruit.

The feeling only lasted for another two hours, when she stepped into the ring against Irric. She danced with a thin teho sword in yet another style he'd never seen.

She lasted a full minute before Irric won the duel.

The unit agreed, good-humoredly, that Hakon still had

the honor of being the newest member of Brynja's army.

LESS THAN A WEEK LATER, Hakon was once again practicing alone in the training yard before the sun rose. He hadn't really done much else since he got here. As near as he could tell, all Brynja's army did was lounge around the fort, train, and occasionally drink themselves into oblivion. He supposed that was all well and good, but how were they helping the empire?

His question was answered by the sudden appearance of a stranger in the training grounds. Hakon felt the burst of teho and almost tripped over his weapon in surprise.

The woman saw Hakon and froze. "You new here?" she asked.

"Joined about a month ago."

She grunted. "Then you can wake Brynja."

Hakon didn't want to die, so he shook his head. "She was up late last night with the section commanders. From what I heard, the dice didn't treat her well."

"Don't care." The woman held up a small leather tube bearing the emperor's insignia.

Hakon's eyes widened. She was one of the emperor's messengers. He gave a deep, apologetic bow that she waved away. "Just go wake her. It's urgent."

Hakon still didn't want to die, but at least now he had the small comfort of knowing it would be in service of his emperor. He ran to the officers' quarters, then froze before knocking on Brynja's door. One deep breath steadied his nerves, and he knocked.

There was no answer, so he knocked again.

"Come in." The voice was sleepy, but fortunately, not angry.

Hakon entered and averted his eyes. Brynja was sprawled out naked on her bed, and she wasn't alone. One very talented swordsman had his own naked limbs entwined with hers.

"What do you want?" she growled.

"Messenger from the emperor, ma'am." Nervousness had brought his old habits back.

She swore and stood. He risked a glance.

She noticed. "Is there anything else?"

"No, ma'am."

"Then why are you still in my quarters?"

"Of course. Sorry, ma'am." He started to bow, cut it off halfway, then scrambled out of the room, clutching what small shreds of dignity he still possessed. His cheeks were burning as he closed the door behind him.

By the time Brynja assembled them, Hakon had cleaned up and broken his fast. All twenty of them were together, standing in a loose circle in the training grounds. Hakon kept looking at Irric, who returned his glances with wide smiles.

The emperor's messenger had departed almost an hour ago, and Brynja was carrying herself in a manner Hakon hadn't yet seen from her. Her slouch was gone, and her gaze was piercing. She glanced around the small circle and began. "As most of you felt, we got new orders from a messenger this morning. There's a small rebel group harassing some of the new settlements in the northwest corners of the frontier. All the usual annoying tactics. They're ambushing supply caravans, attacking farmers as they work in their fields, and spreading propaganda against the emperor."

Hakon clenched his fist. For some reason, the frontier seemed to be a breeding ground for these kinds of people.

He didn't understand how someone could experience the gifts of the empire and then turn their back on it. They deserved the death that was coming to them.

Brynja continued. "They've got at least one kolma with them, which no one knew about until they wiped out almost the whole frontier unit sent to catch them. One survivor reported back. The emperor wants us to end this now. A new caravan of settlers is on their way to the area and due to arrive in a week or two. It's our task to clear out the rebels before they can do any more damage."

"What do we know about them?" one of the section commanders asked.

"Not much, unfortunately. We don't think they're a large group. Estimates range from about twenty warriors to as many as forty. One kolma for sure, although there may be more. They don't have any permanent residence that scouts have been able to find. It's suspected they're living in a camp they move every few days."

Brynja looked around the circle. "Our mission is easy enough. We find them and we kill them. Their numbers are well within our capabilities, but I want us to complete this one wisely. We've got a few new recruits, and I don't see any reason to lose any of our fresh meat to a pathetic group of rebels. Keep your shields ready and set some strong wards at night."

"Any threats from the wilds?" another commander asked.

"None of note," Brynja said. "But we all know that means absolutely nothing. Any other questions?"

No one spoke.

"Good. Gather your gear. I don't think this will take us any more than a day or two. Meet back here in an hour. It's time for us to go rebel hunting."

THE BAND 3

Hakon learned more about the operation of Brynja's army in the next hours than he had in the weeks before. He'd already learned each of the sections within their unit had a kolma capable of transport. But it wasn't until they made ready for departure that he understood how important that was.

His military mind was still stuck in the trainings of his first camps. Camps run by and for ahula. His thoughts about distance, terrain, and supplies were all foolish when considered through the eyes of tehoin who could transport.

He realized that Brynja's army would reform his mind just as much as it did his body.

There was a reason they could afford to spend so much of their time training and drinking in the fort—because they could be almost anywhere in the empire within a few hours.

Though the morning had been like any other, Hakon found himself spending the afternoon walking through the prairies of the far northwestern frontier. They were divided into their four sections, with five kolma each. Brynja served as the fifth member of one of the sections.

Hakon turned to Irric, finally giving in to his curiosity. The swordsman appeared to be waiting for the question. "Really?" Hakon asked. He didn't want to say more, in case anyone overheard their conversation.

"Surprised?" Irric replied.

"It's against regulations!"

Irric laughed. "True, but I think you can acknowledge that the rules don't apply to us in the same ways."

"If someone finds out, you could get in a lot of trouble!"

Irric shook his head. "Sometimes I forget how young you are," he said. "Trust me, we're not going to get in trouble, even if one of the generals finds out. And besides, what's the point of life if you're not having at least a little fun, eh?"

"Serving the empire!"

"I think it's possible to do both," Irric said, his spirit untroubled by Hakon's morality.

"How long?"

"A couple of years. It's nothing serious. We've both had other partners over the years."

Hakon blinked, trying to follow.

"You spent most of your childhood growing up around ahula, didn't you?"

"Everyone in my family was, yes. And then in the military."

"You'll understand better once you've got a few more decades under your belt. Trust me. Some of the things that seem so important when you're younger, they just don't have the same weight when you get older."

Hakon wasn't sure he agreed, but didn't see any point in

arguing. He didn't have enough experience to prove Irric wrong.

Their scout, a man named Somerled, reappeared in their midst. "We found them," he said.

Hakon's eyes went wide. They'd only been in the frontier for a few hours. "You can cover a lot of ground very fast if you have a group of transporting scouts," Irric said, noting his reaction.

Hakon wondered if he would ever get used to this other way of living, so different than anything he'd known before. He'd have to forget so much of what he understood to be true and replace it with new knowledge. Maybe even new ethics. He hadn't halted his own aging yet, and hadn't given enough thought to the myriad ways doing so might change him. No wonder so many tehoin broke off from their families earlier than he had.

Radulfr, their section commander, focused Hakon's attention as he took charge. "Everyone together."

Hakon was joined in his section by Radulfr, Somerled, Ragnbjorg, and Irric. They gathered, and Somerled transported them to where the rest of the unit was waiting. They found the other scouts reporting to Brynja, who listened intently.

When they finished, Brynja used teho to clear a patch of prairie grasses and expose the dirt underneath. A long thin rod of teho appeared in her hand and she sketched out the layout of the camp in the dirt, frequently checking with the scouts to ensure her diagram was correct. When it was done, she gathered the whole unit around it.

Hakon studied the diagram and frowned. He was almost offended. It was nothing more than a couple dozen tents clustered together. Who would choose that sort of life over the bounty of the empire?

Brynja considered the layout for a moment before speaking. Then she sketched four crosses in a rough semicircle around the camp. "I don't see any reason to make it complicated. We'll transport to these approximate locations and attack them as hard as we can from all sides. No need to get close. My signal will be what starts us off, and I'll send some teho high into the sky when we're done. Any questions?"

Hakon grimaced. He hated to have to ask, but it would be irresponsible not to. "What about me?"

"Either you'll have to learn how to throw teho in the next two minutes, or you can sit back and watch," Brynja said. "Sorry, but there's probably not going to be too much use for your sword today."

Hakon had expected no less, and Brynja was kind enough about it, but the words still stung. He felt useless. He was a good soldier, though, so he nodded and kept his regrets to himself.

"Anything else?" Brynja asked.

When there was nothing, she gave their final orders. "They'll know we're coming, so no point in delaying. My section will lead the way."

The sections transported, encircling the camp as the rebels scrambled to respond to the threat. Hakon watched the rebels as they hid behind hastily erected fortifications.

Did they not know what was coming? Their overturned carts would do them no good against the assault that was only moments away. As the others gathered their teho, he had to guess the rebels were clueless. They were still sorting themselves as though preparing for a charge.

Brynja threw the first teho spear in the air. A heartbeat later, dozens of teho darts and spears followed the first.

Hakon swallowed a lump in his throat. He'd never seen a teho assault before, and the attack blazed against his senses.

In the middle of the rebel camp, a kolma tried to form a shield around the others.

In trying to save everyone, he doomed them all.

Spread too thin, the shield shattered after only a few impacts. The rest of the darts and spears fell toward the camp, undeterred.

The rebels never had a chance. Teho shattered their poor excuses for fortifications. Carts splintered and broke apart. Teho passed through wood, canvas, and flesh indiscriminately.

After the first volley, the rebels were broken. A few still moved, lucky enough to avoid the teho that dropped from the sky.

Brynja launched another spear, and the rest followed, flinging teho with abandon. She let them launch into the camp for several minutes before calling a halt.

By the time it was over, Hakon couldn't see a single rebel soul moving. The camp was eerily still, and it was hard to believe that just a few minutes before, it had been the home of dozens of rebels.

Dust hung in the air. Tatters of canvas that had once been tents rustled softly in the gentle prairie breeze.

Brynja ordered them forward, and the section moved toward the ruins. It only took them a few minutes to reach the fortifications. Though no one had given Hakon a direct order, he understood they were looking for any survivors.

He didn't see how there could be any. The falling teho had destroyed everything. The ground was soft underfoot, almost like sand in places.

The rebels looked like they had been in pitiful shape,

even before the assault. Many were too thin. Some weren't even wearing boots.

He didn't understand. There hadn't been a shortage of food for years. The emperor often sent extra food with the expeditions out west, to keep them fed until they could grow enough to support themselves.

Why would they choose such suffering? Most rebels complained of the strict rule of the empire, but didn't they understand that such rules were needed to survive this hostile world?

Hakon prodded a corpse with his boot and shook his head. The dead had no answers for him.

He walked around a tent that had remained remarkably intact. Teho had punched holes in the canvas, but had somehow missed all its supports. Behind the tent, he found Solveig, kneeling with a rebel on her lap.

A rebel that still, somehow, drew breath.

When Solveig looked up, there were tears in her eyes.

Hakon glanced around, but they were the only two in the area. "What are you doing?"

"He's too young!" she said.

He looked down at the rebel, seeing him for the first time. He was young. Though his unkempt hair and emaciated frame made it hard to tell, Hakon would have guessed the rebel was a few years younger than he was.

The young man wouldn't live through the day, though. He'd taken teho through the stomach, and it was surprising he was still able to breathe. But not for much longer.

"I can heal him," Solveig said.

The rebel coughed up blood. He looked up at Solveig hopefully. "My father made me join. Please. I don't want to die."

Hakon felt Solveig begin to gather teho. "You're a healer, too?"

She nodded and put her hands on the young man's chest.

A lump formed in Hakon's throat. He looked around again. They were still alone, but the camp wasn't that large. If Solveig used her teho, it would definitely attract attention.

The emperor had ordered them to kill all the rebels. It had been a simple, clear order, with no room for interpretation.

"I'll give you a quick death," Hakon told the boy.

Solveig looked up. "What?"

Before she could stop him, he drew his sword from the scabbard at his hip and stabbed, careful to avoid Solveig.

His blade went through the young man's heart, and he died a moment later.

Solveig stared at him, frozen in place.

"Get up," he said. "If anyone finds out you were trying to heal a rebel, you might lose everything."

Which was an understatement. Their orders had come straight from the emperor. Hakon couldn't guess what Brynja's attitude toward discipline was, but she wouldn't be out of line to kill Solveig for her misguided efforts. Hakon refused to disobey the emperor, but he understood Solveig's impulse.

He managed to get Solveig to her feet just as Radulfr came around the corner. "Anything wrong?" he asked.

Hakon shook his head. "No, sir. We just found a rebel who was still alive, is all." He held up his bloody sword as proof of what they'd done.

"Good work." Radulfr smiled. "Glad you could help out."

He turned and left them alone.

Hakon tried to escort Solveig back to the others, but she slapped his hand away and stomped off.

He didn't follow. She wanted nothing to do with him, even if he had saved her life.

He cleaned his sword and sheathed it, then looked at his hands.

He'd just killed a man, barely out of boyhood, who'd been no threat to anyone.

It wasn't how he'd envisioned his life in service of the emperor starting.

THE BAND 4

The next few years passed quickly. What Hakon remembered were bright moments, both of joy and of pain.

FOUR DAYS after their first battle, Hakon brought Solveig a package of tea, a variety he knew she enjoyed.

She'd used every trick to avoid speaking with him since the battle. She joined their meals late, so there'd be no chance of letting him sit next to her. Whenever he was free, she seemed to be in the middle of something important.

Training sessions were particularly painful. She couldn't avoid him, but she could make her feelings well known. Despite Irric's instruction, she was still a better sword than him, and he had bruises across his arms and torso from their "practice" duels. Even his enhanced healing couldn't keep up with the damage.

He purchased the tea from the town outside the fort and waited for a moment to speak to her.

Eventually, he found her alone, reading in a quiet corner

of the fort. She saw him coming, but had no escape. He raised his hands in supplication. "I'm sorry," he said.

Her glare forced him to a halt. "For what?"

A simple question, but one he found he had no answer to. He wasn't sorry he'd killed the young man. It was the emperor's will, which wasn't a matter of debate.

He still felt like he'd done something wrong. Guilt gnawed at him, but he couldn't say why. "I'm—just sorry."

He held up the tea as an offering.

She moved so quickly he had no time to react. Her thin blade of teho sliced the bag of tea in two. She left a cut across his arm, too.

And she was certainly good enough that she hadn't had to.

"Never speak to me again," she said as she stormed away.

AFTER SIX MONTHS, Hakon received his first extended leave. He traveled home, a small village about four day's riding from Mioska. His mother, Helga, greeted him with a smile and a warm embrace. Then she stepped back and took a look at him. "You finally put some meat on those bones," she said.

It was something of an understatement. As a youth he'd been lean and tall. But in Brynja's army, under the twin influences of plentiful food and constant training, his shoulders had broadened enough that when he stood before his mother in the early afternoon sun, she was completely shaded.

"Mind helping out your father in the field while I finish up the cooking?" Mother asked.

She told him which field his father was in, then took his

small bag of belongings inside while he went searching for his father, Knut.

Hakon found him right where Mother said he'd be. He was pulling stone from the field in preparation for the next planting. Father's back was to him, and Hakon paused to watch for a moment.

He was struck by the disorienting feeling of being in the wrong place, of being in the wrong time. The last year of his life, of training and his time with Brynja's army, became like a dream he was waking from. It had been about this time last year when Hakon had left, and it was like no time at all had passed. His father's life had frozen while he'd been gone.

Father finished carrying a stone to the cart at the edge of the field. As he dropped it into the cart, he caught sight of Hakon. He waved, and Hakon returned the gesture. The feeling of being unmoored in time vanished, and he stepped forward to help his father with his work.

They spoke little, but the silence between them was familiar. Knut had never been a man of many words, and it didn't seem as though he'd become loquacious in the time since they'd said their farewells. Working together, they finished the field before sundown and returned home.

Warm smells from the hearth greeted them on their arrival, but when Hakon stepped through the door, that feeling of time freezing in place caught him again. Everything in the house was exactly as he remembered it, and he found it eerie. The rooms were the most familiar places in the world to him, and yet he didn't belong here.

He was home, but it wasn't home anymore.

They sat down for the meal, and Hakon stared at the food for a moment before eating. He couldn't remember serious hunger from his childhood, but the thin stew before him wouldn't last him long anymore. Still, he smiled, and honestly complimented his mother on the flavor.

"Aasveig is engaged to be married this spring," Mother said. "Do you think you might be able to return for her wedding?"

Hakon hadn't thought about Aasveig for at least six months. She was a good girl—woman, now, he corrected himself—who his parents had thought would be a good match for him. Like him, she was honest, and a hard worker well respected in the village. If Hakon had planned on staying, he very well might have married her. Of the limited choices for marriage in the area, she was certainly the one he had liked most.

But he felt nothing at the news. "Who is she engaged to?"

"Oyvind," Mother said, then leaned in conspiratorially. "But I hear she's not entirely pleased. She had hoped you would propose, you know."

Hakon wasn't so sure. He and Aasveig had always gotten along without problem, but there'd never been anything more. And despite his mother's hopes, he had no plans to return home and steal her away. This place had never felt smaller, and it wasn't just because he'd grown bigger.

Father snorted. "He's not going to come to the wedding, Helga. He'll be too busy fighting and dying for the empire."

The warmth of the room vanished, replaced by a chill no fire would banish.

Father was a loyal imperialist. Hakon had no concerns on that front.

But they'd never agreed on Hakon's decision to leave home. Knut believed in hearth and home, in a hard day's work in the fields followed by a quiet night at home with loved ones. He didn't even travel to Mioska unless circumstances demanded it. He simply wasn't capable of understanding what inspired Hakon to leave.

Mother tried to placate Father. "Knut—"

Father was having none of it. "I didn't raise my son to be a killer."

He hadn't. Father had never even raised his hand against Hakon growing up, and there weren't many boys nearby who could say the same of their parents.

Hakon's stomach twisted. He'd hoped that in time Father would make peace with his choice to leave. That hope died as he watched Father struggle with his emotions.

He wondered if it was perhaps best to just leave again. It would shatter his parents' hearts, but maybe a clean break was best. The easiest wounds to heal were from the sharpest cuts.

Then his father took a deep breath. "I'm sorry, son." He looked like he might say more, but the apology ended there. He changed the subject. "Why don't you tell us what you've been up to this past year?"

Hakon saw how much the apology cost his father. They would never agree, but they could at least live in peace. He swore he'd do nothing to upset that peace, for all their sakes.

He thought back to his first action, to the waves of teho crashing down on the unprepared rebels. He thought of killing the boy, younger than him. The memory still woke him at night sometimes, a confirmation of all his father's fears.

But he'd also seen the wilds, and understood why the empire had to act as it did. He wore his sword so that Knut could live his life of peace.

He regaled them with humorous tales from training, and told them stories of the corners of the empire few people got to visit. He spoke nothing of violence, and they didn't ask.

Three days later, he left, and his heavy heart told him he would only rarely return.

Brynja was often involved in his most powerful memories.

She wasn't the sort of leader he'd expected when he joined the military, but after months of serving under her, he couldn't imagine respecting any other officer as much.

She allowed no slack in their training. Her expectation was that their bodies and minds were always ready for the next messenger from the emperor. But she had no patience for the rituals that defined much of the ahula military. Hakon grew accustomed to wearing his hair however he chose, and when his muscles grew to a size that his old uniform didn't fit him anymore, he didn't even bother requisitioning a new one. She drank with them at night, and Irric often disappeared with her once the sun was down.

When they were out in the field, Brynja was much closer to the type of leader he'd originally envisioned being the best when he was a younger man. She was always the first into battle and the last to leave. He knew, without a whisper of a doubt, that she would never ask something of him she wasn't willing to do herself.

Soon he grew to love her the way the others did.

Months passed. Their missions continued. Despite Brynja's efforts, they lost friends. Their sections changed and new tehoin were recruited. In time, Hakon became a veteran new arrivals looked up to.

Solveig joined the same section as Hakon. She remained cold towards him, but he resolved to treat her no differently than any other member of Brynja's army.

They found themselves, one day, in fields surprisingly close to Hakon's home, skirting the edges of the great forest that sat near the heart of the empire. It was only their section today, as Brynja had decided no more were needed.

As usual, they were chasing tehoin. A mother and son, it seemed. Hakon didn't know the details of their story, but they'd raided two imperial stores. From the accounts Brynja possessed, neither was particularly strong, but they were still tehoin, capable of wiping out an ahula unit.

Solveig and Hakon were teamed up, a blatant effort on Radulfr's part to get them to mend their differences. Neither was pleased about the situation, but they uttered no complaint.

They skirted the edge of a grove of trees, senses alert. The early morning sun warmed the cold air, fighting a valiant but losing battle against the forces of winter marshaling to the north. Hakon smelled the fire before he saw it, the familiar scent of roasting meat causing his mouth to water. He signaled Solveig, and the two crept together closer to the smell.

They found a small camp buried between tall oaks. A woman with long dark hair and an awkward gait was working around the camp, periodically holding her hands up to the dancing flame to warm them. Huddled around the fire, she barely seemed a threat. Hakon stepped forward, hand on his sword, but Solveig grabbed his shoulder to stop him. He frowned, and she whispered, "the son."

A good decision. Hakon assumed the son was in the tent, but had no evidence. Better to wait until both were in sight.

They didn't have to wait long. A boy emerged from the tent. Together, the family made for a pitiful sight. Their thick furs made them appear more well fed than they were.

When the boy extended his hand toward the fire, Hakon saw how skinny his wrists were.

Why?

Like on his first mission, he had to wonder what had led these tehoin to steal from the empire. Especially with their gifts there was no lack of work.

Why starve, or steal, or suffer at all?

Maybe soon he would be able to get answers from them.

Solveig put her hand on his shoulder again. She leaned close, her breath hot against his ear. "He's too young."

Hakon looked more closely. He hadn't noticed at first, but Solveig was right. The son wasn't even close to manhood yet.

And already a criminal.

"You don't need to kill them," Solveig hissed.

He knew that, and hated that such was her first thought of him. Their orders were to capture or kill. No doubt, Brynja didn't expect them to return with prisoners, but it wouldn't matter much if they did. "I won't kill them unless I have to."

Solveig shook her head. "Look at them. Unless one of them is secretly a stamfar, I don't think you need to worry much. You could crush them without teho."

He growled.

The information they'd received didn't give them all the details they wanted. The mother was almost certainly tehoin, but they didn't know about the boy.

The wise choice would be to find the rest of the section and gather them. The five of them together could attack virtually risk free. But Solveig was right. Unless these two were far more powerful than they appeared, he and Solveig were more than enough. And if the whole section attacked, the odds were much more likely that the criminals died.

Which was probably why Solveig wasn't arguing for them to find the others.

He had another reason, too, one that was less noble. Rumors were swirling that Radulfr was in line for a transfer to command of another unit. He deserved it. He'd been in service to the empire for nearly thirty years, and he was an excellent section commander.

If the rumors were true, Brynja would soon need another section commander, and she preferred to choose from tehoin already a part of that section.

Hakon knew Irric was interested in the role, but so was he. He kept calm during stressful situations, and he believed people naturally listened to him because of his size and confidence. Taking these two on their own might earn him more serious consideration from Brynja.

With soft whispers, the two of them formed a plan, such as it was. They split apart to come at the criminals from different angles. Solveig, with her ability to form teho into spears, would signal the attack. She would wound them, then Hakon would move in and subdue them before they even knew what had happened.

Simple and easy.

Hakon reached his position without incident. Despite his size, he moved like a wraith. He waited for Solveig's attack.

Instead, the snap of a twig startled him almost as much as it did the two fugitives. They both straightened, alert as deer. Hakon saw them tense as they began to form teho into long swords.

Both of them.

He broke from his hiding place with a yell, drawing his sword as he did. They were on him in an instant, faster than he would have expected possible. Off in the distance, he felt

Solveig's own teho, but she held her attack ready, unwilling to launch her spears with the three combatants so close together.

He swore at her. Of the three of them, he was the only one who would survive her attacks relatively unscathed. If she threw, their problems would be over.

But it didn't occur to her. His abilities were too unusual, so why should it, especially in the heat of battle? If anything, Radulfr bore the responsibility for putting them together when they weren't that experienced.

Teho blades sliced at him.

Both of them possessed strong teho and quick reflexes. But like too many tehoin outside the army, they'd never learned to wield their swords like true weapons. They were used to cutting through anything they swung at.

His body filled with teho, his own reactions were otherworldly. He turned aside their cuts and slid through the spaces they couldn't reach. Two moves would be all it would take to bring them down for good.

Solveig's hope stayed his murderous intent. He swiped his sword at the mother's head, twisting it at the last moment so he struck her with the flat of his weapon. She crumpled like a rag doll.

The boy screamed for his mother, but the moment of distraction was all Hakon needed. One more swing brought him to the ground to join her.

Solveig rushed forward, full of apologies that Hakon waved away. "Do you have drugs?" Tehoin were notoriously hard to capture, as no building could withstand their assaults for long. Common practice called for them to be kept unconscious until a formal trial could be formed. The result of most trials was death. Tehoin couldn't reasonably be imprisoned, so death was simply expedient.

Hakon reconsidered his mercy as Solveig soaked a cloth in a liquid and held it to each of the fugitives' faces. Brynja would probably be furious at having to deal with these two until their trial.

But when Solveig looked up at him, he knew he'd made the right choice. She was about to say something when they heard a flurry of footsteps. The others had felt the bursts of teho.

He gave her a single quick nod, and just like that, they began their long journey toward friendship.

THE BAND 5

One morning a messenger appeared, his face ashen. He hurried to Brynja's quarters empty-handed. Hakon and the others gathered in the training ground, preempting the order they all expected.

Brynja appeared a few moments later. "Five minutes. Gather everything you need, combat only."

The unit ran to the bunkhouses. They changed into their sturdy boots. Some slipped on light armor. Hakon had experienced quick deployments before, but this one felt different. The messenger's attitude. The lack of sealed orders. The bunks were quiet except for the sound of the soldiers preparing. He wasn't the only one who felt it.

Even Irric was speechless, and he rarely missed an opportunity to display his wit. He had good reason, though. After Hakon finished preparing his own gear, he made his way over to Irric's bunk and laid a hand on his shoulder. "You'll do well," Hakon said. He added a forced smile. "And if you make a mistake, I'll be sure to tell you. Loudly."

His attempt at humor fell flat. Irric shook his head. "It's a big one."

Hakon had the same feeling. They all did. "Probably, but we've been training together for a month under you. We're ready."

Irric nodded. "Thanks."

This was their first mission since Radulfr's transfer. Their first with Irric as their new section commander. It was unfortunate it had to be a mission that felt so rushed.

Brynja's decision had stung Hakon's pride, but Irric had a significant edge in experience. Hakon needed to put in more time. His opportunity would come. Hakon, judging that Irric wanted space, retreated and let his friend have a moment to himself.

They assembled back in the training grounds well inside of five minutes. The messenger had already disappeared. Brynja's briefing wasted no time.

"We've got dragons," she said.

The circle of warriors fell perfectly still. "Dragons?" Irric asked, emphasizing the plural.

"Yes. Perhaps as few as three, maybe as many as seven."

The silence around the circle was almost painful. It wasn't that their typical missions weren't dangerous, but a handful of dragons was by far the most dangerous task they'd ever attempted, at least during Hakon's time with the army.

Irric broke the tension. "You probably should have waited to tell us that until after we transported."

Several of the kolma chuckled.

Of course, Hakon had trained for this. They all had. Dragons were humans' greatest predator. Fortunately, they didn't appear often, and when they did, it was typically on the far western frontier. He'd yet to see one in person. There'd been attacks during his term of service, but other units of tehoin had been sent into battle.

It was a rare day when a full unit returned from those orders.

Another commander spoke up. "Even if there's only three, that's too many for us to take on."

"We're not going in alone," Brynja said. "They're sending in three tehoin units."

Sixty tehoin, assuming they were all fully recruited. Hakon swore silently. That was almost half of the tehoin units the emperor had.

Brynja asked, "Anything else pressing? Otherwise, we need to reach the rendezvous soon."

Brynja told the transporters where they were going. Hakon recognized the location. It was on the western frontier, but closer to populated areas than he expected. There was a town nearby with a few hundred settlers, if he remembered correctly.

A few minutes later, Hakon appeared in the plains west of the great forest. Despite his familiarity with transporting, the fact he could travel nearly the whole width of the empire in the blink of an eye never failed to instill a moment of awe within him.

Brynja ordered them to move. Hakon fell into his role of scout, using his teho-assisted muscles to roam ahead of their unit. Brynja had found him particularly useful for the role when the unit didn't want to announce their presence with frequent transporting.

They made the rendezvous without problem, but Hakon couldn't tear his eyes away from the billowing smoke several miles to the west. The town was on fire.

Brynja's army was the last unit to arrive, and as soon as they did, Brynja took the section commanders to a quick strategy discussion with the leaders of the other units.

Under other circumstances, Hakon's curiosity would

have overwhelmed him. He'd never been on a joint mission with the other tehoin units, and he wondered how similar they were to Brynja's army. Today, though, he sought the comfort of the familiar. Irric's section stayed tight together, finding a patch of grass in the sun they could call their own.

From the looks of it, they weren't alone in their choice. When Hakon ran his eye over the gathering, he noted that the tehoin tended to cluster in groups of four, with sections of a unit keeping closer together, too.

Solveig sat down next to him. The strength of their former enmity had transformed into an unbreakable friendship. He was even closer to her than to Irric.

"Nervous?" she asked.

He nodded, then shook his head. There was no point in lying to her. "Closer to terrified."

"Glad it's not just me," she said.

There wasn't much else to be said. Their company was all that was needed. When the orders came, they would march without question. Whoever lived in that town needed aid, and they were the only warriors in the empire who could provide it.

The commanders didn't give them much time to stew in their nerves. Irric returned from the meeting after only a few minutes. He looked almost as pale as the messenger that had arrived in their fort earlier that morning. He sat down among the rest of the section, and for several long seconds he didn't speak.

Finally, he took a deep breath and launched into their orders. "We've got better information now than before. Our best guess is that there are five dragons in the town. They're attacking as we speak."

Hakon bit down on his outburst. Five?

Solveig, her mind always sharp, asked the clarifying

questions Hakon knew he should be thinking about. "Do we know how old the dragons are, and why they're attacking?"

"Yes." Irric looked like he was chastising himself for not telling them that right away. Hakon didn't think he'd ever seen the swordsman so uncertain. "At least one elder. One might be an adult or maybe an elder, but they aren't sure. The other three are definitely younglings."

Hakon tried to swallow the fear that rose in his throat. *Elders?*

He swore. Even with so much strength gathered here, he wasn't sure it would be enough.

Irric answered Solveig's second question next. "We think the attack was due to a case of bad timing. A caravan recently arrived, but they had a stamfar with them. One who gathered their teho when the dragons were passing close enough to sense it."

No one knew why dragons hated tehoin so much, but the measure of their hate seemed to increase the measure of the tehoin's strength. It was no wonder the dragons attacked, and no wonder why the town still had a chance.

Hakon felt the first glimmer of hope at the mention of a stamfar. With that power, the gathered tehoin just might have a chance against the dragons. "What's our plan?"

"There's not much of one. We'll head out soon, as quick of a march as we can. The units will keep close to one another. No point in spreading out and diluting our strength. Primary targets are the elders. There's some slim hope that if we manage to kill them, the younglings might flee."

"How about our unit, specifically?" Hakon asked.

Irric thought for a moment. "Attack them with everything?" He looked at Hakon. "I can't ask you to stay back, but I would ask that you do your best to defend us while we try to pierce their hides from a distance."

Hakon gripped his sword tighter but said nothing. What tactics the imperial tehoin had developed against the dragon often boiled down to "stay far away and aim for weak spots." Using such tactics, Hakon was next to useless. But he could act as the first line of defense if a dragon came too close.

As Irric promised, they were on the march soon after, the town growing steadily closer. Before long, Hakon could see flying shadows. Even from a distance, they were terrifyingly large.

As they neared, Hakon felt the stamfar in town fighting back.

Brynja, as was her way, led her unit from the front. They were at the center of the force, with one unit north of them and the other south. Several hundred paces short of the town, she came to a stop and summoned her teho. That was the signal for them to do the same up and down the line.

The sheer strength of their numbers rivaled the power of the stamfar. Hakon imagined the unit commanders hoped their arrival would deflect the dragons from the town. They waited nearly a minute, but no dragons emerged from the town to do battle. The stamfar, it seemed, remained more interesting to them.

The units didn't wait long. When no dragons took the bait, Brynja formed an enormous sword of teho, nearly twice as long as Hakon was tall. She shouted and brought the sword down, ordering the charge. Her voice was joined by dozens of others, and Brynja took the first step forward.

Alone, Hakon didn't know if he would have possessed the courage. The energies at the heart of the town were the strongest he'd ever felt. Every instinct in his body screamed at him to run the other way.

But he wouldn't leave Brynja behind. The shame would be unbearable.

Nerves made his fingers tingle, and the thought of fearing shame almost made him giggle like a child.

Funny that he was more motivated by looking a coward in front of his friends than by death.

Then he was in the streets of the town, and the dragons were no longer ahead of him, but in the skies above. It was the younglings overhead, darting down to pick off unsuspecting targets. Hakon couldn't tell how successful their hunts were. Fortunately, their jaws were as empty on the ascent as they were on the descent.

Brynja, of course, threw the first spear, aiming for a youngling's head as it dove toward an adjacent street. Her attack bounced harmlessly off the dragon's scales, but it certainly caught the creature's attention. It shifted toward them, and nearly twenty spears followed that of their leader. They landed with equal result.

The dragon passed overhead, skimming just above the top of the roofs as its long neck reached for an appetizer. They ducked low and the dragon passed, as hungry as it had been a moment ago.

It had to be too big to be a youngling. Hakon had seen paintings, but none of them did the creatures justice. Even the youngling was as big as several homes put together. What would the elders be like?

Most of the town seemed abandoned, although Hakon had no trouble imagining some of the collapsed homes held bodies inside. However this attack had started, it looked like many people had been able to escape.

Brynja waved them forward. They reached a corner and

turned, and Hakon got his answers about the elders. Two of them roamed the town square, and between them, they almost filled the enormous space. Hakon could only see parts of the predators from his position in the street.

Again, Brynja formed a spear, and her action was mirrored by almost everyone in her army. As one, they threw.

All that power, and the spears broke as if they were nothing against the armored scales of the elder dragon. It felt like they were children, trying to destroy a mountain with nothing but sticks.

Their attack did cause the dragon to rise, giving Hakon his first full look at the beast. It stood ten, maybe fifteen times as tall as him, and it regarded the charging tehoin with an ancient gaze. It considered for a moment, no doubt deciding between the stamfar fighting in the square and the new arrivals.

It twisted toward them.

If not for his forward momentum, he would have run. There was no shame in running from this.

The dragon snapped forward, filling the whole street with its head and neck.

Somehow, Brynja found the courage not to run. She stood her ground and formed another spear, daring the elder to do its worst.

And so Brynja's army began their fight against an elder dragon.

THE BAND 6

Spears sped toward the dragon, but again, they did little more than tickle it.

Too late, Hakon realized their first mistake. The street acted as a corral for the tehoin. The environment favored the wide jaws of the elder dragon.

"Shields forward," Brynja cried.

Nineteen tehoin acted as one, and the elder dragon's skull met a wall of pure teho. Again, Hakon was useless, unable to support his friends in any way that mattered.

Miraculously, the shield held.

Hakon's hopes soared. If they could coordinate their efforts, perhaps they stood a chance.

No one saw the youngling approach from the rear. Every eye was forward, on the elder dragon.

The youngling swept in unopposed. It picked up a tehoin in each claw and bit off half of Somerled's body with its powerful jaws. It was past them by the time anyone realized what had happened. Hakon turned around just in time to watch Somerled's legs topple to the ground. He looked around, searching for their transporter. Then he stared at the legs, uncomprehending.

The roar of the elder dragon returned him to his senses. It retreated from the teho shield, but the retreat was only to give it more space. It thrust its head forward again, and this time, the shield couldn't stand. It shattered, sending several of Brynja's tehoin to their knees.

Hakon looked to the sky. The youngling was circling around behind them again, close to making another pass.

They were trapped. Somerled was gone.

Red creeped into the edges of his vision. He'd always considered himself relatively peaceful. He fought when necessary to protect his friends and his empire, but he considered that a far cry from being a violent man.

But now, perhaps for the first time in his life, he *hated*. He'd thought he'd known hate before, but those feelings had only been a pale imitation of the all-consuming fire that burned in his veins. Teho filled his limbs, not because he controlled it, but because it had to. He leaped forward, above the heads of the stunned tehoin.

His sword was in hand, though he didn't remember drawing it. He brought it down, an extension of his arm and his hate. Teho met dragon scale with a sickening *thunk* he felt in his bones.

Scales shattered like the shield had moments before, exposing the muscle beneath. Hakon landed on the dragon's snout and stabbed at the exposed muscle, but the dragon jerked back.

Hakon fell backward as his footing was yanked out from under him. He hit the ground hard, but with so much teho raging within, he barely noticed.

Behind him, Irric saw the hole in the dragon's armor,

and like a true swordsman, refused to let the opening pass him by. "After it!" he ordered.

By the time Hakon returned to his feet, Irric was already a dozen paces closer to the town square, teho sword in hand. Behind Hakon, Brynja shouted, "Irric, wait!"

Irric didn't slow. Her voice was either lost among the roar of the dragons or the blinding focus of Irric's revenge.

Hakon looked back at Brynja, then to Irric's advancing form, and then back to Brynja again. She saw his gesture and shook her head, shouting at him, too. He saw her lips move and could guess well enough what they said, but like his section commander, he heard nothing.

He sprinted after Irric, teho filling his legs. Every step of his was worth two of Irric's, but Irric's lead was too great. With a sinking heart, Hakon knew he wouldn't reach Irric in time to divert him.

Footsteps slapped against the cobblestones behind him, and a glance revealed that Solveig and Ragnbjorg were right behind him.

Fools.

The least they could do was save themselves. But he had no time to argue with them. He turned forward and focused on the scene before him.

Hakon's powerful blow had thrown the battlefield into disarray. The weakened elder dragon roared, the power of the sound alone almost enough to bring the homes around them down. The sound agitated the other dragons, and the younglings dove into the streets, unafraid of whatever resistance rose up to greet them.

Hakon reached the town square three steps behind Irric. The two elder dragons still filled the space, and Hakon glimpsed his first stamfar warrior. She looked a few years older than him, but there was no telling the age of a stamfar by appearance alone. She was tall and thin, and her outstretched arms were braided with sinewy muscle. If not for her teho, she would have looked exactly like any of the hundreds of road-weary settlers Hakon had crossed paths with over the years.

But her control of teho marked her as someone special.

Hakon had met with some of the few remaining stamfar before. Torsten, the emperor's chief advisor, was one, and he'd attended Hakon's graduation from training camp all those years ago. But he'd never been around one as they expressed the full extent of their power.

After years of being around kolma, Hakon had come to believe that teho had a uniform feel to it. Different warriors manipulated teho in different ways, but every manipulation felt like a variation on a theme.

The stamfar's use of teho had as much in common with the kolmas' efforts as an enormous waterfall had with a quiet trickle of a tiny stream. Her teho possessed a texture, an identity. It seemed like she was barely managing to contain a torrent of power rushing through her. It was a power to level towns, a strength that even the dragons respected.

Irric swung his sword at the dragon, seeking an angle that would allow him to strike at the wound Hakon had inflicted. But the elder dragon was no fool, and it protected its weak spot. Alone, Irric had no chance. Together, though, they just might. The sight of the elder dragon retreating before Irric gave Hakon hope. He saw an opening and leaped high into the sky, grinning like a madman as he saw the wound.

The dragon twisted, faster than Hakon thought possible. Its tail whipped out and caught Hakon in midair.

For the half a heartbeat that he spun violently through

the air, Hakon cursed his own foolishness. His body was already filled with teho, so there was nothing for him to do except tuck his limbs in and hope he didn't die.

He smashed through the wall of a house.

When he came to rest, he cautiously opened his eyes. He found himself in the middle of what had once been a dining room. He shook his head and stretched his jaw to clear the sound of ringing in his ears. Irric was calling for him. He tried to croak out that he was fine, then closed his eyes and let his head fall back until it rested against something hard. Nothing felt like it was broken but a nap had never sounded more appealing.

Just a quick snooze, then he'd join the battle again.

A shadow crossed over his face, blocking the warm sun. He cracked open one eye and saw Irric framed in the doorway. A moment later he saw a blur of movement, and Irric was gone as though he'd been wiped out of existence. For another moment, Hakon stared at the place Irric had once stood, uncomprehending.

Then realization hit him almost as hard as the dragon had hit his friend. Hakon shouted and fought his way back to his feet. The room spun around him, but he stumbled forward anyway. By the time he reached the hole in the wall that had served as his entrance to the home, he saw that the square was getting crowded. Solveig and Ragnbjorg were standing near the edge of the square, hurling teho at whatever targets presented themselves. Brynja and the rest of her army weren't far behind. Combined with the efforts of the stamfar, they were laying down waves of teho that could have reshaped an entire coastline.

The dragons kept flinching back, retreating one small bit at a time from the overwhelming forces. Whenever one tried to reply to the forces arrayed against them, a withering barrage of teho would knock them back.

Hakon looked left and saw Irric in a ball in the corner of the square. Some of his limbs were at unnatural angles, but for now his chest still rose and fell, which meant it wasn't too late to save him. Hakon returned his attention to the wounded elder dragon. Its attention had been seized by the arrival of so many new warriors. Hakon stood behind the beast, forgotten in the chaos.

With one cut, he could end this. He flexed his fingers along his sword and waited. The moment would have to be perfect, and he wasn't sure he'd get another. Wave after wave of teho broke across the dragons, and there it was, the opening he'd been waiting for.

Summoning teho once again into his tired limbs, he leaped into the air, his body protesting against the effort. This time, the dragon didn't notice him. Two errant spears of teho passed underneath his feet.

Then he saw the wound again, wide open and inviting his strike. Hakon thrust his sword in and planted his feet on either side of the wound, twisting and yanking the sword in every direction, hoping that it might sever something vital.

The dragon let out a howl of agony. It thrashed back and forth, and Hakon could only hold on for a few moments. Eventually it threw him off, but blood and bone followed. The dragon let out a sound Hakon had never heard. It couldn't be called a roar, because the pitch was too high. The sound pierced Hakon's eardrums and he curled around his head in a futile effort to protect himself.

Then the dragon fell, and it wailed no more.

Hakon's surge of elation was short-lived. The other elder in the square fell into a frenzy. Its movements, which had before been smooth and sinuous, were now jerky and frantic. As it lost control it gained strength. Its tail smashed through houses as though they weren't even there. Its jaws snapped on whatever was close at hand, and the teho emanating from it blasted those in the town square backward.

Nor was the elder alone. Movement in the sky pulled Hakon's gaze upward. Two younglings plummeted to the square. One trailed blood from a wound, but both spasmed as though they'd lost control of their bodies. They crashed into the cobblestones and immediately unleashed their fury on the tehoin gathered there.

One by one, Brynja's army fell against the onslaught of claws and teho. Hakon pulled himself upright using the wall of a house for support. He found himself in a small alcove.

He ordered his legs to run, to join the fray and help the others. But when he looked at the storm that had fallen into the center of the square, he knew there was nothing he could do. He'd given everything he had to kill the one elder, and its death had doomed all his compatriots.

Brynja's army acquitted themselves well. One of the younglings fell as the battle raged, and it looked like, for a moment at least, they might still win the day.

One tail swipe from the elder dragon changed all that. It took out three of the remaining tehoin, one of which was Ragnbjorg. Her eyes had been turned the other way, focused on a youngling, and she never even saw her death coming.

Other tehoin began to arrive in the square. Hakon recognized them from the other units, and they looked battered. But they added their teho to the fight. Combined with the efforts of the stamfar, who was unleashing torrents of power, they succeeded in driving the last elder into the sky.

Brynja threw herself at the last youngling without regard

for her own safety. She launched spear after spear, focusing the dragon's attention on her. Hers was a unit filled with talented warriors, fighters who danced with their swords and spears better than anyone else in the empire.

None came close to Brynja's final fight. For nearly a minute, she seemed untouchable, and her spears always found their mark.

But the youngling was fast. It lunged out and grabbed her with its massive jaws. As its mouth began to rip her body in half, Brynja formed the longest teho spear Hakon had ever seen in battle.

She thrust it, and even in her moment of death, her aim was true. It pierced the dragon's eye and destroyed the beast's brain.

Warrior and dragon fell together, and neither rose again.

THE BAND 7

The elder dragon circled in the air above town, as though an uneasy truce existed between the remaining tehoin and it.

Hakon watched it soar overhead and wondered if it felt more peaceful up there, high in the sky. Down below, the survivors were at each other's throats.

From what Hakon gathered, none of the units assigned to the mission had fared well. At the sound of the elder dragon's first wounded roar, the younglings had grown far more aggressive. It had cost the smaller dragons their lives, but far too many tehoin had died in exchange. Of the nearly sixty warriors who had marched on the town, there were only seventeen left.

Seventeen tehoin who couldn't agree on what came next. All three unit commanders had been killed, and only a few section commanders remained. Most wanted to use the remaining transporters to return to their respective forts and report to the emperor.

If not for the stamfar, they might have run.

But she stood among them, her eyes fixed on the sky. Her courage hadn't yet failed her, though Hakon imagined that if she was strong enough to stand in a square surrounded by two elder dragons, she had little to fear. "Your orders were to kill the dragons," she reminded them.

The section commanders disagreed. They argued that they'd never received written orders. They claimed the emperor would want to maintain the numbers of tehoin more than he'd want to kill a single elder dragon, especially one that wasn't currently attacking anyone.

The stamfar, named Nanna, didn't budge. Hakon didn't blame her. Like the others, he desired the safety and familiarity of their fort. But he wanted revenge, too. Brynja and the others watched from the other side of the gates, and he wouldn't flee like a coward.

He turned his attention to his most pressing concerns. Solveig had healed both himself and Irric, and now she was exhausted from her efforts. Irric was physically whole, but the battle had wounded him in ways Solveig couldn't heal. The tall swordsman was sitting against a wall, arms wrapped tight around his knees. His eyes were sunk deep into his skull, and his thoughts traveled dark paths.

Hakon had tried to talk to him earlier, but he would have had a more invigorating conversation with a blade of grass. He supposed it was time to try again. Irric was their section commander, and the only one not currently involved in the argument about what to do next. He sat down next to the swordsman. "We need you, Irric."

Irric shook his head vehemently.

"You're our commander, Irric. We need to know what to do."

He shook his head again. "No."

Hakon was at a loss for words. How could he argue against outright denial?

Irric met his gaze for the first time since the battle. Hakon felt as though he was falling into a deep hole, a bottomless pit from which there was no escape. "I watched her die. I watched—everything." He somehow wrapped his arms even tighter around his knees. "We were only in that square because I ordered us to charge."

Irric shook his head again. "Never again." He shuddered. "The section is yours. You wanted it. It's yours. Now please, leave me alone."

Hakon put his hand on Irric's shoulder and squeezed, a reminder he was around if Irric wanted him. Then he stood and looked around. It wasn't how he wanted command. Not at all. But he'd keep Solveig and Irric safe. He swore it.

Now the only question was how.

Two tehoin chose that moment to approach their section. Hakon welcomed them, and they introduced themselves as Meshell and Ari. Ari was a transporter, and Meshell walked with a grace that reminded Hakon of Brynja in her final duel.

"Our section is dead," Meshell said without preamble, "and our commanders, too. You're the one who slayed the elder dragon, right? The one who uses teho within his own body?"

Hakon nodded, cautious. In other circumstances, his deed might be worthy of a song. But these soldiers knew what the elder's death had led to. Depending on where one stood, he was either the bravest hero of the day or the greatest villain.

He wasn't sure which side these two stood.

"Can we join your section?" Meshell asked.

"Why?"

Ari shrugged. "Three of you. Two of us. Makes us full strength. And you're the only one who looks like you're actually thinking about the problem instead of wasting your time arguing."

"I'm planning on helping Nanna kill the elder dragon." Hakon didn't realize he'd already made the decision until the words tumbled from his lips.

Meshell's smile was vicious. "We were hoping you would."

Why not? Ari was right. It would bring them up to full strength, and they needed someone who could transport, anyway. "Well, welcome to our section," he said.

THE FIVE WARRIORS sat in a loose circle while the commanders bickered nearby. Hakon was lost in thought, his eyes focused on the elder dragon circling high above them.

When he had made the claim that he was going to help Nanna, a seed had sprouted in his mind. He tended to it and nurtured it gently, carefully considering the repercussions. He wanted to tell someone else. Ideas, like soldiers, were always better after they had been battle-tested. He needed someone to either tell him he was a fool or that he was a genius. Because it was certainly nowhere in between.

But the two new arrivals kept to themselves, part of his section and yet not. Solveig slept, and Irric was too lost in his own grief to be any help.

His wondered if this was leadership or a suicide pact.

He closed his eyes and ran the previous battle through his thoughts, over and over. He watched his friends die a dozen times, just to grasp the smallest detail that might help them kill the second elder. Eventually, he came to the point where he was certain that there was nothing left for him to learn. He opened his eyes and he felt as though he had halfway escaped from the horror already. "I know how we kill it."

His quiet claim caught the attention of the two new arrivals, who leaned forward. Even Irric unwrapped his arms from his knees.

"Really?" Meshell asked.

"Maybe? At least, I know that the way we were taught will never work."

"Explain," Ari said.

Hakon laid out his reasoning. "The tactics we were taught might work if we were a full unit against a youngling. In such a circumstance, we might be able to overpower them. But even with Nanna on our side, we can't overpower one of the elders. Our teho simply bounces off."

He was relieved to see that both of the new arrivals were nodding, and even Irric had a thoughtful look to his face.

"So what do you suggest?" Ari asked.

"We get in close," Hakon replied.

"You're mad," said Meshell with a smile. She leaned closer forward. "And I like it."

Hakon finished his thought. "I'm not saying that it's going to work, but every time we've killed one of the dragons, it was because we were able to get in close and strike it in a weak place."

He went to speak with Nanna, whom he convinced to come listen to his idea. The others woke Solveig up. Once they were all together, he told them what he thought. When he finished, all eyes turned to Nanna. Without her, none of it mattered.

She considered for a moment, then agreed that it was both mad, and their best chance for success.

"So, we're doing it?" Hakon asked.

One by one, they nodded.

"Then we need to tell the others. I'll see if I can get them all to listen."

It took no small amount of doing. Hakon's dual status as hero and villain did him no favors, but by claiming he was gathering them on Nanna's behalf, he was eventually able to get them together.

Once he did, he explained his plan one last time. With every retelling he became more convinced his way was the only way. Unfortunately, the other section commanders weren't convinced.

At all.

Instead of bringing them together to fight the dragon, Hakon stood, openmouthed in surprise, as the other commanders made the hasty decision to leave the battlefield. It seemed his idea was just the excuse they needed to leave for good.

Once the commanders made the decision, the tehoin exited quickly. From the way they kept glancing toward Nanna, it was clear they thought she might try to stop them by force.

She let them go, though.

The others were gone minutes later, and Hakon stared at the place where they had once stood, unable to believe his eyes. They were sworn to protect the empire. How could anyone think of leaving?

His section remained. Though they'd been given the opportunity to join the others, they chose to stay. The town, which had once been a hub of activity, now housed only six living souls. The others had claimed that they would seek reinforcements, but Hakon wasn't holding his breath for those.

He felt the red returning to his vision as he looked at the places the tehoin had been. They had broken their vows.

He didn't think he had any space in his heart to forgive them. He clenched his fists, swearing to use his newfound hate in service of the empire. In service of those that had fallen.

They prepared silently. Hakon gripped his sword, and he realized he was actually looking forward to the battle to come.

They gathered and left, off to kill a dragon.

THEY MARCHED BACK into the center of town. Hakon forced down the recent memories, ignored the blood on the street he knew belonged to his friends. Once in the square, Nanna wasted no time. She summoned teho, and overhead, the dragon altered its flight for the first time in hours.

Hakon cast one glance over at Solveig. Of all of them, she looked the most exhausted, and was also the one Hakon worried about the most. "You don't need to be here. It would be fine if you waited a ways away to see if any of us need healing."

Her answering glare was enough to silence him.

The dragon gave them no more time for conversation. The group scattered as the creature plummeted to the center of the square, landing with such force that the cobblestone rippled outward and exploded from where it lay. Hakon held up an arm to protect his face.

Then he charged.

It had been a promise he made to himself prior to the battle. Whatever happened, he'd always move forward.

The dragon's jaws snapped at Nanna, and she formed a shield around her. The jaws crunched, and for one heart-stopping moment, Hakon worried the battle had been lost before it even had an opportunity to properly begin.

But the jaws slipped off the smooth surface of the shield, and Nanna formed a spear of teho in her right hand. She flung it forward and the dragon twisted its massive snout out of the way. For a heartbeat, it was on the defensive.

In that space, the rest of them attacked. Meshell cut at the dragon's face. Ari transported to a roof surrounding the square and launched three teho darts at its eyes. Hakon stayed low. So long as he stayed in contact with the ground he thought he might be fast enough to evade its blows. He didn't want to leap and be stuck in midair like before. He dashed forward and stabbed his sword back toward the dragon's head. It slid under the interlocking scales, and Hakon drew the first blood of the battle.

The dragon twisted and snarled, snapping and swiping at Hakon. He danced around the beast and looked for another opening.

Hope pounded in his chest. Though they lacked the sheer power of their previous assault, his plan was working. They had already wounded the dragon.

Now, they just had to finish it before it was too late. In this battle, time was no friend. Surviving required all their focus, and the dragon could endure many more mistakes than they could.

Nanna continued her barrage of teho. While Hakon and the others cut and scratched at the dragon, she bore the brunt of its assaults.

Hakon's initial optimism faded. Yes, they were still alive, and yes, they were causing some small damage to the elder, but it wasn't nearly enough, and a single mistake would kill them fast. He felt the initiative sliding from his grasp.

Every moment seemed to give one of them a brush with death. Ari transported away less than a heartbeat from being broken in two by the dragon's tail. A claw ripped through Solveig's left shoulder. Once, Hakon hesitated between moves, and was certain the dragon would catch him in one of its claws.

Meshell saved him. She darted in, swiped at the claw with a powerful teho sword, and knocked it away.

Hakon feared that if even one of them fell the others would be sure to follow.

Once again, the dragon's jaws closed on Nanna, and this time, Nanna could no longer protect herself. Her shield shattered and the jaws closed. She flinched away, and the razor-sharp teeth sliced clean through her right arm.

The stamfar fell, and for one precious moment the scene seemed frozen in time. The dragon swallowed the arm in one gulp, then darted forward, jaws hungrily searching for the meal it had sought for so long.

Hakon saw the end. Without Nanna, their fight was over. The kolma had no chance against an elder dragon.

Then, impossibly, Meshell was there. She slid right in front of the dragon, holding a teho spear three times the length of her own body. She stood in the path of the dragon's jaws without fear, as though it were just another day of practice in the training yard.

She flung her spear, and Hakon saw that she did so with all her strength. She collapsed as she released it.

The spear went down the dragon's throat, tearing at the vulnerable organs inside.

It spasmed, missing Meshell and Nanna completely.

That same wailing cry tried emanate from it throat, but

its torn esophagus strangled the sound before it could be born. Perhaps it was a fatal blow, but the rest of them took no chances. A moment later Irric and Ari were on opposite sides of the dragon, stabbing into its eyes and into its brain with long teho swords.

The elder dragon fell, not with a roar, but with a whimper.

THE BAND 8

Hakon led the others through a set of calisthenic exercises. They ground out repetition after repetition, sweat pooling in the cracks between the stones of the training grounds. Their grunts were the only sound he heard.

Though they'd joined him for the past several days, it still felt strange to have company. For years, his morning workouts had been a solitary endeavor, the one time in his day when he was almost guaranteed privacy.

The day after Ari transported them back to the fort, out of the horror of that town, Hakon had woken up before the sun, as he always did. Lacking any better use of his time, he'd gone out to the training ground to complete his routine. But his movement woke up Meshell, and the others weren't far behind. None of them had slept well.

He'd given them no order. They'd followed him silently. Then they'd joined him in his routine, and then followed him for the rest of the day. None of them wanted to be alone for long. Hakon understood. Before the town, he would have been bothered by the constant company. Now he welcomed it.

The five of them rarely broke apart. The were held together by the twin glues of sorrow and achievement. They'd all lost friends. And together, they'd brought down an elder dragon.

The fort was too quiet. Once it had housed twenty-one boisterous souls. Now it held only five broken ones.

They bunked together and cooked meals together. No one from the empire had yet come to them. Ari and Meshell debated returning to the survivors of their own units, who had abandoned them in the town. Neither seemed enthused by the prospect.

As Hakon led them through his routine, his mind wandered. By this time, he could do the routine in his sleep. They needed direction, and after Irric's abdication, he decided it was his responsibility.

First, they needed closure. Once their exercise was done, he said, "Tonight we need to have some sort of memorial for those who died. For our friends." The others nodded, but the idea didn't seem to lift their spirits the way Hakon had hoped it might.

Irric helped. "There's a special cut of meat still in the pantry. I'll prepare it tonight."

That was enough encouragement for Solveig. "I know where a few people were hiding their liquor. I'll grab all of it."

Hakon asked Ari and Meshell if they'd be willing to gather enough wood for a long fire. It wasn't much, but it would give them a way to contribute. They agreed, and they went their separate ways for the first time since coming together in the town. Part of Hakon feared that now that the spell had been broken, Ari and Meshell might return to their units.

The day passed quicker than any since their battle with the dragon. They threw themselves into the preparations, and by the time the sun fell below the wall of the fort, they'd prepared a feast large enough for a whole unit. They attacked the food as though it had insulted the emperor, and before long they were sprawled out around the fire, hands over full bellies.

Hakon told the first story, of Radulfr, who was always getting in trouble for hiding food. Though she was one of the thinnest women he'd ever met, she ate more than most families put together. Brynja was always yelling at her for hiding food in the bunk room, encouraging vermin to find their way in.

Irric followed, telling stories of Brynja. Funny stories. Hakon had known the two were close, but he didn't realize how little he'd actually known his commander. In the years under her command, he realized he'd come to love the image she projected more than the person. Irric was the opposite. He'd seen behind the facade, and he'd loved her.

He still blamed himself. It was obvious in the way he spoke, in the anger that lurked behind the sorrow. Hakon didn't know how to help him, though, so for tonight, he simply let Irric tell his tales of the woman Hakon thought he'd known.

Solveig, Ari, and Meshell told stories of loss, too. They spoke late into the night, until the fire burned low.

THE NEXT DAY, Hakon announced another decision. "I want us to start training together," he said. He continued before Ari or Meshell could interrupt. "I intend to write to the emperor and request we be kept together as our own section. I know I don't want to be split apart again. Do you?"

No one did. Hakon only stated what they'd all been feeling.

"Then let's get training."

He ran them through the same exercises Brynja had drilled into them every day. They practiced fighting as a section, and Hakon was surprised how easy commanding them was. They simply listened, and although he'd assumed the role of their leader, it wasn't like any section Hakon had been in before. They discussed everything together, and all ideas were treated equally.

Two days later, a group transported into the training grounds. Hakon recognized their visitor, though he didn't quite believe what he saw. Their guest was an older man, gray hair pulled back into a tight braid. His eyes were sharp, and he was accompanied by two others.

The people he traveled with were almost as interesting. One was a young man, and the other an even younger girl. Strange traveling companions for a visit to a tehoin fort.

Irric took a knee. Hakon and the others followed suit.

Torsten stood before them.

He was the second most powerful individual in the empire, behind only the emperor. And there were whispers that Torsten was actually first on that list. That he was the one who actually ran the empire.

The stamfar's eyes ran over the assembled group, and Hakon suppressed a shiver as their gazes met.

"I came to congratulate you on your efforts against the dragons," Torsten said. "I know your losses were incredible, but Nanna has vouched for your courage. I know what you did for the empire, and your emperor himself thanks you."

The words were exactly what Hakon had hoped to hear. But coming from Torsten, they seemed to lack heart. Torsten wasn't congratulating them because he cared. He was congratulating them because he knew, somewhere in his calculating mind, it was the appropriate thing to say in the situation.

The section bowed their heads. When Hakon looked up, the older man's eyes had settled on him. "You're Hakon, correct?"

"Yes, sir."

"Nanna tells us that it was your leadership that led to the death of the final elder dragon. In thanks, the emperor has named you commander of the new unit here."

Hakon bowed his head again, but his thoughts were jumbled. Unit commander? Before he'd even had any real experience as a section commander?

Torsten continued delivering his orders. "Ari and Meshell, you will be returned to your own unit. Each of you will be given your own section, as befits your actions."

Though no one made a move, Hakon sensed his friends' discontent. The past days had brought them together, and now they were being torn apart. He didn't like it, but obedience froze him in place.

After another moment of deliberation, he cursed at himself. If he could face the rage of an elder dragon, he could stand up to an old man.

So he did. He stood up, quickly.

The reaction from the two youth Torsten traveled with was instant. They both summoned teho, and surprised Hakon in the process. The young man was kolma, and a strong one at that. But the younger girl, she was stamfar. Hakon swallowed the lump in his throat. He didn't believe his senses, that someone so small and so young could contain such a power. And yet she stood there, all the evidence he needed.

Torsten held up a hand. "Peace, Isira." The older man glanced at the boy. "And you, too, Damion. I don't believe that Hakon has any intent to harm us." He turned his attention to Hakon. "You have an objection?"

"I believe I speak for all of us when I say that we do not wish to return to our normal units. We've become our own section since the battle, and before your arrival, I was planning on traveling to the emperor and asking if we might remain together."

Torsten shook his head. "The experience you gained fighting the dragon is too valuable. That knowledge needs to be spread among the rest of the tehoin."

"Then we will train them, as you wish. But together."

Torsten set his lips in a tight line. Hakon had the feeling this was not a man who was used to being argued with. But it was too late to turn back now.

"You know how the units work, Hakon. Experience is spread among the various section and unit commanders. It's a system that has worked well for years. Between the five of you, there's over fifty years of combat experience. That's far too much for a single section."

It was hard to argue against the weight of tradition, and Torsten had the right of it. Spreading out their experience made more sense.

The memory of Hakon's unit being attacked by the youngling returned, bringing with it the counterargument. "I agree that it's worked for many years, and there is wisdom to it. But perhaps the empire needs a section like us. A small group of experienced warriors eager to take on challenges others won't." Hakon looked at the others. None of them were looking at him, but he felt as though they agreed with what he said. "Besides, none of the others want leadership positions."

He was guessing at that. For Irric he felt pretty safe making the claim, but much less so the others.

Torsten finally tore his gaze away from Hakon. "Is that true? I would hear it from each of you."

Irric spoke first. "It is certainly true for me, sir. I will give my sword and life to the empire, but I am not fit to lead."

"No one would want to follow me, sir," Meshell said.

"I work best in the shadows, sir," Ari announced.

All eyes turned to Solveig. Hakon knew she was ambitious, and of the five of them, seemed to have the temperament most suited for command. In many ways, she was probably even a superior choice.

Except she didn't step forward.

"I have no desire for command at this time, sir," she said.

Torsten rubbed at his chin as he studied the group. He said nothing for a very long time. Then, finally, he nodded. "Very well. It is an experiment worth trying. I will let this section exist as it is for one year, and then we'll revisit the question."

Hakon expected Torsten to stay, to talk with them for a time. But his purpose at the fort was over, and he turned to his strange compatriots. They held hands, and a moment later, vanished.

With the emperor's advisor gone, Hakon's face broke out into a huge grin. They'd done it. They'd given themselves a year to prove themselves.

In that time, he was certain he could prove they were worth the risk.

CHAPTER 24

Hakon took a deep breath, then let it out slowly. "And that is how the band was born. Torsten gave us our year and we made the most of it. No task was too big, too challenging, or too risky. By the end of the year we'd made a name for ourselves, and it was agreed that we would stay together."

The old warrior looked almost shaken by the retelling of the story, and Solveig picked up the loose threads. "There's not much relevant that need be said about the next few dozen years. There are enough legends of our exploits, and while the details may have grown in the retelling, the substance of the stories is true enough. We fought against small rebellions, pushed back the wilds, and protected new settlements as they built their walls."

Valdis looked like she was close to fighting someone. "What does any of this have to do with where we are now?"

Hakon's answering gaze was sharp. "Zachary asked for the truth. This is how it began, and its important, because I hope it helps you to understand the next part. Why my oathbreaking carries such weight, even today."

Hel, always the peacemaker, spoke up. "I believe it would be good for us to take a short break. We can stretch our legs, grab a bite to eat, and resume in an hour. I need to speak with some of the other council members to ensure that Aysgarth won't fall apart while we speak."

"And when we return," Valdis added, "I expect to learn why you betrayed the empire. Why you killed Torsten."

"I will," Hakon promised.

The group disbanded, and with Hel gone and busy, Zachary found himself standing next to Irric. The swordsman had a distant look in his eyes and Zachary suspected that at the moment he saw only the past.

"How are you?" Zachary asked.

The question startled Irric out of his reverie. "Sorry. Just lost in the memories of a time long ago." He gazed meaningfully at Hakon, who was leaving the room with Meshell. "I was just thinking that even though hundreds of years have passed he really hasn't changed at all."

"How so?"

"Everything he does, he always does with his whole heart. Never once have I known him to take a more moderate path, a reasonable path." Irric pressed his palms gently against his eyes, then ran them through his hair. "Do you know what I remember of that day? The day that Torsten came with his orders?"

Zachary shook his head.

"I thought we were all going to die. Between Torsten and Isira, they'd come with two stamfar and a strong kolma. They could've crushed us like ants underfoot and been done with us. I'd had a few run-ins with Torsten before that day, and I can assure you that no one spoke to him like Hakon did that day. But the fool just charged forward. Then he spent the next year charging every problem put in our way.

And we always followed. We followed him when he was devoted to the empire, and we followed him when he wasn't. Even now, it feels like we're simply trailing in his footsteps. Though I don't think anyone else has figured that out."

"What do you mean?"

Irric sighed. "When he was awoken, he left us all behind. The rest of us stayed in touch, coordinated our efforts across the six states as much as we thought we could without attracting Isira's wrath. But he never tried to find us. He left us for good. Solveig kept a watch on him, so we always knew what he was doing, but he never once reached out. He was done with us."

"With his whole heart," Zachary finished.

Irric nodded. "Always. And that hurt, maybe even worse than the original betrayal. We knew that things would never be the same, but we didn't think they'd get to be so broken between us. Then Cliona disappeared and his necessity brought us all back together. Now, he's still chasing her with every bit of strength and will he possesses, even though she's dead. And it doesn't matter. We still follow." Irric shook his head "I don't know why we follow."

A sad smile grew on his face. "You know the worst part?" He didn't wait for Zachary to guess. "Somehow, I wouldn't have it any other way. He's led us to more triumph and more tragedy than seems possible somedays, but my life is just so much richer when he's in it." Irric shook his head. "Sorry. Listening to that story makes me think of things I haven't thought about for a very long time."

Zachary didn't mind. But Irric had said something he couldn't let go of. "You think Cliona's dead?" Generally, he believed that, too. But when he was around Hakon, he still held out hope she might return, and that he could apologize for the wrong he'd done.

Irric looked at him, and Zachary had never seen those eyes filled with so much sorrow. "I'm sorry, boy. I know what it's like to lose somebody you care for. But she's dead. I don't understand what hope Hakon holds onto. In our lives we have seen so many things that one could call impossible, but I've never seen anyone return from the dead. It's a hopeless quest."

The words landed like stones falling from the sky on Zachary's heart. He wanted to argue, wanted to protest, but after hearing what Irric had gone through himself, he realized that there was no one in a better position to tell him the truth.

The truth hurt. But it was a sharper and faster pain than the scab he kept picking at. And suddenly he felt as though he was lost in the wilderness, surrounded by trees with not even the sun to guide him. "Do we just give up on her, then?"

"I don't know. It's the sort of question you can only answer for yourself. But I can tell you one thing. I've seen the way you and Hel get along. There's something special between you two, even if you haven't realized it yet. Don't let the memory of the past prevent you from seizing the present."

With that, he left, leaving Zachary in the room by himself. Stunned, he sat down at the table and let his thoughts wander while he waited for everyone to return.

ZACHARY WAS STILL SITTING in the chair when the others began to trickle back in. Hel, thankfully, brought with her a small plate of food. She set it down in front of him. "I didn't see you outside and figured you might be hungry."

"Thank you." He felt as though he was looking at her

with different eyes, as though Irric had pulled a veil off his face.

"Are you fine?" she asked.

"I will be." And he thought it was true.

Once they had all taken their seats, Hakon resumed his story. "So, now you know the story of how the band came to be, and all of you have heard enough of our legends to know more or less what happened next. But before I talk about my decision to kill Torsten, I want to let you know about our decision to join the rebellion, because it all ties together."

Hakon took a sip of water. "It's hard for those of you who weren't alive to understand what it was like back then. The governments of the six states are completely different than that of the empire. Sure, there are governors here who take a dim view on people speaking out against them, and certainly lives have been lost by vocal critics. But in those days, if you so much as whispered a word against the emperor you were putting your life and the lives of your family and friends at risk.

"For a long time I believed in the empire. I believed in it even longer than I should have, simply because I thought it could do no wrong. I recognized that some of the actions it took could be construed as evil, but I viewed it all in service of the greater good. A servant of the empire would always have food to eat and a roof to sleep under. Perhaps the food wasn't great, and perhaps the roof was in a state of disrepair, but it seemed better than nothing. I believed in what we were doing.

"We served under three emperors. None of them were tehoin, and so lived and died natural human lifespans. But it was under the third emperor that the cracks in the empire began to widen.

"There were always rebellions, small groups of people

who thought they somehow could do better than what the empire provided. Some of them turned violent, and when they did, we put them down. But the rebellions kept growing, kept nibbling away at the edges of the empire and slowing our westward expansion. As the years went on, more of our missions dealt with rebellions than they did with the settlement of the west. What's more, we began to realize that the little rebellious fires we were putting out across the frontier weren't isolated events.

"They were connected. They were organized. Many tehoin had joined them. They had supply trains, and they had a plan. We didn't see that at the time, but it was becoming more obvious with every passing month."

Hakon took a deep breath. "This was about the time that I started to suffer doubts. I was no longer as certain of what we were doing as before. But, I still considered myself a loyal servant of the empire. Until the night that Damion returned with new orders."

Hakon looked around the table, resting his eyes for a moment on Valdis. Then, he took them into the past again.

BETRAYAL 1

Hakon shuffled the papers around his desk, then leaned back in his chair and stretched. Another long day of training followed by a long evening of reading.

It wasn't strictly necessary that he read the reports. In fact, as far as he surmised, few commanders actually did. The role of the tehoin units was to go where the emperor commanded, when the emperor commanded them. Then they were to do exactly what the emperor told them to.

It should be that easy. Though the memories were old now, he was pretty certain that was how Brynja had run the unit. And perhaps she'd been right to do so.

But the stories were concerning, and Hakon believed it was important to read the latest news. What was within the reports was almost as worrying as what was left out.

The empire wasn't what it once was. Of that, he had no doubt. But that didn't mean all was lost. There were more people than ever who pledged their loyalty to the emperor. Compared to his own youth, the empire was larger, more populous, and more prosperous.

So why didn't he feel like it was a success?

He glanced over at the mirror in his office. He'd chosen to stop the aging process in his early thirties, and by all appearances, he was in the prime of his life. But he felt a weight on his shoulders that his responsibilities alone couldn't account for. Sometimes, he wondered if it was nothing more than the accumulation of years.

They all knew the stories of stamfar who had chosen to end their own lives after hundreds of years. These days, more stamfar died from suicide than by battle. Late at night, when drink and companionship had loosened tongues, kolma often speculated whether or not humans were meant to live so long. Ahula looked upon the tehoin with a great jealousy, but sometimes Hakon wondered if it was deserved.

Learning one was tehoin didn't mean life was without struggle. It was just that the nature of the struggle changed.

He rubbed at his chin, watching the reflection in the mirror do the same.

Someone knocked softly at the door, and the sound brought a hint of a smile to his face. "Come in."

As he'd guessed, Meshell was on the other side. She sauntered in and sat on his desk, scattering his organized papers in every direction. "I thought you said you weren't going to be long."

"Sorry. Got distracted."

"Hmm. Must have been some distraction." She lifted up her legs and spun so she was facing him. Hakon watched as his papers lost the last semblance of their order. She leaned forward. "I think you deserve a break, commander."

And just like that, his worries about the world faded. Their lips met, and he pulled her off his desk and onto his lap.

Teho bloomed out in the training ground. Hakon

groaned as Meshell stood quickly. She gave him one tantalizing smile, then made her way to the door. "Better clean your desk for company. They won't be pleased by your lack of organization."

She left, and Hakon scrambled to pick up the scattered papers. He'd just finished putting them in a single pile when there was another, firmer knock on his door.

Hakon had expected a messenger, so he was surprised to see Damion enter. The kolma had quickly become Torsten's chief aide, a loyal sycophant if there ever was one. Hakon had never really liked the younger man, and the dislike had only grown over the years.

Solveig said that it seemed like Damion was missing something essential that made people human. Hakon agreed. He was missing a heart, just like his master. Both approached life like a game to be beaten. People were nothing more than pieces, and logic meant far more than emotion.

If Damion sensed Hakon's opinion of him, he gave no sign. He wouldn't care, regardless. Just so long as Hakon acted as Damion predicted, all would be well. "You're ordered to join me on an assault, immediately."

"The orders?"

"There are none. But rest assured, the command come from the office of the emperor."

Clever wordplay. Not from the emperor, then, but Torsten, most likely.

He had the right to refuse the orders. Without a signed and sealed document, Damion's instructions weren't binding. Hakon's skin prickled. He should just refuse. His instincts were screaming, but they always did around Damion.

And although he had the right, it didn't mean there

wouldn't be consequences. If Hakon's guess about the origin of the orders was correct, Torsten would be very displeased if they weren't carried out. He could disband them with a wave of his hand, and there was nothing Hakon could do to stop him.

"What's the mission?"

"Assemble the band. I'll tell you all at the same time."

Hakon kept his expression bland. He had nothing to gain by picking a fight with Damion, as satisfying as it might be. "Very well."

He brushed past Damion on the way out.

Damion's arrival had alerted the others, so summoning them took no time at all.

Damion laid out their mission in short, terse sentences. "We've found a new rebel hideout. They have cleverly disguised themselves as a merchant caravan, and our scouting reports indicate there are several tehoin embedded within the group."

"You know their location?" Hakon asked.

"I do. I will take you there now."

Hakon didn't bother to hide his surprise. "You're coming with us?"

"It is an important matter. I will join you in the assault and ensure the rebels are all killed."

Hakon's gaze traveled to Solveig. He suspected she was thinking the same as him. More than once over the years the band had let rebels escape without much in the way of pursuit. No doubt, Damion and Torsten had guessed as much. Was their loyalty being tested?

Hakon hated that those questions even came up. It was a sign of how far the situation had deteriorated that he would even have to worry about such matters. Decades of service, and it earned him nothing.

They joined hands, and as promised, Damion transported them. Hakon saw that he was now standing among the rolling plains of the southwest. Though he couldn't say for sure, the surrounding geography put him in mind of a small cluster of villages they'd defended against wilderness attacks two or three years ago. Damion pointed south and took off without another word. The band shared a look and then followed. Less than an hour at a quick march brought them to the crest of a small hill. Down below, off in the distance, a cluster of wagons gathered around a campfire. Hakon watched it for a few moments, but had to admit he saw nothing out of the ordinary.

"There it is," Damion announced. "We'll get within range and then will drop so much teho on them they won't have any chance to react."

A lump formed in Hakon's throat. The strategy was by no means uncommon. It was the most efficient way of fighting a group of soldiers whose tehoin were far outnumbered, and it kept his own people out of harm's way. He'd ordered the tactic himself a dozen times, but it still reminded him uneasily of that very first mission.

That memory never truly faded, no matter how many years had passed in the interim.

They advanced silently, avoiding detection. The other four tehoin coordinated their assault and Damion assisted. Hakon kept an eye on the whole caravan, checking for stragglers. The teho fell, fast and almost without any warning. If there had been tehoin in the caravan, they had no chance of defending against the assault.

As soon as the deed was done, Damion gave them orders. "I am going to check the scene first," he announced. "Then I must return with all haste back to the capital. Thank you for your help."

He didn't wait for any sort of acknowledgment, but simply disappeared.

Irric spoke first. "You know, I never did like that guy."

Soon they felt another blooming of teho, and then the night was completely silent. Damion was gone.

"Good riddance," said Meshell.

"Do you think we should take a look?" Hakon asked.

The question cast an even deeper pall over the already gloomy group. Normally they were responsible for looking for survivors after such an action, but Damion had provided them a way out. He had already checked the area.

"I suppose we should," answered Solveig. They reluctantly agreed and made their way to the shattered remains of the caravan.

They swept through the camp in a straight line, kicking aside debris with their feet. Hakon examined the bodies, the damage, and any signs of what the rebels might have been planning.

His stomach twisted in knots as he surveyed the damage. If these had been rebels, he could find no evidence of it. There were no swords, not even a long dagger among the deceased. Hakon saw two knives, but that was it. They looked for all the world like they were settlers. To his left, Solveig stifled a cry. He looked over as she dropped to her knees before the body of a child.

Hakon turned away, the truth of the matter hitting him harder than any whip of a dragon's tail. He swallowed hard. He might not have personally dropped any of the teho upon these people, but he'd given the order. He'd followed Damion out here.

This was on him.

A grunt from Ari caught his attention. He looked over, afraid of what he might see. Fortunately, the assassin seemed to be studying a bloody patch of dirt with intense scrutiny. "What is it?"

"Someone was here." Ari sketched the outline of a body in the dirt. I think Damion took a body back to the capital with him." Hakon clenched his jaw and nodded. Red creeped into the edges of his vision, the first time it had ever happened outside of combat. This hadn't been an action against rebels.

This had been an assassination. Damion had taken a body back to show his master.

"Come on," he said, more loudly than he intended. "There's nothing more for us to see."

If he ever got the chance, he was going to kill that man.

CHAPTER 25

Hakon looked around the room, at the band and the others gathered to listen to their story. Eventually, he locked gazes with Valdis, but if Damion's disciple had any feelings on the subject of her former master's orders, they couldn't be read on her face.

Of course, Hakon wasn't sure that she would be surprised. Damion had never bothered to hide who he was. He never believed it was necessary. He had the strength of conviction behind him, and could point to a long history of the empire supporting people exactly like him, doing exactly the sort of things he was doing.

Though he didn't know Valdis, he could guess her type well enough. If she'd become one of Damion's aides, she would have understood her commander. She would have believed in him the same way Damion had once believed in Torsten. For some reason, be it power or some misguided hope in the future, she had considered Damion the way forward.

All he could do was tell his story, and hope she saw reason.

Hakon broke his eyes away and addressed the rest of the party. "That was the beginning of the end for us. Eventually, thanks largely to Ari's work in the shadows, we were able to figure out exactly what happened that night. There was a woman in that caravan who'd been speaking out against Torsten. Apparently, she'd said enough to make him want her to disappear. Torsten feared that she was being escorted by tehoin who were powerful, and so enlisted our help. He made us unwitting accomplices in his scheme."

The worst part of it was, what happened to her had been happening to so many others. But because it didn't happen in front of him, he was able to ignore it.

Sometimes, there was regret. That he didn't act as quickly as he could have. With the benefit of hindsight, everything seemed so obvious.

How many lives could he have saved if he'd acted sooner? The emperor, and Torsten in particular, had been making people disappear for years by the time Hakon and the others stood up against them.

What kind of difference would they have made, if he hadn't been so blind to what was happening inside the empire he loved?

Hakon took strength from the faces of his friends around the table. What they'd done in the aftermath still felt right, even knowing all that was to come. "It wasn't an easy decision. Despite what you may believe of us now, each and every one of us was a loyal servant of the empire. But we'd seen firsthand how that power had become corrupted, and innocent people were being punished. We argued about it for days."

"Weeks," Irric corrected.

"Why did you join the rebellion, instead of doing something else?" Hel asked.

"Because we couldn't think of anything else that mattered," Hakon said. "Strong as we were, and as well known as we were at the time, there were still only five of us. If we'd settled for only speaking out, we believed we would have been silenced. And, at least in the beginning, we didn't think the war would grow as large as it did. We believed, wrongly, that the empire would be willing to part with a section of the western border. We predicted a small conflict followed by treaty."

When Hakon watched their reactions, he didn't see much belief around the table. The war had been the most destructive years in recorded history. Again, perhaps in hindsight, their foolishness was easy to spot. They hadn't realized that the empire fought, not for land, but for minds. It couldn't afford to let even a small section of land secede.

He pushed on. "What happened after that is also mostly known. It's been told both by legend and by the historians of that time. As before, the stories are more or less accurate, but are good enough for our purpose today. The whole land was at war, and we spent years at the tip of the spear, fighting as hard or harder than anyone else to bring a new world about."

Hakon wondered what else to say. Left unchecked, he could spend years talking about the war, about the trials and tribulations. He'd lived lifetimes in the span of years, and that conflict had shaped him into the person he was today. But none of it really mattered. Not for this.

He shook his head at the unbidden memories. He didn't like thinking about those times. Necessary as they might have been, he'd never seen violence like it before or since. Belief, it turned out, was the most dangerous opponent of all. Family had turned against family, trading blows where once they'd traded kindnesses, and Hakon hoped he would never live to see such times again.

"I suppose," he said, "that if I wanted you to know one thing, it was that those battles were unlike anything I'd fought in before or since. The rebellion quickly amassed incredible numbers, but they were fighting against much-better-trained troops, and Torsten was a strategic mastermind. But it wasn't just the scope of the violence that still haunts my memories. It was the intensity of it all. I'd never seen so much hate in so little time."

He focused on the story. Perhaps, he thought, he was just delaying because he really didn't want to tell the next part. To this day, it was the greatest regret of his life.

But Zachary was right. They needed to know. They couldn't break free of the past if they didn't understand it.

"Anyway, the fighting was terrible, but for the most part it has been well documented. Battle by bloody battle we won the war, but it is not a time that I would ever wish to live through again. And now, I suppose I come to the crux of the story. The end of my tale."

And then, one last time, Hakon took them into the past.

BETRAYAL 2

Hakon stared into the ruins of Taunka. Once, it had been the largest city in the empire, its streets filled with the shouts of merchants, the smells of dozens of kitchens, and a wider variety of goods than could be found anywhere else in the world. Before the rebellion, the band had often visited between their assignments. Taunka's smiths were among the best, so it was here they turned to repair and replace their weapons.

Solveig had enjoyed getting lost in their libraries. Hakon and Irric had whiled away more afternoons and evenings in the taverns than either of them cared to admit. Meshell had sparred with the arena combatants. No one knew what Ari did on their visits, but even the dour assassin had walked with a lighter step when they left.

Someday, Hakon hoped that the delights of the city would return. But that day was years away.

His more recent memories of Taunka were far less pleasant. Fighting within the city had been brutal. Archers camped out in high windows, raining down arrows on unsuspecting warriors. The tight alleys, sharp corners, and dark alcoves hid frequent ambushes. To drop your guard, even for a moment, invited a quick death.

And the tehoin had unleashed a destruction here the likes the empire had never seen. The strongest among them had no problem using teho to fell buildings like they were saplings. Any survivors who hoped to live here would be digging out bodies from under piles of rubble for months to come.

Hakon was certain his own nightmares would last just as long, or longer.

It was a city that held little but fear now. The battle for Taunka had been waged one street at a time, the front lines a constant, shifting mess. Hakon's last full night of sleep had been weeks ago.

Yesterday, though, they'd finally breached the walls of the imperial keep. The main forces of the rebel alliance had pushed forward in a suicidal charge, forcing Torsten and his imperials to commit to the defense of their last fortification. The band used the opportunity to break through the wall in a different location. Hakon didn't think he'd ever forget the look of achievement on Irric's face when he finally ripped through the last six inches of stone with a teho spear.

With the wall breached, victory had only been a matter of time. Rumors claimed that hundreds of rebel prisoners were being held in the imperial dungeon. If the band could free them, it would bolster their forces at a crucial moment. Even if they couldn't free the prisoners, the imperials were running out of warriors and land to defend.

Solveig joined Hakon as he stared into the ruins. "Do you think it's true?"

"Not even Torsten can think his way out of this," Hakon said. "But it doesn't matter. If his offer of a treaty is real, the war is over. If it isn't, we'll be there, and we'll end the war ourselves."

The messenger had arrived this morning, under a flag of truce. A promise of peace after years of war.

A memory, decades old, resurfaced. Torsten, visiting the band after the battle with the elder dragon. Nothing Hakon had learned of the man in the intervening years had changed his opinion of the stamfar. That he was brilliant was beyond question. Without Torsten's leadership, the empire would have fallen at least a year earlier against the overwhelming numerical advantages of the rebellion.

But the man had no heart. The whole world was nothing but a puzzle for him to unravel in the most efficient way possible. He didn't care about people. It probably didn't even occur to him that he should.

The crunch of boots over gravel caused both Hakon and Solveig to turn around. Groa, the rebellion's top general, stood there, wearing her cleanest uniform. She looked profoundly out of place. The rest of them were dusty and blood-soaked from the past days of battle. "Ready?" she asked.

Hakon nodded. "Orders?"

After years of war and matching wits with Torsten, Hakon always expected Groa to look more exhausted than she did. Somehow, the well of energy she drew from never dried out. Even today, she looked like she'd just risen from a long and relaxing sleep. If Hakon hadn't seen her meeting with her commanders just three hours ago, he might have believed it.

Her focus and will were the reason the rebellion stood to win.

No one else could have led them so successfully.

This morning, her eyes were sharp, and wary. But he thought he saw hope flicker within. "Protect me."

Hakon echoed the same question Solveig had just put to him. "Do you think it's true?"

Groa nodded. "If the fight goes on much longer, he won't have the strength to demand any concessions. I don't think he has any more tricks up his sleeve."

Solveig raised a doubting eyebrow at that, and Groa chuckled, a deep and throaty laugh. "Fair enough. I don't think he has any more tricks worth worrying about."

"He could be waiting for this moment to spring Isira on us," Hakon said. The young and mysterious stamfar had vanished months ago, and no one knew where she'd gone. Rumors claimed she and Torsten had argued, but Hakon would have been a fool to accept that without evidence.

"Possibly," Groa admitted. "But we can't not hear him out." She stopped the questions. "The time draws near. Gather the band, and be wary."

Hakon collected the others and met Groa near the edge of the camp. She brought a few clerks with her, but otherwise traveled alone. She saw no reason to risk her whole command structure on such a meeting. At this point, she trusted any of her generals to finish the fight she'd started.

They walked slowly. Ari transported ahead of them, scouting the area for potential ambushes. The streets of Taunka remained quiet. Those citizens who had both decided to remain and still survived hid deep in whatever holes they had created for protection.

Hakon struggled to maintain his spirits as they walked deeper into the destroyed city. His eyes searched for traps, but all he saw was evidence of the destruction he'd had no small part in creating. He believed, with his whole heart, they could build something better than the empire. A place where people could live free.

But there were plenty of days like today, when he questioned whether freedom was worth the cost they paid. If peace was actually at hand, he'd do anything to see it through.

Still, he was almost surprised, as they went deeper into the city, that more traps didn't await them. There were no proper battle lines here. The city had been fought over one neighborhood at a time. Eventually, though, they passed from an area where the rebellion largely held control to one frequented by Torsten's remaining loyalists.

Ari appeared in front of them. His face was twisted, a sight even more frightening on the normally implacable man. Hakon reached for his sword, but Ari appeared to be in no haste. Hakon let his arm drop back down by his side, stomach knotting.

Of course, Torsten would have something prepared. "What did you see?"

When Ari met Hakon's gaze, his eyes glistened. "Our friends."

Hakon pushed past Ari and into the next street. He froze as he understood the assassin's warning.

This last leg of the journey carried them along a tree-lined boulevard. Tall maples, planted dozens of years ago, ran up both sides of the street. In the autumn, this street was a wonder to behold. Gold and velvet leaves seemed to fill the sky. The harvest festival here was one of the greatest in the empire.

In the cold of winter, the trees had dropped their leaves. But they had acquired new, grotesque decorations.

From where Hakon stood all the way to their meeting place, the trees were lined with hanged bodies. They hung from short ropes, too short to offer the mercy of a quick death.

Torsten had ordered all the prisoners strangled. A slow, agonizing end. The signs of struggle were evident on every body nearby.

It didn't take much to imagine the scene. Torsten had to have done it last night. There'd been no whisper of this during the fighting the day before. He would have taken a few prisoners at a time, brought them out, bound and accompanied by more guards than they could hope to overpower. They might have struggled, but it didn't matter.

Hakon recognized faces. Men and women he'd fought beside over the years. A few he'd seen in the past week or so, no doubt captured recently.

Down the street, a tent had been erected, covered to protect those within from both the elements and observation. No doubt, Torsten was in there, smug grin on his face, waiting for them.

Three lines of imperial soldiers stood guard around the tent, but the boulevard was otherwise deserted. Crows pecked at the corpses.

Hakon drew his sword, but before he could advance a step, Groa's commanding voice stopped him. "No, friend."

She was the only one in the world he would have listened to at that moment, but even then, he almost broke away from her. He would kill them all. Anyone who had anything to do with this. The edges of his vision turned red.

Groa stepped beside him and put her hand on his wrist. He tore his gaze away from the tent and saw that her face was pale. Her hand trembled on his arm. Not in fear. Not Groa. Her rage was nearly as great as his, and that, more than even her order, kept him in place.

"This is the last sacrifice the rebellion makes," she said.

She gripped his arm more tightly. "If Torsten believes anything else, I promise I will unleash you and never ask you to stop again."

It was good enough for him.

Together, they walked toward the tent where Torsten waited for them, under the watchful eyes of vengeful ghosts.

BETRAYAL 3

"You squeeze that cup any harder, and that'll be the last pour you get from me," Irric said.

Hakon looked down at the battered cup in his hands. His knuckles were white around it, and he'd bent the pliable metal. He swore under his breath and tried to put the cup down on the table, only to realize he'd bent the bottom, too. Wine sloshed over his fingers and he picked the cup back up.

Following the conclusion of the treaty negotiations, the band had found an abandoned tavern in a relatively intact neighborhood. The door had been busted open long before, the owner nowhere to be found. But deep in the cellar, Meshell had sniffed out an unopened cask of wine.

The band had cracked it open about an hour ago.

The night should have been a celebration. In the streets outside, it was. The treaty wasn't signed yet. Groa still had to convince the rest of the generals, but the war was as good as done. The generals couldn't turn down Torsten's offer. As usual, Hakon had the feeling the stamfar was playing a completely different game than they were.

Most of the rebellion soldiers hadn't seen the boulevard, either. Word had spread, of course, but there was a world of difference between hearing about an atrocity and witnessing one firsthand. Hakon didn't begrudge the rebellion troops their celebrations. They'd earned tonight, and many more nights of celebration besides.

The band had broken open their own cask with the expectation of celebrating the victory, but not even Irric seemed in a mood to toast their exploits.

Whenever Hakon closed his eyes, he saw the bodies on the trees, followed immediately by the sight of Torsten negotiating the treaty as though nothing had happened, as though it was any other agreement.

Torsten had brought Damion to the negotiation, but the younger kolma's presence did little to restrain Hakon's bloodlust. Not drawing his sword was one of Hakon's greatest accomplishments of the war. And it was probably one that would be spoken of the least.

A knock at the door ripped the band from their collective reveries. Groa stood there. "Mind if I join you?"

"You're always welcome," Hakon answered.

Groa stepped in and took a seat at the long table the band shared. She was ahula, and yet one of the only people Hakon knew who showed no hesitation approaching them. Part of it, certainly, was the long years they'd spent together, but it was more than that. Somehow, she was the only ahula Hakon knew who could look past their legends to see the people beneath.

Irric poured her a cup of wine, and she took a long sip. "The other generals have agreed to the terms of Torsten's treaty. The official signing will be in two days."

"They didn't ask for anything more?" Solveig asked.

"No. The treaty will be accepted, word for word as Torsten presented it."

Hakon slammed his cup on the table. "We didn't fight for years for Torsten to declare final terms."

Groa took another long sip of her wine. Then she held out her cup for Irric to pour her another one. He obliged. "I agree. But this is Torsten. Every objection was predicted and accounted for. As much as I hate it, the treaty he presented is more reasonable than anything we would have created. If we're serious about granting freedom to the people, this is how we do it."

Hakon stood and paced. "What about Torsten?"

"He'll accept voluntary exile in Aysgarth."

"He should die," Hakon insisted.

"I argued for it," Groa said. "But the other generals disagree. His threat of Isira avenging him is too great a risk. The generals believe having him exiled beyond our lands will be sufficient."

Hakon closed his eyes, hoping to calm himself. Instead, he saw the hanged prisoners. He opened his eyes, cursed, and threw his cup against the wall.

The others watched, but did nothing to stop him.

Hakon resumed pacing, and Irric picked up the thread of the conversation. "I thought winning this would feel better."

Groa nodded. "I believe it will, in time. For now, the fighting and the horrors are still too fresh in our minds." She finished her second cup in another fast gulp, then set it down, waving off Irric's offer of a third. She stood. "I need to go and make the rounds among the others. But I wanted to let you all know, first. Thank you for the wine."

Groa walked to the door, but before she left, she turned around and addressed them all. "And thank you for everything else. I can't say what the future holds, but I do know that if not for all of you, the rebellion never would have succeeded. You've given us more than we can ever thank you for."

Her words dulled the sharp edge of Hakon's anger. She had a point. Despite everything, they'd won, and that was worth recognizing.

Groa left for more cheerful celebrations, and the band raised cups in her honor as she left.

Hakon returned to the table and sat down next to the others. An idea was forming in his mind, one he never would have uttered with Groa nearby. He leaned forward and spoke softly. "I think we should kill Torsten."

When no one responded, Hakon wondered if they'd heard him.

Then Solveig shook her head. "Out of the question."

"Why?"

"He needs to be alive to sign the treaty."

"Obviously. After."

"No."

Hakon pounded his fist on the table, then pointed vaguely in the direction of the boulevard. "Our friends are still hanging from the trees out there. He had no reason to kill them, especially knowing he was going to sue for peace this morning. He killed them out of spite, nothing more. Don't you think he deserves to die?"

Solveig didn't budge. "Absolutely. But he positioned himself in such a way that we can't kill him."

"Of course we can!"

"No one knows more about the workings of the empire than he does. He's promised to answer all our questions and help us establish the framework for our new governments. He's pledged to order all imperial loyalists to assist us. We might have won our freedom, but rebuilding the land will take years. With Torsten's help, we'll establish stability that much faster."

"The only work he'll do will eventually benefit him!" Hakon shouted. "It's all he's ever done. One subtle move at a time, he'll worm his way right back into power, and everything we fought for will be for nothing. Everything they died for will be for nothing."

"Then it will be up to us to build something better than the empire, something that doesn't give him the opportunity to return," Solveig argued. "Besides, if we even try to kill him, Isira will hunt us down."

"So he says," Hakon pointed out. "But she hasn't been seen in months. It feels like a bluff to me."

"Is it a bluff you're willing to call?" Solveig asked.

It was the first question that made Hakon doubt. They'd had a few run-ins with Isira over the years. The only reason they lived was that she wasn't much of a warrior. But her strength was terrifying. Whenever they scuffled, it was the band that ended up retreating with their tails between their legs.

Without a better argument, he turned to the others. "What about you all? What do you think? Ari, certainly you'd love another opportunity to assassinate a stamfar?"

"I would," Ari admitted. He slowly spun his cup between his fingers. "And few would be a more satisfying kill. But I'm afraid I agree with Solveig. Assassinating Torsten is likely to hurt more people than it will help."

Irric chimed in. "He's promised us peace, Hakon. And I'm tired of fighting. I don't trust him, but if he offers us a way forward, I'm not going to endanger that. I won't move against him unless I'm convinced he poses an imminent threat."

Hakon turned to Meshell. If anyone in the band would agree with him, it was her. They saw the world the same. For a long time, she was silent. "I also want him dead. But to kill him now would be an act of naked revenge. We need to give him a chance to help us establish the new government."

Her answer broke his heart.

He buried his disappointment, though. They'd all see soon enough he was right, and then they'd make their move.

For tonight, though, he stood up, got himself another cup, and let Irric pour him a glass of wine.

BETRAYAL 4

After years of fighting that had felt like lifetimes, the next several months passed so quickly that Hakon sometimes felt as though they were a dream flashing from one scene to the next.

The band couldn't have known it at the time, but that somber night in the destroyed tavern was one of their last nights together. With the rebellion officially over and no single government yet in charge, there was little need for the band.

Solveig became involved in the formation of the new governments. She was the real reason the band never suffered from a lack of supplies, and her mind was naturally organized. When Hakon spoke with her, he couldn't help but notice the enthusiasm in her demeanor. She had found a calling, a task that made her eyes sparkle when she recounted the steps they'd taken to found what was to be six separate states, each with their own governor.

Peace suited her. As strong a warrior as she was, it was the exercise of her mind that brought her the most satisfaction. It also gave her a chance to be the leader she naturally was.

Irric, to no one's surprise, became a weapons instructor. Rumors claimed he gave personal lessons to almost as many women at night as he did students during the day.

Ari returned to the shadows that were his natural home. Sometimes, Hakon wondered out loud if Ari had been raised in some deep cavern. Solveig claimed to have some knowledge of his activities, but Hakon heard nothing.

He and Meshell remained together. They patrolled the western frontier, continuing the fight against the wilds. Humans might have stopped killing humans, but the wild never relented. The years of rebellion had been particularly brutal for the frontier settlers, as soldiers and resources had been pulled from the borders to the interior of the empire.

Humanity had lost ground against the wild, but Hakon hoped they would eventually recover it and more. During the day, he and Meshell drove back shadow wolves, bears, and predatory birds. Occasionally they clashed with a wandering dragon, though those were rare. Most had been driven far to the west in the days of the empire, to wherever they came from.

At night, they would build their campsite and talk about what came next. The frontier was a fine place to be, but they weren't sure they wanted to spend their lives there. But they were in no rush. For now, the peace held.

At least for others.

Hakon held onto his hatred of Torsten. Some nights, with Meshell sleeping next to him, he tried to let go. It was in the past, and as the rest of the band had insisted, back in that tavern, he was helping the world return to normal.

He suspected Torsten was winning the others over. Though the development of the new governments wasn't easy, no one could claim Torsten had failed on his end of the bargain. Hakon listened closely to news from across the former empire, and Torsten had been nothing except a model of a man dignified even in exile.

Seven months after the signing of the treaty, Hakon and Meshell ended up joining an expedition to Aysgarth. Torsten had apparently promised supplies for the struggling border towns, and the travelers needed protection from the wilds between the frontier and Aysgarth's location high in the mountains.

The first time Hakon saw Aysgarth, he almost couldn't believe his eyes. The forested valley was being cleared for farmland, and a fortress was being built into the side of the mountain.

Hakon kept his distance from Torsten, afraid that he wouldn't be able to still his sword again should they meet. He skipped the meals welcoming the caravan to Aysgarth, opting instead to explore the area.

He recognized a stronghold when he saw one. Torsten might be in exile, but he'd brought along no small number of followers, and there were soldiers everywhere in the valley. Before long, this place would be even more secure than the keep in Taunka. Hakon left with a growing sense of unease.

Torsten had gotten off too easy.

Others forgot that Torsten was stamfar, and effectively immortal. He hadn't surrendered. He'd only delayed his dreams. Aysgarth wasn't exile. It was the capital from which he would eventually launch another assault.

It was all so clear to Hakon.

The caravan left three days after it had arrived, laden with gold from Aysgarth's mines and seed for the upcoming year. Hakon sometimes caught himself staring at the wagons. Torsten had bought himself an enormous amount of goodwill with this caravan, and he was helping.

That was what Torsten did. Somehow, he managed to put you in a position where no matter what you did, you were helping him.

He kept his fears to himself, but when they returned to the six states, Hakon sent a messenger to Solveig, asking if they could meet together as a band once again.

She put it together for him.

THE FIRE CRACKLED and threw up sparks, illuminating the space that had once been their training ground. Weeds had grown through the cracks in the stone, and Hakon couldn't shake the feeling that the ghosts of the past watched them here. What would the younger versions of themselves think of the people they'd become?

For a while, the reunion had been jovial. They'd all enjoyed catching up on the exploits of the others. But eventually the small talk had subsided, and they were left staring into the flames.

"So," Solveig asked, "why bring us here?"

Hakon saw little point in playing coy. "Torsten."

Solveig shook her head. "We talked about this."

Hakon held out his hands, begging them for patience. "Meshell and I just returned from Aysgarth, and I saw things that were very concerning."

That caught the attention of the others.

"Just give me a few minutes, and I think you'll agree." When no one objected, Hakon told them of their visit, of the fortifications he'd studied and of the soldiers training there. He finished with the inescapable conclusion. "Torsten didn't actually surrender. He's just biding his time."

His case made, he gave the others time to agree with him.

Instead, Irric just laughed. "I'm sorry, Hakon, I really am. But really? Of course he's building a fortress. Aysgarth is the farthest into the wild anyone has ever built, and I'm sure it'll be visited by dragons soon."

"Already has," Solveig confirmed.

"And the same goes for soldiers. I've been in that valley, and if he wants to develop it at all, it's going to require a significant force to hold against the wild," Irric finished.

"That's not what it looks like to me," Hakon said.

Irric's smile fell. "The war's over, friend. You need to let it go."

Hakon let his gaze travel around the circle. He didn't need to ask the others what they thought, for their expressions said enough. They looked at him with pity, as if he was the one who was somehow misguided.

How could they not see? He felt his rage, so familiar and yet absent these last seven months, build again.

He stood up, not wanting to unleash that on his friends. "The war's not over until Torsten's dead." He marched out of the training area into the cool night air. Trees lined the road leading from the main gate, and Hakon imagined the bodies hanging from the limbs. He knew he was right, but how could he convince others to see the truth?

Meshell approached him a few minutes later. She let her company be enough, and eventually he shook his head. "I'm so sure of it."

"You might be right," Meshell said.

Hakon started. "You believe me?"

She shook her head. "I do. I don't trust Torsten, and would sleep better at night if I knew he was dead. Perhaps, someday far in the future, he might try something again. I wouldn't put it past him. So, yes, you might be right."

"But?"

"But for now there's peace. It's not perfect, but all across the six states, people are returning to their normal lives. Loyal imperialists are a big part of that recovery. I don't think you understand that if you even try to kill Torsten, it puts everything we've fought for at risk. We're slowly building this delicate glass structure and you want to throw it at the ground and see if it'll shatter."

Hakon swallowed her rebuke. It carried more weight than the others. "I do understand. But I'm also looking out farther than the rest of you. The greatest threat to peace is Torsten. Maybe we get a brief respite, but he will destroy our efforts. The pain of transition might be difficult, but it's the only lasting path to the world we want to build."

"You're not going to try to kill him without us, are you?"

Hakon wondered if she knew how close she was to the truth.

The foundation of their relationship had always been honesty. When they fought as often as they had, there was little point in deceit. There was never any telling when the final battle might happen, and they both believed it best to pass to the gates without regrets. The practice had served them well from the very beginning of their relationship.

But no matter how hard he tried, he didn't think he'd ever convince the others. It only left him one option, ugly as it was.

He met her gaze, his decision made. "No," he lied.

CHAPTER 26

Hakon continued his story, but Zachary found himself losing interest. Hakon had prepared for Torsten's assassination relentlessly, telling no one of his plans. Zachary wondered if the others had suspected. Based on their reactions, he didn't think so.

They sat woodenly, looking anywhere but at the man who had once led them.

The distance between him and the band had never felt wider. Not because of the time or strength that separated them, but the way they lived their lives. Growing up, direct truth was far rarer than gold. Tutors gave him good marks, regardless of his actual ability, to please his father. He never knew whether the boys he played with were friends or not. Did they enjoy his company, or were they only enduring his presence in the hope that one day they might advise someone high in the courts?

Years of uncertainty had built a shield around his heart. Finding someone honest, someone who didn't care about the trappings of his station, someone like Cliona, was the exception. Had he been in the place of one of the band, he might have been momentarily hurt by Hakon's betrayal, but it would have been one of a thousand shallow cuts.

Not so for the legendary warriors.

They had trusted, and maybe for the first time, Zachary caught a glimpse of what that actually meant. That he had lied to them, repeatedly, still broke their hearts over a hundred years after the fact.

What would it be like, to trust someone so completely? To expose yourself to such an injury?

He couldn't say. No doubt, that trust was part of the reason the band had accomplished as much as it had. But it had brought tragedy as well as triumph.

Zachary saw, too, the weakness in Hakon. The man never did anything in half measures. Back then, he'd been unable to move past the horrors of the war. It couldn't be over for him until Torsten died. Just like his search for Cliona might never end.

Hakon told of his eventual assault on Aysgarth. How he'd slaughtered guards by the dozens, and how he'd dueled with Damion high on Aysgarth's walls. He'd almost killed the other kolma then, but when Damion had fallen, broken, from the height of the walls, Hakon hadn't pursued. A small choice in the moment, but one that would have dire consequences over a hundred years later.

"And that's the story," Hakon said. "I went into hiding after. But Isira found us and imprisoned us, and we disappeared into myth."

Zachary frowned, risking a glance toward the stamfar. "But that doesn't explain why you won't help us now."

Hakon pulled at the collar of his tunic, looking decidedly uncomfortable. "Well, you see..." He trailed off, looking to Isira to save him from having to explain.

"I loved Torsten," Isira stated simply.

Zachary swallowed hard and suddenly decided he really didn't need to know any more.

Isira took up Hakon's story. "As Hakon said, Torsten and I parted ways before the end of the rebellion. I still loved him, but I lacked his conviction, his belief the world could be made right. I'd seen firsthand the cost of the war, and the longer it continued, the more I came to believe it, along with all human endeavors, was ultimately pointless. I chose to remove myself from the fight, and, as much as I was able, from the world."

"If that's true, why come back to imprison the band?" The question came from Valdis.

"Mostly, because Torsten deserved justice. He'd finally authored a treaty, and before the year was done, was dead. But also because I believed that humanity would be better off without the band."

"How?" Zachary asked.

Isira bit her lower lip. "Torsten had already realized, even back then, that teho was slipping away from humanity's grasp. Those with the power we called kolma weren't born anymore. Even those who were tehoin, who had the strength we now know as nelja, were less common than before. Torsten worried that within a handful of generations, there might not be any tehoin alive. It was a belief that motivated him, because he believed the order of the empire was the best way to organize what strength humanity had left. It was also one of the reasons I'm sure he surrendered. He couldn't stand the sight of tehoin killing other tehoin."

The stamfar paused, considering her next words. "I disagreed. Before the rebellion I was like Torsten, placing my faith in the strength of tehoin. But I walked one too many battlefields where a handful of kolma had slaughtered a far greater number of ahula." She glanced pointedly at the band. "I came to believe, and I still believe, that tehoin shouldn't use their power. That it's not natural. That our deaths, when they come, will only be best for humanity. And perhaps, I'm not that different from Ava in wondering if this planet wouldn't be better without any humans around."

"So why didn't you just kill them?" Valdis asked. "We know you could."

"Because Torsten wouldn't have wanted me to," Isira answered.

Zachary wasn't the only person at the table blinking in disbelief.

Isira explained. "Had my decision been my own, I might have killed them and called it justice. But Torsten always had a measure of respect for the band. They fascinated him, the way they always completed assignments he thought would kill them. He believed, even as the band tore his beloved empire to shreds, they would have a role to play in the future of humanity."

Isira took a sip of wine. "Imprisoning the band was a compromise between my desire to kill them and Torsten's spirit."

"Then why did you release them?" Again, the pointed question came from Valdis, who sounded more and more frustrated with Isira's decisions.

"Because of Damion. He made me realize that no matter what I did with the band, I couldn't stop humanity from destroying itself. I saw him gathering strength in the west, and I saw history begin to repeat once again. War was coming, and Damion's would have been worst of all, because it would have pitted tehoin against ahula. So I released the band, one at a time, with a promise they wouldn't use their power to rule the six states. Then I retreated, wanting nothing to do with any of what followed."

Zachary leaned back, digesting everything he'd learned.

This was more of a mess than he realized. Valdis hated the band and wanted Hel's leadership of the council as her own. The band feared Isira, and Isira didn't want anything to do with any of them.

What hope did they have against Ava? It was a small miracle they weren't drawing their weapons against one another in this room, and they were all ostensibly on the same side.

For a moment, Zachary let himself wallow in despair. How fragile was humanity, that a single stamfar could be such a threat?

He forced the thoughts aside with a vicious shake of his head. It didn't matter. No matter what they faced, they would stand up to it. Even if it meant his death, better to die standing up than die in despair. "So, what do we do?"

Isira stood from her place at the table. "Whatever you want."

She turned to leave. To Zachary's amazement, the others didn't stop her. Zachary, too, watched as she left and shut the door behind her. The sight of the door closing broke the spell holding him in place. He was out of his chair and racing around the table when Irric's grip arrested his motion.

"Better you let her go. She's impetuous at the best of times, and I don't think sitting through Hakon's story made her any friendlier."

"That's a risk I'm willing to take."

Irric shrugged, then let him go. Zachary charged out the door, catching a brief glimpse of Isira before she turned a corner. He ran after her, then almost collided with her when he turned the corner himself. She had stopped and waited for him. Her stare was colder than the glaciers atop the highest mountains. "What do you want?"

"I don't believe you," he said.

One of her eyelids twitched, and Zachary almost dove back behind the corner for cover. But there was no point stopping a charge halfway through. "I think you care about humanity. And we need you, more than we ever have. We don't have the power to fight Ava."

Isira turned her back without answering.

"What about when everyone is dead? What will you do then?"

"Enjoy the quiet," she said.

"She'll come for you. Though you don't seem to believe it, you're a part of humanity, too."

"And then I will die. I've lived long enough." There was something in her answer, an emotion Zachary couldn't quite pin down.

She kept walking away, but Zachary couldn't let it go. Perhaps he had more in common with Hakon than he cared to admit. He shouted after her. "If you don't help, you'll be worse than Hakon when he betrayed his friends. At least he believed in something."

His words froze her in her tracks.

He never saw the blow. Her teho manifested and flew at him before he could react. She launched him off his feet. By the time he'd stumbled to a stop and returned to his feet, she was gone.

WHEN ZACHARY RETURNED to the meeting room, his mood was already dark. As he opened the door, he was greeted by several voices trying to shout over one another. He stood there, door open, unable to believe what he was seeing.

"We need to return!" Hakon shouted. "We know the dragons are linked to Ava, somehow."

Valdis stood on the other side of the table. "You simply want to abandon us to die!" She pointed an accusing finger at Hakon.

Hel shouted, too, but her voice was drowned out by the others.

He only watched for a few moments, but that was enough. Teeth grinding, he formed several small teho darts, then flung them at the table.

Irric cast a lazy teho shield between Zachary and the others, stopping Zachary's attack without problem. But it did have the desired effect of quieting the table.

"Sit," he commanded Valdis. She was halfway to her chair before she remembered he had no authority here. She sat down anyway, so as not to appear foolish.

Isira had broken something in him. Not a bone, but some sense of restraint that had held him back these past months.

Like her, he just didn't care anymore.

"Grow up!" Zachary said.

He knew lecturing this group was the height of foolishness. Anyone in this room could kill him without breaking much of a sweat. But he'd been pushed too far. "Between Ava, dragons, and the wild, humanity isn't just in trouble. We're on the edge of extinction. And none of you seem to remember that."

Hakon opened his mouth to respond, but Zachary stopped him with a glare. "No. You're more concerned with finding a ghost than you are with the future of humanity.

What's in the past is past. Painful as it is, this is our one chance to save ourselves."

Zachary strode toward the table. His initial outburst hadn't been planned, but now that he had their attention, he would use it. His mind worked again. For all his father's mistakes, he'd raised Zachary to handle situations exactly like this. "First, let's list the problems. Ava is one. The dragons are another."

"Food for Aysgarth," Hel added.

That problem seemed easy to solve. "There's plenty of food in the six states. I know none of the court in Mygar are going hungry."

Valdis scoffed. "And they're just going to give it away?"

"No," Zachary answered. "In exchange we'll need units of your tehoin to help guard our walls, to provide some basic defense against Ava and the dragons."

"You can't promise that," Valdis said.

"Actually, he can," Hel replied. "He'll be a leader among the court as soon as he returns. If anyone can forge such a deal, it's him."

"We can't defend you against either Ava or the dragons," Valdis said. "And why would we defend you when our home is here?"

"You're more than we have now." Zachary thought back to Hakon's story, how the young warrior had realized war was different for tehoin. His own experiences bore that out. They could have it both ways. "You don't even need to walk the walls. We just need to agree that you would transport tehoin to our cities in case of an attack."

Valdis didn't look convinced, but she stopped arguing. He'd count that as a victory for now.

"And us?" Hakon asked.

Zachary considered that for a moment. Then he shrugged. "Up to you. Obviously, your help will be appreciated wherever you decide to lend your strength. Maybe you can find out a way to kill Ava. That would solve one of our problems, at least, and no one else around here has a better chance."

Though he couldn't believe it, they were listening. He didn't delude himself into thinking it would last long, but it was a step. It had given him a chance to say what he needed to. His frustration had blown away.

The discussion shifted. They accepted the broad outline of his plan and started debating the details. They would fight. He would help them find the way.

And it also determined his own future.

When there was a break in the discussion he made another announcement.

"I'll start packing my things," he said. "It's time for me to return home."

CHAPTER 27

"Kid's got some spirit," Irric observed.

Meshell snorted. "He's lucky Isira didn't give him any more than bruises. Thought for sure she'd break every bone in his body."

"He'd probably still talk, even with a broken jaw," Ari said.

Hakon laughed at that. "Say what you will about him, he spoke true. Got us to put aside our differences, at least for a bit."

Even after Zachary had left the room, the conversation had remained productive. Hel asked for permission to be named Aysgarth's representative to the six states, so that she could accompany Zachary and hopefully strike a deal in Mioska. Valdis readily agreed, once Hel promised to install her as the temporary head of the Aysgarth council while Hel was gone.

Hakon worried about that choice, but he also believed circumstances forced Valdis' hand. Though the woman might want to kill them, she couldn't until Aysgarth was on more stable footing.

Only one pressing problem remained. It was the reason the band had reconvened in Solveig and Ari's room. They passed a pitcher of wine around, and Hakon couldn't help but think of that broken tavern from so long ago.

"I suppose you're going to try to convince us to explore a den of dragons, right?" Solveig asked Hakon.

Hakon scratched at the back of his neck. "I was."

Solveig extended her arms wide as she leaned back. Then she made a show of drinking a sizable portion of wine. "Very well. Make your argument."

"I believe Cliona is alive, inside the dragon we met at Husavik. I know it's in that den, because I heard it while Meshell and I were there. I felt it in my own teho. And even if all that is false, we still need answers about what is happening with the dragons. They're connected to Ava."

He supposed he could surround his argument with fancy words, the way scholars liked to. But among his friends, there was no point. It wouldn't have helped back then, and it didn't today.

"Is that it?" Ari asked.

Hakon nodded.

"Really thought you'd be talking for longer," Ari said. "Poured myself a full glass."

"Is there any way of killing Ava? Something more sensible than us investigating a den of dragons?" Solveig asked Ari.

The assassin considered his cup. "There's always a way. Her flesh should be easy enough to pierce. She's wary, though, and sensitive to teho. I might succeed one chance out of five."

Solveig looked to the others. "Do we risk the dragons?"

Hakon had arguments, but he bit his lip. He'd only be repeating facts the others already knew.

No one answered, and the minutes passed in silence. Then Meshell finished her glass with one long swig. "Oh, why not? I was getting bored anyway."

Irric raised an eyebrow at that, but let the observation pass without comment. "I've always wanted to ride a dragon the way Hakon did above Husavik. If you promise me that, I'm in."

Hakon rolled his eyes. "I'll see what I can do."

Solveig's and Ari's gazes met, and the two of them held a silent conversation. Eventually, Ari gave the slightest of nods.

"I guess that's it, then," Solveig said. "I'll let the council know."

"Force them to let me transport back here," Ari said. "Otherwise I'm not going to be much use if they need us quickly."

"Agreed," Solveig said. "I'll tell them we plan on taking the fight to the dragons, but if the battle goes poorly, we'll transport back here."

"They might not take kindly to us just leaving," Irric said. "They do want us to guard their walls."

"They don't tell us what to do," Solveig answered. "Besides, if Hakon is right, there's a chance our fight saves them anyway." She stood. "No point delaying the inevitable. I'll go talk to Valdis."

Ari stood to accompany her.

"I don't need a guard," she said.

He shrugged and followed her anyway.

Solveig's departure marked the end of their gathering. Irric returned to his own room, and Hakon asked Meshell if she wouldn't mind joining him on a walk around the walls of Aysgarth. She agreed, and they climbed the stairs until they reached the top of one level of the fortress.

The sun was setting on what had proven to be a long day. Though most of what he'd done was sit in a chair and talk, digging up the past had leeched the strength from his limbs. By the time he reached an overlook, he felt as though he'd climbed a high peak. He rested his arms on the stone wall and looked over the valley.

Despite the damage, the tehoin of Aysgarth soldiered on. Though the hour was late, the sounds of hammers, chisels, and axes filled the air. The dragons might destroy, but humans would always rebuild.

"What's on your mind?" Meshell asked.

"I had hoped never to have to tell that story again. Thought I might have to tell Cliona at some point, but never imagined I'd have to confess to everything publicly. Got me thinking."

She leaned on the wall next to him and waited.

"First, I'm sorry—"

She cut him off. "I don't care."

Hakon swallowed. Lost in his own shame, he'd forgotten the story might have been just as painful for the others.

"All I want to know is that you'll never break your word again," Meshell said. "All I need to know is that I can trust you."

Hakon wanted to blurt out that she could, of course, but it wasn't so simple. "This feels an awful lot like then," he confessed.

She nodded. He wasn't surprised the same thought had occurred to her.

"You don't believe me, not really." The truth felt like a cut against his skin, but better the injury now than a mortal wound later. The band might be back together, but they weren't whole, not like they had been before he'd lied to all of them.

"Can you blame us?" Meshell asked.

He couldn't. He understood how they viewed him. Understood that the claims he made sounded like the ravings of a parent consumed by grief.

And he was. He swore he saw Cliona whenever he turned around. By now he was almost used to expecting to see her, then suffering the disappointment of realizing he was mistaken.

His hope was a thin thread. A series of guesses tied together by the slimmest shreds of evidence. Still, the feeling in his heart was that he was right, and he didn't believe it was just wishful thinking.

Of course, any parent would probably feel the same in his place.

"I don't want to be forced to choose between you and the band, and her," Hakon said.

"Because you know you'd choose her," Meshell said.

"How could I not? She's my daughter."

"You're still thicker than these walls," Meshell said, rapping her knuckles against the stone.

"Huh?"

She sighed. "It's not about what side you choose. Never has been. It's about telling the truth about your choice. Of course you'll choose Cliona. If you didn't, you'd be a terrible father. Just don't pretend to us you might set her aside for our sakes."

He reached out and took her hand. He felt the calluses on her palm, felt the strength in her grip. "You'd think after all these years I'd learn something approaching wisdom."

"You'd think."

He kept holding her hand as they looked out over the valley. "So, you ready to explore a nest of dragons?"

She grinned. "For all your shortcomings, dear, I will say this: life is far more exciting when you're around."

CHAPTER 28

Hel transported them to a location about five miles away from Mioska. She claimed Aysgarth maintained closer transport locations, but there had been some concern about letting Zachary learn of them.

He didn't mind, ignoring the fact Aysgarth's secrecy was due to their former plans to conquer the six states. Plans some had difficulty letting go of. His destination was his family's estates, but he hoped to wander a bit before arriving. His father was the sort of man who defined reality by his own terms, and once Zachary entered his sphere of influence, his perception would be colored. Better to study Mioska with his own eyes first.

The walk from the transport location to one of the main roads leading into Mioska was a short one, and they soon joined a steady flow of travelers journeying towards the largest city in the six states. Their light packs were an unusual sight among the merchants and the farmers, but Zachary didn't see anyone too interested in either of them.

The road was a familiar one. Though Zachary's father

rarely left Mioska, he'd frequently sent Zachary on short trading routes with trusted merchants. At the time, Zachary had believed he was learning everything he needed to know to one day take over his father's projects. With the benefit of hindsight, he suspected the trips had been a way for his father to kick him out of the house for a few weeks at a time, hoisting the responsibility of raising his son on lesser allies and merchants who sought favor.

The road hadn't changed much in the years Zachary had been gone. After his time along the frontier and at Aysgarth, the familiarity of the scene jarred against his sense of propriety. He understood that the concerns of the frontier were distant, but this was as though he'd jumped from the world of the present to the world of the past. Though some of the shops along the road had changed owners and names, everything was just as it was in his memories. More than once he even saw collections of children playing out in the fields.

It was as if the wilds didn't matter a bit.

They ate lunch at a shop about a mile from the city walls. Tables sat outside, with nothing and no one protecting them. He had yet to see a single tehoin standing guard. Both he and Hel enjoyed the sandwiches, and Zachary let his attention wander from table to table.

Two merchants to his left were discussing rates they hoped to earn at the open markets. A farmer and his wife behind Zachary were traveling to Mioska to finalize the sale of their land to a neighbor. A few tables away, a young woman sat and watched the scene with a sharp eye, sketching the scenery with a stick of charcoal. Her hand moved with smooth, confident strokes.

"How long has it been since you've been here?" he asked Hel.

"Last year, just before Husavik. I was escorting a cartographer."

Zachary figured that with Hel alone, he might get answers he wouldn't otherwise. "How close was Damion to invading the six states?"

"Not very. Defeating the ahula armies wasn't necessarily the hard part. We might have been able to do that. It might not mean much to you, but Damion didn't want to "conquer" the six states. He wanted to bring them together as an empire, and he knew he didn't have the strength to control them. He learned that lesson from the rebellion well enough. That was why he sought statehood for Aysgarth, searched for Ava, and why he tried to kill any kolma who stood in his way. He intended to use every path possible to seize control."

Zachary wasn't sure he saw much of a difference. But, if it had held Damion's hand from rash action, he wouldn't question it.

"He was right, you know," she said.

"Who?"

"Hakon. This came from Damion, so that's probably worth remembering, but I'd heard Damion speak about how Aysgarth was always meant to be the place where the empire rebuilt its strength. Eventually, Torsten would have tried to reclaim the empire, had Hakon not intervened."

Zachary wondered if that would make any difference to Hakon or the others. He suspected, in the intervening years, the fact that Hakon had been right mattered little. Regardless, he'd lied to his friends.

They finished their meal. The whole time, Zachary hadn't even heard a whisper about events at the frontier. Considering it hadn't been that long since a dragon had appeared over Vispeda, that was a useful piece of information.

There was no trouble at the gates. Though guards stood watch, there was no attempt to control the flow of people in and out of the walls. They stepped through the gates and into yet another world.

He noticed the noise first. Merchants near the gate loudly proclaimed their wares, and Zachary heard so many smithies at work he wondered if an army was about to march. He pushed past the crowds near the gates, ducking into familiar alleys that looked exactly the same as he remembered them. He began to doubt that he'd been gone for years.

Hel followed as he left the bustle behind. The deeper one got into the city, the quieter it became.

At least for a while. If they continued traveling east they would eventually find themselves at the harbor, the only place that rivaled the gates for noise and activity.

The harbor could wait for now. He navigated the turns with ease, Hel close on his heels. Eventually, she noticed they weren't heading for his family estates. "You have a destination in mind?"

"An inn, run by an old friend."

"Not sure we have time for reunions."

"We do for this one."

As Zachary had hoped, the inn still stood, and although the sign had been repainted since he last visited, the name on the front told him that ownership hadn't changed. That was good.

Though he would have preferred a more dramatic entrance, he pushed the door open gently and gestured for Hel to enter first. All eyes would be on her, which might prove useful.

The interior was brightly lit, and the tables and floors were impressively clean.

Sometimes the dirtiest business took place in the tidiest rooms.

Given that it was the middle of the afternoon, there were almost no customers within. A short, thin man stood behind the bar, cleaning its already pristine surface to a shine. Zachary's hope that Hel might distract the innkeeper only lasted a moment. His sharp eyes examined her for a moment, then turned to him.

Seeing them go wide was worth the trip alone.

The mask only slipped for a moment, and then Ingolf was all business once again. "Didn't think I'd ever see you here again." Zachary didn't think he imagined the corner of Ingolf's lips turning up in the barest hint of a smile. "Though I suppose there's been some rumors in the air."

"Care to tell me about them?" Zachary sidled up to the bar.

"Maybe. You here to kill your old man or save him?"

"Not save him. Undecided on the first part. How bad is it?"

Ingolf shook his head. "Don't think you can afford my rates anymore." He poured two glasses of ale and slid them across the bar.

Like the city itself, Ingolf didn't change. The man lived on information the way others did on food and drink. He never parted with any unless some was offered in return. Zachary made a show of being reluctant to spill his secrets, but this was a dance they'd done dozens of times. "I'm here to take my father's place."

"That's either the bravest thing you've ever done or the most foolish."

"So, how bad is it?" Zachary repeated.

"Bad. Your old man is hanging on, but it's costing him every favor he's built up over the years. The other nobles are circling him like shadow wolves around an injured deer. They know he doesn't have long left, and your brother is as ignorant as always. Spends more time thinking about clothes and parties than he does the great game."

That had always been Ingolf's term for it. The constantly shifting alliances of nobles and powers that ruled Mioska, and in turn, a large part of the six states.

Zachary hadn't missed the game. In fact, he hated it almost as much as his younger brother ignored it. The simplicity and struggle of frontier life held a much greater appeal. But if playing the game could help the six states, Zachary intended to play once again.

And if he played, he intended to win.

He leaned forward. "Tell me everything."

CHAPTER 29

Hakon sat on a bench, wringing his hands together. Sleep had eluded him last night. Whenever he had closed his eyes he was back at the structure, the dragons circling far overhead. He heard the dragon roar as if it were in the room with him.

Eventually he'd given up. He'd grabbed his gear and climbed to the top levels of Aysgarth, watching the sun rise over the mountain peaks. The air was cold, and Hakon basked in the feeling.

This journey instilled a sense of finality in his heart. Soon, he would have answers to the questions that had torn him apart for the better part of a year. And if it ended up being the last journey he would take, well, that was fine, too. He'd lived a far longer life than was allotted to most, and he felt little need to extend it farther.

By the time the sun was high over the peaks, Hakon felt at ease. His heart beat steady.

As the time of their departure neared, he left the high places of Aysgarth and dropped into its bowels, where their transport locations had been built. He was still the first of the band to arrive, so he passed the time on the bench, his anticipation growing with every minute.

Meshell was the first to arrive, followed soon after by the others.

"Thanks," he said.

"You promised a dragon ride," Irric replied. "You better not disappoint."

A grin crept across Hakon's face. "I think you'll be suitably impressed."

After one last check of their gear, they joined hands and Hakon closed his eyes.

I'm coming.

As always, there was no sensation of movement when they traveled from one place to another. Hakon knew Ari had transported them thanks to the fresh breeze on his face, as well as Irric swearing under his breath. "Impressed yet?" he asked.

"What is this?" the swordsman asked.

Ari's transport point was almost underneath the structure, and all of them craned their heads to take the sight in. No one had an answer to Irric's question, though. Hakon had held out some slim hope that Solveig, once she saw it, might have an idea. But she was as speechless as the rest of them. Not even her libraries had the answers, then.

"Let's find out," Meshell said. She led them to the door she'd found earlier, and it opened at her touch. Torches were lit and passed around, and one by one they clambered into the structure.

They'd argued, briefly, about this last night. Hakon wanted to march straight to the mountains, but the others had outvoted him. Between the lack of damage and the proximity to the dragons' den, the others wondered if there was a connection between the structure and the dragons.

Besides, they were curious, and none of them could be convinced that spending a few hours exploring the structure would matter one way or another.

Hakon's objections faded the moment he climbed into the structure. Torchlight illuminated a long hallway, the walls smoother than even the constructions of the stamfar. Hakon ran his fingertips along the wall. The material felt like nothing he'd ever touched, either. It was solid, but was neither stone nor steel.

Meshell and Solveig were focused on a portion of the wall that looked different than the rest. There were symbols, and Solveig was trying to read them.

Hakon joined them, though the symbols meant absolutely nothing to him. "What do you think they are?"

"They are very similar to the texts of the early stamfar," Solveig said, "which, unfortunately, I can't read. If Cliona were here, she might be able to."

Meshell reached for the symbols, and though Solveig objected, pushed one.

Nothing happened.

Solveig sighed in relief. "You need to be more careful! You have no idea what they might do."

Meshell shrugged and pushed another symbol.

Light erupted from strips of the ceiling.

Irric yelped in surprise, earning judgmental looks from the rest of the band. "Sorry," he said, blushing slightly. "I wasn't expecting that."

"Teho?" Hakon asked. He'd seen similar lights in old stamfar structures, powered by a small infusion of teho.

Meshell shook her head. "It's like the door outside. Whatever causes it, it isn't teho."

Ari snuffed out his torch. "Guess we won't be needing these for now."

"Hold onto them," Solveig said. "I'm not quite ready to trust these lights yet."

No one argued with that.

They explored the structure together. The odd angle complicated matters. It was clear the structure was designed to be horizontal, and the angle was steep enough they were either half-slipping down the slope or struggling back up. But the material on the floors gripped well against their boots, so except for a few embarrassing falls there were no major problems.

They found more symbols at regular intervals, as well as symbols next to every door. A bit of study revealed that one symbol opened doors. Another closed them, and the third, when it appeared, made a sound on the other side of the door that reminded Hakon a little of a bell.

Most of the rooms appeared to be living quarters. There were bunks and desks, the functions easily recognizable, even if the design was unlike any Hakon had ever seen.

Generally, they moved downward, toward whatever had once been the front of the structure. Their search was largely fruitless. The rooms that weren't living spaces appeared to be storage rooms or small workspaces. It wasn't until they explored deeper toward the interior of the structure that they encountered more mysteries.

There was one room that wouldn't open to their touch. It had the same symbols as any other room, but when they pressed the "open" button, all it did was growl at them with a harsh buzzing sound. They briefly considered trying to force the door open, but decided against it.

They continued on, opening all other doors as they went.

Irric led the way. He opened a door, but instead of

glancing briefly as he usually did, he froze in place. His eyes went wide.

The others crowded behind him, and their reactions were variations on a theme. Instead of a small room, Irric had opened a door on a large chamber. Inside the chamber were cylinders, forms that all of them had seen before, and that none of them had fond memories of.

They were the same types of cylinders Isira had once forced them into. The places where they had spent dozens of years in captivity, locked in dreams that never ended. The same type of cylinder that had once held Ava, and even now most likely held Cliona's body.

Hakon guessed there were about forty, lined up in nice rows. All were open, and there was no sign of anyone.

"What is this place?" Ari whispered.

No one had any answer for that question, either. They wandered up and down the chamber, but nothing provided them the clues they so desperately sought. There was a door on the other side of the chamber, which they used to exit the space.

The sight of the cylinders had cast a pall over their exploration. They continued up the structure, but barely glanced into the rooms they opened. Eventually, they reached the top. Hakon stepped into one of the rooms with a window that faced the mountains.

A mile away, dragons flew in the air, circling their mountain. Protecting it from intruders.

Hakon watched, ignoring the others as they found places to sit and spread out a quick lunch. His eyes didn't leave the mountain.

I'm coming. Just hold on a while longer. Soon, Father will be there.

CHAPTER 30

Zachary rang the bell outside the main entrance to his family estate. Through the wrought iron he could see the gardens, which his father believed were proof that he had wrestled the wild into submission. The property was walled with thick stone, protecting the gardens and house from whatever unpleasantness the average citizen of Mioska had to endure.

It took less than a minute for a groundskeeper to answer the gate. Zachary didn't recognize the man, but the man certainly recognized him. After several rounds of obsequious bowing, Zachary was escorted into the building that he'd once called home.

A familiar face appeared at the top of the stairs leading to the second floor from the entrance.

Zachary felt his heart skip a beat when he saw her. She was older, of course, but still every bit his little sister. Her smile could light a room better than any stamfar invention, and she graced him with it today. It was probably the only genuine emotion he could expect on this visit.

Edda. The reason he'd become a murderer, and the

reason he'd been exiled. He hadn't seen her since the events of that night, but to see the smile on her face, he knew that everything he had endured was worth it.

She ran down the stairs, her footsteps light, and leaped from a few stairs up into his arms. He caught her easily and swept her around in an embrace. His ribs ached where Isira had struck him, but he barely felt the pain. "Sister, it's good to see you."

She hugged him fiercely, as though afraid if she let go he might disappear again.

He held her just as tight. He couldn't promise he wouldn't leave again, but it would never be like before.

Eventually, they broke apart, both of them blushing. Such a display of emotion probably hadn't been seen in this house for the better part of a decade. She gathered herself quickly. "Are you answering Father's summons?"

"Not exactly," he confessed. When her face fell, he rushed to say, "but I am back, at least for a while."

Edda glanced around the house. "Will you escort me through the gardens?"

He probably should call on his father, but if there was one person in the house he could trust, it was Edda. Besides, his father would likely wait to summon him anyway, to give the impression he was consumed by important work. Father never missed an opportunity to remind others how little he thought of them. "Of course, although I'm afraid not for long. I must call on Father soon, lest he think me rude."

Edda rolled her eyes, a silent acknowledgment Zachary had spoken for the benefit of the housekeepers no doubt listening in. They would report everything back to Father.

Zachary didn't like how quickly old habits reasserted themselves.

His concerns vanished when Edda took his arm and

pulled him back out the door. They stepped into the gardens and slowed to a stroll. Edda's eyes roved quickly around, ensuring they were alone. Once she was certain, she asked, "It is truly good to see you, but your arrival couldn't have come at a more chaotic time. How much do you know?"

"Of what's happening at court, plenty." He and Ingolf had talked for most of the evening last night, which was the best education he could have asked for. "Of what's happening here, very little."

Edda nodded. "Father will be grateful that you're here, although I'm sure you'll never guess it. Tollak will not be."

"I've heard much about him."

"Little good?"

"Unfortunately. What's become of him?"

"He inherited all of Father's traits but none of his ambition. He's manipulative, cruel, and petty. His only desires are women and drink, and the other nobles are more than happy to keep him supplied with both in exchange for his support at court."

"I'm surprised Father hasn't been able to stop him."

Edda hesitated. "You've heard he's sick?"

"I have."

"He's dying, and not quickly. Every time I see him, I think it'll be the last. But he keeps holding on. He started introducing Tollak as his successor. It's not official yet, but the nobles act as if it is. They'd much rather have Tollak than Father on the council."

"So, I probably shouldn't be waiting for a warm welcome from the other council members?"

"I'd go so far as to say you should avoid leaving the grounds without protection."

Ingolf had said something similar the night before. Zachary didn't like that his sister confirmed it.

"What do you intend?" she asked.

"There's danger on the frontier, and I fear it may reach as far as Mioska soon. I've come to prepare the city, as best I can."

"I've heard rumors, but is it bad?"

He decided to tell her everything. If he couldn't get her to believe him, he'd have no chance with anyone else. He told a brief version of his story, including his time with the band, and the fact stamfar were real, and one wanted to destroy humanity. When he was finished, they walked in silence for a while.

"If you were anyone else, I'd call you mad," Edda said.

"I've often felt that way." In Mioska, stamfar and dragons were little more than myths, and the wilds rarely more than a nuisance. Even the band, a much more recent historical event, was considered by most to be long dead and gone. "But at the very least, I need to take Father's seat on the council. Maybe it won't be enough, but it's all I can do."

"That, at least, I can help you with."

They rounded a corner of the garden, and through the trees, Zachary saw a small stone structure with a heavy door. It looked like a cellar, except guarded as though it were a keep. "What's that?"

Edda's eyes lit up. "I suppose you don't know! It's one of the more exciting things to happen around here recently. They discovered tunnels and caverns under this section of Mioska, with walls of stone smoother than anything we can build. Scholars believe they were built by the stamfar. Sometime, I'll have to take you down there."

"Why the thick doors?"

"They're an open secret. Only a few families have

entrances. They've become something of an escape for the nobles. Father's peers might be fools, but they're nothing if not paranoid. They sealed the entrances when they heard rumors of Vispeda being attacked by bandits."

"Is that what they believe happened?"

Edda nodded. "Makes more sense than your story."

He supposed he couldn't argue that.

They finished their tour of the gardens, re-entered the house, and parted ways at the top of the stairs. "You'll find him in his chambers," Edda said. "See me when you're done."

"Not his office?"

She shook her head and let him go. He walked through the familiar halls, his memories surprisingly fresh. The place hadn't changed much in his absence.

He stopped outside his father's chambers and froze, his hand halfway towards knocking. His heart pounded in his chest. Down the hall was his father's office, where they'd argued after Zachary's deed. Their argument still seemed to echo in the hallway.

This was foolish.

He'd faced down dragons, kolma, and even argued with a stamfar. His father wasn't even tehoin. What did he have to fear?

And yet, he couldn't force his hand to move.

He growled and knocked on the door, harder than he intended.

"Enter."

The voice was frail and old, so soft Zachary barely heard it through the door.

It still froze his blood solid.

Slowly, he forced his hand to grab the knob, to twist it, and push open the door.

His father lay on the bed, covers pulled up nearly to his chin. Though Zachary couldn't see much of his father's body, his face said enough. His cheeks were hollow and sunken, the flesh hanging off his bones. For a man who'd once prized his appearance and the strength it projected, it was no wonder his father never appeared in court. It was surprising he'd even let Zachary see him in such a state.

Still, it would be a mistake to underestimate him. His eyes were as sharp as ever, like two animals caged in a dying body.

"I take it you are familiar with the situation?"

Zachary grunted. Not that he'd expected an embrace like the one Edda had given him, but he'd thought there might at least be some mention of his years of exile. Perhaps even a simple "hello."

But he supposed this was easier. Better to focus on the court, even to the old man's last breath.

"I am."

The fear that had held him on the other side of the door loosed its grip. His father was brilliant, and dangerous in his own way. But Zachary had outgrown him.

"Tollak left the premises as soon as he heard you were here. You'll need to move fast to outmaneuver him."

"What will he try?"

"Tollak?" Father laughed bitterly. "He'll do the only thing he knows how to do, which is suck at the teats of the other nobles. But they'll do anything to protect their investment."

"Name me your official heir."

Father's glare was rebuke enough. "You know it wouldn't matter at this point."

Zachary shrugged. "Is there anything you can do?"

"I can guarantee your safety within these walls."

Zachary shook his head. "I'm sleeping elsewhere."

"It's likely they'll attack you."

"Let them try."

Father was about to argue, but then his eyes narrowed as he studied his firstborn. "That's not an empty boast anymore, is it?"

Before Zachary could answer, there was another knock at the door. A servant entered, bearing a message with the seal of the governor. He ignored Zachary and delivered the message to Father, then quickly retreated. Father tore it open, then raised an eyebrow as he offered it to Zachary. "That was quick, even for them. One might almost think they were waiting for you to return."

Zachary read the message. He was summoned to the governor's mansion, tomorrow at noon, "in regards to the disposition of his father's seat" at court.

"Good," Zachary said. "We'll be able to finish this quickly. There are more important issues at hand."

He handed the missive back to Father, who continued to watch him with a curious eye. "Unless there's anything else, I'll see you tomorrow after it's done."

"They'll try something," Father said. "Before."

"I know," Zachary said. "It's good to see you again."

He didn't lie. For years, he'd feared this moment. Only now did he realize his father no longer had any power over him. He turned sharply on his heel and took his leave. He wanted to stop by Edda's room before he left, and then he needed to return to Ingolf's, and quickly.

He needed Hel and his good pair of boots.

CHAPTER 31

Hakon nibbled at his food while he stared out the window of the structure. Like sleep, his body didn't seem interested in sustenance, either. He ate because he knew he would want the strength, but he felt no desire.

Behind him, the quiet conversation of his friends was like a bee buzzing around his ear. He could ignore it easily enough, but he still wished it was appropriate for him to ask for silence.

The longer he watched the mountain, the more he longed to be on his way. While they had explored the heart of the structure, he'd been able to push his daughter from his thoughts. Now, looking out the window, she was the only thing on his mind.

He couldn't explain his beliefs. That was why they were beliefs.

But she was out there.

She was waiting for him, somewhere near the top of that mountain.

From the safety of the structure, he could watch without

fear, and that watching revealed facts that would be helpful for the band. Hakon couldn't guess at the exact number of dragons, but he suspected it was at least a dozen, and most of them were younglings.

At least two were always in the sky above the mountain. Hakon guessed they were sentries. They had no set pattern, but swooped, dived, and floated like oversized birds around the peak. Eventually, a dragon would return to the mountain and disappear from view, and another would emerge.

Hakon noted the places they disappeared into. That was where he needed to go. From this distance, he couldn't see anything, but he trusted it wouldn't be too hard to find. Dragons didn't exactly fit in mouse holes. He traced routes to the top of the mountain.

Meshell came and sat next to him. "What are you doing?"

"Mapping out possible routes to the top of that peak."

She frowned. "Why?" She jabbed a thumb at Ari. "We have him."

"I think you all should leave, or continue exploring this area."

"Not a chance."

"I think there are far more dragons up there than there are of us."

"Not that surprising. We knew what we signed up for."

The conversation around the room had faded. Everyone was looking at him and Meshell. "I can't keep asking you to join me like this," he said.

Irric yawned. "I never thought I'd say this, but I think I preferred it when you just ordered us around and expected us to listen."

The others nodded. Solveig spoke for them. "We chose to be here, Hakon. Don't try to take that away from us, too."

Hakon thought of what Meshell had told him back in Aysgarth. "If it comes down to it, you all should know I'm going to do everything I can to save Cliona. No matter what." He couldn't bring himself to say he'd abandon them outright, but the implication was clear enough.

Ari snorted. "You think we'd expect you to do anything else?"

Hakon swallowed the rest of his objections. He didn't deserve these friends, but then, he never had.

Irric pointed to the door. "You need to go out into the hallway and have a good private cry before we leave?"

Hakon shook his head, painfully aware that his eyes were indeed moist.

They packed up the rest of the food. Hakon motioned Ari over and pointed out where he saw the dragons disappearing. Ari just nodded, which was all the certainty Hakon needed.

They sketched out their plan. They would return to Ari's transport point outside the structure, drop off their packs, then have Ari transport them to the mountain. After that, the plan was mostly to stay alive while Hakon searched one last place for his daughter.

Before they could leave the room, they felt a bloom of teho. It didn't feel strong, but at the distance they sensed it at, it was far beyond any of their abilities. The others pressed their faces to the window. The figure wasn't much more than a speck, but it floated in the air toward the mountain.

Meshell swore.

"If I was a betting man, and I am," Irric said, "I'd put my money on that being Ava."

The figure disappeared against the mountain. Hakon couldn't say for sure, but it seemed like it headed toward the same entrance the dragons used.

The appearance of the stamfar put a halt to their preparations. Irric, of course, was the one who gave voice to the thoughts they all had. "So, are we still going?"

Hakon knew his answer. "I am. I'm sorry, but I need to go."

"You're being a fool," Meshell said, cutting him off before he could argue. "She clearly arrived from somewhere, and I'm willing to bet she'll have somewhere to go soon enough. We can just wait for her to leave. Until then, we have plenty of shelter and food."

Meshell was right. He was a fool. There was no reason to charge in. If Cliona had survived this long, she would continue to survive until Ava left.

The others quickly agreed, and they took their seats once again. From what little Hakon had seen, it didn't look like this was Ava's first visit to the dragons. Cliona would be fine.

They all felt the explosions of teho at the same moment Hakon felt his heart suddenly ache. He clutched at his chest, but still saw the dragons take flight from the mountain. There were almost a dozen, and they looked agitated.

Hakon grunted as the pain in his heart doubled. He didn't even see Meshell approach, but she was at his side, supporting him.

"What is it?" she asked.

"I don't know. Whatever's happening up there, I'm connected."

Another blast of teho, and this time, Hakon fell to a knee. His breaths came hard, and sweat beaded across his brow.

He couldn't explain it.

But he needed to get to the top of that mountain. "You don't need to come with me, but Ari, could you drop me off there, now?"

The rest of the band shared looks. Irric shook his head. "He really was more entertaining back in the day. I think becoming a father broke him."

The band gathered, grabbing hands in preparation for the transport. It took Hakon a few moments to understand, but he had the good sense not to object. Irric would just mock him more.

He was the last one to join the circle. He took their hands, and they looked around, giving each other one last check.

Then they transported to battle.

CHAPTER 32

Zachary woke to the sound of boots on the stairs. Five or six pairs, though he couldn't be quite sure. He transitioned from sleep to wakefulness in a moment, a habit he'd picked up in his wanderings around the frontier. Across the room, he saw Hel's eyes reflecting the light of a lamp turned down low. They watched the door. She leaned forward, ready to spring into action.

Ingolf was as good as his word, then. After they'd returned from their short expedition, Zachary's old friend had set them up in this inn, a decrepit building closer to the day it fell over in a strong wind than the day it was built. Then he'd spread the word, quietly, that Zachary had returned to compete for his father's seat. Moreso, Ingolf had whispered, he knew where Zachary was staying, hoping to remain incognito.

He might as well have painted a target on Zachary's back.

But Zachary couldn't afford to make it too hard for Tollak. His younger brother still probably didn't know which end of the sword went in the enemy, so it was best to keep the assassination attempt simple to plan.

From the pounding of the boots on the stairs, his brother hadn't exactly hired a professional group of killers, either.

They broke down the door, never even checking to notice that Zachary had kindly left it unlocked for them.

This was why they used a different inn. Zachary had worried about the damage to Ingolf's place, and didn't want to waste his friend's favor.

Two broad-shouldered bandits both tried to be first through the door. They got stuck, and Zachary used the moment to launch a teho dart at each. The two men went down, clutching the wounds that had opened in their chests.

The two behind were slightly smarter than the first pair. Not clever enough to realize the trouble they were in, but at least smart enough to come through the door one at a time. A teho dart greeted each one, and they joined their companions on Zachary's bloody floor.

He'd spent so long among other tehoin, where his strength was nothing special, he'd forgotten how strong he was against ahula.

Which led to the next thought. His brother, at least, knew he was tehoin. And he hadn't even bothered to bring a vilda along?

Zachary was almost offended.

Tollak followed the second pair, stopping in the doorway when he realized his plan wasn't proceeding the way he expected.

That was good. His father and sister had worried enough about him leaving the grounds that Zachary was pretty certain he could attract an assassination attempt. He hadn't been sure his brother would join or be content to give the order.

But Edda had said Tollak had inherited many of Father's traits, and Father always supervised important projects personally. It was a bit of a gamble, but Zachary figured if Tollak didn't show for the attempt, he wouldn't be too hard to find.

And given Tollak's clothing, that seemed doubly true. His brother had grown in the years of his exile, filling out a powerful, muscular frame. But he wore a silk tunic and a garish white cape, fastened with a thin chain of gold. His weapon was a jewel-encrusted dagger that rested in an equally jewel-encrusted sheath.

Tollak had just enough time to sneer at Zachary before Zachary punched him once.

Zachary didn't consider himself that much of a brawler, but Tollak collapsed from the single hit and didn't rise again.

Not willing to take any chances, Zachary stripped the dagger from his brother's belt and searched him for other weapons. Then he bound him and gagged him for good measure.

Hel watched as Zachary finished. "I thought that would be harder," she observed.

"As did I, but I won't criticize my brother's foolishness tonight. Ready?"

She nodded. "What about them?" She gestured to the men on the floor. Two weren't moving, but the other two were curled around their chests where the teho darts had gone in.

The wounds Zachary had inflicted were on the edge of fatal, depending on where exactly they'd hit. But they were painful wounds, too. It might be a mercy to kill them.

"Leave them," Zachary said. He had no desire to kill more people than he had to.

She reached out her hand, and Zachary took it. Then he grabbed his brother, and Hel transported them away.

Less than an hour later, it was done. The night wasn't even half over.

He spoke with Brenda, the matriarch of this village, far on the edge of the frontier. "Thanks again for taking him."

"After all you did for us, it's the least we can do." Her eyes twinkled. "Besides, given what I've seen of him thus far, it looks like you might have actually gifted us a great deal of entertainment." She held up the jeweled dagger and sheath. "What are you even supposed to do with this? Blind your opponent?"

Zachary shook his head. "I have no idea. But regardless, I thank you, and I'll do what I can to get more caravans sent out this way. You're sure you're fine, otherwise?"

They'd spoken this afternoon, when Hel and Zachary had found the place after a bit of wandering. It wasn't as far west as Aysgarth, but the village was about as far west as you could be and still claim to be in the six states. Brenda had reported dragon sightings, but so far, the village had been left alone. Zachary hoped it remained that way. He had fond memories of this place.

"I'm sure," Brenda said. She looked back at the hut where they'd left Tollak. "What if he tries to escape?"

Zachary shrugged. "He's not your prisoner. Let him do as he pleases. Maybe warn him of the dangers, though." Zachary remembered his own journey to and from this village, and he wouldn't wish that upon anyone. And he was a tehoin. "Otherwise, if he wants to leave when a caravan does come through, let him."

Zachary didn't need to kill his brother. All he needed was Tollak out of the way.

Who knew, maybe his brother would even learn something out here.

They said their goodbyes, and Hel transported them back, straight to Ingolf's inn this time.

That night, Zachary got one of the best sleeps in recent memory.

The next morning he spent an extravagant amount of time preparing, indulging in one of the hottest baths he'd enjoyed in a year. Hel's company didn't bother him, either.

"Are you sure you don't want me to join you?" Hel asked.

"I'd enjoy your company, but there's no guarantee the other nobles won't have other schemes in motion. I'd rather know you were safe here."

"Seems more like a reason to stay somewhere near you," she said.

He considered. She had a point. She was stronger than him, and he hardly needed to protect her. "I stand corrected."

He was admitted to the governor's receiving chambers at exactly noon. There were other nobles present, members of the governor's council, but no one else. A valuable piece of information. Usually, the nobles couldn't even visit an outhouse without a crowd to perform for.

They weren't sure what he would do, and so they wanted this quiet.

He'd been forced to leave Hel in the room on the other side of the doors. The guards had made it clear this was a private affair. Zachary knew, though, that if he embraced teho, she'd come through the door to join him.

Zachary strode into the room trying to project a confidence he didn't feel. The governor could only make one rational choice, but he had no guarantee the governor would make that choice. The noble who relied on reason and logic to protect them usually found themselves in exile before long.

Zachary could attest to that personally.

He supposed this was out of his hands, though. He'd done all he could. Now, like a gambler, all he could do was roll the dice and see what number came up.

The nobles eyed him warily, but they let the governor speak. "Where is your brother?" he asked.

Agnar had been the governor of the state nearly as long as Zachary could remember, and the years had been kind to him. He'd put on weight, and his gaze didn't seem quite as sharp as it once had.

The structure of power served the nobles in Mioska well, and in a time of peace, they governed well enough. They could have done more, but most of the people who lived here had roofs over their heads and food on the table.

But they weren't ready for Ava, and they needed to be.

"He decided he needed to take a trip to the frontier," Zachary said. "My father believed it would do him good to see how the settlers were expanding our borders against the wild, as it did me."

No doubt, everyone in this room knew Father had exiled him, but they knew they couldn't dispute the story publicly. Father was already spreading the word that he'd sent his younger son to follow in the footsteps of the eldest. The old man had practically cackled with joy when Zachary told him of Tollak's fate.

"You lie," said one of the nobles.

Zachary produced a note, sealed by his father not an hour ago. "You have the word of my father, too."

Then he produced another note. "And this one, which is also being sent to the council, says that I have once again been named the heir of my father's council seat."

If looks could kill, Zachary was certain he would be dead soon. But the corner of the governor's mouth turned up in a smile, and some of the spark returned to his eyes. "I was under the impression you had forsaken your claim when you left for your studies."

"A necessary precaution, sir. My father was worried something might happen to me and didn't want any questions surrounding the proper succession of his seat."

The same noble who'd accused Zachary of lying earlier, whose name he now remembered was Hallr, flew into a rage. "This is preposterous! We all know Tollak was being groomed for the seat. This is nothing but lies and more lies!"

Zachary didn't dignify the outburst with a response. The choice was the governor's to make.

The governor ran his fingers over Father's note. "This is his handwriting, with his seal. His word is clear."

Hallr didn't back down. "I demand we get to the bottom of this!"

"There's nothing to investigate," Agnar said. To Zachary, he said, "Welcome to the council, son. I'm eager to see what ideas you might bring to our state."

Zachary bowed. "Thank you, sir."

He left the receiving room, a member of the council.

CHAPTER 33

Ari's first transport left them buried knee deep in snow and below the entrance into the mountain. From here, though, they could see the top of the mountain was honeycombed with caves. Before Hakon could even ask, Ari transported them again to one of the larger entrances.

Ava was within, and she wasn't alone. The amount of teho leaking out of the cave was staggering.

Unfortunately, Ari's transport didn't go unnoticed. They felt the power take shape deep within the cave, and they dove to the side as a wall of pure teho blasted from within.

Hakon landed next to Solveig. She was on her feet in an instant. "We'll distract her. Go in," she said.

He didn't question the offer. Cliona was deep in these caves. He sprinted into an adjoining entrance just as Ava emerged from the other.

Her appearance was welcomed with powerful teho spears from the rest of the band. They broke harmlessly against her shield, but they succeeded in focusing her attention.

Hakon felt sick as he fled the battle, as though he were a coward leaving his friends to die. It didn't matter that they had chosen this, that they fought for him. He should be by their side.

He ran, hoping that if he was fast enough, he might outrun the curses he called down on himself. His cave soon joined the other, larger one, and after following that for another hundred paces, he jumped down from a ledge into what could only be a dragon den.

Back in the days where they'd wandered the empire, they'd all speculated endlessly on how dragons lived. Now they had an answer, and it was both more impressive and less elegant than Hakon had imagined. It was an enormous hole in the mountain, with smaller alcoves surrounding a communal area.

The size of it staggered the mind. The ceiling of the cave towered over a hundred feet over his head, and the communal area had to be at least two or three times that wide. It barely seemed as though it was underground.

And yet, it was no more than a cave. Enormous as it was, it was just stone. Somehow, he had expected something more from the dragons.

He wasn't here to see their home, though.

As his eyes adjusted to the darker spaces of the den, he saw a shadow move in a corner of the communal area. Two eyes opened, bright in the darkness.

It was her.

Or at least, it was the dragon from Husavik. The one that had once been under Damion's control. The sight of it struck him with almost physical force.

There were other dragons in the caves, resting or hiding in the alcoves. They bore his presence with surprising equanimity. Dragons hated tehoin, and now one stood in their home. He saw shadows move, deep in the alcoves, but none of them attacked. He couldn't guess why, but he wasn't about to waste time questioning his good fortune.

He stepped toward the dragon. Toward his daughter. A snarl rumbled deep in its throat, but it didn't lunge for him. It didn't even roar.

He remembered it as an enormous dragon, an elder. Now, though, it seemed shrunken, like it was somehow lesser.

He stared into the eyes, looking for some sign that his daughter was present, a part of the dragon. That he hadn't been a fool for pursuing this creature for almost a year. No matter how hard he stared, though, all he saw were a pair of dragon eyes staring back at him.

Outside, he felt the exchanges of teho quicken. How long had he been in the caves? Strong as the band was, they couldn't last for long against Ava.

He didn't have time.

But he had no idea what to do. All his plans had been about finding this dragon again, but now that he was here, staring it in the face, he couldn't figure out his next step.

Could he ride it out of here?

He was glad none of the band knew his thoughts. They already thought he was close enough to going mad with grief. That thought would convince them for good.

But he'd ridden the dragon once before. Perhaps it would let him again.

He stepped closer, his approach hesitant. His muscles were tense, ready to dive out of the way of any sudden movement.

The dragon remained still. Almost too still. If not for the steady gaze of its eyes, he might have suspected it was dead. What had Ava done to it?

The dragons in the alcoves roared as he neared, the sound reverberating in the cave, deafening Hakon. The stone walls made the handful of dragons sound like a horde. He grimaced against the pain, but it was only sound. He reached out his hand, and still the dragon didn't respond.

Hakon steeled his body with teho, now too close to avoid any attack. He put his hand against the dragon's neck, and it didn't resist.

The tenor of the battle outside the caves changed. Ava was fighting harder, unleashing even more teho. She'd heard the dragons roar, too. She knew something happened within, and it frightened her.

Why?

Hakon closed his eyes. He felt the teho within the dragon, swirling like a turbulent storm. It was almost the same as in his own body, but magnified hundreds of times. Something about the flow struck him as wrong, though.

The battle outside became desperate. He knew the techniques of his friends almost as well as they did, and they were flinging everything at Ava, to no effect. She approached.

Hakon swore.

She'd figured out the rest of the band was nothing but a distraction.

Hakon couldn't escape. Ari couldn't transport in here, a place he'd never seen, and Ava was at the main entrance.

The only way out was to figure out what was going on. He took a deep breath and closed his eyes. Though it was nearly impossible, he pushed everything else out of his mind.

He remembered that day in Husavik, connected to the dragon as though it was a part of his own body. Hakon tore down the barriers between him and the dragon.

Teho rushed into his limbs, and he felt like a wineskin filled to bursting.

But he didn't just take from the dragon. His own teho mixed with that of the dragon. Though his was just a drop in an ocean, it connected them.

And he felt *her*, another drop in the endless ocean.

Except not a drop. He was a drop, maintaining a semblance of identity as he was tossed about in the deep waters of the dragon's teho. She was everywhere, one with the dragon.

Hakon knees weakened.

After all this, to come so close, only to find out it was meaningless. He couldn't imagine a way of separating Cliona from the dragon. He could tear away, return to his body.

What remained of Cliona was part of the dragon now. There was no return.

In his grief, he felt her gather around him, her teho embracing his. He felt no sorrow from her presence. Only gratitude, and determination. He held onto her tightly, unable to let go.

Then she was gone, scattered once again in the turbulent teho. In a moment of clarity, he understood why the dragon hadn't attacked him as he neared. He understood the turbulence that raged within the creature. And he knew what he could do to help Cliona.

Within his own body, teho flowed smoothly, circulating through his limbs in a never-ending stream. Such was the natural order. When he was injured, that flow was interrupted, and his body fought to heal it.

Something similar plagued this dragon. He felt the trio of dark hooks, pinning the dragon in place. Its teho, and

Cliona's, raged against the hooks, but to no effect. Ava held them in place.

But Ava was dealing with the band and the dragon at once.

Even stamfar had limits.

Hakon imagined reaching out and grabbing one of the hooks. The dragon and Cliona joined him, using his will to focus their strength. As one, they pulled. The hook slid out easily, and in the physical world, he felt the dragon shift under his palm.

Perhaps freeing the dragon wasn't wise when he was standing next to it. But he didn't care. It was Cliona.

He turned to the next hook, and once again, the three of them pulled. It slid partway out, but not nearly so easily. Ava's will opposed theirs.

Hakon strained, not knowing exactly how he did what he did, but knowing that it felt right. The second hook released, and Ava's scream of frustration was drowned out by the dragon's roar at the taste of freedom.

Hakon hoped his friends still lived, because he didn't think he could remove the last hook without help. They needed to distract her for another moment.

As if his thought had summoned them, he felt them in the caves. Ari transported in circles around Ava, attacking her from all sides and disappearing before she could respond. Meshell and Solveig unleashed every attack they had, and Irric—

Well, Irric was attacking the dragons in the alcoves. His provocation was enough to make them overcome whatever fear had held them in place, and they joined the battle, attacking anything with teho.

Ari transported the band out, and the dragons focused

their efforts on Ava. They'd always hated the stamfar the most.

Hakon gripped the third hook and pulled. Ava's resistance was even stronger, and Hakon felt as though he was trying to pry a boulder up using only his fingernails. He gritted his teeth. Every bit of his strength joined with the teho of the dragon and Cliona, and together, they were able to move the hook. One inch, then another.

Every bit calmed the dragon's teho more. As the turbulence faded, the dragon gained strength, and the hook moved another inch.

Finally, Hakon pulled the final hook free.

The dragon flexed, and some instinct told Hakon to jump on the dragon's back once again. He obeyed.

The moment he was on, the dragon rose, spreading its wings and stretching as though it had woken from a long slumber. It took a deep breath, then blasted teho in all directions.

It rose smoothly, and with a single flap of its powerful wings, blasted out of the cave, snatching Ava in its jaws as it did.

She formed a shield just in time, and the jaws closed on a sphere of teho, which cracked under the enormous pressures. But Ava remained alive.

The stamfar struck the dragon with a teho staff, and Hakon felt as though he'd been punched in the face. The dragon lost both altitude and its grip on Ava, who quickly righted herself in the air.

The dragon launched itself higher, though a wispy cloud and into the pure blue sky above. Hakon could do little but hold on. His teho and its were still joined, and he felt the same rush of freedom that coursed through its veins.

He felt, more than heard, the order that came from Ava.

Go.

The command tugged at the dragon Hakon rode, but with the hooks gone, and Hakon and Cliona both connected, the dragon could ignore the order.

Dread gathered in Hakon's stomach, though. They'd suspected a link between Ava and the dragons, and now it was confirmed. Somehow, she'd learned how to command them.

The control wasn't perfect. The dragons' attacks on her in the cave were proof enough of that. But that was a slim hope.

Hakon risked a glance below, and he saw that the dragons who had been circling chaotically around the mountaintop all turned east.

Toward the six states.

They sped away, racing as though they were being chased. Hakon couldn't imagine the destruction so many dragons would unleash. But he couldn't fight them all. They were moving far too fast.

But Ava remained, and even from up here, he could feel her eyes on him. They could at least try to kill her. Perhaps that would be enough to disperse the younglings.

The dragon seemed to agree. It banked into a dive, and Hakon fell toward the woman who dreamed of killing them all.

CHAPTER 34

If Zachary learned one lesson on his first day on the council, it was that he wasn't going to bring any changes to Mioska quickly. He'd arrived at the meeting with a long list of ideas and proposals, ready to get to work.

Instead, the other council members had insisted on spending the whole day arguing about the best way to celebrate the elevation of their newest member. There was talk of parades, feasts, or hosting a "quieter" celebration involving only the nobles and a few dozen guests each. They'd quibbled for hours, though it was clear after about five minutes they were going to choose the smaller option.

It would be their opportunity to bestow favor on their chosen few, as well as yet another opportunity for the ever-expanding court to fight for that favor. Zachary saw it all as clear as day, and yet there was nothing he could do. He felt as though he was standing in the way of a falling boulder, hoping that by shouting at it he might change its direction. Any suggestion that they use the time and funds for other purposes was ignored, and he was told in no uncertain terms he couldn't bring any new business to the table until the current matter was resolved. They weren't even interested in discussing an alliance with Aysgarth, the item that sat at the very top of his list.

So he stewed in his frustration and used the time to observe the others. He knew of all the noble families, but he only knew some of the current council members personally. He noted the flows of power: who spoke most and who was listened to most closely. Though it seemed pointless now, someday he hoped to turn that knowledge into his own strength.

His studied the governor most of all. For Agnar to survive and rule as long as he had, Zachary knew he was no fool. He kept himself aloof from most of the debate, only offering opinions when directly asked.

Coming so recently from listening to Hakon's tale of the past, Zachary marveled at how this mess of a system was a direct result of actions taken over a hundred years ago. Torsten had been the one to suggest the formation of six loosely affiliated states, each given to a faction of the rebel alliance.

Holar, the state which controlled the city of Mioska, was long considered the jewel of the six states. Or, at least, that was the way Zachary had been taught history. Now he suspected students in the other states learned their own states were somehow superior. But it and Garor, to the south, maintained the closest ties to the old empire. Most of the nobles who sat around this table could trace their lineage back to a family member who had served the last emperor. Zachary was no exception.

Each state had been free to choose their own style of government, but, especially out east, the emperor's favored had been the only people with the money and influence to help rebuild the six states after the rebellion.

How different would the world have been if the band hadn't disappeared? If they had shaped the six states more directly?

It was an interesting question, but one without an answer. For all the wonders in the world, one couldn't turn back time.

Zachary returned his attention to the discussion around the table. The sun would be setting in a few hours, and at the very least he wanted to bring up the possible alliance with Aysgarth. Hel was waiting back at Ingolf's for news, and he wasn't sure how he could confess that they'd talked about throwing him a party all day.

An urgent knock at the door was a welcome relief.

Hallr, always one to observe proprieties when they suited him, sputtered, "Who dares interrupt us while we're in session?"

Zachary hadn't thought much about the interruption, but when he looked around the table, he saw he was alone in that reaction. The others seemed quite disturbed that someone would have the gall to knock on the door.

The door opened, and a man wearing the uniform of Holar stepped in. From the rank insignia, Zachary realized he was staring at a general. The man gave a stiff and hurried bow. "I'm sorry to interrupt, but our outposts to the west have just lit their warning flames."

The anger at the interruption quickly turned to confusion as the other council members glanced at one another. Zachary's stomach twisted in knots. He'd hoped there would be more time. A lot more time.

Hallr spoke for the nobles. "Is this some sort of prank, General Amund? The fires haven't been lit for generations."

And for good reason. Mioska was almost as far from the frontier as one could get. It was hundreds of miles away from the nearest other state, too, though they were rarely involved in more than minor border disputes. Torsten had divided the states up well, giving them little reason to attack their neighbors.

So Zachary knew there was only one reason why the fires would be lit today.

Amund gulped hard. "Giant creatures have been spotted in the air. They're coming this way."

Hallr scoffed. "Your soldiers lit the fires to warn us about birds?"

Amund paled. Zachary felt for the soldier. But the news had to come from the general. The others would never believe Zachary. "Dragons, sir."

Hallr laughed and waved his hand. "Amund, as of this moment the council relieves you of your duty. You're mad, general."

Amund's eyes darted around the room. The man had come, hoping for direction, and with a single line, Hallr had doomed the entire city to chaos. Zachary gripped the edges of his chair. It would be easy to sit, and to let it all happen. No matter what happened, his position would be safe.

He was ashamed to admit he felt the temptation.

He stood up. "I believe you, general. I survived a dragon attack on Vispeda."

Hallr growled. "Sit down!"

Zachary ignored him. He spoke to Amund. "How many tehoin do you have, and of what class?"

Amund replied instantly, relief etched in every line of his face. "Maybe four or five vilda, sir."

Zachary's eyes went wide. He knew tehoin had been leaking away from the military, where they weren't terribly welcome, but he hadn't realized it had gotten so desperate. "Then you can't do anything to protect the walls."

His mind raced. He was cognizant of all the eyes on him, the barely contained glee on the face of Hallr as he waited for Zachary to make a mistake that would get him removed from the council.

They couldn't protect the city. All the arrows in the world wouldn't do more than irritate a dragon. So what did they do? They didn't have any place to run and hide.

Except—they did.

The answer came in a flash, and he said a silent thanks to Edda for her tour of their house. Then he suppressed a smile as he thought about just how angry he was about to make his father. "I want you to organize your soldiers and evacuate as many citizens as you can to the caverns underneath the city."

"Sir?" Amund looked around the chambers, looking for some form of confirmation.

Hallr, of course, disagreed. "It's a foolish idea. Better they shelter in their homes."

The ground shook beneath their feet, causing several of the nobles to sprawl across the table as if they were afraid they would fall out of their seats. Zachary grimaced. They didn't have time for this. The dragons were already here.

Zachary turned to Agnar. "Sir, we don't have the forces here to fight against the dragons. The best we can do is save as many as we can, and I suspect the passages underneath the city are the safest we have."

Hallr protested. "Sir! Our house treasures are down there! We'll be robbed blind!"

"If the others object," Zachary said, his voice cold, "I am happy to open the gates in my estates." He held the governor's gaze, curious how the ruler would decide. If Agnar couldn't even do this, Mioska didn't have a hope.

"Do it," Agnar said.

Amund nodded. He left the council in a hurry, and a stunned silence lingered in his wake.

Hallr rose a few moments later. "Sir, with your leave, we must see to our families."

Without waiting for a response, the nobles were hurrying out the doors, practically nipping on Amund's heels.

"You've made an enemy today," Agnar said.

Zachary chuckled at that. "Not much I could have done to avoid that. And I'd rather fight him than what's in the skies above."

"You spoke true, about Vispeda? Even I doubted the reports."

"I did. It's best you find shelter, sir."

Agnar nodded. "You're welcome to join me, if you wish. There are safe rooms here in the keep."

Zachary formed a teho sword in his hand, giving it a few practice swings. The invitation was an honor. Private time with the governor was treasured more than all the gemstones in the city. But Zachary refused to stay hidden. Better to die on one's feet, fighting until the last breath. "If it's all the same to you, sir, I'll head out into the streets to see how I can help."

CHAPTER 35

Ava formed a spear of teho and launched it at the falling dragon. In less time than it took to blink, the dragon twisted, and the spear flashed past Hakon. He gripped the dragon's back tighter. The creature might have survived the impact, but that spear would have ripped through him, even with his body filled with teho.

The dragon aimed straight at Ava, but before they reached her, she vanished. A moment later she reappeared, hundreds of feet above them. She formed nearly a dozen teho darts and flung them down.

Hakon swore as the dragon spread its wings, sliding between the darts with ease. All he could do was watch as the darts passed by him and cratered into the ground. Stone cracked and trees shattered where the teho impacted.

The dragon banked around the last dart, then shot higher into the air. Hakon held on and let teho flow freely between his body and its. He felt stronger than ever, as though he were part dragon as well.

They weren't even halfway toward Ava when she disappeared again.

It reminded Hakon of his more frustrating training duels with Ari. Few transporters could focus their minds enough to transport and fight, but it was a powerful skill. Though he rode an elder dragon, it made no difference if they couldn't reach the stamfar.

Against Ari, Hakon had learned to endure, to absorb the assassin's attacks until Ari tired enough to make a mistake.

Ava reappeared, hundreds of feet away, at nearly the same altitude. The dragon turned toward her, and Ava formed a spear. She snapped it at them.

It flew too fast to dodge. Hakon felt it, but couldn't track it with his eyes. The dragon lifted, but even it wasn't quick enough. The spear caught it below the neck.

Hakon almost lost his grip on the dragon as his chest spasmed in agony. The dragon's smooth flight stalled, and Hakon feared the worst. The dragon's wings no longer caught the air. They plummeted together. Mountain and sky spiraled in a dizzying dance, and Hakon couldn't tell where one ended and the other began. He clutched tightly to the dragon, nothing more than a helpless rider.

He couldn't see Ava, but he felt her. She gathered teho and flew at them.

Come on, girl.

Teho spears filled the air. Not Ava's work. They were too weak for that.

His friends, protecting them with their last strength. They'd rejoined the battle to help how they could.

Ava broke away, unleashing her fury on the mountain below.

The dragon's wings finally snapped open. They caught the air, and Hakon had the breath knocked from him as the dragon pulled up, not a moment too soon. Its claws tore through aged pine trees as though they were dead grass.

Hakon got his first look at the battlefield in several precious seconds. The mountain where the caves had been was a shell of what it once was. Ava's last attack had blasted a good part of the peak away. Snow hung in the air, and once again, Hakon feared the worst for his friends. The power of the stamfar was just too great.

Teho spears punched holes in the clouds of snow. Against Ava, they felt like someone was throwing pins at a giant, but they reassured Hakon that somehow, his friends lived.

But if they were to have any hope of defeating Ava, it rested on him, his daughter, and the elder dragon.

They clawed back the altitude they had lost, but Hakon's heart was as heavy as it had ever been. What could he do? For all the power of the dragon, it wasn't useful against Ava's abilities.

They turned toward Ava again, wind snapping Hakon's hair straight back. They weren't even close when she turned her attention to them. She created even more spears this time, filling the sky. The dragon twisted and banked, finding gaps Hakon couldn't even sense.

Ava didn't relent, though, and even the most nimble dragon could only dodge for so long. Another spear struck the dragon close to its right wing. A pinpoint of fire erupted near Hakon's corresponding shoulder.

The dragon fell again, but this time caught itself well before crashing. It banked away as Ava hurled another set of spears.

The spears hadn't broken through the dragon's armor, but he felt its enormous strength starting to fade. He couldn't forget it had been a prisoner not that long ago.

One of their next attempts had to succeed. But he had no idea how to approach Ava. Between the deadly walls of teho and her ability to transport away, closing with her seemed nearly impossible.

When the idea came to him, he laughed out loud, the sound lost to the rushing wind.

It was a shame their battle was so far away from any witnesses, because if this worked, it deserved a place among the greatest tales ever told. He hugged the dragon close, felt the blending of the teho running between them. Despite everything, he felt lighter than he ever had.

It wasn't as if he spoke his command. Whatever he shared with the dragon, and maybe even with Cliona, it went deeper than language.

It understood him.

The dragon banked again, returning to the battlefield. The rest of the band still fought Ava, but it didn't look like they could survive for much longer. For every attack that launched from the ground, a dozen fell from the sky.

Just a little longer.

As before, Hakon and the dragon caught Ava's attention early. She turned to them and launched spears, and the dragon dove toward the ground. The spears passed overhead. The dragon spread its wings, nearly brushing the tops of the trees as it passed.

Hakon glanced behind, seeing the trail of broken trees that marked their path. No matter how old those trees were, no matter how deep their roots went, against such power, they had no choice but to break.

He saw his friends then, and his heart soared to see that all four still stood. Irric limped, and part of Meshell's right arm was gone, but they stood.

Hakon gripped the dragon tightly, his fingers locked in between two scales and his heels hooked against the scales as well as he could. He let teho fill his body, borrowing liberally from the dragon's nearly endless supply.

The dragon rotated so it flew upside down. It weaved back and forth as Ava rained spears down around it. Hakon extended his free hand and locked his gaze on Ari. There had been no way to let the others know his plan, but hopefully, Ari would understand.

From the way that the assassin's face paled, Hakon figured he knew.

The others dove, protecting themselves from the incoming force. Ari braced himself and raised his hand.

At the last moment, the dragon slowed. Instead of ripping Ari's arm from its socket, they clasped hands and Hakon pulled Ari toward him. The dragon rotated, and after a bit of scrambling, Ari was sitting on the dragon, swearing up a storm, riding behind Hakon. Then they were accelerating, weaving away from Ava's attacks. The mountain of the dragons rumbled, as though it was contemplating simply falling over under the continued attacks from the sky.

Hakon told Ari what he intended, and for once, Ari's silence wasn't by choice.

He found his voice eventually, though. "That's mad!"

"Do you have any better ideas?"

Ari shook his head. "But I'm also not sure I'm strong enough. That fight took it out of me. Only reason we're still alive is I kept transporting everyone away."

Hakon had feared as much. If Ari wasn't sure he had the strength, there was a better-than-even chance he didn't. "There's not much choice, old friend."

"Does it understand?"

"I believe it does."

Ari shrugged, a small gesture laden with meaning. He'd

always had a fatalistic streak, and so there wasn't much argument.

The dragon banked, and once again they flew toward Ava. She'd gone silent after they'd passed over the band, as though waiting to see what trick they unveiled. A wall of spears appeared over her head. Hundreds. More than ever before.

One way or another, the battle was ending with this pass. The elder dragon sped up, and she hurled her spears.

Hakon grimaced. There was no chance of dodging them. He strengthened himself again, filling every pore with teho. If nothing else, he could act as a shield for Ari.

He watched his doom approach. He could meet his fate with open eyes.

Just before the spears hit, Ari transported them. Warrior, assassin, and dragon all.

It was the most sickening transport Hakon had ever experienced. His body had no idea what had happened, and the urge to vomit almost overwhelmed him.

But they were right behind Ava.

The stamfar barely had time to react. She'd lost a precious heartbeat of time trying to figure out what had happened, and Ari had transported them close. Ava turned, and dragon met stamfar.

From his position on the dragon's back, Hakon couldn't see what happened. But the dragon stopped, as though it was a mere human running full speed into a thick stone wall. In the instant before they were thrown, Hakon felt bones within the dragon shatter as the impact traveled through its body.

Then he was airborne. He tried, desperately, to grab one of the dragon's enormous horns, but he was too slow.

Filled as he was with teho, he might survive. But they were high, and he didn't like his chances.

Ari appeared beside him, and he clutched at Hakon's tunic.

The last thing Hakon saw before Ari transported them again was the dragon, his daughter, falling and broken, and Ava still floating triumphantly overhead.

CHAPTER 36

Bravery had come a lot easier to Zachary when he'd been safely ensconced in Agnar's keep. The rumbling of stone, disconcerting as it was, wasn't enough to frighten him.

Stepping out into the sun and seeing the damage the dragons had already wrought on Mioska, though, certainly did. Smoke rose in the distance, and the streets were pure chaos. For several long moments, all he could do was watch, frozen in astonishment.

He looked to the sky. It didn't take long to spot the dragons. For the moment, they seemed content to wreak their havoc on the western edges of the city.

No doubt, the destruction would be terrible, but Zachary was also grateful. The western edges of the city were the least populated. As they kept working east, there would be even greater losses of life. But this gave them at least a little time to react.

Where would he do the most good?

Watching the dragons swoop down and destroy another building, it was sorely tempting to say he'd do the most good hiding in his parents' estate, helping funnel people into the caverns beneath the city.

But that was blatantly foolish. There would be plenty of others capable of doing that. He was tehoin, which meant he had a responsibility to fight the dragons.

Granted, he was just a vilda, so he wasn't going to be anything more than an annoyance, but it was still something.

He thought of Hel, and wondered what had happened to her. But he knew she could look after herself. If nothing else, she could transport back to Aysgarth and be back in time for supper.

He ran toward the west wall, sticking to narrow alleys and abandoned side streets. He hoped to avoid the crush of people fleeing east, but he was only moderately successful. It still took him far too long.

As he neared, he was surprised to feel other tehoin fighting against the dragons. Their attacks weren't strong, but at least someone was fighting back. Zachary angled toward the source of the teho.

He found two soldiers standing, all alone, in a wide street. They were flinging teho spears up at the dragons, and so far, it didn't look like the dragons had even noticed they were being attacked.

Not knowing what else to do, Zachary joined the soldiers. They spared him a glance when he arrived, but when he started flinging teho, they let him join without complaint.

His joining them accomplished nothing. He scored a few direct hits against the dragons, but his teho broke harmlessly against their scales. Even worse, now that he saw them up close, he realized just how small they were. These were younglings—perhaps even hatchlings.

Something about their behavior seemed wrong, though, but it took him a few moments to figure it out.

They weren't attacking him back.

Which, on one hand, he supposed wasn't that surprising. It wasn't like he was a threat.

But it went against everything he'd learned about dragons. They *hated* tehoin. And so they should be attacking him, no matter how weak he was. They shouldn't be ignoring him.

He didn't have time to answer the question, though. The dragons shifted toward the east, swooping down and destroying buildings with a casual disregard for any lives within. Zachary chased them, flinging teho as though it would do any good.

That spark of rage returned, his fury at always feeling so pointless.

If the band were here, they'd be able to do something.

But Zachary, once again, did nothing. Could do nothing.

He heard screams ahead.

Zachary set aside his self-pity and ran. He saw several houses down, a group of families cowering in a corner between two buildings. Maybe nine or ten people, including two mothers holding young infants.

His first thought was to yell at them. Why hadn't they run when the orders had come?

But that wasn't helpful, either. There were a dozen reasonable explanations. All that mattered now was that he find a way to get them to safety.

Behind him, a dragon crashed into a building, wood splintering as armored scale and teho tore through it. The dragon, not content to destroy a single building, kept crashing down the street, shattering building after building. Zachary risked a glance back and saw that sure enough, the dragon was heading straight to where the families were hiding.

He ran, wishing he had Hakon's ability to funnel teho into his muscles, to run faster and be stronger than seemed humanly possible.

But he was just a weak vilda.

He slid to a stop beside the families, the dragon only three buildings away. He took a quick breath and focused his teho. Shields still didn't come naturally to him. He needed to focus, and it was very hard to focus when a dragon was tearing up your city, approaching you with nothing but destruction on its mind.

Zachary tried and failed.

And like a fool, he'd put himself in danger, too. If he didn't get a shield up, he'd join the families in their fates.

He thought of Cliona, and of Hakon. So different in so many ways, but they shared one characteristic.

The will to change the world.

He closed his eyes.

Though the world might collapse around him, he would remain steady. He was calm.

The shield appeared around them. It was, he believed, one of the best he'd ever made.

The dragon passed overhead, and Zachary felt the wave of teho press against his shield. Then it was past, and the buildings were collapsing. Thick wooden beams struck his shield, as well as hundreds of sharp, deadly pieces of shrapnel.

The children clustered behind him screamed, but it felt to him as though the sounds were coming from far away. Despite the volume of debris landing on his shield, he found he could hold it without problem.

A few moments later, the assault was past them. The

dragon focused on other buildings. He didn't think the creatures had a plan of any sort—they were just attacking and attacking, destroying the city.

He let his shield drop. "They're letting people into the caverns from the entrances around the council district. If you make a circle south around the dragons, you should be able to get there and take cover."

The grateful families nodded and ran.

Zachary dusted the debris from his shoulders and watched the dragons. He thought for a few moments, but there was no changing the facts of the matter. He wasn't strong enough to turn them aside. All that he could do was help individuals whose lives were in danger.

But for Mioska, he could do nothing but watch the dragons destroy it.

CHAPTER 37

Hakon crashed into the dirt, stone, and exposed roots of the mountainside. Ari tumbled limply to a stop next to him, unconscious. Perhaps it was due to injury, but Hakon suspected the assassin had simply given everything for that last set of transports.

He raised his head and searched the sky.

Ava, floating.

Cliona, falling.

It had all been for nothing. Hakon had felt the dragon's bones, cracking one after the other as the two incredible forces met. There was no way the dragon could survive. It seemed impossible that he was still alive.

Hakon supposed he'd have to buy Ari a drink for that sometime, though at this point it was getting hard to keep track of how many times they'd saved one another.

As the dragon fell, all Hakon could think was that it didn't look right. Its massive neck was bent at a strange angle. Limp wings fluttered in the wind. He held his breath, hoping he was wrong.

He could imagine it straightening out and taking back to

the air.

But the dragon crashed into the ground, maybe a half mile away from where Hakon lay. It never moved.

Had he just killed his daughter for good?

He refused to believe it. That was an elder dragon. One of the greatest powers on this planet.

She was injured, certainly, but this fight wasn't over.

Hakon turned his eyes up to Ava and felt the first glimmers of hope. Yes, she was floating, but when he looked closer, he saw that her left leg was missing. Blood dripped from the sky.

Then he realized the reason he could make out such details was because she was floating closer to them. She gathered teho, and while it wasn't nearly as much as before, it made no difference. It was still enough to kill the band several times over.

For the first time, he looked around the place where they'd crashed. Ari's last transport had brought them back to the band. Irric was sitting on the ground, watching Ava approach with a resigned look. He'd taken a nasty gash across the forehead, and one of his eyes was caked shut with blood.

Meshell shuffled close to Hakon, and his eye couldn't help but be drawn to her wounded arm. If they lived through today, it would eventually regrow, but it would take considerable time, and he was fairly certain they wouldn't even live to see the sunset. She shook her head when she saw the look on his face. "I regret nothing," she said. "None of us do. Don't you dare try to steal that from us."

Hakon swallowed and nodded. Even he knew there were times not to argue.

Solveig looked to be in the best shape of anyone, but she still bled from at least a dozen wounds. She collapsed next to Ari and pulled his head onto her lap. She began playing with his hair.

It was the first time he'd seen a physical display of affection between them. It wasn't their way, not in front of the others.

Hakon took Meshell's left hand in his right.

There was a part of him that still wanted to fight. Nothing short of death would rob him of that. But it was an empty gesture. He'd rather spend his last few moments with Meshell's hand in his own.

He had no words for his friends who had followed him here, knowing full well something like this might be the conclusion. Nothing he said would do them justice.

And they already knew everything he would say.

Ava threw her teho, shaped as another enormous wave of spears. Hakon watched, and Meshell squeezed his hand tighter. None of them made any move to escape.

The teho hit a shield and shattered.

Hakon looked down and saw the small form of Isira standing before them.

For a moment, he thought he was having some sort of death vision. Isira, of all people, would never raise a hand to help them.

Then Isira formed her own attack and hurled it back at Ava. Teho darts shattered Ava's shield, and the enemy stamfar fell from the sky, shrieking in agony.

Ava landed between the band and the fallen dragon. She supported herself with teho, but she'd never looked weaker.

Still, she was a stamfar, and far, far stronger than Hakon and the others. She raised her hand, and small needles of powerful teho sped toward them.

Isira's shield handled the attack with ease. She strode toward Ava.

Ava launched waves of teho against the childish figure. Any one would have leveled the band.

But Ava's attempts didn't even have enough strength to slow Isira's advance. The band couldn't beat Ava, but with the dragon's help, they'd weakened her enough for Isira to finish the task.

Hakon felt teho building above him. He looked up to see a spear, which had to be at least a quarter of a mile long. In all his years, he'd never seen anything like it. Isira aimed it straight for Ava's heart.

And Ava vanished, transporting away.

Hakon looked around, expecting her to reappear behind them. But she was gone.

They waited another minute. Even Isira looked as though she expected Ava to reappear somewhere behind her. But eventually, the truth became clear.

Ava had run.

Hakon swore. They'd been close, closer than ever before. And now, again, all their efforts were for nothing.

The spear above them disappeared, and Isira turned her attention to the band. She took two hesitant steps, then she collapsed.

The band watched, in stunned silence. But she didn't look like she planned on rising anytime soon.

Hakon pushed himself to his feet. He stumbled toward her, feeling weak. When he reached her, she was lying on her back, staring up at the sky.

Something about her looked pitiful. It engaged some long-dormant parental instinct in Hakon, and he kneeled down next to her. He picked her up and cradled her in his arms. She was too light.

How could such power be held within such a frail body?

"You helped us," he said.

"Blame the boy," she said. Her voice was hoarse.

"Wondered why you didn't just kill him. But why help now?" He looked at her, checking for a wound he hadn't seen earlier. Had one of Ava's attacks broken through Isira's shields?

He saw nothing, though. There was no blood anywhere. "And what's wrong?"

She tried to sit up, but grimaced and failed. "Same answer to both questions." She let herself relax in his arms. "I'm not quite who I've led you to believe I am."

"What?"

She shook her head. "Time enough for explanations later. But I'm far older than you think." She raised her hand and pointed at the structure where they'd made their camp. "I'm old enough to know what that is. I'm old enough to remember the First Empire."

Hakon knew he was repeating himself, but he couldn't believe her words. "What?"

She shook her head again, making Hakon feel like a fool. "Later. Just know, I'm dying, and that damn boy finally convinced me to make one last effort to change something."

Hakon was about to ask a whole series of questions, but she stopped him with a single word. "Cliona. There's something happening there I've never experienced before. And that's truly saying something. Go to her, now. All of you. I'll be here when you return. I'm not ready to die, yet."

It took Hakon a moment for the import of her words to settle in. Isira believed. She'd called the dragon by his daughter's name. And she believed the dragon still lived.

Hope pounded in his chest. Strength returned to his limbs.

He laid Isira down gently and led the band toward his daughter.

CHAPTER 38

Zachary groaned as he lifted the stone. He pressed harder with the tips of his fingers, willing his grip to hold for another moment. The older man, recently pinned beneath the rubble, scrambled out between Zachary's legs, and the moment he was through, Zachary let the stone drop again.

The man thanked him profusely, but Zachary couldn't hear him. His body ached, and his muscles screamed for rest.

But Mioska was only falling faster. As he watched the dragons, they reminded him of nothing more than children, wrecking everything they could get their hands on while their parents were gone. They even took breaks, flying up into the sky and circling around, chasing one another exactly like tireless toddlers.

The western side of the city was simply gone. Every building had been destroyed, and there was a gaping hole in the wall large enough to walk an army through, with room maybe for a circus alongside. And now the dragons were beginning their work closer to the heart of the city.

If there was anything positive about the day, it was that the dragons had been as thorough as they had, and that they'd focused on the west like they had. It gave the majority of citizens time to evacuate, and assuming Zachary's orders were obeyed, most of them were in the caves.

Zachary wasn't sure the caves would protect the citizens, but there was no better place for them.

He imagined them, huddled in the dark. They'd woken up this morning having no idea what threats gathered over the horizon. By the time the sun set on the destruction, many would have their lives destroyed for good.

The thought pushed him to continue his search for survivors, while to the east, the dragons continued to demolish Mioska, a city that had stood proudly for almost five hundred years.

He'd be considered a pretty poor council member if the city was destroyed on his first full day on the job. If he was remembered at all.

He shook his head to clear it. The longer he remained on his feet, the harder it was to focus. He found his thoughts wandering more and more, and if he pushed on for too much longer, he'd be falling asleep as buildings collapsed on top of him.

He walked east, toward some of the more recent damage. To his right, he saw a dusty arm sticking out of some rubble, but when he grasped it, he found it cold and stiff. He continued on, listening for any cries of help.

For now, though, the streets in this neighborhood were silent. The dragons were on one of their breaks, circling in the sky above.

An enormous bloom of teho behind him caught his attention. He turned back, toward the west and the light of the setting sun.

Zachary almost ignored the new arrival, but then there was another bloom of teho, and another.

Unable to ignore it any longer, Zachary summoned what little strength he still possessed and ran west. They weren't far away, and soon he saw a new sight, something else he'd never expected to see, but he'd dreamed of.

Hel stood there, at the head of several columns of Aysgarthians.

His first thought, that he was ashamed of, was that they had come as conquering heroes. But then she stepped toward him, her eyes wide when she saw how he looked, and he knew that help had finally come.

Humans, banding together against the wild.

He wanted to run and embrace her, only stopping himself because he knew she was here as a commander. Instead, he bowed as she neared. "You're a sight for sore eyes."

"You're—not," she said. "But we're here to help."

He took in the columns. It was more tehoin than he would have even hoped for. They waited for Hel's orders. Despite the destruction of the city and the dragons flying off in the distance, they stood tall and firm. Their faces might have been carved out of stone.

He felt tears welling up in his eyes and he brushed them away.

"Then follow me," he said.

Hel relayed his orders, and he found himself marching by her side, nearly a hundred tehoin behind them. The thought occurred to him that with this strength, he could just take the city. Council politics meant nothing with this kind of power.

He let himself bask in the dream for a bit, then focused his attention on the problem at hand. If he thought like that, he was no better than the emperors or Torsten.

As the tehoin advanced, they caught the dragons' attention. Apparently, even these ambitious, city-destroying younglings couldn't ignore an entire army of tehoin.

They dropped from the sky, roaring as they swooped toward the columns.

As they rushed toward him, he felt a sudden and nearly overpowering urge to run. If not for Hel, standing by his side, he might have.

She gave her warriors their orders, her voice clear and loud. "Spears, ready!"

A hundred teho spears appeared in the hands of the tehoin. Hel joined them, and Zachary looked on in wonder. How could she stand, so certain, against the dragons?

The street was filled with teho. Enough strength to level a city wall.

Enough strength to make him understand the truth. Alone, he was nothing special. A vilda born to power. By himself, though, he would never achieve legendary feats like the band.

But he didn't have to.

He wasn't alone.

He never had been. Humanity pushed deeper into the wild because they could cooperate. Together, they had a chance to fight. A chance to declare to this world they belonged.

Perhaps no stories would be told of his incredible deeds. But as he felt the teho gathered here, he knew he was at least partly responsible for giving the city a way to fight back. He had helped bring them together.

He stood tall, next to Hel, and formed his own teho spear. It wasn't much, but it was one of over a hundred.

The dragons picked up their pace, racing toward the columns.

"First wave, southern dragon!" Hel shouted. Then, "Release!"

The spears launched into the air, and Zachary threw his, too. He wasn't sure how much longer he could hold onto it.

He'd seen the sight of dozens of spears in the air once before, back when they'd escaped from Aysgarth. The power of a single tehoin was considerable, but when they worked together, the results were devastating. No single spear pierced the dragon's armored scales, but the combined force brought the southern dragon crashing down to the street.

The second youngling broke off, not wanting to share in its sibling's fate.

"Second wave, release!" Hel ordered.

Another wave of spears filled the air. This time, a few seemed to slip in cracks in the fallen dragon's armor.

Blood dripped onto the cobblestones. But the dragon fought to its feet and roared at the tehoin, its jaws painted red.

Hel didn't even waste the time needed to give the order. She snapped her arm and spear forward, and the tehoin in the front ranks next to her did the same.

They were all nelja, Zachary realized. The best and strongest Aysgarth had left.

They aimed for the open mouth.

The youngling's roar turned into a gurgle, and it fell to the street, unmoving.

A vicious cheer went up from the columns. This was revenge, not just for Mioska, but for Aysgarth, too.

Zachary searched the sky for the second dragon. Their work was only half done.

This time, half done was good enough. The second youngling fled, flapping its wings and flying west with as much haste as it could manage. Zachary watched and allowed himself to believe.

They'd done it.

They'd banded together. And though he couldn't bring himself to call the day a victory, it was a start. A very promising start.

"What now?" Hel asked.

Zachary looked over to the dead dragon. His father had taught him never to waste an opportunity, and the one before him was the greatest he could have asked for. He turned to Hel. "Don't suppose you'd help me carry this back to my home?"

She looked doubtful, and he turned to the columns, hoping it would be forgivable to bypass her authority this once. "Will you help me carry this east? As recompense, I will open up my family's *very extensive* cellars."

Within a moment, a hundred small platforms of teho were lifting the dragon high, so that all could see. Zachary marched ahead of it, Hel by his side.

In ones and twos, citizens of Mioska came to watch, emerging from cellars and dark corners to peer at the procession. As word spread, crowds began to gather. Zachary could guess what the stories from today would sound like.

Zachary reached out and grabbed Hel's hand. She didn't pull away.

He was looking forward to introducing her to his father.

CHAPTER 39

Hakon led the band down the mountain. Their pace was slow, their steps shuffling. Ari had awoken, but only walked thanks to Solveig's constant support.

It felt like a funeral march.

They heard the dragon before they saw it. It had landed among tall pine trees, which blocked their view. But its breathing was labored, uneven, and wet. Hakon feared what they would see when they finally stumbled upon it.

They picked their way through the last line of trees.

It lay before them. At rest, out in the open, its true size was apparent. From snout to tail, it had to be seven, maybe eight times Hakon's height. That something so massive had ever taken flight defied all reason.

It didn't look like it would ever take flight again. Limbs lay at unnatural angles, and every breath sent a shudder down its body. Its eyes tracked the band, but it made no move toward them.

Did dragons heal like kolma and stamfar? Hakon

couldn't guess. They'd fought the creatures back for years and still knew so little about them.

If dragons didn't, this one had no hope.

The thought cracked his heart.

The others stopped, but Hakon continued. One step at a time, he neared the creature, his hand outstretched. It watched him, and Hakon swore he saw expectation in those intelligent eyes. He finally came close enough that he could put his hand on the creature's neck.

The dragon's reservoir of teho remained deep, but it lacked the vitality Hakon had come to expect. It felt more like a placid lake, the water almost perfectly still. He let his teho blend with that of the dragon. He dove into the placid lake and let it fill his body.

Sensation washed over him. Emotions wrapped around his heart. They weren't his, but felt as though they were. And each was magnified, focused almost to an unbearable purity.

Anger, at him, for having lied for all those years. That feeling, at least, was familiar, echoing his own regrets.

Wonder, at a vast world filled with mystery.

The emotions subsided, and in the ensuing calm, memories surfaced. Him, holding her against his chest as she gently fell asleep. Teaching her how to manipulate her teho. The memories were warm.

Then more recent memories, cold and unfamiliar. He saw himself in the forest with Meshell, protecting the travelers. Felt the pull of the elder dragon on the youngling, a manipulation of the connections that existed between all dragons.

A manipulation Cliona had learned from Ava, the first human who had understood it.

Haken nodded. He saw why the dragons had fought

with one another, and why they'd exhibited such strange behavior over the past months. It was the same way Ava had escaped captivity, the same way she'd ordered the dragons east.

Hakon bowed his head. "It was supposed to be me watching over you, girl. Not the other way around."

Warmth flooded his limbs again. A brief memory of him catching her as she fell from a tree.

Then all was still, leaving him with a deep sense of peace that he'd never felt before. It was the absence of everything, but yet he didn't fear it. It was nothingness, but still welcoming.

An arch appeared in his thoughts, glowing a pale blue. The darkness within the arch was deeper than any night sky he'd ever studied, but he wasn't afraid of the gate. He hadn't, not since he was a young man. Not since he'd encountered that first elder dragon, the day the band had been born.

Then he felt her, standing beside him. And she was embracing him. Forgiving him.

He never wanted the moment to end.

But it did. She let him go and turned toward the gate. Her steps were light and confident, without a trace of fear or hesitation.

He wanted to call after her, but he was being pushed away. Being pushed out.

He filled himself with the dragon's teho, hoping it would give him the strength to stay. But it wasn't enough. He was expelled, his teho forcefully separated from that of the dragon and Cliona. He opened his eyes and realized he'd been crying.

He tried again, hoping to force the connection with the dragon. But he couldn't. A wall stood tall between his teho and its, and there was nothing he could do to climb it. The dragon's teho was still and calm on the other side of the wall, but he didn't think it would ever let him swim in those waters again.

He saw a much younger Cliona in his own memories, asking him for just one more story. She hadn't learned to read yet, and so relied on him to tell the stories of the past. Like him, she was relentless, never stopping until he really put his foot down about going to bed. She would just keep going, and going, ready to listen forever.

And now she was going where he couldn't follow.

But she needed his help.

He didn't know why. But he couldn't ask, and he trusted her.

He didn't grieve for her. She'd shown him what was waiting, and there was nothing to fear.

Hakon fell to his knees, hand still pressed against the dragon's neck. He let the tears fall.

He grieved for himself, for not being able to watch his daughter grow up. For not treasuring the moments he'd had with her *enough*. If he'd truly realized how few moments they would have, he would have fought harder to stay near her when she'd tried to leave him.

He grieved for the future he would never have with her.

He shook his head. There had to be a way. He'd never given up on anything, and he certainly wasn't going to give up on his daughter now. He would search to the ends of the world until he found a way to reunite Cliona's soul with her body once again.

He wouldn't end her life. Not while even the faintest hope remained.

He was so lost in his own thoughts, he didn't hear Meshell come up behind him. Didn't even know she was there, until she put her arm around his shoulders.

He took a deep breath. "She wants me to kill her."

Meshell held him close. "I'm sorry."

He shook his head again. "I can't. I can't give up on her. There's got to be a way. We can find one."

Meshell was silent for a moment. Then she said, "You've got to let her go."

Her words were the final blow of the chisel that shattered the stone around his heart. He slumped, silent sobs wracking his body as he clung desperately to the dragon's neck.

He couldn't.

Hakon didn't know how long he stayed like that, but it was the dragon that startled him out of his grief.

Without warning, it rolled. Hakon heard the bones crack, snapping like tree trunks. A pained hiss escaped from the creature's sealed lips, but it didn't release the expected roar. It exposed its torso, revealing a hole in its armor. Its intent couldn't have been more clear.

Still Hakon didn't move.

Meshell squeezed tighter. "If you want, I can take this burden from you."

No.

He knew he couldn't ask such a thing. He couldn't imagine being the one who sent his daughter to the gate, but he knew, beyond a doubt, he couldn't let anyone else, either.

She'd trusted him with this last task, and he wouldn't be the one who failed her. Never again.

He stood up, his body feeling heavier than ever before. He reached back and drew his sword, which had seen so little use on this devastating day. Teho trickled from his hand up the blade.

The hole in the dragon was wide and deep. He guessed

Ava had struck the blow as the dragon had taken off her leg. He'd never seen such a wound on a dragon, but it made this next part easier.

He closed his eyes. He saw Cliona sitting with him as a small girl, snuggled up on his lap as he told her stories. True stories, as it turned out, of his life, though she'd thought they were just legends at the time. Though, now that he thought of it, he wasn't sure she hadn't suspected, on some level, the truth.

He saw her learning how to mix herbs from her mother. She'd learned quickly, and if shown a recipe once, she could recreate it without problem.

He relived the days they'd spent training together. Cliona had his gifts, and though he hadn't wanted her to follow in his footsteps, he was not-so-secretly delighted that she learned his skills almost as easily as her mother's.

And their argument outside Vispeda.

Painful at the time, but now, he appreciated it. Because after that argument, she knew better who he was. There were no secrets anymore, and all had been laid to rest between them.

He opened his eyes and stabbed his sword straight into the dragon's heart.

CHAPTER 40

Zachary's stomach clenched as he looked out over the hall. Long benches had been moved in, and each and every one was filled with the great and mighty of Mioska. To no one's surprise, *they* had survived the dragon's assault with little difficulty. The damage had been focused in the western quarters of the city, and though the death toll was staggering, and still growing hourly, those who lived farthest east looked like they'd barely been inconvenienced.

He wanted to hate them, and there were a few he did. Surprisingly, though, when the orders had come to open up the caverns, most nobles had obeyed without question. Zachary had even heard stories of several sharing food and clothing with the citizens hiding under their estates. A handful still left their entrances to the caverns open for the newly homeless to sleep in while the city was rebuilt.

Others, of course, hadn't been so kind. Hallr's entrances to the cavern that day were protected by a series of locks the household staff suddenly couldn't find the key to.

But that was all a problem for another day.

Today, he had to pretend like he was glad to be here, celebrating their survival, when there was still so much work to do.

If not for Hel, he might have abandoned the whole event and borne the costs later. But she was here, looking as beautiful as ever in her Aysgarthian uniform. And she had correctly pointed out that he needed to be here. He needed to be seen.

Agnar droned on, saying something about the power of friendship and alliances, and of how everyone was stronger together. True words, maybe, but empty in the context of this space. This audience didn't care much about cooperation, because they still didn't understand, deep in their bones, the danger they were in.

They hadn't seen their homes destroyed.

He met Hel's gaze, but they both kept their faces carefully neutral. Here, every small facial tic would be pored over by nobles with nothing better to do than try to figure out what plans the two young leaders had.

The dragon attack focused Zachary. It made his future clear. The thing he could do? He could gather the disparate threads of humanity and weave them into a force capable of standing tall against the wilds.

And nothing, dragon or noble, could stop him.

Finally, Agnar finished speaking. He invited Hel to join him, and she did, turning to face the crowd. Her words were brief, and even emptier than Agnar's. She praised him for his wisdom and expressed her gratitude to be of service to the people of Mioska.

They signed the treaty.

Food for defense.

Hel's tehoin already patrolled the walls, and the first

shipments of food had already been sent to Aysgarth. Both cities would survive, hopefully.

There was polite applause, and then it was his turn.

Again, a speech by Agnar, speaking of bravery, sacrifice, and bold leadership. It all felt a bit heavy to Zachary, but he bore the list of his accolades with a firm expression. Now, more than ever, every eye was upon him.

Agnar invited him to speak, and taking his cue from Hel, he made his remarks brief and bland. He said only that he was proud to be of service. They'd decided beforehand. They would let their actions speak.

There was polite applause as Agnar gifted him a new sword, a jewel-encrusted monstrosity that put him in mind of his younger brother. Zachary smiled and said his thanks.

Then the ceremony thankfully concluded. Zachary wanted to speak with Hel, but she was quickly mobbed by all the nobles curious about the new arrival to the city. By the end of the day, he suspected she would have a dozen offers of minor alliances. Possibly a few marriage proposals, as well. He decided he wanted to be nowhere close to those conversations. He silently wished her well, then found his way to a balcony. The fresh air was a relief.

He hadn't been out nearly long enough when he heard the sound of footsteps behind him. He looked back to see Agnar step onto the balcony and shut the doors behind him.

Zachary gave a small bow. "Sir."

Agnar waved it away. "No need for any of that when it's just the two of us."

Together, they looked out over the city. The damage was extensive, but Zachary couldn't help but think it could have been so much worse. Already, the sounds of repairs reached their ears.

"Not one to bask in your glory?" Agnar said.

"I didn't do much, and there's more left to be done."

"You started the alliance which just saved the city. So I'd say you did quite a bit."

"That was mostly Hel, but I appreciate it."

"The stories about you are already spreading. How you went from house to house, freeing those who were trapped. Quite a few people are making comparisons to the other nobles, who ran straight to the caves. You're the hero of the people, at the moment."

Zachary decided that Agnar was on his side. The side of the people. "So, how do I use that to prepare us for what's coming?"

Agnar offered a hint of a grin. "Off the top of my head, I have no idea. But I'm excited to see what you come up with." He tapped his fingers on the stone railing, then said, "A warning, though. You've made an enemy of Hellr, several times over now, and that's a risky position to be in."

"You think he'll try to assassinate me?"

The governor shook his head. "Nothing so crude. He'll turn any friends you make against you, start rumors about you. Those who stand tallest are the easiest to topple, and you're standing very high now."

"I appreciate the warning."

Agnar nodded. "I very much look forward to our next council meetings," he said as he excused himself.

Zachary turned back to the view of the city, but got no time to himself. Before the door closed, Hel slipped through. "I can see why you left the city," she said. "The nobles here," she searched for the right word, "are very intense."

Zachary laughed at that. "Congratulations on the treaty," he said, and he meant it. The food would save Aysgarth, and hopefully, the tehoin would help Mioska, too.

"Thank you. It keeps my position as the head of the council safe for a bit, much to Valdis' dismay. We have a small window to plan out what we do next."

Zachary nodded, but his thoughts were wandering again. "Any word?"

Hel's expression was answer enough. "I'm sure we'll hear from them soon, though."

Zachary wished he could feel some of her confidence. For all the difficulties he faced, it seemed like the band still had the greater fight ahead of them. He wondered if they'd finally chosen a battle they couldn't win.

"You want to get out of here?" he asked.

"I was starting to think you might never ask," she replied with a sly grin.

Her touch sent a thrill up his arm, and he took one last moment to look over Mioska before she transported them back to Ingolf's inn.

Let the wilds, the dragons, and rogue stamfar come.

Humanity would find a way.

EPILOGUE

The fire crackled as the band sat in silence around the burning logs. A few feet away, Isira was curled under a pile of blankets, snoring with a volume that would have woken a dragon. She'd promised answers, but hadn't even had the strength to stay awake long enough to eat supper.

Hakon didn't care about Isira, though.

Truthfully, he didn't care about much of anything at the moment. He went through the motions of living, but he wasn't alive. His heart had died with the dragon. He rubbed Cliona's necklace between thumb and forefinger, and imagined her spirit imprinted on the warm metal.

Experience taught him that, in time, feelings would return. After Sera's death, he'd become exquisitely familiar with the ebbs and flows of grief.

Somehow, he would keep going. It was what he did.

Solveig, who had stood tall up on the mountain, now looked as though someone had hollowed her out. She'd spent hours healing Meshell and Irric's wounds, and though she could only do so much, she confirmed both of the warriors were out of immediate danger.

Ari didn't allow Solveig to heal him, nor did Hakon. Ari was more exhausted than injured, and Hakon had survived the battle remarkably unscathed. Tiny pangs of guilt troubled him when he looked at Meshell and Irric, but they'd volunteered.

They'd sacrificed themselves for him, again.

The mood around the fire was almost as dark as the cloudy, starless night. They roasted their food but ate without hunger.

Hakon helped Meshell with her food, grateful to have something he could do with his hands. Something he could focus on that wasn't the memory of driving the sword deep into the dragon's heart.

The snoring behind them changed pitch, turned into a snort, then a cough. Isira stirred and sat up. Her eyes were glazed, and when she looked around, she seemed surprised to be around others.

Hakon didn't think he would ever understand the mysterious stamfar. Trapped in the body of a child and possessing a power he could barely comprehend. It was almost impossible not to treat her like a little girl, and yet she was possibly the most important person in the world.

"We've got food," Irric said.

She threw off the blankets and crawled toward the fire.

Hakon never saw her like this. When she came to the band, it was typically with teho firmly embraced. Now she held none. He still wasn't bold enough to try killing her with the knife in his hand. Had he believed killing her was right, he would have done it while she slept.

But she'd never seemed more like a little girl. He saw

how thin her limbs were, how her clothes practically hung from her body.

Ari offered her some meat, and she chewed at it hungrily.

In time, her pace slowed and she looked around the circle. "You killed the dragon?"

Hakon frowned. Isira was passed out when they'd returned to her, and he assumed she was unconscious when the dragon died. Had she been awake, or had she guessed something? "It was what she wanted."

Isira turned to Hakon, clearly surprised. "You were able to communicate?"

"In a way. Memories, emotions."

Isira shook her head. "Remarkable."

The first embers of rage sparked deep in Hakon's chest. This was his daughter she was talking about. If not for his exhaustion and grief, he might have flown into a fury. Tonight he settled for raising his voice. "What do you know, Isira?"

"Know?" Isira gave a bitter laugh. "Oh, so much and yet not nearly enough."

Before Hakon's rage could build, she met his gaze. "I cannot tell you specifically what happened to your daughter. As I'm sure you've guessed, she managed, somehow, to blend her teho with that of an elder dragon. What you don't know is that there are tehoin who have tried to achieve that feat for hundreds of years, always without success. For her to unlock the secret, it's nothing short of remarkable."

Isira kept her eyes locked on Hakon's. "I assume it has something to do with your unique ability to manipulate teho within your bodies, but I don't know. If I was sure of the answer, I'd be flying up there," she pointed to the sky, "instead of remaining trapped in this body."

"Why would you want that?" Solveig asked.

"The same reason everyone has searched for it. As a way to defeat death."

"It didn't help my daughter," Hakon said.

"Didn't it?" Isira challenged. "Cliona should have died in Husavik. Instead, some part of her, perhaps the *essential* part of her, lived on, experiencing wonders no human has ever known before. At the very least, that is something. And I am not so sure her story ended today."

It took every bit of restraint Hakon possessed not to grab her and shake her until she talked sense. "What do you mean?"

"I mean that the gates are a mystery we still don't understand. The greatest mystery of all. And Cliona approached them today with an incredible power and will." Isira sighed. "I'm sorry, Hakon. I can't tell you what happened to your daughter. She's exploring paths no one has before. And I don't know what that means."

"Maybe," Ari said, his annoyance obvious, "you can start with something you do know. Like what this is?" He pointed to the structure towering behind them.

"Hmm. Yes." Isira wrinkled her nose as she looked up at the structure. Then she stared down at the fire. Hakon got the sense she was deciding whether or not to tell them what she knew. That she was reconsidering her earlier promise to tell them more.

She played with the dirt in front of her feet with a stick, drawing random shapes while the others waited for an answer. Had it been anyone else, their patience would have ended long ago.

Finally, she tossed the stick into the fire. "I suppose it's time for someone else to know." She paused a moment. "That, right there, is a ship. One of many that carried us here many, many years ago. It's the reason why the wilds attack us to this day. The reason why I can never decide what to do with the strength and time remaining to me. We don't belong here."

Silence greeted her announcement. Hakon didn't understand what she was saying. As usual, Solveig's mind moved quickest. "From where?" she asked.

"Where what?"

"You said that the ship carried us here. From where?"

Isira pointed up at the cloudy skies.

"From the stars."

THE ADVENTURES CONTINUE!

Top o' the morning!

I hope that wherever you are in the world, and whenever it is you're reading this, that you're doing well.

First, as an author, let me thank you for reading *Fall of Forgotten Gods*. Whether this is the first book of mine you've read or my twenty-first, I hope that you enjoyed it. There have never been more ways to be entertained, and it truly means the world to me that you choose to spend your time in these pages.

If you enjoyed the story, rest assured the adventures of Hakon and the band are far from over. They mysteries of their world remain, but the truth isn't far away.

Look for the final installment of *The Saga of the Broken Gods*, coming fall 2022!

And if you're looking to spread the word, there's few better ways to support the story by leaving a review where you purchased the book!

Thanks again!

Ryan

February 18, 2022

DIVE DEEPER INTO THE STORY

Throughout *Fall of Forgotten Gods*, there are references to Zachary wandering the frontier on the western edge of the six states.

Someday, I hope to chronicle more of his solo adventures, but I did write one as a bonus short story, which also helps explain the backstory of the place he left his brother.

It's a story I really like, taking place a while after the events of *Band of Broken Gods*. If you haven't read it yet, you can download it for free here:

www.waterstonemedia.net/lone-wolf/

And if you pick it up, I hope that you won't mind staying in touch. I typically email readers once or twice a month, and one of my greatest pleasures over the past five years has been getting to know the people reading my stories.

If I'm being honest, email is my favorite way of communicating with readers. Whether it's hearing from soldiers stationed overseas or grandmothers tending to their gardens, email has allowed me to make new friends all over the world.

Email subscribers also get all the goodies. From free books in all formats, to sample chapters and surprise short stories, if I'm giving something away, it's through email.

I hope you'll join us.

Ryan

ALSO BY RYAN KIRK

Saga of the Broken Gods

Band of Broken Gods

Fall of Forgotten Gods

Last Sword in the West

Last Sword in the West

Eyes of the Hidden World

A Sword Named Vengeance

Oblivion's Gate

The Gate Beyond Oblivion

The Gates of Memory

The Gate to Redemption

Relentless

Relentless Souls

Heart of Defiance

Their Spirit Unbroken

The Nightblade Series

Nightblade

World's Edge

The Wind and the Void

Blades of the Fallen

Nightblade's Vengeance

Nightblade's Honor

Nightblade's End

Standalone Novels

Blades of Shadow

The Primal Series

Primal Dawn

Primal Darkness

Primal Destiny

ABOUT THE AUTHOR

Ryan Kirk is the bestselling author of the *Nightblade* series of books. When he isn't writing, you can probably find him playing disc golf or hiking through the woods.

www.waterstonemedia.net
contact@waterstonemedia.net

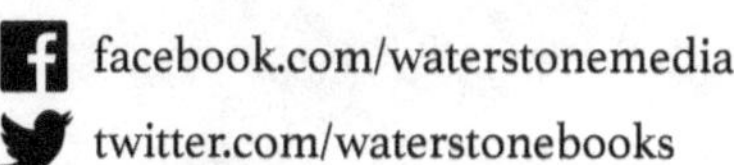

facebook.com/waterstonemedia
twitter.com/waterstonebooks
instagram.com/waterstonebooks